I0583299

ruth (noun):
1. compassion for the misery of another
2. sorrow for one's own faults

•

synonym: mercy

•

antonym: cruelty

ADDITIONAL BOOKS BY

CHRISTY LANDERS TALLAMY

Sipping Mercury
The Second Book of Ruth

Releases February 2026

What Was Done to Me
The Third Book of Ruth

Releases September 2026

The First Book of Ruth

SUGARCANE SAINT

Christy Landers Tallamy

Bendings Publishing, LLC
Leesburg, Virginia 20176
https://www.christylanderstallamy.com/bendings

for my mother

Author's Note

My part of this story is finished. A strange thing to say on the first page of a book, hmm? Well, it is. I did my part. I ran away. I cut them off. I married a strong man with hearty roots and gave birth to a girl. I raised her to be fierce. I protected her from the shadows at no small cost. I erased the shame and humiliation from her blood. I was and continue to be merciless in this. Perhaps sparing one beautiful life away from the chaos of Ruth's legacy was my life's purpose. I put her feet on an undamaged path so that through her there would be redemption.

It isn't time to share my story yet—from its start to finish. My story comes much later—somewhere toward the end of the third book. This story—the first of three—begins with Ruth. My grandmother. Though I never knew her as such. I only knew of her. She died protecting my mother long before I came along. I struggle with Ruth. Ruth conceded to and aided unimaginable violence that was visited upon her children. Ruth allowed a horror to take root in a family that vibrates through three generations—to this very day. But Ruth is said to have been beautiful. Loving. Gentle. A good mother.

My mother's ten brothers and sisters are dead now. She is the only one that remains. This is important because this story couldn't be told when the brothers were alive. No one would allow it. No one would even admit to it. But the week after she buried her last brother, my mother gave me permission to tell it. The best I could.

The memories are in pieces. Fractures. Snippets. Many of them fall from traumatized minds and bodies. I've pieced them together for you. The violence and sexual abuse you will encounter here is real. Horribly, painfully real. The bones of this story are all real. All of the characters you will encounter are real. Carefully researched. The fluidity of the story required embellishment in conversations, settings, and some relationships. Many names have been changed to protect the wounded, if not the innocent. My goal, as I write, has been to understand Ruth. Understanding her has meant some assumptions had to be made. Understanding her meant going all the way back to the day she was born and reconstructing her path. All to answer my mother's unanswerable question: Why?

I began researching in 2019—wrote, sought counsel, and did a considerable amount of thinking over the five years it took to create a picture of what Ruth's life may have been like and why she may have made the choices she did. At the end of that time, what was intended to be one book became three. In a deliberate attempt to define how a destructive culture can form within a family, I broke the manuscript into the three phases of the abuse cycle: Seduction, Isolation, and Destruction. *Sugarcane Saint* is the beginning. The falling. The seduction of Ruth.

Christy Landers Tallamy
Granddaughter of Ruth

Prologue

Bibb County, Georgia—Summer 1950

Sonny heard the girl's screams before he even reached the porch. He hesitated. A defeated sigh escaped him. He paused at the bottom step. His hand loose on the crooked wooden railing. He listened to her cries. Her fighting. He heard the familiar thwack of a leather belt and the slurred hum of a man's voice. He wouldn't go in. He hated himself for it. But the hate was mingled with a sewer of stagnant apathy. He'd encountered that belt—most specifically the heavy steel buckle end of it—and had been laid into many foggy, pain-ridden days of flickering consciousness by it. The man. The belt. Their might suffocated his memories.

He trudged up the stairs. The heavy Georgia summer lay on the wooden slats of the porch—rippling with the sound of cicadas and tree frogs. The damp earth and rot wrapped around him. The low buzz of mosquitos hissed from the massive dripping trees. The porch sagged. The red earth below gulped at the crumpling house as if it were trying to swallow its horrors. An old swing sat still on its chains—inert in the lifeless air.

Sonny paused by the dirty window. The screams were louder. Vicious and desperate all at once. He already knew what he'd see. He'd seen it all before, but the tug of curiosity as to who lay victim to his father's cruelty overpowered his ability to look away.

He looked through the window just as his father raised the belt and struck Sonny's eldest sister mercilessly on her bare thighs. She was sprawled on the floor, kicking and clawing; her thin legs were useless weapons against the leviathan strength of his intentions. Her red hair raged around her face. Her dress was hitched well above her hips. Sonny could see the welts rising on her skin. Welts Sonny had borne himself. Welts that would later be hidden. Explained away. Denied.

His father splayed his hand on the girl's belly, holding her down. The edges of his grizzled face hardened. The skin about his eyes was bulbous and puffed. Freely consumed moonshine filled the skin from underneath. His dark hair flopped in greasy strands across his forehead, and his chest heaved with exertion.

"Ruth!" His voice held the purple haze of intemperance.

A woman came into view. Sonny stumbled backward. This he hadn't expected. He couldn't reconcile the woman's presence nor the sudden rush of fear he felt for her. His sister, writhing beneath his father's hand, became no more than the afterthought in the room. It was his mother that rooted his heavy boots in place and fastened him to the window.

"Ruth. Hold her." His father ordered. The girl stilled, breathless. She craned her head back on the floor and looked up for help. In horror, Sonny took in the stillness of their mother—the woman who had cradled him after every beating, who'd hidden him in closets and under porches and around corners to protect him from his father.

Her hands were hidden in a towel. Her faded cotton dress grazed her knees. Her auburn hair lay in thick, round waves about her slumped shoulders. She looked at her daughter through glass green eyes.

"Mama . . . ," the girl pleaded. "Mama, please . . ."

Sonny watched his mother set the towel aside. She knelt on the wood planked floor, placing chafed hands on the girl's shoulders and running them along her arms until she had captured them within her own, as if she were offering her comfort rather than restraining her. The green in her eyes shifted, replaced by a gray flatness. She leaned down and whispered in her daughter's ear. Despite the impossibility, Sonny strained to hear her words. He needed to walk away. Needed to not see this. To not know this. Yet the screaming in his head to run from it held no sway over the waves of crushing realization that had pinned him to his place.

Whatever their mother had whispered reignited the girl's wailing. She thrashed against her mother's embrace. Bile rose in Sonny's throat as his mother turned her face away. From his sister. From his father. From him. As if the peeling paper and the ancient glue crystalizing into small drops of amber against the crumbling surface of the walls held some fascination.

"Now gurl . . . you will learn to respect yer daddy."

Sonny shuddered. He'd been taught to respect his father in much the same way.

Only in a woodshed.

Where no one knew.

He paused to adjust his thinking. He thought no one knew. He watched his father unfasten his pants, pushing them aside enough to release himself. The girl bucked her hips—fighting every move. He took her by the knees, forcing her legs open. Splitting her. Ripping at her. Her screams taunted Sonny with his own cowardice; shame and humiliation vibrated around him; and then in the smallest corner of himself, he fastened onto a pitiless thought. He too had suffered, and no one had rescued him from his father. None of them had been rescued from him. No one defied Leonidas Brantley.

His father pushed himself to standing, adjusting his pants before shoving his daughter out of the way with the toe of his boot as he walked past her. A stone settled onto Sonny's chest. The time for intervention had passed, and he wrestled down the threat of regret, told himself that had he stepped in, it would have been worse for his sister, for his mother—who now loosened her embrace but didn't release his sister. She leaned in and this time he made out her words.

"It's over now, baby. Let's get you cleaned up. I need a hand in the kitchen."

She touched the snarled mess of the girl's vibrant hair.

"You shouldn't upset him like that. You know better."

Sonny's mother turned, slow and cumbersome. The rounded bulge of the baby she carried in her belly weighed heavily on her. She faded back into the shadows of the kitchen.

Sonny watched his little sister unfurl her bruised body. She moved gingerly—favoring her right side—using her crumpled underwear to wipe between her legs. Her expression rearranged as he watched. Finally settling into an impassive, tight-lipped resolve. She tugged at the edges of her dress before wiping the back of her hand across her face. She smoothed the skin about her nose with her fingers. She looked up, and her eyes met his. They held each other. A thousand words passed between them and nothing at all. They could not save each other.

Sonny stepped away from the window and sagged onto the old porch swing. He pulled the parental consent form from his pocket and stared at it. Along the top, in evenly spaced capital letters, it read, Consent of Parent or Guardian for Enlistment in the US Army. He was six weeks shy of his eighteenth birthday. He held the image of his mother in his mind, rummaging through and discarding the violence and pain until all that remained was the thought of her embrace, firm and comforting, and the inevitability of her tears when he told her he was leaving.

The porch swing creaked as he pushed it back and forth, considering his options. Face his father now or wait six weeks. He folded the paper and stuffed it back in his pocket. The cicadas continued their song. The Southern sun began its liquid descent. The distant lilt of female voices—his mother and his sister baking the week's bread—drifted from the kitchen.

PART ONE

A Legacy of War

(1918–1924)

On April 6, 1917, President Woodrow Wilson gave an impassioned speech to Congress asking that American forces enter a "war that would end all wars." By June, American forces were in Europe side by side with the Allied armies battling German troops—who were referred to disdainfully as the Huns.

For the southeastern part of the United States, war and the wounds it inflicted were part of life. The Huns were merely a new foe to fight. Five decades prior, the American Civil War (referred to in this manuscript as "the States War") crippled the South's economic and social structures, leaving Southerners at odds with themselves. Reeling from grief and devastation, the people of the American South—the formerly enslaved, the former enslavers, and the great many who were neither—spun in a maelstrom of social evolution they were ill-equipped to navigate.

From 1865 to 1877, the former Confederate states were occupied as a hostile part of the precariously reassembled Union. The former ruling class of wealthy white patriarchs was forced to accept the Union's authority, fly the Stars and Stripes, and acknowledge the political participation of formerly enslaved persons. Those who refused to pledge allegiance to the Union risked losing what little remained of their assets.

Powerlessness among those who were once all-powerful simmered into a violent rage that poured down through the middle- and lower-class Southern white families—boiling and brewing into a legacy of racial violence. By the late 1870s, the Union occupation had eased, and in its wake, political corruption radiated from the Southern capitals, most notably Atlanta. From this corruption, bargains were made among the men in power, resulting in the Jim Crow laws that dominated the region for the better part of the twentieth century.

In 1898, an overwhelming number of Southern men marched to war again, this time to the faraway Caribbean. The conflict, later known as the Spanish-American War, saw former Confederates fighting alongside the same Union soldiers who had once vanquished them. These soldiers—fathers and sons raised on tales of past glories—sought redemption for the humiliation of their forebears. Forebears who still sat at their breakfast tables and told tales of what used to be until yesterday became grander than it ever truly was. Forebears who had witnessed the enslavement of other humans and who saw land as the only enduring form of wealth.

In 1915, two organizations set their sights on Stone Mountain, Georgia—the Knights of the Ku Klux Klan (KKK) and the United Daughters of Confederacy (UDC). Historically, the granite outcropping had been a ceremonial ground for the Indigenous Creek and Cherokee people until the land was retained by the federal government as part of the Indian Removal Act. The land was purchased by the Venable family from the State of Georgia in 1887 and became private property. It was a place shrouded in mystery and sacred ceremony, lifting its smooth granite face high enough that it could be seen for miles, a pulpit established by God beckoning those with a (not so) righteous cause.

The KKK, an all-white male supremacist group, lit their inaugural bonfire atop the mountain on Sunday, November 25, 1915, and would continue holding their Sunday gatherings there until 1958. The UDC, a female-run organization devoted to the support and remembrance of the Confederate veterans, commissioned the Yankee-born sculptor Gutzon Borglum to transform the flat face of Stone Mountain into a memorial to the great Confederacy. In the hands of Borglum, the UDC envisioned a ninety-foot relief of General Robert E. Lee and his horse Traveller etched into the stone. However, two years after the memorial project began, fund-raising efforts were put on hold as resources shifted toward managing America's involvement in World War I (referred to in this manuscript as "the new war").

By 1917, as President Woodrow Wilson raised the American battle flag, the South remained largely rural, populated by war-hardened agricultural communities. Yet, within the region, another kind of battle was unfolding—the clash between tradition and modernization. Urban expansion was devouring the agricultural way of being, particularly in Georgia, at a crippling rate.

Coastal cities like Savannah and railway hubs such as those in DeKalb, Fulton, and Bibb Counties were becoming centers of war-driven progress. Key US military encampments for ground troops, aviation training, and naval embarkments were planted along the same railway and port systems that had been immobilized by the States War. German POWs were under guard; French troops were being equipped; soldiers from across the country were being funneled in and prepared for deportment.

Advancements like electricity, indoor plumbing, and education reform bloomed under the energy of war. These changes reached the bedroom communities of Atlanta and extended southward along the red-dirt Dixie Highway into Macon. But beyond the railways and port cities, much of Georgia remained cloistered, enraged, and resistant to the forces of change.

Lamentations 2:1, 4
KJV

How hath the Lord covered the daughter of Zion
with a cloud in his anger, and cast down from
Heaven unto the earth the beauty of Israel,
and remembered not his footstool
in the day of his anger!

He hath bent his bow like an enemy:
he stood with his right hand as an adversary,
and slew all that were pleasant to the eye in the
tabernacle of the daughter of Zion:
he poured out his fury like fire.

Chapter 1

January 1918

Ruth woke with a start. Gray-blue moonlight spilled into her bedroom window. It was far from morning, and yet something had tugged her from her dreams. Then it came again—a banging from the porch.

Ruth heard the creaking of their heavy front door as it swung open. Her father's voice, gruff with sleep, sounded loud in their quiet house.

"McGurdy?"

"Bill. Bring the boys. And every bucket ya got."

Frantic shouting. Stumbling feet on wooden stairs.

Ruth burrowed into the worn quilts—hiding from the unseen. Her eyes scanned the dark. Her ears strained against the night. Her little sister's body, warm beside her, stirred. She lay a hand on

Ruby's back, humming reassurances. Her sister settled. Ruth tucked the blankets tighter around Ruby, protecting her from cold and fear. Undisturbed breathing from the nearby crib assured Ruth that baby Clara May was unaware of the tumult.

Swinging lamp lights blazed by her room—bursting flashes of orange light carried by broad shadows. The acrid stench of lamp oil and the rumbling of men filled the house. Doors slammed. Horses snuffed and hooves pounded against the earth outside. The frankensteined Model T—pieced together from spare parts by Ruth's father—sputtered to life. The horses neighed in angry protest at the rattling sound of the engine. Then all was silent.

Ruth lay listening. Had the Huns come here? To Georgia? The soft swish of women stirred, and the glow of the kitchen lamp crept down the dark hallway—its rhythmic undulations softer and more reassuring than the emergent lights of the men.

The scent of oak burning in the cooking stove skulked through the rambling farmhouse. Fleshy dough slapped against wood, nudging the house from its slumber. Murmured prayers, like ancient spells, wafted from the kitchen. Slap. Slap. Slap—percussed over susurrated sound. Ruth felt the gnawing of fright as familiar as breathing.

She closed her eyes. She could tell by the height of the moon that dawn was still a ways off. She whispered, "Our father who art in Heaven, hallowed be thy name . . ." drifting back into a fitful and shallow sleep.

She dreamed of guns and raw voices. Of blood disappearing into the red earth. Of ropes swinging heavy with the damned. Of black, smoky engines roaring through the halls of her house.

She ran. She hid. She was trapped. Trees surrounded her on every side. Roots heaved beneath her. She curled herself into the writhing roots. She sank beneath the trees into the dark earth.

Graveled voices broke through her nightmares. The caustic burn of smoke and charred wood and sweat-soaked flesh wrestled with the aroma of fresh baked bread. Ruth slipped out of bed, careful to tuck the blankets around Ruby—pausing to check on Clara May. She snuck past the mounded form of her older sister Bessie, whose cheek rested on the open pages of *Betty Policeman.*

In the kitchen, her father was surrounded by soot-covered men. All four of her brothers were there—Wheeler, Tom, and Riley, right down to seven-year-old Earl. Her grandfathers—Papa Jefferson and Papa Perkins. Four of her father's five brothers. They were tight-skinned sacks of muscle and bone, sagging against the surfaces of the room. Sporadic coughing and the clank of metal coffee cups punctuated the unformed morning. Ruth felt small. Her insides were fog.

"Most a'it's gone," her father said, his voice raspy and forced. "We only managed to save what we did cause a'the Sanders and Rhodes boys—planted themselves right up on the roof a'the bank. Kept our water line movin'. Mighty lucky those boys were on furlough. Mighty lucky."

He took a draught of sugar-thickened coffee. He laid a hand on his chest. His breath labored from the billows of smoke. His audience—the men who had been by his side and the women who had kept watch for their return—waited for his recounting.

"Flames were a'risin' all about. Blisterin'. We saved twenty or so a'McGurdy's stock. Got 'em out a'the barns 'fore they went up. But Britt's? Most a'the bank, Miz Dorothy's . . . Tuggie's . . . ? Nothin' left."

Ruth's mother laid a gentle hand on his arm. She refilled his coffee and leaned in to him as if the sound of his words were a steady reassurance of her own safety. Ruth's eldest sisters, Dollie and Bea, assisted her in her ministrations. Dollie moved from the shoulder of one man to the hand of another—soothing, tutting, pouring. Her shadow, Bea, scuttled by the stove.

"Pass me your cup now. Let me fill it up. More sugar?" Dollie cooed, reaching behind her with the expectation that Bea would hand her the sugar bowl. The faded day dresses and morning aprons of the women appeared bright next to the gray mounds of male bodies.

Her mother tore away from her father's side to pull a pan from the oven. She placed a chipped platter laden with steamy biscuits and salted pork on the table. Dollie leaned in and out and in between, laying out bowls of jams and butter, weaving through pipe smoke and dirty limbs. The men, with their sinewy hands and black fingernails, reached for the fluffy white biscuits.

Father carried on, as much to himself as to the room. Ruth wriggled between elbows and shoulders and pilfered a biscuit. A streak of soot appeared on her pale nightsleeve when she grazed against her father. He reached for the butter bowl and placed it in front of her—the corner of his mouth lifting in her direction.

"I'll be dayumed if them Southern Bell folks didn't keep answerin' the lines—lettin' folks know what was happenin'. Never mind that fire roarin' toward 'em. We kept it from 'em, though. By a hair."

He paused, searching for words. He spoke as if he alone were responsible for the damage done before the fire was extinguished. "Couldn't be stopped. Finished one wall and ran right up the next. Took out two blocks 'fore we could even slow it down."

He laid a hand on Riley's bone-thin shoulder. Angry red welts glistened from beneath the soot on Riley's skin. Blisters bubbled along his jawline and down his neck. Riley winced at the slight touch of his father's hand but refused to cry out.

"This boy a'mine worked as hard as any man out there. Timber caught him when the stables came down." A nervous chuckle tinged his words. "The boy hightailed it outta there right 'long with them long-legged colts. Might as well been one a'em, he moved so fast."

Mother laid a cool wet towel on Riley's wound.

"Doll-baby? Hand me the salve," she instructed. Dollie passed Mother the burn salve—a concoction made of hog fat, marshmallow root, and calendula flowers. Ruth and her sisters collected the marshmallow roots by the creek bank in the summer and harvested the sunny yellow calendula flowers every fall. They were hung in the garden shed to dry and, once dried, crushed into powders. Her sister Bessie, under the tutelage of their mother, had a knack for medicinal combinations. The burn salve was one of her creations.

"That lil'un there?" Father cocked his head in Earl's direction. "Ran buckets faster than a horse with a tail full of bees. All you boys fought hard."

Earl and Riley beamed under their father's adulations. Tom and Wheeler, grown men as tall and strong as their father, elbowed their little brothers in agreement—relief passing between them. They'd all emerged breathing from the grip of night and fire. A round of grumbling affirmation vibrated from around the room.

Ruth's mother tutted with reassurance, "Not a thing a'one a'you could do, Bill, not one thing . . ."

Silence descended. The men stared into their coffee cups, aware of their good fortune—and their defeat. They were grateful for her words.

The soft-pillow biscuit melted in Ruth's mouth. She curled near her father's feet with her knees to her chin. She leaned against his chair leg, fending off the trembling in her bones. His hand rustled her thick auburn curls as if one of their farm mutts had settled by him. She could hear a faint whistle from his tired lungs.

Fire had visited their town. Ruth imagined it had crept out along the railway and slithered its way down the trolley lines from Atlanta. She knew the stories well. People still talked about the fire that swept through Atlanta last year, burning through the entire Fourth Ward and damaging her cousins' properties. There was the massacre on Decatur Street before that, and then there was the monster Sherman.

Not a soul in Atlanta would ever forget General William Tecumseh Sherman and the devastation he wrought. Especially considering that Papa Jefferson had seen it with his own eyes and spit out his terrible memories at regular intervals—stories of horses with their tails on fire and women screaming and houses bigger than their own farm crumbling into great bonfires and men being run straight through with the bayonets. Papa Jefferson saw every last bit of it. Every time Ruth heard it she wanted to cry.

Ruth's own brother was named after General Joseph Wheeler— the Southern hero who had tried and failed to stop the fires set by Sherman. Ruth snuck a peek at her oldest brother. Wheeler had his eyes closed and his chin dropped into his chest. He was soot-covered, and the counter he leaned against appeared to be the only thing holding him upright. He resembled more of a whipped foot soldier than a general.

Ruth's great-grandfather had settled their family in Stone Mountain, a farming hamlet that lay ten miles outside the capital city of Atlanta. By 1918, a nickel and a trolley brought people back and forth between the bustling city and their sleepy village every day. Ruth's family ties stretched thick between the two. It suited them that a few of their own worked for the Atlanta Trolley Car Company, and on occasion, rides from one cousin to another could be snuck in for free.

Ruth had learned from her father that Stone Mountain herself had been born of primordial fire. A sixteen-hundred-foot monolith of granite and quartz jutted from the village center, formed by a prehistoric volcanic eruption. It had the appearance of a stone bubble that had half broken from the earth before freezing in place.

On one side of the granite edifice, a rolling green lawn beckoned Sunday picnickers. On the other, Venable Lake, named after the owners of the mountain, was a regular temptation for those needing solace from the unrelenting heat of Georgia summers. In a land of lush, tangled vegetation, the rounded rock face stood out stark and odd—a natural wonder both revered and feared. It is the biggest piece of exposed granite in the world. A wild and unfounded claim that suited the Southern vernacular. Ruth preferred Arabia Mountain, a hidden place behind the great stone bubble that only the local children knew about—a place where Ruth and her younger siblings often wandered under the watchful care of their older sisters.

Huddled safely beneath her father's hand, Ruth tried to imagine a fire that swallowed buildings and chased animals, this crawling thing that had reduced her father, her grandfathers, her uncles and brothers to blackened heaps. She thought of the controlled burns in the fields and the cackling of their mammoth fireplace, a cavernous hearth fashioned from the same mountain granite that loomed above their village. She thought of the nurturing flames of her mother's cooking fires and the ease with which those were put out. She wondered why some fires couldn't be stopped. Why some could not be contained.

The kitchen door flew open, and a wild-haired girl stomped in. Ruth clamped her hand over her mouth to keep from snickering. Her sister Lola Bell looked as if she'd taken a roll in the mud.

"Mama! That new dairy cow is a beast. A right mad woman." Lola shoved her way to the table and grabbed a biscuit. She was as grimy as the men and not the least bit happy about it. "Though I cain't say I don't respect a mad woman."

"Take a tumble in the pigsty, Lola? Mornin' chores gettin' the best a'ya?" Tom leaned back in his chair and took in the disheveled sight of his younger sister.

"I did not tumble with the swine, Tom. I went to blows with that feral heifer you bought off a'Richard Sams. I was not bested—am I ever bested? I managed a full pail before I let her teets rest."

A giggle escaped Ruth, and Lola, now aware of the girl at her feet, bent over sideways to meet her eye to eye. Lola tapped her nose.

"You know what teets are, don't ya, little sister?"

Mother stepped in and set Lola aside, giving her a scolding look.

"Ruthie? Ruthie baby. Why don't you go on ahead and get a head start on feeding the hens?"

Lola winked at her and took a bite of her biscuit. The stove fire snapped in harmony with the one in the Great Room. The kettle whistled in readiness. Bea rushed to its rescue while Dollie waited for her to steep the next pot of brew. Night had fallen into day, and the men would run on thick, sweet coffee.

"Yes, ma'yam."

She unfolded herself from the floor, grabbed the Carhartt coat her mother kept by the door, slid her feet into a pair of hand-me-down boots, and headed outside to the hen run—a large, sturdy outbuilding inhabited by a mean old rooster named Max, a peacock named Francis, and countless colorful laying hens. It was one of her favorite places. Free of the crowded confines of the kitchen, she held out her arms and twirled in a circle. Twirling and twirling until she reached the fence post where the feed bucket hung.

She would be six years old in a few more weeks. Within those few years of living, she had learned that twirling—and rock kicking and frog hunting—helped chase away her frightened thoughts.

She was Ida and Bill Shurlington's ninth child, born into a world already in chaos. The coloreds hid within the dark fringes of the village in a place called Shermantown. Tornados, droughts, and plagues came at random, rolling them between feast and famine. The Yankees roamed among them—leftover interlopers from the States War. A new war—an invisible war—in a far-off place called France had spurred the rising of the military camps. These sprawling, barbed-wire complexes designed for training and deploying and even imprisoning swallowed her uncles and cousins. They were full of fighting soldiers from France and New York and captured soldiers from Germany, all with strange accents and curious ways. She could see the encampments anytime she went into town and hear the faint popping of their military exercises throughout the day.

Ruth blew out a hoary breath and watched it fade before huffing another in its wake. She was a great dragon hiding in the heart of the Stone Mountain blowing smoke instead of fire. Harmless. She sifted through her picture-card thoughts, stopping on the brighter news of yesterday.

There was going to be a new baby in the fall—rounding out the Shurlington family offspring to an even dozen. Her mother had told them during evening readings. Grinning, pipe held tight between his teeth, her father had rubbed her mother's belly with affection. Ruth rolled it over in her mind. She loved babies. She wanted it to be a boy because she already had two little sisters—Clara May and Ruby.

In the distance, the Stone Mountain commuter train thundered down the rail line. The ground beneath her shuddered, and the sleeping fields exploded with tiny, frosty lights. It was a cold blue morning heralded by a fiery sunrise. In the distance, gray puffs of smoke from the village fire were etched against the sky by the first rays of the morning. Lacy bits of silver and black ash floated on the breeze. A peppery snowfall. She slipped the latch on the hen run and ducked inside. Clucking. Chasing. She let the cracked corn slip from her fingers in swirling patterns and giggled to herself as the chickens followed her bidding, forming circles of pecking, dancing feathers. There was power in being the keeper of the grain. She set small patches here and there. Watching them follow the food. Forgetting the night in favor of the day.

Bibb County, Georgia—1918

Leonidas Brantley settled himself by the old wood-burning stove that dominated the main room of his one-bedroom shanty. He reached into his front pocket and pulled out a gold ring, sliding it back in place on his left hand. He admired the red stone overlaid with the square and compass signet. His Mason ring. He removed it when he worked, for safety reasons, but otherwise it was always on his hand.

He reached back into his pocket and pulled out an old tin that held a half dozen hand-rolled cigarettes and a handful of matches. He flicked his nail against the match, and a tiny orange flame burst to life. He sucked the flame through the open end of the hand roll, pulling smoke into his lungs and holding it there a long while before letting it out in perfectly formed rings.

He watched the rings drift around him through half-closed eyes. He was a machinist at Schofield's Iron Works—a trade he'd learned from his father and his uncles. The work was hard and the days were long. He was black with grease, and his nose twitched from the caustic smell of overheated iron that clung to his clothes. His shoulders and his back hurt. He could feel the itch of metal splinters embedded in his fingers. He was only twenty-three, but the monotonous days of working the lathe for the steam engine builds aged a man past his years.

He stretched his back and shook off the humiliation of the day. He'd had to admit he couldn't read to his foreman. He'd never been able to make sense of the letters that floated on a page. Most days he could get by without it causing a problem. But every now and then, there was no way around it. Today had been one of those days. There was a note added to one of the blueprints. A specification change that hadn't been drawn into the pictures yet, and he'd screwed up, mis-machined a key part and brought the whole line to a halt. His foreman, once he'd figured out the truth, had been kind enough to explain the details that Leonidas needed, but that sound of pity, the dismissal in the voice of his superior, simmered in Leonidas.

From the corner of the room came a mewing that quickly expanded to a wail. He watched his child squirm in the cradle, rubbing her face against the sheet, and wake in a fit. He stared at her. Crawford had named her Helen. Her cries agitated him. He laid his head back against the threadbare couch.

"Crawford! Crawford!"

He could see his young wife outside pulling the laundry off the lines before the night freeze set in. She was wrapped in one of his old coats and had on fingerless mittens. She turned her head toward the house, toward his voice, when she heard him calling, and he was pleased to see that she didn't hesitate. She made quick work of piling the sheets in her basket before trotting through the back door.

She headed straight for the cradle and hefted their daughter into her arms.

"I'm sorry, Lee. I thought for sure she'd sleep another hour," Crawford repented and added quickly. "Supper's near ready."

She bounced Helen on her hip, shushing her as she unbuttoned her top and settled her into nursing. Crawford sank into the chair opposite Leonidas, avoiding his eyes, her knees brushing his. Leonidas smoked his cigarette, blowing smoke rings in her direction, watching her.

"I brought ya somethin'," he said finally. He reached into his pocket and pulled out a brown box. Crawford lit up—Hershey's Sweet Milk Chocolate Kisses.

"Figure since it was yer birthday and all."

She reached for the box, and he moved it out of her reach, a glint in his eye.

"How old are you turnin' anyway, Crawford?"

The smile on her lips faded, and she feigned disinterest in the box of chocolates. She blinked a few times, wondering where he was leading her.

"Seventeen." She spoke to the top of her daughter's head, making a fuss with her blouse. Helen was a waif of a babe. At seven months old, she was no more than a sparrow nestled in the crook of her mother's arm. "You know that, Lee."

"Seventeen," he repeated. "You were a purty thing when I married you. What? Last winter?"

Crawford nodded. Leonidas opened the box and pulled out one of the silver-wrapped chocolate drops. He opened the candy and put it in his mouth. She kept her eyes on Helen, waiting.

"Look like a dayum sow now," he mumbled under his breath, examining the box and biting into the chocolate. "That's right tasty. I get why ya like 'em."

He opened another and leaned closer to her.

"Open yer mouth."

Crawford closed her eyes and emptied her mind. His comment hurt her.

"Com'mon, Crawford," he cajoled. "I was teasin' ya. Yer still purty as the day I first saw ya. Purty little gurl with purty yella curls.

Open up. Let me give ya a'birthday chocolate."

Crawford opened her mouth. He held the chocolate close to her lips, letting her smell the aroma of it. She did love chocolate and rarely had the pleasure of enjoying it. She tried to bite it from his hand, and he pulled away laughing. She knew these taunting games pleased him, and so she opened her mouth a second time. He dropped the chocolate on her tongue and immediately followed it with a kiss.

"Mmm . . . still tasty too, ain't ya?" He gave her free breast a squeeze. "Finish up with that young'un and get m'supper on."

Psalms 139:13-16
KJV

*For thou hast possessed my reins: thou hast covered
me in my mother's womb. I will praise thee;
for I am fearfully and wonderfully made:
marvellous are thy works; and that
my soul knoweth right well.*

*My substance was not hid from thee, when I was
made in secret, and curiously wrought in the lowest
parts of the earth. Thine eyes did see my substance,
yet being unperfect; and in thy book all my
members were written, which in continuance were
fashioned, when as yet there was none of them.*

Chapter 2

The snow ash from the village fire fell for days, covering the ground in a fine white dust that turned black when you rubbed it. Riley and Earl took to running their fingers in it and painting their faces like Indian warriors, which frustrated Mother because it meant she had to change Riley's bandages more often. The acrid scent of charred wood lingered in the air with the faintest edge of something more sour—Riley said it was roasted animals and took to recounting his narrow escape from the falling timbers of the town stables. With each telling he became more heroic and immortal.

The morning train, with its inescapable clacking, was louder in the cold months, cracking against the stiff air, with nothing more than winter pine to dampen the harsh sound. Ruth imagined the shrill caw of the crows and the piercing sound of the train whistle came from the same creature—morphing them in her mind into a broad-winged flying machine that flew low over the land.

"It's black as night with yella fire for eyes and a skinny black body made a'metal. If you touch it, you'll turn black as a soot-covered darkie. It don't fly straight, neither. It wiggles and slides like a sidewinder. It's got wings long as tree branches sewn on either side, and they don't flap like regular bird wings. They go back and a'forth like the catfish fins. Has a belly full a'granite, and black smoke puffs from its mouth."

Ruth watched Ruby and Clara May's eyes grow wide. The sun had yet to rise, and the three girls were outside stomping on stiff, frost-bitten blades of grass, caped in colorful patchwork quilts about their shoulders. A night terror had roused Clara May earlier than usual, and no amount of cajoling could convince her to return to her dreams. Ruth, accustomed to soothing her younger sisters in one way or another, decided it was too early for breakfast but too late to keep bothering with sleep. Grass-breaking and storytelling seemed the finest way to pass the time until the rest of the house stirred.

"Where's it live? Cain't be up in the trees," Ruby challenged, scanning the sky. Ruby was about to turn four and had started asking too many questions for Ruth's comfort. Ruth, secure in her superior storytelling prowess, narrowed her eyes and leaned closer to her sister, lowering her voice as if the monster might hear.

"Course it don't live in the trees, Ruby. Don't be coo-coo. It lives deep in the mountain most a'the time. But when it gets cold enough? When the creek freezes over and you can see your breathin'? It comes flyin' and spittin' rocks."

Ruth flapped her arms back and forth. Clara May, who was hardly more than a baby, clapped her hands at Ruth's antics. Crows cawed in the distance, and Ruby's gaze darted across the horizon in search of the fantastic creature. The long wail of the train whistle blew. Ruby squealed in fear, dropping the quilt from her shoulders and running into the house. Ruth, pleased that her tale had produced the desired impact, hefted Clara May onto her hip, rubbing her nose with her own.

"Eskimo kisses," she declared to Clara May, who giggled and tucked her head into Ruth's shoulder. Ruth struggled not to tilt under her weight as she followed Ruby up the porch steps.

The Shurlington family farmhouse, with its raging hearths and tightly sealed windows, held heat and ash with jealous determination. Both levels of the house were filled with bodies, coughing and scratching. Fetid mounds of flesh stirred and stumbled over each other. Indoor plumbing had been installed the previous year, but the outhouse and the side of the barn were still used, most frequently in the morning, when all thirteen of the house's inhabitants needed to relieve themselves. Bathing happened only on Saturdays in preparation for Sunday services.

"Your body is a temple to the Lord and must be presented holy in the Lord's house," Mother said every Saturday.

The girls weaved through the waking adults—Ruby wailing in the lead and Ruth swaying behind her with Clara May perched on her hip and clinging to her neck. Ruby was heading straight for Mother, and Ruth knew it would be advisable to be present for her own defense when Ruby tattled.

"Our Lord in Heaven is listening to you, Ruthie—and He is very disappointed that you went and upset your sister this way." Ruby nestled in their mother's skirts, looking devastated.

"A child a'God speaks with wisdom, and kindness is perpetually upon her tongue," Mother chastised, calling on her endless knowledge of the Proverbs.

"She's bein' a baby, Mama. Twas just a story. Daddy and Papa Jefferson tell 'em all the time. She don't go rattin' them out."

Ruth stuck her tongue out at her sister, who was smiling

through crocodile tears.

"I have no say over your father or your papa, but I do have say over you, young lady. I expect you to be my big girl and take care a'your sisters. Don't let me hear a'you scaring 'em again."

Ruth hung her head, seething at Ruby for tattling and wishing she could tell stories the way she wanted without risking retribution. Clara May twisted her body toward Mother, reaching and whimpering. Ruth battled to keep her footing while holding onto her baby sister, reluctant to admit she was failing in the endeavor.

"Yes, ma'yam." And with reluctance: "I didn't mean to scare ya none, Ruby."

"What are you girls doing outside so early, anyhow?" Mother scooped Clara May from Ruth's arms and handed her a piece of toast.

"Clara May was havin' night terrors. She couldn't sleep." Ruth, relieved of her sister's weight, reached up and patted her on the back.

"See now, Ruthie. You are a good girl, baby. Taking care a'Clara when she was scared."

Mother tucked Clara May onto the shelf of her hip and handed Ruth the egg-gathering basket, swatting her and Ruby back out the kitchen door.

"Y'all go on—and be good to your sister, Ruthie."

Outside the train whistled as it left the depot. Ruth turned to Ruby, flapping her arms like catfish fins and widening her eyes in mock fear.

On the horizon, past the fallow fields, the vigilant mountain blended into the low-hanging sky, casting shadows over the countless acres of Shurlington family land. Ruth's father and brothers and a handful of hired hands spilled from the porch, coughing and muttering, out into the fields and barns. Ruth and Ruby went about their chores until their chores faded into adventures that sprawled from the house to the outbuildings and brought them stumbling and laughing upon the men working in the cold afternoon.

They made a habit of searching out their father. His patterns were easy to follow, and by midafternoon they knew they'd find him by the grazing fields, where they plopped themselves on the fence line he was mending with Riley and Earl as his helpers. Father had grown up in the shadow of the mountain and knew all about the goblins and dragons that lived deep within its caves. His stories were endless.

As the oldest boy of twelve children, their father held a rather significant place in a Southern family. The further down the birth order a boy fell, the less he mattered. If you happened to be a girl, like Aunt Alice, who was really the firstborn, it didn't really mean much when you showed up—as long as you were pretty enough to marry well. Their father was lucky—or so one assumed—to be the eldest son of Robert Jefferson Shurlington, whom they called Papa Jefferson, and Mary Tressa Hahn. Ruth only knew Mama Mary by name, as she died when Ruth was only a year old and had gone on to be with the Lord.

Papa Jefferson told hateful tales of the mountain. The ugly kind that would get Ruth in serious trouble with her mother. He told of Yanks hiding among the crags, waiting to get their hands on Rebel children. He had a cold, distant demeanor honed by war and want. His gray beard hung in a scraggly triangle to his chest, and he kept a pipe clenched in his few remaining teeth. He smelled of dirt and corn whiskey. Papa Jefferson had been fourteen years old when his regiment, the 63rd Georgia Infantry, faced the Union army in Atlanta, and he had no use for Yanks or blacks or girls—then or now.

"That mountain?" Father said, taking off his hat and pointing toward the gray mass. He coughed and paused to catch his breath—a habit he'd had since the night of the fire. "Why, it goes miles and miles below the ground. Deeper than the turnip roots. Deeper than the graves up at Mount Zion. Deeper than anything you girls could reckon. What you see there is not more than a mole's nose pokin' from the ground."

"Deeper than the swimmin' lake?" Ruth asked suspiciously.

"Deeper than the swimmin' lake. And I'll tell you—there's caves too. And there's goblins that live in them caves—protectors of the village. I hear tell they're ol' Rebs who refused to surrender. So they retreated so far down that they couldn't find the way back up. They're guardin' an ol' Confederate treasure for when we need it again." He smiled down at his children.

"Papa says it's Yanks up in there," Riley challenged.

"Your papa's never gotten over the war, Riley. Still thinks there's Yanks behind every tree and stone. He's one of those that refused to surrender."

"I thought we were the losers. Ever'body had to surrender," Riley countered. Father leaned against the fence and gave him a half smile, his expression taking a faraway look.

"We mighta had to step down for the betterment a'the country, Riley, but I don't suppose we were losers. And it is the Gawd's honest truth about your papa. My daddy and near 'bout his entire regiment would not surrender. Officially, anyway. Wasn't til the gov'ment threatened to steal the land right out from under him that he signed the allegiance papers."

Ruth, having caught the burr of agitation in her father's voice, rolled the two conflicting stories around in her head before blurting, "Maybe there's both up there. Maybe they made friends and decided the whole thing was so coo-coo they'd rather live up in the caves than fight anymore."

"Well, that don't make no sense. You don't go makin' friends with somebody you're trying to shoot," Riley snapped.

"Maybe they did make friends, Ruthie. Not unheard of," Father said, ignoring Riley and lifting Ruth and Ruby off the fence, setting their feet to the ground. "I will say. If you squint your eyes as the moon rises, whatever's up in there—be it goblins or Rebs or Yanks—can be seen marchin' long the crevices."

Ruth squinted her eyes at the mountain, nose wrinkled and chin jutting forward. Gray and green lines marred the sloping granite so that it appeared to be weeping metallic tears. Occasional tufts of emerald trees dotted its surface. Ruby, Earl, and Riley followed suit. All four squinted and stretched their faces forward to make out the goblins.

"I think maybe I see somethin'," Riley said. The tight sheen of a burn was still pink along his jaw and pulled the corner of his mouth down ever so slightly, making him look serious even when he smiled. Mother covered it in salve every morning—which didn't prevent him from scratching at it.

"It only works when the moon is high," Father said, laughing and scrubbing their heads. "Now y'all scoot on. Your brothers and I got to finish up. Cain't be havin' 'em missin' more than a day a'school over this fence. And I'm willin' to bet a wooden nickel and a slice a'pie that your mama could use your hands."

Now that they were part of a new war, half the hired hands had enlisted or been drafted. To make up for the loss, Riley and Earl stayed home from school more than their father wanted. Their cousin Elmer and their father's youngest brother, Uncle Ephraim, had enlisted too. Ruth liked having Riley and Earl around more, even if it seemed to worry her parents. She did not, however, care for the absence of Uncle Ephraim. It made her father sad.

Day by winter day, the farm heaved through the biting cold under the labor of too few men. Evening came fast, engulfing the house and the land and the magic mountain in inky blackness broken only by the brilliant blanket of stars that hung overhead. In those brief, dark months of winter, the earth fell into a heavy torpor, refusing to wake to such an inhospitable chill.

The days were made all the darker by the burned-out buildings in the village. Ruth, tagging along on her mother's town errands, stumbled along the sidewalk, her head swiveling to take in the cavernous black spaces that only weeks before had been a millinery and a barn and a pharmacy, vibrant with colorful hats and snuffling horses and shelves filled with shiny glass bottles. The Granite Bank was streaked in long black whips of soot, and a hodgepodge of crates and tables formed a makeshift grocery.

The fire had burned up all the colors.

The tiny bell on the door of the pharmacy, the one Ruth rang by closing and opening the door until her mother made her stop, was silenced.

The smell too had changed. There was a bright metallic tang that tickled at her nose. Overwhelmed by the changes, Ruth ran to catch up to her mother, wrapping her fingers in her skirts. Even the people had changed. There were soldiers in all different kinds of uniforms, crowing and calling to each other. She peered closely at their faces, looking for Uncle Ephraim.

"Mama?" Ruth tugged at her mother, who turned with thinly veiled frustration. "Mama? Maybe we'll see Uncle Ephraim?"

Sadness softened her mother's face, and she knelt down until she was eye to eye with Ruth. "No, baby. We won't see Uncle Ephraim. He's in France. He and your cousin Elmer both. There's no need for us to worry on it. They are taking real good care of each other."

Elmer was Lola's beau. He'd gotten all excited about the idea of fighting Huns, and since he was eighteen and too young for the draft, he went ahead and enlisted last Christmas. Lola had been crying ever since. Ruth looked at the scuffed toes of her shoes and whispered.

"Will Daddy go too?" Her mother laughed the way she did when the storms came up fast and the windows were still open. She wrapped Ruth tight inside her arms.

"No, no, no, baby. Daddy won't be going anywhere. Daddy's a farmer. So are your brothers. The farmers gotta grow the food to feed your Uncle Ephraim and Elmer. Your daddy's staying right here with me and you."

Ruth nodded, clinging to her mother's words as if she'd spoken them from the church altar.

That winter in particular, time was equally divided between preparing the fields for spring planting and helping rebuild the burned-out village. Father relied on his oldest sons, Wheeler and Tom, to conduct the necessary farm tasks while Riley and Earl, along with most of the town boys, were kept from school to help with building repairs. Father then migrated between the farm and the village—supervising, advising, teaching.

Ruth begged to join her brothers in the village during the days, but Mother needed help with Ruby and Clara May—so instead she was allowed to go in with her father in the afternoons after dinner when Ruby and Clara May were worn out and resting. Ruth was satisfied with this arrangement, as she was given an important job. Mother gave her extra burn salve to bring to Riley, who rejected any tender concerns over his wounds but appreciated the midday relief from the itching.

It was an unexpected pleasure to be side by side with Riley and

Earl—to help her brothers without being shoved away. A pleasure she felt guilty for feeling, since it might mean she was happy about the fire and maybe even happy that Riley had been burned—which she was not. The fire repairs meant she was no longer separated from her brothers by boy chores and girl chores. It meant she could leave Ruby and Clara May behind and be a part of Riley and Earl's adventures—which had always appeared much more interesting than her own.

Every day, their father doled out repair jobs to the three of them. They swept the floors of the damaged buildings or helped clear out charred clutter. Riley showed her his copy of *Thurston's Easy Pocket Tricks*. Magic had fascinated him ever since he'd seen the magician and escape artist Harry Houdini escape from a tank full of Coca-Cola in Atlanta two years prior.

"He coulda drank it. Drank up all the Co-Cola and taken his time escapin'. Ain't like you can drown in Co-Cola," Ruth remarked when Riley started talking for the millionth time about seeing Houdini.

"Don't be daft, Rue," Riley snapped, who, given his miraculous escape from the village fire, credited himself as being an expert on the subject. "You cain't go drinkin' that much Co-Cola. They filled the whole tank with it. Plus it splashed out when he got free."

He reached behind her ear and produced a blackened piece of wood, raising his eyebrows as if his and Houdini's magic were connected by his mastery of the trick.

"I bet you could drown in Co-Cola. Same as you can water," Earl added.

"So it was like he took a bath in Co-Cola?" Ruth snickered. "That's coo-coo. You gotta take another bath after that. Co-Cola baths make no sense."

"I'd take a Co-Cola bath," Earl said as he swiped black ash

across his cheeks and waggled his eyebrows at Ruth.

Ruth and Earl broke into laughter at the idea of taking a bath in Coca-Cola. Riley let out an exasperated sigh and returned to collecting debris. By some divine hand, which Ruth was sure to include her gratitude for in her nightly prayers, her brothers made room for her, and the pair of two grew to a pack of three.

Most of the damaged buildings and businesses had belonged to the McGurdy family, and from time to time, Mrs. McGurdy came by with a fresh pie or basket of sweet corn muffins in appreciation.

"Thank you, Miz McGurdy. It's very kind a'you to be thinkin' a'us."

Ruth was careful to mind the manners her mother had ingrained in her and to keep her posture straight. Mrs. McGurdy was a fine lady. You could tell by the pearl brooch she wore at her throat and the smooth white gloves that covered her slim fingers. The whole town felt sad for her. Nevermind the fire had burned up her sister-in-law's hat shop and her husband's stable. Word had come that her son wouldn't be coming home from the new war. He'd died in France.

Despite her best effort to give Mrs. McGurdy her full attention, Ruth couldn't help but be distracted by Riley and Earl, knowing they were waiting to gobble down the muffins. They too were working hard to be young gentlemen—removing their hats and greeting Mrs. McGurdy whenever she visited. She had a way of lingering on Riley and Earl ever since she'd received the news about her son, and it seemed Riley and Earl knew they were reminding her of something she'd lost, so they stood tall and respectful and let her look at them.

"Please pass on to your mama and daddy that we are so grateful for your family's help," she said in her sad, singsong voice.

Ruth liked Mrs. McGurdy because she was one of the few adults who spoke directly to her. She made her feel important—tasking her with delivering both messages and muffins alike.

Ruth gave Mrs. McGurdy a curtsy.

"Yes, ma'yam."

It was good manners to express your gratitude for the help of others, even if it was expected that men like Ruth's father would lend a hand to the finer families such as the McGurdys. Everyone understood their part. As long as everyone minded their place, the community meandered along in peace. Mrs. McGurdy was kind and generous, but she and Mother had never sat down to tea, nor would either have expected such an invitation. While Mr. McGurdy shook hands with all the farmers, it was the Coca-Cola makers—the Candler boys—that he invited to dinner.

Job 37:9-10
KJV

Out of the south cometh the whirlwind; and cold out of the North. By the breath of God frost is given, and the breadth of the waters is straightened.

Chapter 3

By February, the pale yellow wood of new construction gleamed along Main Street. Two days before Saint Valentine's and just as Miss Dorothy's millinery shop reopened, Ruth turned six. The biting cold made her glad to be excused from her responsibilities. Ruth and her eldest sister, Dollie, shared their birthday celebrations. They were born fourteen years and four days apart. Dollie had told her this exactly and said she didn't mind that they celebrated on Ruth's actual day instead of her own, which only rooted Ruth's regard of her.

On their birthday morning, the two sat in their parents' twin rockers by the fire, rocking in rhythm and making a show of being warm and cozy as the rest of their siblings headed out into the cold. Skipping chores and having Dollie by her side, even for those few minutes of morning, made her winter birthday somewhat acceptable. Ruby and Clara May, who shared a birthday month, had both been born in the spring—exactly two years apart. Riley and

Earl too. There were more flowers in the spring. More flowers and fruits and sun.

"Dollie?" she said. "Why did you pick February for your birthday?"

Ruth couldn't recall picking her own birthday month but was certain it had happened, and she had forgotten doing it. Dollie laughed her perfect laugh—wind chimes caught in the slightest breeze.

"You don't get to pick your birthday month, silly goose. It just happens. Same as rain or sunshine or a twister coming through. You wake up and look outside and that's the way the day will be. Mama woke up one day in February and there you came, like a rain shower happening."

"I wish I'd happened on a sunny day."

Ruth kicked her tiptoes against the roughhewn wood floor and sent the rocker into a vigorous sway.

Dollie studied her. "Winter birthdays are special birthdays, Ruthie. Warm and cozy. More starlight than sunlight. Starlight twinkles. Like you."

Dollie reached over and tapped her on the nose, tilting her head the way she did when she was mothering rather than sistering. Dollie practiced mothering a good deal, which at times confused Ruth as to who Dollie was supposed to be.

"Com'mon now. Let's go see what kinda cake Mama's making, hmm? Maybe she'll be making it with starlight this year."

Ruth scrunched her face. "You cain't cook with starlight!"

"Mmm . . . I don't know. She's got her special secret ingredients. Who says it cain't be starlight?" Dollie winked at her, standing from her rocker and scooping down to hoist Ruth onto her hip. "Goodness child, you are getting big. I believe this might be the last time I carry you anywhere. It is official. You are turning six and practically grown."

Ruth wiggled and slid off her sister's hip easily, darting toward the kitchen to find Mother. She called back over her shoulder, soothing the sting of leaving Dollie, "I'm plenty big already! Big enough to beat you there!"

Mother ruled their world from the kitchen, conducting the business of their house on a tight schedule with lists of chores doled out over breakfast. She shifted, with organized precision, from one task to the next with no time for dallying. It was rare to have her full attention. But on Celebration Day, she started the day by your side, baking a cake and singing hymns under her breath.

She commemorated all her children's birthdays with a freshly baked cake served after supper. One cake for all the birthdays in the month—thus eliminating any need to serve the cake on anyone's exact day. Ruth suspected this was in part because she found it easier to remember her children's birthday months, rather than the day of a new baby's appearance. Not to mention there was a birthday in every month save July and March so she could bake one cake a month, hold it out, and wait for whoever had a birthday to claim it. If no one claimed it for their birthday, she could assign it to a holiday or church gathering in that month. However you looked at it, Mother's method meant there was cake at least once a month for one reason or another.

Since the new war had started, they had to have a different kind of cake—made with cornmeal—because all the regular flour went to the soldiers at Camp Gordon and Camp Jessup, which was fair as far as Ruth was concerned since cakes made with regular flour would make the soldiers less sad about being away from their families. Every Sunday, her mother clipped the cornmeal recipes from the *Atlanta Constitution* and tucked them into the green grease-stained recipe box she kept on the kitchen windowsill.

"I've never tried a cake made with cornmeal. Cornbread, sure. But not a cake." She leaned down to Ruth and tweaked her nose, leaving a grainy yellow smudge of cornmeal on the tip. "Your Aunt Alice passed it on to me. She told me little Elly loved it so much that she ate the whole thing in one sitting."

She squinted at the recipe card. "We're gonna use corn flour to make a sponge cake. I suppose it's gonna taste a bit like sweet corn cake with sugar icing. But that doesn't matter much, does it, Ruthie baby?"

"No, ma'yam. I like sweet corn cake." Ruth grinned.

Aunt Alice was her father's eldest sister, and her daughter, Elly, was one of Ruth's favorite cousins. Aunt Alice and Elly lived down the road, and Ruth and Elly often met at the creek between their two houses to play. If Elly loved it, she'd love it. Besides, she didn't care what they made as long as she got to join her mother and her sister in the kitchen.

Ruth cracked and separated the eggs into two milky-white bowls. She stirred the sugar into the yolk bowl while her mother whipped the whites to stiff peaks. Then she helped marry all of the ingredients into one big glass bowl. Sweet peaches, canned the previous summer, sat waiting to top the spongy confection. The peaches were so bright and sunny that Ruth begrudgingly thought her mother had figured out how to capture the sunlight, not starlight, inside the jars.

Just as it was time to lick the batter bowl, which was her most favorite part, Riley and Earl tumbled through the kitchen door. Riley snatched the spoon from Ruth's hand and gave it a big lick, his eyes rolling back in his head at the pleasure of it. Earl clammered at Riley—grabbing at the batter spoon—nudging Ruth away. Father, who made a habit of swinging through the kitchen for refreshment between his early and late morning chores, ambled into the kitchen behind his boys. A fresh cup of chicory coffee and a bowl filled with red-eye gravy and a sopping biscuit perched on the side was waiting for him.

"What month we in?" He winked at Ruth. Ruth's father was tall and had roiling dark eyes, a square jaw, and cheekbones so high they cast shadows on the side of his face. "This'd be Riley and Earl's birthday month, then?"

He fixed his attention on the boys, whose faces were covered with dirt and cake batter. Riley and Earl had been born in May. She knew this because she was already very good at math. She had been born in 1912. Earl in 1910 and Riley in 1908. It would have been nice to share a sunlight month with Riley and Earl, but she had decided starlight months were just as fine. It was the one thing she had in common with her eldest sister—and her mother, who had been born in December.

"No, s-sir. No, sir. It ain't," stammered Riley, guiltily handing Ruth back the stirring spoon. Earl sank behind his brother, staring at the floor.

"Isn't . . . No, sir. It isn't." Mother corrected him.

"Maybe it's Ruby and Clara May's, then?" he continued, looking decidedly confused and feigning the need for forgiveness. "There's been lotsa babies, Ida darlin'—hard keepin' track, ain't it?"

She pursed her lips at him and refilled his coffee.

"No-wah, Daddy," Ruth wailed. "It's mine. Mine and Dollie's. Me'n Dollie's ya Valentine gals, 'member?"

He laughed and nudged Dollie with his shoulder. He pulled a coin from his pocket and handed it to her. She blushed and thanked him.

"Figured with Miz Dorothy reopenin' shop this week, you might want a new hat or somethin'. I hear tell there's been a flurry a'deliveries from New York. Saw a bunch of boxes bein' unloaded myself."

Everybody knew Miss Dorothy McGurdy, the poor spinster sister-in-law of Mrs. McGurdy, ordered all her merchandise from New York. It was her life's mission to keep the ladies of Stone Mountain fashionable.

"Thank you, Daddy," Dollie said, brushing his cheek with a kiss.

"I'll have a little somethin' for you tonight, Rue. After cake. I'm meetin' Cousin Frank down at the trolley station to pick up your best present."

With that, he sopped up the last of his gravy, ruffled Ruth's hair, and swatted his wife on her generous behind. She snatched the kitchen towel from her shoulder and popped it with false indigna-tion in his direction, missing him by a mile.

"William Shurlington! You need to watch yourself!"

"Oh, and Uncle Henry'll be joinin' us too! So all y'all need to be on your most Christian behavior," he called as he disappeared through the kitchen door with Riley and Earl at his heels. His satisfied chuckle lingered in the air.

Ruth's mother married her father in the 1800s—December 20, 1895—on Mother's eighteenth birthday. She was the youngest daughter of Nancy and John Perkins. There were only two other children in her mother's family, which Ruth found odd. Aunt Norah lived down the road with Uncle Lovett, a confirmed bachelor. Aunt Norah was a widow with two daughters who were older than Wheeler. Ruth had only ever heard stories of her Grandma Nancy because she passed when Mother was still a baby. Papa Perkins, a widower with three small children, married a spinster named Ann very soon after Grandma Nancy's passing. Mama Ann, Papa Per-kins's second wife and the only living grandmother Ruth knew, lived with Papa Perkins next to Aunt Norah.

Papa Perkins, a gentle soul with a small round body and a ruddy face, stopped on his way to his cobbler's shop in the village and often came bearing some confection Mama Ann whipped up. If there were shoes that needed mending, they were to leave them in the basket by the door, and Papa Perkins would take them to his shop—returning them the next morning in finer condition.

Ruth had heard many times how her parents' families thought that Ida Perkins and William Shurlington made a good match. Anytime the story came up, her father would say, "And a good match its been."

Combined, the Perkins and Shurlington family farms took up several miles and a near century of history along the Stone Mountain car line, the ten-mile byway for car traffic between Atlanta and Stone Mountain.

"I bet you're excited about having Elly and Lizzie over tonight," Dollie said. Ruth knew she had reached the end of her allotted time with Dollie by the way her sister's voice had taken on an edge of distraction. "They sure are sweet girls. I think you're awful lucky."

Ruth felt her grin stretch into her ears. "I got everything ready. Even saved the paper doll cutting for tonight. Lizzie's bringing her book a'paper dolls—it's very nice—but we're gonna add the ones from the magazines too and have a whole bunch a'outfits."

Dollie leaned down and whispered, "I know where there's a box full of old paper dolls. Wanna use those too?" Ruth nodded with such vigor her neck hurt. Dollie laughed and went off to find the box of her old paper dolls.

The best part of Celebration Day was the sleepover with Ruth's two favorite cousins: Elly, who lived a skip away from Ruth, and Lizzie, who rode the trolley in from the city on Sundays for church services at Mount Zion Baptist Church.

Elly had her same given name—Ruth Elizabeth. Her cousin Frank's daughter, Lizzie, was also called Ruth Elizabeth. It got confusing to have the same name as two of her cousins who were also her same age. They were three persons—but one all at once. When the three of them were together, they made a joke of all answering every time somebody called out the name Ruth. Then they'd fall into a pile laughing. They talked about who was the overall best Ruth Elizabeth—which of course was Lizzie because she lived in Atlanta and wore the prettiest shoes. Elly was the smartest Ruth Elizabeth. She was a whip with numbers and read at least one new book every month. Ruth, they agreed, was the sweetest Ruth Elizabeth.

Lizzie's father, Cousin Frank, brought Lizzie with him once a month for an extra visit when he came into Stone Mountain on behalf of his Atlanta construction company. He came to haggle with the men at the Stone Mountain quarry office over stone purchases for his construction projects. This month he'd been kind enough to be sure his quarry business and Ruth's Celebration Day coincided.

It was this sweet anticipation of an overnight visit that fueled the better part of Ruth's day. She organized and reorganized the room she shared with her sisters, pulling in extra quilts and lining up her personal treasures. Her sister Bessie—who was a whole seven years older but still had to share a room with her—poked at her for her putterings.

"Best stay off my side a'the room," she warned, lifting her head from her book. She'd finished *Betty Policeman* and had started *The Return of Sherlock Holmes*—a book loaned to her by Uncle Lovett, Mama's brother. Uncle Lovett fancied himself to be a man of literature and made a habit of loaning books to the girls in their family, which was the only time Ruth ever saw him—when he was delivering books or helping in an emergency.

"I'll know if you bother any of my things."

Uncle Lovett had told Bessie she had a detective's eye. Bessie took this compliment to heart. Ruth stuck out her tongue and made a mental note to move Bessie's shoes to see what sort of detective she might be.

It was dusk when Father finally set out for the quarry to pick up Cousin Frank. Just as he left, Elly came bounding up the driveway. She'd run all the way from her house and, upon catching sight of Ruth, slowed to a trot, catching her breath and pushing at the stitch in her side.

"I thought Aunt Alice was bringing you!" Ruth giggled at Elly's red face.

"No-wah," Elly said with agitation. "The buggy'd been un-hitched already cause that old horse needed tendin' again. Mama said I had to walk." Elly lifted a bag made from a bright yellow square of scrap fabric in Ruth's direction.

"Looks more like you ran the whole way," Ruth said and took the small bag and untied the ribbon. It was full of penny candies.

"I been savin' 'em for you. Maybe took some from my brothers too. Plenty there for sharin' tonight," Elly said, cutting her eyes sideways in case anyone overheard her confession. Elly was the same as Ruth—the ninth child in a family of eleven—and felt she could justify the occasional thievery from her elder siblings as compensation for her undesirable birth order. Ruth gave her a quick hug, and the two girls planted themselves on the front step to wait, playing a hand-clap game to pass the time.

The blast of the car horn announced Lizzie's arrival, and the girls squealed in delight, tumbling down the steps and into the yard. A car door swung open before the wheels came to a stop, and a bright blond girl in shiny black Mary Jane shoes scampered toward them.

"There's a passel a'piglets on my porch," Mother laughed as she stepped outside.

Cousin Frank unfolded himself from the small car, and Ruth was hit, as she often was, by his resemblance to her own father. The two men looked more like brothers than cousins. Though, she supposed, there wasn't much difference between a cousin and brother. Behind them, a third man appeared—Uncle Henry. As Uncle Henry rose from the car, stretching into his full, towering height, the girls quieted to whispered shrieks, all three taking note of Uncle Henry to be sure they weren't disturbing him. Uncle Henry was kind but stern and had little use for children who were too happy.

"Frankie! Henry!" Mama cooed in her most melodious voice as the three men strode onto the porch. "You com'mon in here and have yourself a bite. Bill took down a big ole six-point buck that's been feeding us for weeks. I've fried up some nice deer steaks for y'all. We got gravy and mashed potatoes. I sure hope you didn't let those quarry boys take you for a ride."

"Aww, no Ida. You know me better than that. Got a better deal on a load a'stone than the last time." Cousin Frank surrendered to her embrace. She half released him and began squeezing at his limbs.

"That city wife a'yours has you down to skin and bones, I see." Cousin Frank waved her away.

"Aww . . . it's none a'that, Ida. We've a passel a'young'uns we been chasin' round. Our own Ringling Brothers." With that he nudged Lizzie away from the other girls. "I don't believe you've said your hellos to your Aunt Ida, Elizabeth."

Lizzie blushed and gave a small curtsy. "Good evening, ma'yam. Thank you for having me."

"Oh, the manners on this one! I take it all back. You be sure to tell your lovely wife she is doing a mighty fine job. Y'all com'mon in here, now."

She stepped back and waved them all into the house. Uncle Henry leaned down and gave her a kiss on the cheek, and she returned the gesture with a slight curtsy. Mother's manners, as did Ruth's own, shifted from casual to reverent when the old folks came around.

"Jeff comin' round?" he asked Mother, looking over her shoulder for any sign of Papa Jefferson.

"He said he'd drop by a little later, Henry."

Uncle Henry and Papa Jefferson had started life as a pack of eight brothers and had been whittled down to two. They gravitated toward each other. Like the clock pendulums—swinging with the same weight in the same time.

Ruth's brothers extended a firm handshake to Cousin Frank as they came into the dining room, followed by the same reverent deference to Uncle Henry that Mother had shown.

Uncle Henry was touched by God. He'd saved two of his brothers during the States War, taking on wounds he still bore the marks of. A thick white scar on his shoulder proved he was a hero—a saint saved for greater things. He started a good number of his sermons with a description of that day in June 1862 when he stood on the battlefield in Cold Harbor, Virginia, and, infused with the righteous wrath of God, refused to let the Yankees kill his brothers. He'd said more times than anyone could count that the minute the bullet ripped through his shoulder was the very same minute he decided to take up the cross of preaching.

Once respects had been duly paid to the presence of Uncle Henry, conversation about the quarry and the new war and the frenetic energy building in Atlanta dominated. At the end of the table, far from the drone of the adults, Ruth made room on her chair for

Elly while Lizzie sat little Ruby on her lap. Lizzie was used to little sisters. She had a four-year-old little sister too.

"Found some treasure at the quarry," Lizzie said, leaning in. She reached into her pocket and pulled out three rocks. They were sapphire blue and shaped like several cubes that had stuck together. "Found one for each a'us."

Lizzie slid the biggest rock to Ruth and a smaller one to Elly. "Daddy says it's called tor'leen. You can have the nicest one Ruthie since it's your birthday."

"Tourmaline. It's black tourmaline," Elly corrected as she inspected her stone. "You found such pretty ones. I have a few, but none nice as this."

Ruth gave Lizzie a squeeze and pocketed the gem. She had a box full of treasures from the mountain.

At the head of the table sat Ruth's father with his back straight and his arms spread wide enough to encompass his wife, his eleven children, and his extended family. His pride was barely concealed. His rich baritone voice commanded their attention.

"Bow your heads. Uncle Henry? Will you provide us with the blessing?"

Ruth silently groaned. Uncle Henry was a long-winded preacher who prayed long-winded prayers. It was a consequence of being touched by God. Supper would be cold by the time he finished.

"Our dear heavenly Father. We are humbled by the riches you have bestowed on us and give thanks for all your blessings. We ask that you look down upon your poor servants and lay a hand of protection about Ephraim and Elmer. About all our boys who will brave the battle of this holy crusade. We ask that you infuse your wisdom into President Wilson, into our generals and lieutenants, and that you inspire the will to rise among our foot soldiers. Bless this food we are about to eat and the hands that have prepared it.

Make us ever mindful of the needs of others. Amen."

Father and Cousin Frank added their own "Amen" to affirm the prayers of Uncle Henry. Lola sniffed back tears. Ruth shrugged at Lizzie and Elly.

"She's coo-coo," Ruth explained in a too-loud whisper. Mother reached over and touched Lola's hand.

"Elmer is covered by our prayers, Lola Bell," she soothed, giving Ruth a sharp look of rebuff. Ruth, mortified that her words had been heard, looked at her hands.

"A good boy. Strong boy. Got his Uncle Ephraim right there with him," Uncle Henry added with a righteous token of compassion and a rub to the ghost wound on his own shoulder.

An appropriate extra beat of quiet was given in respect to Lola's fear over losing Elmer to the Huns. With that, chaos erupted as heaping dishes were passed from one hand to another. Conversations layered over conversations.

"I've been thinkin' about comin' back," Cousin Frank lamented as they settled into their meal. "There's more people crowdin' the streets every day, Bill. People cain't make up their minds if they're walkin' or drivin' or ridin' their horses. Even the dayum train keeps runnin' folks over. Never mind the new trolley line bein' put in by the house. A street over! I have a small crowd gatherin' at the end a'the street on the daily. Not safe for Lucy and the kids. She's expectin' again soon too."

He gave a shy smile to the women at the table, who fluttered at the news of a new baby. His deep-set eyes tarried with concern on the girls—his daughter and his nieces—huddled together in conversation at the end of the table. It was a constant conversation among the Shurlington men—stay in the idyllic farming fringes of Stone Mountain or move into the heart of the city?

"You think that village fire did some damage? You know that

three hundred acres over in the Fourth Ward that burned last year? Stone's throw from my house? It's been taken over by the negroes and the poor whites. Buttermilk Bottom they've been callin' it. There was a big typhoid outbreak that left a bunch a'em dead with no means a'buryin' the bodies. The stench's been right near unbearable."

"I couldn't do it myself, Frank. Livin' shoulder to shoulder. All that noise."

"I tell him the same, Bill," Uncle Henry added. "I told him he and Lucy could take over the farmhouse. With Mother's passing and all you kids grown, it's too big a place for me. Told him I'd move on into the cottage house."

Ruth, Lizzie, and Elly perked up. If Cousin Frank moved back to Stone Mountain, they'd all live on the same road within a mile of one another.

"These girls here." Uncle Henry gestured toward them, a twinkle in his eye. "I'm gonna guess they wouldn't be heartbroken to have my granddaughter livin' closer."

"Please . . . please . . . please . . . ," the girls started to clamor but just as quickly quieted when the sparkle left Uncle Henry's expression. He preferred they kept their excitement to themselves.

"We'll talk about it, Daddy." Cousin Frank nodded toward Uncle Henry. "We're seriously considering it. I'm gonna guess you wouldn't be heartbroken none either to have us back?"

"Naw, naw . . . cain't say that I would be." Uncle Henry shifted in his seat as if it had grown too hard for his comfort. A sharp bang of the screen door rescued him from further confession.

"Bill! Ida!" Papa Jefferson's voice growled, "Where y'all at?"

Papa Jefferson was more accustomed to being greeted on the front porch after supper. He made a habit of wandering over after the supper hour to smoke a pipe with Ruth's father on the porch.

The family visit had caused supper to run late.

"In here, Jeff," Uncle Henry called. "Ida's just gettin' to puttin' out the cake."

Mother, Dollie, and Bea began clearing the table as Papa Jefferson strode into the room. Ruth exchanged glances with her cousins. Papa Jefferson was the dark side of Uncle Henry, right down to his grizzled appearance. Uncle Henry sucked a flame into the bowl of his pipe and pushed out a chair for his little brother. Cousin Frank sat up straighter. Ruth's father took out his whittling, his shoulders turning in toward the small figure he'd been carving the last few days. Ruth cocked her head. The room. Her father. Cousin Frank. Everything shrank a little when Uncle Henry and Papa Jefferson came together.

"We were just discussin' how it was high time Frankie brought that family a'his back where they belonged. Maybe you can talk some sense into him, seein' as how your boy Bill here didn't up and desert you," Uncle Henry remarked, pulling himself from the sop of his feelings back into a more comfortable tone of authority.

"We'd love to have you back on this side of the car line, Frankie," Papa Jefferson groaned into the chair and took out his pipe. "Your fam'ly'd be safer here. Trolley line comes all the way out now. It'd be easy enough for you to head into the city when you need."

Mother reappeared from the kitchen with a tray of small glasses filled with clear liquid. Dollie followed her with the flat cornmeal celebration cake.

"You sure do know how to lay a satisfyin' table, Ida," Cousin Frank said as he took a nip of peach moonshine. "The aperitif isn't all that bad either. Though I am aware you aren't the responsible party for this indulgence." He raised his glass to Papa Jefferson and Uncle Henry.

"Not a thing wrong with the enjoyment of an unlawful indulgence . . . if only for special occasions, Frankie." She winked at him before turning to Dollie and fussing with passing around cake slices.

"Who we celebratin', Ida?" Uncle Henry asked over a mouthful of cake.

"Our Doll-baby . . . and little Ruthie there."

Uncle Henry sat back and made a show of inspecting Dollie.

"I remember the day you showed up. Bright. Sunny. Cold day. But sky as blue as a cornflower. Pretty little cornflower you've turned into. I hear there's a soldier courtin' you? Your daddy keepin' an eye on him, I hope?"

Dollie nodded, blushing, and thanked her Uncle for the compliment. Ruth waited for her memory, but Uncle Henry turned back to his cake without another word. Ruth scowled at the idea that Dollie had been born on a sunny day. A day that even Uncle Henry remembered.

"Drys are makin' some progress. Might be unlawful in the whole dayum country before long." Uncle Henry, having exhausted his interest in his nieces, shifted his conversation. "When'd Georgia go dry, Jeff? Was it '05?"

"Naw, naw . . . it was '07. Right after all them gawd-dayumed niggah riots in A'lanah?"

"It was right before Riley was born." Ruth's father leaned forward into the memory. "I remember. Ida lookin' like she'd swallowed a watermelon. It wasn't no time for a man to go without the occasional refreshment."

"The law's never put a stop to a man's desire, now has it?" Cousin Frank winked. "Don't mean you shouldn't be careful 'bout that still, though, Uncle Jeff."

The men broke into a laugh and clinked their glasses. The girls looked between each other—giggling at the scene. There was a still in every creek in the county. Everybody knew that.

"Daddy's no more fool than Uncle Henry here." Uncle Henry shifted in his chair, and Cousin Frank gave a sideways look at his father. There was a bleeding gray line between saint and sinner that had to be respected, making it acceptable to call out Papa Jefferson's still but best to leave Uncle Henry's in the shadows.

"Well," soothed Cousin Frank, sitting up straighter, "there's not a Probi man alive gonna get the best a'our daddies."

Uncle Henry chuckled at the compliment and gave an affectionate lift of his chin to his brother in blood and arms. Ruth's father blew the last of the shavings from the wooden figure he'd been whittling, passing it over to Ruth. The small wooden bunny fit perfectly in her palm. It had tall, thin ears, and its face and paws were finely detailed by his pen knife.

"Hop along now, you three. On up to your beds," he said, chuckling at his own joke and rising to indicate that his need for company had been sated.

Ruth woke while the house still slept. She loosened herself from the pile of cousins and sisters on her bed. She snuck outside barefoot to feel the frost-stiffened grass break against the soles of her feet, wakening her. She preferred the morning when she was alone—not with Ruby and Clara May—because she could hear the tiny silver shimmer of sound the blades made when the ice shattered under her weight. She knew her birthday meant winter would end soon.

"For as the rain comes down, and waters the earth, it gives seed to the sower and bread to the eater."

Her father's voice quoting his favorite Bible verse startled her. She was wandering through the bare kitchen garden, brushing her hands over the dark, dormant rosemary bush, the faintest scent of summer stirring from the needles. A crystalline dampness clung to her nightgown and nipped at her fingers and toes.

"I wish it didn't die like this," she said, watching him shyly, lest she be in trouble for her early wanderings. "I wish Mama's garden bloomed all the time."

"If it bloomed all the time, Rue, the land would never rest." He knelt down and shifted some of the leaf mulch that blanketed the square plot. "There'd be no chance for it to be restored. See this?"

He showed her the dark mash of old leaves and food scraps that were decomposing into the ground beneath. When she came closer, he tweaked her bare feet and gave her a look of mock displeasure.

"Uck!" She wrinkled her nose and curled her toes under.

"That uck, m'girl, is makin' a right fine home for the worms. The more it rots, the more it's feedin' the land. Like a warm wormy stew." He wiggled his fingers in her direction. "When the land is well-fed and rested, it brings better crop. Mama's kitchen garden gives more beans and tomatoes. The winter—the dyin' a'things—is necessary. Gawd's divine order."

Ruth examined the thick layer of decomposition. She envisioned pale green shoots in perfect rows popping through. In a few short weeks, she would help her mother plant this garden with a bounty of vegetables. The herbs would come to life with a heady perfume. This garden was different from the endless stretches of cotton and wheat and corn that flanked their house. This garden was for their family, and it was her favorite.

"Mama says we have to pray over it."

He nodded. "We do—cause the thing is we can do ever'thing right. We can clear out the rocks . . . hoe the rows . . . plant the best seeds—and there will still be times when our plants don't grow or maybe the bugs make a meal of a whole field or maybe the twisters come through and rip it all out. So we pray. We pray that Gawd will see the work we do and He will do His work too—if He sees fit."

He reached for her and hefted her onto his shoulders—making his way back to the house. "Winter reminds us that we need Him, Ruthie. It reminds us a'how pretty the garden is when it's a'bloomin' and how warm the sun is when it's a'shinin'." He paused. Thinking.

"Sometimes the darkest winters are the price we pay for bein' born sinners. Those are the times when we have to pray the hardest."

Ruth propped her chin on her father's head. In a shiver, she looked for the face of God in the puffy white clouds, with his long white beard and gray-blue eyes, blowing the cold air down from the Yankee states onto their earth and freezing the edges of the creeks with a thin, glassy fringe of ice. She promised herself she would memorize his Bible verse and say her prayers and work hard to be good. For if winter were the price of sin, then perhaps it could be shortened by those who chose to be righteous.

The regular coming and going of the train, vibrating beneath her feet, was a clockwork of monotony—clacking the morning into the afternoon and back into the evening. Morning chores. Games with Ruby and Clara May. Village repairs. A telegram—for a friend or a neighbor. A boy called up. A soldier coming home. A soldier never coming home. Washing up for supper. Saying prayers by her bedside. Tickety-tick. Clackety-clack.

On Sundays, she dressed in her good dress and sat with her sisters and her mother in the Shurlington family pew in the back rows of Mount Zion Baptist Church. From her vantage point, she studied the slick-backed heads of her father and her brothers several rows in front of her. Mother promised that the farmers were special. The farmers had to stay home. Her father and her brothers were farmers. Except maybe Wheeler, who didn't want to be a farmer.

The Shurlington women sat right behind the minister's wife and her daughters and just in front of the Hollingsworth women. Across the aisle, there were more pews of Shurlington women, including Elly and Lizzie's family. Ruth and Elly and Lizzie made faces at each other across the aisle on a regular basis. Discreetly.

Their minister, Brother Johnson, had filled their pine pulpit since long before Ruth was born. His own four sons dutifully sat in the front pew. Brother Johnson waved his worn Bible high in the air when he called upon God and the American soldier to avenge the sailors lost to the German submarines.

"Victory belongs to the righteous. To the redeemed. The Huns, harbingers of all that is evil, will not stand in the face of God's holy vengeance."

He'd get so excited about his words that he'd take time to whoop—dance a holy jig and then mop his brow with a yellowed handkerchief carefully embroidered with an ornate letter J. Sometimes, he wound himself up so hard on the glories of the Almighty that his face turned bright red and spittle glistened on his lips. Ruth leaned forward, fascinated by the changing color of his skin, waiting for him to explode into a holy light.

"And if thou hath sinned, my brothers and my sisters." His words ran like rabid mice through the congregation. "I invite you to this altar. I invite you to fall upon your knees and cry holy, holy, holy unto our Lord. For He will forgive you. Children . . . He who sees All. Will forgive you . . . Of All. Come. Come and lay your burdens here."

Brother Johnson spread his arms wide, as if he too were willing to be nailed to that old rugged cross, and lifted his chin to the sky. The congregation rustled. One by one they made their way to the altar, women to the right and men to the left, kneeling and weeping and confessing—cleansing themselves of wrong and responsibility.

Ruth, rooted to the hard pine pew, bowed her head in feigned prayer. She peered up through her lashes as her mother knelt in contrition at the altar. What sins must her mother feel the need to confess? She watched her father lay his calloused hands on the forehead of a neighbor and pray for the mercy of salvation. The neighbor, now cleansed, reached out and prayed for her father's redemption in return. Her sisters, entranced and hands raised, rocked gently back and forth, moved by the breath of God. All except Lola, who was picking at her nails and staring out the long arching windows, as if she might see Elmer walk up through the cemetery that lay sprawled around the church grounds.

After church, more often than not, the ladies, all sisters in Christ, spread a bountiful dinner in the Fellowship Hall. Their children, a hodgepodge of farm kids and town kids and preachers' kids, formed their own congregation of believers devoted to pranks and capers and general devilry.

It was Homecoming week or Full Gospel Sunday or there was a traveling evangelist in town or somebody had married or somebody had died. Either way—and Ruth wasn't always sure why they were gathering—there was good reason for the brothers and sisters of Mount Zion Baptist to break bread together immediately following a Sunday service.

Ruth loved Sundays. Especially in the winter—as they broke the drone of the dull days. There was an intensity to it all—Brother Johnson's demonstrative message, the weeping at the altar, the wonderings about sin, the hugs and kisses, a neighbor's new dress, a parishioner arriving in a car when only the week before they'd trotted to service in a carriage, the slight paunch of a new baby growing in a young girl's belly. Sundays were full of glory, indeed.

On Sunday evenings, Ruth sat knock-kneed on the bottom step

of the porch, watching the kaleidoscope sun set over the mountain. The light held a little longer each night, and with it, her breath came easier, as if she herself were being refilled by the orange elixir. Her father and her brothers stayed later and later in the fields—setting in the crops that would feed the dairy cows and that they would sell in Atlanta. She watched their shadows rise over the horizon, emerging from the land itself—heavier and slower now that the day was done.

The faint sound of pots and jars clanged in the kitchen. The clatter of the Singer sewing machine droned through the house. The cattle and the horses snuffed. Her brothers whistled down the livestock. The orchestra of the winter farm echoed day after day until it was drowned out by its own repetition. But if you asked Ruth, she'd tell you the winters were terribly quiet.

The lights of her family's homes winked all along the car line, and she formed a picture of her cousins and aunts and uncles settling down for the night. She squinted at the small yellow windows that she knew to be Elly's house. She smiled at the thought of Lizzie's family moving back—of her cousin being among the night lights she could see from her porch step.

Proverbs 30:10
KJV

Who can find a virtuous woman? For her price is far above rubies. The heart of her husband doth safely trust in her, so that he shall have no need of spoil. She will do him good and not evil all the days of her life. She seeketh wool, and flax, and worketh willingly with her hands.

Chapter 4

Ruth watched with envy as her four eldest sisters bundled up in blankets and snuggled into the carriage for their weekly volunteer duties at Camp Gordon. Camp Gordon was by Peachtree Creek—a skip north of their farm. It consumed near two miles of dairy land—which had been purchased at a premium, given that farmland in DeKalb County was worth twenty dollars more per acre than any other land in the state. The camp included a rifle range along its south side. Out of spite for her tattling, Ruth told Ruby that the gunshot-cracking sounds were the black-winged creature stomping through the woods.

The military camps sprung from the ground overnight with unquestioned authority and imposed without apology into their daily routines. Despite her mother's reassurances that her father and her brothers were farmers and therefore recused from the draft, the possibility of her family being sucked into the camps so frightened Ruth that she abandoned any consideration of it. Except when Lola missed Elmer so bad she'd start crying over nothing or when they drove by the old BBQ grounds and she saw the soldiers marching in formation or when there was no regular flour for her celebration cake or when Riley went walking around town selling the war stamps he was given at school or, like now, when her sisters were bundled into the carriage and spending the day away from the farm.

The new war had been going on as long as she could remember. Even before there was an official war, there was talk of it. Not only did Uncle Ephraim not wait for the draft, he hadn't waited for an official declaration of war. When the Germans started sinking American ships last winter, he said he knew it was coming and went straight to the enlistment office, ready for a fight. Wheeler had wanted to go with him, but Mother had put her body right in front of the door and her finger in his face. Wheeler wasn't quite old enough for the draft—he had to be twenty-one, and he was only twenty—but he was itching to be somewhere other than the farm. Mother told Wheeler he had been called by God Himself to be a farmer, and even President Wilson was wise enough to recuse the farmers. "Are you questioning the wisdom of God and our president?" she'd said. Wheeler, wise enough in his own right, backed down. Ruth figured it had nothing to do with God or President Wilson. He was scared of Mother.

Once Uncle Ephraim enlisted, he left her father shorthanded during calving season. Then Cousin Elmer stopped coming over for Sunday dinner. The most concerning part was that Uncle Ephraim and Elmer had been added to the prayer chain—which was not something that happened when there was only a bit of fighting going on. Ruth would know. Riley and Earl fought all the time, and nobody added them to the prayer chain. The McGurdys' son had been on the prayer chain, and that hadn't worked out at all.

The rise of Camp Gordon—and the wakening of Camp Jessup

and Fort Mac—unsettled everyone in their town. The camps were full of Yanks and foreigners, the blacks and sinners—especially Fort Mac. In good Baptist service to the Lord, Ruth's mother and her sisters made weekly rounds between the hospital at Fort Mac, where the white-capped Red Cross ladies were overwhelmed with the incoming wounded, and the YMCA House at Camp Gordon, where they distributed provisions, mended uniforms, and read letters to those preparing to deploy. Mother had said most of the soldiers couldn't read—which made Ruth feel particularly accomplished as she had recently mastered her whole alphabet and could read a dozen words as long as they were the small ones.

"Be sure to head on up Clairmont Road," her father instructed Ezra. Ezra was one of their sharecroppers in the back fields—a former Virginia slave who served as their carriage driver and took up smaller jobs about the farm when needed. "There's only the colored entrance if you head up Buford. You head that way, and it'll take you an hour to make your way back round to Clairmont—Buford Highway's no place for my girls. Y'hear?"

"Yessuh." Ezra nodded. Ruth averted her eyes from him and pretended to help Ruby tie back her hair, not because Ezra was colored but because his face was disfigured with the scarring of his slave days, making her wonder if he wasn't more goblin than man.

"Don't stare," she admonished Ruby, who was gaping at their hulking, scarred carriage driver.

"Take the horses into the barn when you get back and give them a wash down. Carriage too," Father reminded him. "Then come by the kitchen a'fore you head home. Ida has some extras she thought you might could use. She'll leave 'em on the back step."

"I will, suh. And don' you worry none 'bout the young ladies."

Father patted the flank of the horse, and the carriage jolted to a start.

Ruth scowled. Dollie, Bea, Lola, and even Bossy Bessie were young ladies. It gave them a vantage point—a front-row seat to life. Ruth bounced on her toes and wiggled in between them just to catch a glimpse of the world over their heads. The only advantage to being left behind was that in their absence, she became Mama's helper and was the one in charge of her two younger sisters.

Dollie was Mother's second-in-command, and it was only a mission as sacred as this that would see their mother without her oldest and most reliable daughter by her side. Dollie, with her round moon-face and light auburn hair, was being courted by one of the soldiers, Maddox Grant. Maddox's family had returned to the county from Alabama when he'd been called into Camp Gordon to guard the German prisoners. Maddox, a young farmer and aspiring minister, was not on the prayer chain. His job as a prison guard at Camp Hancock meant he could still come to Sunday dinner to see Dollie. His brother Arthur, on the other hand, was a career soldier and was sent to France with the first deployment. Dollie dutifully included Arthur in her prayers as a sign of loyalty to the whole Grant family.

Bea, two years younger and as fair as Dollie, taught Sunday School and was resourceful by nature. She took in mending, providing a small inflow of coin to the family finances. She was a dependable fixture in their Great Room, rocking and mending and peacefully listening to the worries and wonderings of her siblings.

Lola, not quite fifteen, favored their father in appearance the most. She was lean, intense, and more vain than pious. Her dark hair was as unruly as she, and her sun-kissed cheeks betrayed her penchant for escaping house chores. She loved all things French and would even put on a fake French accent. She had a small bottle of Bourjois Lily of the Valley that had been a Christmas present from cousin Elmer before he left for France. He'd bought it up at

Smith's Drug Store for two dollars and swore to her it was the real thing. Daddy had disapproved of the extravagant and somewhat inappropriate gift, but he'd let Lola keep it in consideration of Elmer's impending service to their country. She'd use the smallest touch of it on Sundays and waft herself by her sisters with a certain joie de vivre.

Bessie was ambitious and older than her years. She coiled her hair as if she were a grown-up and nudged her way into her older sister's world at every opportunity. Ruth made it a habit to step back when Bessie flounced into a room for Bessie had a way of singling in on the thing you hadn't done—like brushing your hair or tying your shoe. She had an uncanny knack for knowing who hadn't done their chores and gave no hesitation in reporting the offender. Riley openly mocked her bossiness—and when Bessie turned her slitted vengeful eyes on him, Ruth waited for some invisible force to knock Riley clean out.

"Ambush! Take no prisoners!" Earl shouted, pulling Ruth's attention from the receding carriage and breaking through her sullen thoughts. Earl, running straight for them with Riley by his side, flipped between being a soldier with Riley and playing games with his little sisters. Today, they were enacting war games. Riley's recounting of the night he was burned had expanded to include a narrow escape from a Hun prisoner who was hiding in the stables. He referred to the scarring on his face as a badge of honor. Ruth tucked Ruby behind her.

"Who you fightin, Riley? The Huns or the Yanks?" Ruth toed nose to nose with her brother. Her chin lifted as high as she could manage. This was the one place Ruth felt equal to her siblings. Ruby and Clara May were her charges. Earl and Riley her coterie.

"Bunch a'Yanks, looks to me," Riley retorted. "Yanks fight like a bunch a'girls."

Four years older than Ruth, Riley was lanky and spry—the oldest of their small clan of young ones. He threw back his head and gave a long, keening howl. Clara May, who had been playing in the dirt by Ruth's feet, began to cry. Ruby scooted around Ruth and gave Riley a pinch. Riley shoved her in return, and she landed hard on her backside. Grinning, he cantered backward away from them, flipping a coin in his fingers and making it disappear and reappear.

Ruby and Clara May sat crying in the dirt. Ruby's hands were scraped and a trickle of blood oozed from her skinned knee.

"Riley Shurlington!" Ruth shouted. Riley spun around and gave his sisters a wink before dashing on to the barn.

"Victory!" he wolf howled into the air. That howl was getting under Ruth's skin more and more by the day. She wished Papa Jefferson had never taught him the Rebel war cry.

Earl hesitated, looking from his wounded sister to his Rebel brother. He gave an apologetic half grin to his sisters and sprinted into Riley's wake. Howling.

Ruth leaned down to her little sister. "Don't worry none, Ruby. He didn't mean it. You know he's playin'." Ruby reached to wipe away her tears. Her four-year-old fingers closed around one bloody palm, and she pulled away from Ruth, putting her arms around Clara May and glaring at Ruth in accusation.

Late that evening, when her sisters returned from camp, the family gathered round the Great Room fire for scriptures. The older boys lounged by the windows, and the girls settled into the couches with mending or embroidery or lace tatting in hand. "Idle hands make for the Devil's work," Mother recited.

Ruth, resting her chin on her knees and listening to the slowing of her family, poked at the coals, watching the orange light slither through the blackened embers. Her father, his baritone drawl edged with the burr of pipe smoke and punctuated by his now habitual cough, began with scripture readings. His sinewy bronze fingers navigated the old King James Bible as he delivered the Word from the first book of Psalms. While their mother preferred Proverbs, the Psalms were his favorite to read to them.

"Blessed is the man that walketh not in the counsel of the ungawdly, nor standeth in the way a'sinners, nor sitteth in the seat a'the scornful. But his delight is in the law a'the Lord; and in his law doth he meditate day and night. He shall be a tree planted by the rivers a'water, that bringeth forth his fruit in his season; his leaf also shall not wither; and whatsoever he doeth shall prosper."

He paused, looking at each of them. He told them often that they were like the trees planted by the boulder-strewn banks of the Stone Mountain Creek—strong, resilient, and capable of thriving on the land where they were born. Ruth found it helpful when her father explained his readings since the scriptures used words she could not piece together in any sensible way.

"The ungawdly are not so: but are like the chaff which the wind driveth away. Therefore the ungawdly shall not stand in the judgment, nor sinners in the congregation of the righteous. For the Lord knoweth the way of the righteous: but the way of the ungawdly shall perish." He closed the book. "The word of Gawd for the people of Gawd."

"Thanks be to God," they replied in unison.

At the end of scriptures, the cartoon sections from the paper were passed to Ruth, Riley, and Earl, who lay on the floor and laughed at *Moon Mullins* and furrowed their brow over *Dick Tracy*. Ruth snickered when her older brother Tom sat cross-legged next to her—drawn to the cartoon antics as much as the crop news.

Tom was pretty much a grown-up, and Ruth thought he looked odd sitting on the floor, chin in hand, half smiling as he read. He was born a farmer—like their father—and had the uncanny ability to read the land. He seemed to know what to plant in what fields—what crops were going to earn the biggest return, what the livestock market would demand. He knew the strength of a plant from its first greening to its bearing of fruit.

Father had insisted he stay in school until he learned to read and master his sums. Once he'd completed the eighth grade, he moved on from the classroom and spent every waking hour coaxing life from their fields. Ruth had often seen him kneeling in a field, sifting through the soil as if he were reading a book—a book that was starting to confuse many of the farmers. No matter what they did, the crop yield was declining.

"I heard they're building a special house just for the Jew boys—for their services and such," Bessie giggled. She poked Lola with an elbow. "Or at least that's what Lola found out when she was batting her eyes at some blue-eyed dream from Alabama."

Lola raised her eyebrows in indignation. "Oh pish-posh. I was not doin' any such a'thing. I was talkin' only 'bout Elmer and askin' if there was any news from France." Lola paused. "And he was not from Alabama. He was from Flah'da. He was tellin' me all about how his people do not celebrate Christmas. His people have a different holiday. Called Hanukkah—which I thought sounded delightful."

"They do not celebrate Christmas, Lola, because they do not believe in our Lord and Savior Jesus Christ. They are blinded by the lies a'Satan," Dollie chastised in clipped, disapproving tones. "It's probably best you reserve your conversation for your own kind."

"Amen," Bea murmured.

Lola cut her eyes at Dollie. She'd been born curious of all things—people among them. Dollie was the polar opposite and preferred the familiar.

"Least I don't walk 'round moonin' over some borin' preacher boy. All the way home . . . Maddox did this and Maddox did that . . . ," Lola poked. Ruth giggled. Lola winked at her.

The pop of the paper snapped their attention. Mother cleared her throat.

"Is the whole top of Stone Mountain about to be blown off by a terrible explosion, overwhelming the town at its base and scattering death and destruction in its radius?" A pall fell as Mother began reading.

"Such a dread catastrophe may conceivably occur, and a number of mysterious and widening crevices, which have appeared on the north side of the mountain where Gutzon Borglum planned to carve his gigantic memorial to the Southern Confederacy, have created an alarm which has been in no ways allayed by the discovery that an expert has been on the scene for months, quietly investigating the probabilities of such a terrible occurrence."

Ruth and her brothers looked up from the comic and stilled as she continued. Riley's face darkened. Tom leaned back on his hands—a muscle in his jaw twitched.

"A row of shafts were sunk across the summit of the mountain to a great depth, tunneled, charged with explosives, wired, filled with cement, and simultaneously fired by electricity. The amount of explosives used is inconceivably great."

The titanic mound of granite followed them every day from the farm fields to school. Ruth visualized the explosives buried miles and miles below, like the scientist said. She could see its peak fracturing into millions of stones that would rain down on her family. Were Yanks hiding out inside, building fires to keep warm, waiting until the circumstances were ripe to detonate? Maybe the mountain really did reach to the center of the earth—to the very gates of Hell.

"Seems this scientist claiming there's dynamite in the mountain is a foreigner by the name of Mr. Omigosh Itsonow." Mother paused, letting it sink in. She referred to the article again. "He's the son of the celebrated seismograph expert, Dr. Betchu Itsonow."

"Oh heavens, Mama!" Bessie was the first to wake from the stunned silence. Dollie and Bea returned to the mending that had frozen in their fingers. "What'd you go and do that for? Ruthie and Ruby are a bug's lash from cryin'!"

Mother laughed gently—pointing to the hoax article buried on the tenth page of the paper. "Why, it's in the paper, baby. So it must be true. There must be dynamite ready to detonate in the mountain. Dr. Itsonow is renowned throughout Europe."

"I think what your Mama is sayin' is maybe don't believe ever'thing you read, hmm? There is no dynamite in the mountain. Even these papers are full a'misdirections."

"I don't know, Daddy," Wheeler said from his spot by the window. "Little bit a truth in ever'thing—wouldn't surprise me one bit if them dayum Yanks didn't leave a shaft full a'dynamite for some poor sap to stumble on."

Wheeler—who at twenty years old was the firstborn son and heir apparent—was a stout man with a wide forehead and a permanent scowl on his face. He had the look of his namesake—a bull-headed general. Wheeler was full of ideas on how to make money and modernize their lives—advocating most often to sell the farm and move into Atlanta with the more successful Shurlingtons. Wheeler had an air of self-declared superiority that placed him at odds with Tom and their father on nearly every decision about the farm. Wheeler's solution when trouble rose was to sell. As land prices had escalated and crop yields had declined, his voice only became louder.

"Maybe that ol' mountain is booby-trapped," he continued,

enjoying the fear on the faces of his siblings. "And the quarry's a tickin' time bomb. Maybe it's a matter a'time 'fore them Klan fires trigger an explosion. Tick. Tock. Tick. Tock."

Ruth narrowed her eyes at the mention of the Klan. She'd seen the faint flickering of the bonfires on top of the mountain every Sunday night and was curious about the white-sheeted men who gathered there. Snatches of conversation reminded her of the stories about the mountain. Her brothers talked of dragons and goblins and the Wizard Simmons. She wondered if the imperial goblins of whom her brothers spoke and the goblins of her father's stories were one in the same.

Mother waved her hand at him. "Hush now, Wheeler—you really are starting to frighten the little ones."

Ruth glared at Wheeler and then swiped at her tears, avoiding Riley and Earl's mocking faces.

"I knew it was a joke," she pouted and returned to Moon Mullins.

When the cold gave way to the greening of the trees, all the soldiers stationed at Camp Gordon hiked through the village center and set up a camp at the old BBQ grounds. Ruth had seen them do their war exercises at the BBQ grounds before—high stepping and gun spinning—and knew the American soldiers were the ones in khaki.

The town officials planned a whole weekend designed to celebrate the soldiers' military expertise. Tents were pitched in rows and rows of perfect white triangles, lined side by side along the edges of the BBQ grounds, reminding Ruth of the zigzag stitch her sisters embroidered into the edges of their handkerchiefs. The center of the grounds was left open for the soldiers' exercises.

The Shurlington women had spent the days leading up to the weekend preparing baskets overflowing with sandwiches, cold pieces of fried chicken and hand pies. Mother said they were serving their country by bringing dinner. A devoted member of the UDC, Mother approached these visits with the same solemnness with which she attended church. The soldiers' grounds were sacred.

"Mama?" Ruth tugged at her mother's skirt. She was staring at a small circle of men, whose uniforms were blue rather than khaki and whose words made no sense to her. "Mama? They sound funny."

Her mother looked from her to the blue-uniformed men. She smiled and gave a small wave.

"Those are Frenchmen, Ruthie. They speak French. They've been sent here for training. It's a thing for which we are proud—there are boys from everywhere in the world traveling miles and miles to our town to learn how to be mighty soldiers. Go on, now—take them the sandwiches."

Her mother handed her a basket and nudged her in their direction. Ruth took the basket, her insides trembling. She hadn't encountered too many strangers in her life. Much less ones whose words she couldn't make out. They stopped talking as she approached and looked down at her. They didn't look much different than any of her brother's friends.

"Maybe you'd like a sam'wich? We made 'em for y'all this mornin'."

They glanced from one to the other—their expressions uncertain. One smiled at her.

"Merci, ma petite fille . . . that is very kind of you. And your maman." He reached for a sandwich and nodded past Ruth to her mother. He spoke to the others, and they reached into the basket.

"Maybe you know my Uncle Ephraim? Or my Cousin Elmer? They went to France." Pride surged through her as she called on the names of her uncle and her cousin, connecting herself and her family to the splendor of the day's cause.

"I don't know Uncle Ephraim," the man replied. "But if he is in France—fighting—he must be very brave and you must be very proud."

They spoke to her in their buzzing language. When she lost the thread of their conversation, her confidence faded. She gave a small curtsy, as she'd been taught, and turned and ran back to her mother. Their good-natured laughter followed her. She blushed, proud that she'd been brave enough to deliver the sandwiches by herself.

Ruth understood the camps were good for her family—for all their families. With the camps came new stores, new jobs, and an unending need for goods from the farm. The more goods needed from the farm, the less likely her father and her brothers would be taken away. A bowling alley had even been built next to Camp Gordon. Ruth wasn't allowed to go—but her brothers had been and thought it to be a hoot.

Lola, the first of the dogwood flowers tucked into the coils of her hair, flitted and purred from one soldier to another, laughing and offering sandwiches from her basket. She jumped when the piercing cry of the Rebel yell echoed through the crowds. Among the soldiers were many sons and grandsons of Confederate War veterans—their primal traditions alive in this new generation of footmen. The Frenchmen mimicked their Southern counterparts, and the field erupted into a cacophonous baying. Lola's face flushed in excitement at the sound.

"Thing is, little sister, I want to believe that there's somebody offerin' a sandwich to my Elmer. Some kindhearted French girl. Not a terribly pretty one, mind you," Lola said, absently taking Ruth's hand in her own. "I asked Daddy if I could sign up to work in the war office, even. Wouldn't that be grand? But you know Daddy. He's so ol' fashioned about these things. I might sign up anyway. Daddy wouldn't even notice if I came home late from school sometimes, would he? Bessie'd tattle for sure, but you'd cover for me, wouldn't you, Rue? We could say I was takin' the peacock feathers into Miz Dorothy's for you? Which I would most certainly do. I'd just be a little late makin' it back home."

Ruth worried for Lola when she said these things. Lola had a habit of chattering on when they were together—as if she were talking to herself, for she rarely paused for a reply from Ruth. Ruth imagined herself as Lola's treasure box. She held so many of Lola's small confessions.

"Maybe you oughta just do as Daddy says," she replied. Lola smirked, catching the sight of her more demure sisters across the field.

"I'll leave it to those two to mind Daddy."

Dollie and Bea—contained and womanly—indulged the soldiers who flirted with them, keeping themselves just close enough that the soldiers might brush their skirts with the very tips of their fingers. Docile, yes. Well-schooled in the art of womanhood? Most certainly. Dollie's golden eyes assured them they were strong and brave. Bea, with her nurturing spirit, was nearby. Mimicking. Echoing. Deferring. They were as maternal as their own mother, whose belly was rapidly growing with her twelfth child.

For Ruth and her two younger sisters, Mother, Dollie, and Bea formed a brigade of Southern mothers. Their bosoms and their laps were equally soft and warm. Their voices equally stern. Their womanhood equally demure.

Ruby and Clara May nestled in one of the mother laps during the evening readings. Any one of those voices halted them in their devilish tracks. Unlike bossy Bessie, who was to be avoided, and Lola, who was preoccupied with her own vanities, the mothers were solid and safe.

Ruth lived quiet and compliant among her sisters, observing them. She envied Lola's spirit—and worshiped the saintly nature of Dollie and Bea. In the rare moments she spent with Mother, she soaked in every word. She mimicked the older women when she cared for the two younger girls—trying on each of her sisters' versions of womanhood like a dress to see if it fit—turning this way and that and observing herself in that internal distortion mirror that lines the insides of every sentient being.

Bibb County, Georgia—1918

Leonidas made his way across the yard. He could feel his heartbeat in his face, and he was certain his nose was broken. He paused, leaning his hand against an oak tree, and inspected his house. It was a gray, wooden box with a low-hanging porch. Crawford had hung some ferns from the porch roof to liven it up, and flickering lantern light spilled from one window. He knew Crawford and the baby were already asleep.

He cleared his throat and rubbed at the bruising along his neck. He'd gone by his mama's house after work to give a hand in the barn and found his grandfather there with his little sisters. Two of them. Sitting on his lap, and him rubbing on them like they were genie bottles. He strode right up, pulled his sisters into his arms—they were only seven and nine years old—and delivered them to their room. He returned to his grandfather and punched him square in the face without hesitating. The gold Mason ring on his finger had given the punch an extra jolt. His grandfather was an old Confederate foot soldier and mean as a rattlesnake. It was the only punch Leonidas landed. His grandfather boxed his face until his vision blurred and then pinned him to the floor, his boot biting into his neck, and he might have killed him if his younger brother,

Hoyt, hadn't run into the room, declaring there was an emergency in the field.

His grandfather had released him, growling, "Y'ain't nothin', boy. Useless piece a'shit, ain't you?"

Leonidas pushed himself away from the tree. Useless piece a'shit ringing in his ears. He made his way to the well and pulled up a bucket of water. He washed the blood from his face and ran wet hands through his hair. He found the jug of shine he kept by the porch and took a long, burning draw. He moved silently through the front door and put out the lantern light. He let his eyes adjust to the blue glow of moonlight that spilled into the house.

He slid into his bedroom and watched Crawford sleeping. How fragile she was. How easily he came into the room and she unaware of his presence. He slid his hand in his pocket and felt the cold steel of his knife. Why he hadn't used it on his grandfather, he couldn't say. It was always there. He'd proven many times he wasn't afraid to use it. But his grandfather made him weak. Made him fragile. As Crawford was now.

Crawford awakened to the cold blade of a knife pressed to her throat. Leonidas chuckled, a low humming of amusement.

"I can cut you t'pieces. Anytime I decide, Crawford. While yer a'sleepin' . . . Or cookin' . . . Or fuckin'. Tiny li'l useless pieces. Spread yer bloody chunks through the whole gawd-dayumed county, and won't a'livin' soul miss you. Ain't nobody gonna care. Nobody cares 'bout whores, Crawford."

She wondered how long he'd been watching her.

He leaned in and bit her hard on the ear. His knife pressed against her skin. She held her breath—refusing to cry out. He climbed on top of her, his silver-blue eyes glinting in the moonlight. He smelled of blood and whiskey. He shoved himself inside her.

When he came, he slammed into her hips, bruising her. Her tender skin gave way beneath the knife point. A trickle of blood flowed wet into her ear.

Leonidas leaned over her, his black hair falling over his forehead. Moon shadows made the chiseled lines of his handsome face grotesque. She blinked—uncertain where to look. She hesitated to meet his gaze—hesitated to look away. He slid the knife back beneath his pillow. "'Bout all yer good for, ain't it, gurlie?"

He fell into the bed beside her. She lay motionless until she heard the gentle rumble of his snoring. She curled onto her side, her hand instinctively reaching to the cradle by her bed. She lay a hand on Helen's small back and felt her breathing. Tears slid down her cheeks. She belonged to him. She knew this. Yet somehow she had to figure out how to stand between him and his daughter.

II Timothy 3:1-4
KJV

This know also, that in the last days perilous times shall come. For men shall be lovers of their own selves, covetous, boasters, proud, blasphemers, disobedient to parents, unthankful, unholy, without natural affection, trucebreakers, false accusers, incontinent, fierce, despisers of those that are good, traitors, heady, highminded, lovers of pleasures more than lovers of God.

Chapter 5

Red dust spewed behind the motorcars thundering down the car line from Atlanta into Stone Mountain. Ruth pulled the neckline of her dress over her face to shield herself. She and Riley had convinced their father to let them tag along into town. He and Tom were attending an emergency meeting of the DeKalb Agricultural Association. Harvests of all major cash crops were declining, putting less money in their pockets and less food on their tables, which was a problem when your family was made up of thirteen people and one on the way.

The DeKalb Agricultural Association boasted some of the finest minds in the state for figuring out what was going haywire in the fields. Soil testing and irrigation were new ideas that had folks raising a skeptical brow, figuring God had made the earth and sky just as it should be, but they could not deny that things were looking up for the farmers who learned it. The DAA, alarmed by the crop decline as well as the constant land grabs by Atlanta business-men, was determined to be proactive in protecting their own.

"Is that a Cadillac 57?" Riley gasped, hanging over the side of the truck. The smooth granite ascent of Stone Mountain tempted automobile manufacturers and daredevils from all over the country to test the superiority of their latest vehicles. It wasn't unusual to see the latest models coursing unchecked side by side with the smoky black engine trains.

"That is spiffy! Look at this, Rue!" He pulled her to the side of the truck and waved at the man in the shiny Cadillac. The man grinned and tipped his hat. "That one's got a V8 engine! Can you believe it?!"

Ruth scrunched her face at Riley. "What's the diff'rence? It runs same as ours."

"What do you know? That Cadillac can go as fast as fifty miles an hour! This old Ford barely tops thirty. Saw a Mitchell coupe last week." Riley slumped back against the truck as they pulled into town. Tom and their father got out and headed toward the meeting hall.

"That train won't stop for ya, so don't you get in its way. People comin' in from the city near constant now. Nobody's lookin' down to see if you're under foot," Daddy warned. "Meet me back by the truck in an hour."

Street accidents were commonplace. Cars stalled on tracks or moved too slow, and the train plowed through them. Pedestrians, oblivious to the oncoming engine, were lost to the speeding train. Last summer, the ice truck got hit by the train. The iceman jumped free just as the engine plowed into the cab and barely escaped with his life. Chunks of ice landed all over Main Street, and the children had been charged with rounding it up. The railway, long the life-blood of their community, paused for no one. Town traffic—human or mechanical—was of little concern.

"We'll be careful, Daddy," Riley called over his shoulder as he grabbed Ruth's hand and pulled her toward the depot. They were free to roam. Ruth eyed the winding steel tracks. Parallel silver veins tied by a tight domino path of wooden sleepers came from somewhere and went to somewhere, picking up and dropping off all that passed through her village. She had little understanding of the where those rails came from or where those rails were going, only that they were endless and a constant reminder that there were other places, the likes of which she cared not to conceive.

When she came near to the tracks, she knew the cyclops engine with its black teeth waited around the curve. She ran as fast as she could across them so as not to be mowed down and end up as another sad story that her mother read from the paper. Deep down, she was as afraid of the winged monster as she'd made Ruby.

Riley taunted her, walking along the sleek curve of metal as if it were a balance beam. The rails started to vibrate, and Ruth screamed at him to get off the tracks. He laughed, immortal in his budding manhood, stuffed his hands in his pockets, and strolled back to her, whistling. He didn't even flinch when minutes later they were deafened by the whoosh of his would-be assassin.

Ruth turned away from him. Angry. She covered her ears as the train screeched into the depot. The train—and the streetcars and motorcars—brought plenty of customers to the weekend farm stands and, on occasion, right up to their driveway for fresh eggs or butter. The train carried builders who ordered stone from the yawning quarry and families who picnicked on the great green lawn that stretched out at the base of the mountain. It brought swimmers who cooled themselves beneath the waters of Venable Lake and the winding creeks that snaked around Stone Mountain Park. It brought scientists and philosophers who studied the granite anomaly and offered their opinions on its origins, its powers, and its possible demise.

Past the steaming, heaving train rose the mountain dome where the Klansmen, given easement by the owners, fed their fattening body with regular gatherings along its smooth peak. In her mind's eye, Ruth saw the tepeed bonfire pyre that heralded their meetings—the one she could see glowing from her front porch step every Sunday night. She'd seen the pyre up close when her family had last gathered there for an afternoon picnic. She and Riley and Earl had danced around the towering stack of waiting wood while chanting like Creek warriors. She squinted, certain that she could make out the pointy indent of the woodpile against the far horizon.

Some people said if you were born near the mountain, you'd never be able to leave. The magnetic pull would always drag you back. Ruth decided this one was probably true, as she didn't know anybody who'd managed to get further away from the mountain than Atlanta, and that was only ten miles away. Even from there the mountain pulled on you, calling you, hovering and waiting for you to return. It made sense that Cousin Frank was torn up over whether to stay in Atlanta or come on back home. The mountain was pulling on him. Maybe that was why the comings and goings of the train were so constant—it was God's way of offering a ride back home should you ever be fool enough to leave.

"Do you really think they're gonna be able to carve the face a'General Lee into that mountain?" Ruth wondered aloud. "Mama says that Ms. Plane found a Yankee to do it. She wouldn't shake hands with him, though. Mama said she just nodded at him. Said it wasn't decent to expect a lady like Ms. Plane to shake hands with a Yankee."

"That old Ms. Plane don't shake hands with nobody. She's meaner than a hornet," Riley said, practicing his hand magic with a flat rock he'd scavenged from the train bed.

"She's not so mean. You just ain't so good, so you get yelled at more." Ruth was still mad about Riley teasing death right in front of her.

Helen Plane, the head of the UDC and the mind behind the Stone Mountain memorial project, reminded Ruth of Mrs. McGurdy, though she was a good deal older. She was more polite than kind, and her corset was cinched very tight. Ms. Plane came with muffins too—though she'd only been to the farm once to see Mother, who was the official UDC coordinator for the memorial fund raising at the Stone Mountain school. Mother had set out the china in the dining room for her visit. Ms. Plane wore a large gold locket, and when Ruth asked her about the picture inside, she said it was her husband—murdered by the Yankees in the States War.

"I don't know about that carvin'," Riley said, deciding to side-step Ruth's ill mood. "Maybe they can do it. Seems it might be more chiselin' than any one man can manage. You ever tried to chisel a rock?"

"The injuns carved up the rocks. Made arrowheads out of 'em. I don't see why a Yankee cain't," Ruth reasoned.

Before there were war stamps to sell, Ruth's brothers and sisters had raised funds for the Stone Mountain memorial by presenting patriotic concerts, which had made Ruth proud. Everyone in her family was good at singing. Ms. Plane had recently, and with great reluctance, acquiesced that the schoolchildren should be raising funds for the current war rather than building her memorial fund for the previous one. Ruth cocked her head as she stared at the flat surface of granite. She tried to imagine the great general carved into its side and decided it was an impossibility.

Riley crashed into her shoulder before sprawling on the green bank by the tracks. Ruth shoved him back—biting at her cheeks to prevent herself from smiling at his recklessness. He watched a family of negroes cross the tracks into town.

"People been mighty upset how them darkies been takin' over the lake on Mondays. I heard they're puttin' an end to Blue Monday," he said to her, not taking his eyes off the family. "It's vagrancy. You know what that means?"

Ruth shook her head at him, watching the family now too. The little girl was laughing at something her daddy said. Ruth knew—everyone knew—it wasn't safe to go out to the mountain on Blue Mondays, when the negroes gathered. The green lawns around Stone Mountain filled with colored families taking an unofficial day off to relax. Some said they called it Blue Monday because everybody was hungover from secret drinking on the weekend. But their father said it was because most of the people there wore the blue overalls of poor factory workers.

"Vagrancy means you're hangin' 'round places you don't belong. Mayor says we don't need their services here, so there's no need for 'em to be showin' up." He chucked a rock in the general direction of the family. He let the whooping howl of the Rebel Yell escape from his throat. One might have thought they hadn't heard him, except the father put a protective arm around his daughter. Their pace quickened past the train depot. Ruth shivered at the sight. She had a healthy fear of negro men and could hardly comprehend they made good daddies.

"Papa says they ain't even allowed over in Forsyth County." Riley threw another rock at the backs of the retreating family. "Over in Dawson County they kick 'em out after dark. It's a law—no niggahs after sundown."

Ruth blew the feathery seeds of a dandelion into the air. She watched the tiny, shimmery tufts float into the breeze. Mother had told her she was planting flowers all over the county every time she blew on a dandelion. She liked the idea of planting seeds with one reckless breath. Riley's words annoyed her—disturbed her reverie. She heard Papa's speeches about the negro problem so often she hardly registered them. Ms. Plane told Mama the Klan had the negro problem in hand, and there was no more need to worry about the domination. She didn't see any reason to bother one's mind about it one way or another. She said as much to Riley.

"Them folks don't bother you none, Riley. Why don't you leave 'em alone? Besides, Daddy says the whole thing's all turned 'round anyway. He says it's best we worry more 'bout what's growin' up from the ground than who's livin' on it."

In the summer of 1918, Uncle Henry—veteran and hero of the Great Confederate Cause—passed on. Uncle Henry mattered to Ruth, despite his stern ways. Uncle Henry, one might say, was the most righteous one among the old Shurlington brothers. There had been eight brothers in the beginning. They'd been dying one by one for some time—each passing over in the very dusk of life—until there were only two remaining, Uncle Henry and Papa Jefferson.

"Uncle Henry has gone on to be with our Lord," Mother said. Ruth could not recall anyone she'd ever spoken to who went on to the Lord—though she figured it to be a fairly crowded place, as she'd heard of many of the old folks who had. Mama Mary, Papa Jefferson's wife, for one, and all of Papa Jefferson's other brothers too. There was Papa Jefferson and Uncle Henry's mama and daddy. They were murdered by the Yanks.

Ruth could hardly grasp that Uncle Henry wouldn't be sermonizing over one of their Saturday afternoon family gatherings. She wasn't certain she was sad about this, because as entertaining as he was, he had a way of winding words into one long and arduous storm.

Papa Jefferson said nothing when he was told of Uncle Henry's passing. He fell into an ominous silence that followed him to the church pew on the day of Uncle Henry's funeral. He wore his Confederate grays. His back was as straight and his shoulders as far back as a young soldier first marching to war. His mouth was set in a stony line, and his watery, yellowed eyes stared blankly ahead. Cousin Frank and his family mourned from the opposite side of the aisle.

Ruth shyly walked over to her cousins—a posy of wildflower stems crushed in her hands.

"I'm real sorry 'bout your daddy, Cousin Frank," she murmured. She pulled one of the flowers from the bouquet and handed it to him. She pulled another and handed it to his pretty wife, Lucy.

"That's mighty kind a'you, Ruthie." He tucked the flower in the lapel of his coat. Ruth continued her shuffle down the line of the grieving family, handing a single flower to each of the children until she reached Lizzie. She leaned over and gave her a gentle kiss on the cheek—handing the remaining bouquet to her.

"I'm sorry 'bout your grampy, Lizzie."

Lizzie nodded. "He was really very old," she whispered in reply. Ruth wiggled into the space beside Lizzie and reached for her hand. Pastor Johnson was stepping to the front of the room—albeit briefly.

It was custom in their family for one of their own to officiate weddings and funerals. To honor this tradition, Pastor Johnson gave a solemn welcome and then relinquished his pulpit to Cousin Davis, the eldest son of all the old Shurlington brothers and the most senior of the family preachers, who raged about the need to repent.

At the graveside, a small handful of Uncle Henry's old regiment joined Papa Jefferson in military salute. Ruth caught sight of Pastor Johnson and his family paying their respects from a distance. His family was as large as their own, and his four sons, right down to the smallest, stood in solemn salute to her Uncle's passing.

Ruth held back a giggle when Sister Johnson pulled hard on the ear of one of her boys—one called Quillan. Quillan, distracted by the yo-yo in his pocket, couldn't seem to hold his salute with satisfactory reverence and even less so when his mother yanked his ear. He caught Ruth looking at him and, in his frustration, stuck his tongue out at her. She raised her eyebrows in mock horror, lifted her chin, and made a show of averting her gaze from his misbehavior.

Cousin Davis finished his oration and nodded toward Sister Johnson, who was the choir director as well as the preacher's wife. Before stepping forward, she took an extra moment to give Quillan a hard stare. Satisfied that her wayward son understood the gravity of the situation, she arranged her face in a melancholic smile and turned to the mourners, lifting her hands to direct the closing hymn. Ruth, Elly, and Lizzie—all the women in the family—sang in intuitive harmony from the Baptist hymnal.

> *Let us labor for the Master from the dawn til setting sun.*
> *Let us talk of all his wondrous love and care.*
> *Then when all of life is over and our work on earth is done.*
> *And the roll is called up yonder, I'll be there.*
> *When the roll is called up yonder, when the roll is called up yonder, when the*
> *roll is called up yonder . . . when the roll is called up yonder, I'll be there.*

The pine casket descended into the crimson earth. Cousin Davis pontificated about Uncle Henry ascending to a better place with gates made of pearl and castle walls of jasper. Uncle Henry was up there dancing on the streets of gold. Ruth tried to imagine her tall, solemn Uncle with his finely shaped beard and hitched gait dancing on solid-gold streets. She thought Heaven must surely be a special place if it got Uncle Henry dancing.

"This world is but a testing ground for all of Gawd's children," Cousin Davis eulogized. "And oh, did our brother pass that test! A faithful soldier to his country and his Gawd. A hero to his family. Willing to sacrifice his very life for that of his brothers. Why, we must all long for the day when we can be released from our sinful bodies and rest in the sweet hands of Jesus. Our brother Henry has joined his beloved wife and now waits for us all in that most glorious place."

Cousin Davis nodded to Papa Jefferson at the conclusion of his oratory, and Papa Jefferson walked to the graveside—laying Uncle Henry's war sword on the casket.

Ruth kept her eyes on the gash in the ground. Spidery roots escaped from the perfectly shorn walls of the rectangular hole. Flowers lay strewn, long torn from their nourishing host, on the pine box. The old Confederate sword had been polished and glinted in the sun.

Ruth thought of Uncle Henry waiting for them in Heaven. Heaven was where they all wanted to go. Ruth felt mean and ugly. She had the worst of secrets. She didn't want to die and be put in a pine box. She didn't want to go to Heaven. She wanted to stay right here beneath the shadow of the Stone Mountain—with Lizzie and Elly and her mother and her sisters.

John 16:21
KJV

*A woman when she is in travail has her sorrow,
because her hour has come: but soon as she is
delivered of the child, she remembers no more
the anguish, for there's only joy that a
man is born into the world.*

Chapter 6

All summer, Ruth watched her mother's stomach grow. Having learned that time with her could be stolen in the wee hours, Ruth was the first to rise. In the ripening dawn of the quiet kitchen, she lay her hand on her mother's tummy, feeling the odd squirming of the baby beneath her fingers, awestruck when its elbows or knees made rounded indentations on her mother's skin, as if her protruding belly was a mountain and the baby inside was a moving landscape.

Ruth loved babies. Of all the farm creatures, she thought they were the most perfect. She liked holding them and keeping them safe. She liked the way baby chicks fit into the palm of your hand and the impossible softness of the little lambs. The suckling calves and teetering colts made her laugh in their awkwardness. Mother told her that human babies took a little longer to be born than the goats and the sheep. They were more like the horses and the cows. Human babies came at all different times. Their baby would be coming when the summer was at its hottest.

She loved babies so much that she never minded tending to Ruby and Clara May. It made her feel grown-up. Even Earl and Riley needed mothering, and she was happy to provide them with it when they played Family. She pretended she was the mama, Riley was the daddy; Earl was the son, and Ruby and Clara May were their little girls. Riley set a pipe stick between his teeth and sat on the porch, waiting for his cobbler, which Ruth made by piling fresh blackberries onto an old saucer. He stroked at his imaginary moustache and demanded that Earl and Ruby—whom he decided would have to be a boy named Rudy, since you couldn't have one son and two daughters—go mend the fences.

Ruth took her mothering seriously. She stuffed an old shirt inside her bloomers so that her stomach bulged out with a baby and set about making a meal. She scavenged in the kitchen and returned to the yard with a Mason jar full of sweet tea and stale biscuits wrapped in a tea towel. She sat everyone in a circle as if they were around the kitchen table, gave Riley a wide-eyed command to say grace, and insisted on conversation about the farm business while they nibbled on their crumbling dinner. She lifted her chin and talked nose to nose with Riley about the acceptable asking price for a pound of butter, the same as she'd seen her mother do.

When Riley and Earl got bored, which was right after tea and biscuits were devoured, and ran off to the fields, she took her pretend daughters by the hand and taught them about the henhouse and the kitchen garden. They gathered stray eggs and vegetables in a basket, which, beaming at her own efficiency, Ruth dutifully delivered to the kitchen for later use, receiving a welcome smile and pat on her head for being a good girl.

When the heat of August waffled off of every surface and the outside air felt like you were breathing underwater, the new baby arrived. A sunshine baby. It was Dollie's duty as the eldest daughter to deliver the baby, though Mother had not delivered even one of her eleven babies without her own big sister, Aunt Norah, holding her hand. So when supper ended and the pains started, Dollie and Aunt Norah leaned in to help bring the twelfth baby into the world. For hours, a lowing came from the back bedroom. Ruth knew by then—she remembered Clara May's birth, after all—that her mother's pain was necessary. It was a curse brought on by Eve's betrayal of Adam, but her knowledge of the curse couldn't stifle the rising worry over her mother's situation.

"Can I go in?" Ruth asked, as she watched Bessie make up a pot of skullcap tea. Bessie had gathered the skullcaps without fail in early summer in preparation for the delivery.

"No, you cannot go in," Bessie snapped, swooshing around her as if she were an obstacle to be avoided. Bessie headed down the hallway, passing off the teapot to Bea, who delivered it to Dollie along with a salve made from lard and arnica root.

"What in this world would make you want to go in there?" Lola chuckled. She was leaning against the kitchen counter, eating a peach. The juices dripped around her hand. "Quite the caterwaulin' happenin' back there."

"Mama might need somethin'," Ruth snipped, bewildered by Lola's easy demeanor. Ruth flinched when a fresh wave of lowing came from her mother's room.

"Mama don't need a thing, little sister. She's got Aunt Norah and Dollie and Bea and Bessie flutterin' about. That baby's gonna be caught in a cushion of eight waitin' hands and swaddled up like the baby Jesus."

Ruth grabbed a kitchen towel and swiped at the floor where Lola had let the peach juices drip. Her mother wouldn't want a mess in the kitchen.

"You not worried?" She cut her eyes in Lola's direction. Lola bent down and balanced her elbows on her knees, eye to eye with Ruth.

"I am not. Mama seems to be an expert at baby makin'. I remember when you came out. There was caterwaulin' for hours. And here you are. Fine as a peach." Lola made a face at the peach pit she held in her hand. "I, on the other hand, will not be havin' no babies. At least not a dozen of 'em. Maybe one. Enough to say I did. Figure if I give my husband one, a boy a'course, he'll be happy enough to leave me be about it."

"I'm gonna have a dozen. Just like Mama. And a husband. Just like Daddy."

Lola cocked her head and studied Ruth. She took the tea towel from her and wiped the peach juices off her face and hands, smacking her lips in satisfaction.

"I'm gonna tell you a secret, Rue. You don't have to. Don't have to have babies, I mean. A husband'd probably be a good idea. But you don't have to have one of those if you don't want," Lola whispered. She paused to give the idea of a husband more thought. "Though I cain't reckon anything more horrible than bein' a spinster. Sellin' hats like ol' Miz Dorothy."

"You are coo-coo, Lola," Ruth declared and then added, "You're plannin' on marryin' Elmer."

Lola's face crumpled at the mention of Elmer's name.

"If he comes back, I am. I'd marry him 'cause I want to. Because I love him. And that's what I'm sayin'. You should only get married if you want to. Me and Elmer are gonna move to A'lanah. I'm gonna get a job. A real job. I've got no plans for havin' babies anytime soon."

"Does Elmer know you don't want no babies?"

Lola waved her hands in agitation. "Course not. He'd never agree to marry me if he knew."

Bessie appeared from around the corner holding Clara May at her waist and Ruby by her side. She wedged her free hand on her hip when she saw Ruth and Lola squatting on the floor.

"I have been looking for you, Ruthie," she cooed. Bessie had slipped into a mother voice, and Ruth felt strangely relieved by it, as Lola was offering no comfort to the current situation.

"Com'mon, honey. We gonna go cut out some paper dolls. Uncle Lovett brought by the new *Ladies' Home Journal,* and I saved it for us."

Bessie was the one in between—three older sisters and three younger. It was a treat when she decided to play—especially since she was so good at making paper dolls. Bessie corralled them onto the sleeping porch and channeled her most nurturing self. Her voice was softer and more patient. She refrained from pointing out their errors and instead helped them manage the folding tabs on the paper doll dresses.

When Mother had started her labor, the men stumbled over each other, mumbling, averting their eyes and retreating with an urgency so sudden they were at risk of tripping face first onto the floor. Ruth found it funny that they had no troubles being knee deep in the marsh of a calving but the labors of a woman unsettled them.

Father, Tom, and Wheeler—Riley and Earl—they were all gathered into the Great Room, safely separated from the struggle of childbirth. The windows and shutters were wide open to encourage a breeze, and their voices wafted onto the porch. Their conversation turned to land and money, subjects that brought them to an unending stalemate. Wheeler pressed to sell the farm, and Tom, two years younger than Wheeler, was vehement about preserving their family legacy.

The two men jockeyed their positions to their father. Tom had proven his loyalty to the family by becoming a well-spoken member of the DeKalb Agricultural Association and rooting out solutions to improve the dismal crop production. Wheeler, whose pug face gave him the appearance of an angry bulldog, wanted to ride the rails of urban progress and snatch their fortune from the rising land prices spurred by hungry land developers. He had no interest in acts of heroism or preservation. He preferred profit and progress.

Their father listened with patience, aware that both Tom and Wheeler wanted to take the family legacy forward, but in divergent directions. Riley and Earl, oblivious to the weight of the discussion, sat on the wood floor, mesmerized by Riley's new-to-him hunting rifle. Earl, not yet old enough to have his own gun, watched intently as Riley oiled the lever action of the .22.

"I think Wheeler's got the right idea, Daddy," Riley interjected, enamored by the city's electric lights and Cousin Frank's shiny new car. "We'd all be better off sellin' the farm. Buy us a big ol' house. There's one for sale not far from Cousin Frank. Got three gables on it. Like Mr. McGurdy's."

The discussion escalated. Wheeler raised his voice and started shouting at Tom, undeterred by the aching groans from the birthing room. On the porch, Ruth covered her ears, and Clara May began to cry. Ruby buried her face in Bessie's lap. Bessie gathered the paper dolls into a pile and put on her brightest face.

"How about we go on and catch some lightning bugs, hmm?" Bessie cast a worried glance toward the window and started ushering them off the porch. "Com'mon, babies. Don't pay that no mind. Everything will be fine."

Bessie moved them far enough away from the house that the noise faded to a dull din. Ruth cupped her hands in the air, catching the tiny bugs between her palms. The tickling of bug's feet against her fingers distracted her as she dropped them into the Mason jar that Bessie held open for them. They were making a nightlight to put in their room.

As the night and noise wore on, the twinkling bugs became harder to catch, floating higher and higher until they reached the sky and turned into stars. Then silence pulled Ruth's attention, and she turned her face back to the house. The windows glowed from the lamplight inside. Her father and her brothers, their arguments spent, were sitting in silence, smoking and reading the papers. The wailing had stopped, and the house rested. Ruth couldn't wait any longer. She dashed up the porch steps and straight toward her mother's room.

The new baby was swaddled in the wooden cradle their father had crafted from a single oak tree when Wheeler had arrived twenty-one years prior. The baby slept as if he hadn't caused any pain at all. It seemed strange to Ruth how quiet the room had become. The windows were open, but the air was still thick with heat. Blood and sweat mingled into a pungent aroma. Ruth picked up the flat church fan with an angelic Jesus beckoning from its surface and fanned her mother's face.

The corners of Mother's lips lifted, though her eyes remained fallow. "His name's gonna be Eugene. Eugene Wallace."

Her voice was wispy, and her words fell in a slow drip. Ruth nodded in reverence at the peaceful bundle. His eyes blinked wide and alert. They were blue like her brother Tom's. Ruth made a silly face at him, hoping to make him smile. Instead, his red lips pursed and suckled.

"Hand me the baby, Ruthie . . . careful now."

Ruth put down the fan, slipped her hands beneath the bundle, and cradled him against the flat bones of her chest. She passed Eugene to her mother, who rolled gingerly to her side and tucked the baby into her low-hanging breast. He sucked hungrily at her, as Clara May had. As they all had. Ruth thought of the sow and her piglets in the barn. Mother patted the bed, and Ruth crawled up to sit by her.

"You'll have babies someday too. You'll marry a fine man like your Daddy and have lots a'babies, just as our Lord intended. And. You'll already know how to tend 'em too." Ruth tried to envision herself with sow's teets and a piglet brood. She'd be happy living outside with suckling babes.

"Did it really hurt all that bad, Mama?"

"Well," Mother lolled lazily on the word, "it does hurt. It's a terrible pain. But it passes."

Ruth had never seen her so spent. She couldn't recall a single day when her mother had lain in bed—as she was now—even when Clara May came.

Her face was slack and doughy. Spidery red veins etched her cheeks. Her eyes resembled the thin slits she knifed into the top of her pies. A thin sheen of moisture made the fine hairs along her upper lip and chin more prominent. She'd lost several teeth in the last few years, and her lips were thinner than they once were. She looked older than she had yesterday. Twelve lives had flowed through her veins, nestled in her womb, and been expelled into the world. She'd suckled each at her breast until a new baby started growing in her belly. She'd had a baby in her belly or at her breast for twenty-two years without rest. She had just passed her forty-first birthday.

"There's always gonna be pain, Ruthie. Every day there's pain . . . that's part a'livin. But. Then we pray. We ask the good Lord to give us strength. Just as there's pain every day, we pray every day. If you keep your heart pure? Why, the Lord will gird you up no matter how much pain there is. You understand?"

"Yes, ma'yam." Ruth contemplated a thought, then ventured, "It's lucky, Mama, that he's a boy."

Mother hummed in agreement and ran her hand over the baby's fine-furred head. There was a vacancy to her—a new kind of distance—that Ruth wanted to chase away.

Ruth lay her head on her father's pillow. Eugene slowed his suckling. She could see blue veins running along his skull and the fast pulse atop his head. Mother's body cocooned around him, and his tiny fist lay against her skin. Ruth breathed in with pride. Her mother had brought five men into the world. Ruth knew Eugene would stay with Mother until he was weaned, just like Clara May, but then he'd be hers to watch and keep.

"Will there be another, Mama?"

"Another babe?" She chuckled. "Lord, Ruthie, I think I have been blessed enough, hmm? Go on now. Go on and let me rest a bit." Her eyelids slid shut. The pair of them—her new baby brother and her fading mother—dropped off into dreamless sleep.

Ruth slid off the bed and went out to find Ruby and Clara May. Bessie had just shooed them toward bed, and Ruth caught them by their hands, lining them on their knees along the bedside.

"Ruby. Clara May. I want you to bow your heads. We're gonna pray for Mama's strength. And ours too. We're gonna thank our heav'nly Father for the new baby, Eugene, and maybe tell Him Mama's got enough children. You look inside and be sure you are pure. The Lord won't listen to nobody that's not pure a'heart."

Ruth clasped her hands together and waited for her sisters to do the same. She inspected her heart and all the corners of her mind, for she wanted to be sure her prayers were heard. She stumbled on her reluctance to be in Heaven. She concentrated and told herself over and again she would be happy to die right now if she could be with Jesus. She began to pray the way she'd heard Brother Johnson do at Mount Zion.

"Our Father in Heaven. Look down on me and Ruby and Clara May. We are on our knees before you. Askin' for your ear. Please look down on Mama and make her strong again. The baby, Eugene, has emptied her out. I can make breakfast fine, but we need her back by supper tomorrow. You might wanna know she doesn't want any more babies. They make her tired. And maybe you've seen Daddy and Tom and Wheeler and Riley? They've been fightin' awful. Maybe you can help Daddy when he tries to talk sense into Wheeler. Maybe help Wheeler stop bein' so stupid."

Ruby's head drooped in impending sleep. Ruth gave her a sharp elbow.

"Forgive Ruby for fallin' asleep durin' prayers. Babies don't know no better. We thank you for our Aunt Norah and Aunt Alice. Me and Lizzie and Elly would be very happy if you told Cousin Frank it's high time to move on back here. We'd be extra good together. Send your angels to watch over Uncle Ephraim and Elmer. Bring 'em back home soon. We miss 'em terrible. 'Specially Daddy. I'm not sure a man's s'posed to be without his brother."

Ruby gave a sigh. Her head bobbed between waking and dreaming. Clara May lay on the floor sucking her thumb and listening to the lull of Ruth's prayers. Ruth prayed for all her brothers and her sisters, all by name. She prayed long and hard. Then she and Ruby and Clara May all said "Amen" in unison.

The next morning and the next and the next after that, Mother remained in bed. Aunt Norah came by every day to check on her, assuring them all that she needed rest and nothing more. It turned out Aunt Norah was mostly right. By the time the weather cooled, Mother was back in the kitchen with baby Eugene cradled in a sling against her chest. She moved slower, and there was a shuffling of her feet that Ruth had not noticed before. She was never without Dollie by her side, and even Bea and Bessie buzzed about her more.

"It's all them babies," Lola said one afternoon when she and Ruth were scrubbing the laundry on the washboard. The change in their mother worried Ruth.

"Think of it this way, Ruthie. If making a baby is like making a cake, there's got to be ingredients. Right?"

Ruth nodded, trying to wrap her mind around the idea that she might be made of cake batter.

"Well, let's say Mama has all the ingredients inside of her. She keeps using those ingredients every time she makes a baby. Until she's running low on flour, say. Or butter. Or maybe she runs out of sugar entirely. Or worse yet, the leavener. Mama's like a cake that's got no sugar and no baking powders. She's used up all her sugar and baking powder to make the babies." Lola sat back and raised her eyebrows, satisfied with her explanation.

"Maybe she should eat some sugar, then," Ruth added helpfully.

"Don't work that way, little sister. She's out of sugar. She done baked all her sugar into her babies." Lola grinned, the muscles in her arms tensing as she wrung water from the shirt in her hand. She was fully immersed in her own explanation of baby making.

"There ain't no sugar in Wheeler," Ruth remarked after some consideration of Lola's theory.

"No. I don't suppose there is. But there's plenty a'sugar in you." Lola winked at her, and Ruth blushed. Lola had a way of making the most serious of concerns more tolerable.

Bibb County, Georgia—1918

Crawford dragged herself from the floor and into her bedroom.

Helen was screaming, and Crawford needed to comfort her. She pulled her daughter into her arms and lay her hand alongside her tear-stained face. Leonidas hadn't touched their daughter—he wouldn't touch Helen—but he'd dragged Crawford by her hair into the kitchen over a pot of coffee. She'd let it go cold while tending to Helen. In the kitchen, he humiliated her, making her kneel before him, apologize for being a lazy wife, before calmly putting his hat on his head and leaving for work.

Crawford wondered what her daughter might remember. If she disappeared, took her away, would Helen remember her father? She wouldn't. Crawford was certain of it. Helen didn't have to know about the monster in him. Crawford could tell her stories of when they first met. She could tell her he was a wonderful dancer and knew all about the stars. She could tell her that he told captivating stories and that he built steam engines that carried people all over Georgia. Helen could believe she was born in love. Crawford did love him once. She wanted to believe that he had loved her.

She could take Helen away and tell her that her father had died. She could say he'd been called up in the draft and died fighting the Huns in France. Maybe he would be called up by the draft. Maybe he would be sent to France and die a hero, fighting the Huns. Then she wouldn't have to lie. She remembered how scared she'd been when he'd signed up. Helen had been two weeks old. How she'd prayed he wouldn't be called. Now she prayed that he would. Begged God to have mercy on her and on Helen and call Leonidas away to war.

"Helen," she whispered against the little girl's soft curls. Crawford had named her after a goddess she'd once read about. A goddess whose beauty drove kingdoms to fight for her. Morning light spilled through the windows, and Crawford, Helen held tight in her arms, watched as it spread in bright squares across the floor.

Some very small part of her that she thought irreparable, knitted itself together, tightened and hardened. She knew she too would go to war for Helen.

Crawford unfolded herself from the floor and went looking for the morning newspaper. Women were working now. They had their own money. She knew this because her sister had gotten a job at one of the law offices in town. She took a deep breath. She gently wiped the tears from beneath her eyes with the tips of her fingers. She opened the paper to the classifieds.

II Chronicles 32:6-8
KJV

And he set captains of war over the people, and gathered them together to him in the street of the gate of the city, and spake comfortably to them, saying, Be strong and courageous, be not afraid nor dismayed for the king of Assyria, nor for all the multitude that is with him: for there be more with us than with him: With him is an army of flesh; but with us is the Lord our God to help us, and to fight our battles.

Chapter 7

It was well past dark and Ruth could hear the tense voices of her family coming from the kitchen. She slipped out of bed, pausing when she heard the agitated cries of her baby brother coming from her parents' room. She sighed, knowing she had to check on him. She cracked open their bedroom door, stealing a look inside. Eugene was tiny and fussy. Mother had him snuggled in the crib beside her bed. Eugene was a bump in the middle of the cradle mattress. He wasn't awake at all. He was on his belly, his baby bum poking high in the air, rubbing his face back and forth against the sheets. A dream had him. Ruth tiptoed into the room and patted him on the back until he quieted.

Satisfied that her brother had peacefully returned to sleep, she made her way back up the hallway toward the kitchen. She edged into the dining room, tucking herself into the L-shaped corner that was occupied by her mother's accounting desk, eavesdropping outside the kitchen door. She chewed at her nails and stretched her ears to hear every word.

Mama lied. More than a year had passed since the military camps opened, and now everybody had to sign up for the draft. Even the farmers. Even Tom, who was only eighteen. Worse still, Arthur Grant, the brother of Dollie's beau Maddox, came home from France without his leg and full of meanness. She'd seen him last Sunday at church being pushed around in a chair on wheels.

Arthur was lame, and Uncle Ephraim was lost. Mother had been reading his letters to them at night ever since he went away, but there hadn't been a new letter in weeks. Mother said it was because he'd gotten busy winning the war, but her words and her face didn't match. Mother was lying. This angered Ruth. They thought she'd believe their lying. She knew it was bad manners to snoop like she was doing, but no one would tell her the truth. They kept saying everything was fine even though she knew it wasn't. She could feel trepidation crackling all around her.

Ruth peeked around the corner into the kitchen. It was a long, galley-style room that stretched along one side of the house. On the far end was a round wooden table nestled beneath a picture window. The table had three chairs on one side and a wide bench built into the window on the other. It had enough room for six full-size people and a few little ones. It was smaller than the family table in the dining room where they had their evening meals. This was the Talking Table, as Ruth thought of it. It was where her parents sat early in the mornings and late at night seeking mutual counsel. It was where Aunt Norah and Aunt Alice gathered for gossip and where the men argued over farm business. It was a busy round table whose chairs were never empty.

Tonight, all three of the chairs and most of the bench was filled with Ruth's father, Tom, Wheeler, Papa Jefferson, and Papa Perkins, all enjoying a plate of Mother's cobbler. There was room for her mother, but her mother, though slower than she was before Eugene, rarely sat down. She was circling around them, refilling their cups and interjecting whenever a thought struck her. Ruth knew the warm cobbler was overflowing with the last of the summer peaches. Even with the cornmeal crust from the war recipes, Mother made the best cobblers.

Tom and Wheeler's voices vibrated with hostile tension. Tom said things like "unconstitutional" and fought the idea of being forced to leave the farm. Wheeler shoved back at him, questioning his patriotism and saying they had "a duty." Wheeler had been required to put his name in the month before Eugene came and had been pacing the days away, waiting for his call. "Cowards wait," Wheeler snarled.

Their father, tugging at the ends of his generous mustache, sat between them, reasoning with them both. The older men talked slower and quieter. Concern played at the edges of their voices. Ruth figured of the five men sitting around the table, her grandfather's were the most equipped to be called. They might be very old, but they already knew how to survive a war.

Every time Papa Jefferson or Papa Perkins sat around the table, Ruth heard their stories about the old war and their lives before the Yanks came. Lately Ruth listened to their stories harder than ever. It concerned her that their stories had stopped feeling like memories and were sounding more like advice.

Papa Jefferson talked about a big plantation house in South Carolina called Manchester Forest. He had never been to Manchester Forest, but his daddy, Ruth's great-grandaddy, had told him all about the great house and the cotton-filled land that went on for miles. He told them there were house slaves to do all the kitchen duties and field slaves to keep the crops turning. He told them about the house maid and the two field hands his daddy kept when they came to Georgia. He spit every time anyone brought up the Allegiance papers. Papa Jefferson's war rooted itself in his heart, and he tightened his grip on his guns and his property and his belief that a way of life had been stolen from them all.

"I knew men who ran from the draft in '65, Tom. It's a coward's way. That's not our way," Papa Perkins said, crossing his arms and resting them on his round belly. Papa Perkins was mostly sad when he talked of war—a sharp contrast to the rage that burned in Papa Jefferson. "I never did want to raise a gun to another man. But I was called to it. Like most. Figured running from it wouldn't make it any better."

Papa Perkins had been and still was a shoemaker—a man of commerce who paid fair wages to any man who'd ever served in his shop. His Confederate service was obligatory, and Papa Jefferson never let him live down his request for reparations from the government. Papa Perkins had applied for and received a small sum of money as repayment for the supplies taken from his cobbler shop by Union troops. He'd put that money right back into his business—and he'd been among the first to sign the Allegiance papers. The Perkins family were known to be peace-seekers. When General Lee surrendered, Papa Perkins laid down his arms and began living forward that same day.

Papa Jefferson, who'd often called Papa Perkins a coward for signing the Allegiance papers, scoffed at his advice to Tom but otherwise remained silent.

"Man has to be willin' to stand for his country, boys," Papa Perkins continued. "Willin' to fight for what he loves. For what matters to him. Sometimes the only thing that might matter is your honor. Honor, for country and kin, is what we fight for."

"Thank you, Daddy." Mother extended her hand to Papa Perkins. She gave him a squeeze before clearing his plate.

Ruth seethed, leaning further into the kitchen, and considered marching right up to the Talking Table and reminding them all of the things they'd told her. Fighting can only lead to hurting one another.

Ruth scrutinized her mother as she washed up the dishes in the deep basin sink. There was a window over the sink, and a cast-iron cooking stove warmed the far corner. Open wood shelves, filled with dozens of multicolored glass jars, lined the top half of the walls, replete with the yield of a year's labor.

At the other end of the kitchen, opposite the Talking Table, was a tall, thin closet where the Lysol, the washing powders, and the Palmolive were kept. Past the closet, a door led through the washing room out to the wraparound porch. If you stepped off the porch and went one way, you'd come up on the cellar. If you went the other, you'd come to the kitchen garden, where Ruth often found herself looking back through the picture window at whomever had taken a seat at the Talking Table.

The talk of war shifted and intertwined with the talk of over-burdened fields with too few hands to harvest. Ruth struggled to keep up with their conversation—were they talking of the old war or the new war? Tending the fields or leaving the farm altogether? Her father, her brothers, and all the hands on the farm labored to provide for the family and for the war camps. Who would grow the food for her family and for the soldiers? Wheeler took jabs about selling the land. Mother turned from the sink and snapped back at him.

"Sell the land and everyone a'you might as well march yourself straight to France, Wheeler. Don't be such a fool. It's this farm here that's kept you boys safe so far. As it stands, all they're asking for is a'name. Because a'this farm? Your father's work on it? They've yet to ask for your life."

"Maybe I don't want to be kept here no more," Wheeler mumbled and pushed back from the table. Tom shook his head and ignored his brother.

"That's the whole point here. Ain't it, Mama? Daddy? I sign up for the draft, and what about the farm?" Tom quarreled, working hard to control his temper. Ruth started to wonder if it was wise for Tom and Wheeler to be so close to one another in the kitchen. "I know all they need is a name—they got Daddy's. They got Wheeler's name. Now mine? What if we get called up? We're pullin' twice the harvest what with the soldiers needs up at Gordon. Hogs need butcherin'. Cotton is comin' in. Back field needs to be turned."

Father looked up from his cobbler. He appeared to be made of tree knots. His cheeks, his throat, his knees and elbows—even his hands were a series of sinewy round knots.

"We'll make due, Tom, if need be. I'll call Ezra in to take on some extra work. That man's already lived through one war. He's too old for another. Riley's old enough to help in the back field, and Earl can help with the butcherin' . . . ," he replied.

Ruth pictured the boyish, wiry bodies of her youngest brothers manning the plows and hoisting the massive hogs in the butcher barn.

Mother made her way to the Talking Table and stood sentinel over the men, her brow pinched in thought. The dim light created craters above her cheeks. She looked nearly as old as Mama Ann.

"Don't you worry about the farm, boys. Like your daddy said, we have hands and plenty a'pennies tucked away. The registration age's been lowered. Requirements have changed. You need to go on tomorrow, Tom. Give 'em your name. Your Daddy's done the same. If you do get called up . . . well, the more a'our boys in gray that join up, the sooner this war'll be over anyhow."

"Huns. Yanks. All one in the same you ask me. Fewer of 'em

they is, the better off we are," Papa Jefferson grunted. "You boys take a few out for your ol' pappy."

Ruth had heard the Yankees were colluding with the Germans. Brother Johnson said that Yankees and Germans were a scourge upon their earth. She once asked her father what a scourge was. He said it was a very great calamity, and so she came to see the Yanks and the Huns as simply the Calamity.

Ruth laid her head back against the wall and stroked her doll's yellow yarn hair. She listened to her mother make more promises. She listened to Tom and Wheeler argue and to her grandfathers' remembering. They would be fine, she assured herself. Her mother wouldn't lie. Her mother wouldn't lie.

She pictured her mother standing over the Talking Table. Her mother was as tall as the men. Her ample bosoms spilled round and comforting to the corseted waist of her skirt. Ruth found her mother to be the most perfect place to nestle and had long been jealous of the babies that had taken her place. Envy is a sin, Ruthie. First Ruby and then Clara May and now Eugene. When Mother spoke, everyone did as she said. If she said not to worry, it was usually because she had things in hand. As far as Ruth knew, that included the current war.

Father put down his fork and settled back in his seat. He took in a breath that led to a coughing fit. When he spoke, his voice was raspy and tired.

"Your mama's right. We'll be headin' over tomorrow. There's not much choice—you are both a'age. We're all of age." He raised tired eyebrows at Mother. "They'll pull you away to jail or war one."

Mother cleared his plate, brushing crumbs from the table. She laid a hand on his shoulder. Ruth wasn't sure if she was reassuring him or leaning on him for support. He smiled tiredly at her. Wheeler straightened himself and glanced over at Papa Jefferson.

"I won't be waitin' for them to call my name. I'm tired a'waitin'. I'll be joinin' up tomorrow. Uncle Ephraim did. Elmer too. Got a mind to put a gawd-dayumed bullet through a Hun head."

Papa Jefferson chuckled in approval. "That's my boy."

Wheeler stalked about the kitchen, shaking off his agitation and glancing at Mother, who had raised her eyebrows at his declaration.

"Sorry, Mama."

Tom stood—his bright blue gaze steady on the other men. At eighteen, he was a lighter, less knotty version of his father. He leaned in, square and devoted.

"I'll put my name in, Daddy. But I won't be goin' anywhere 'less I got no choice. They need us to keep sendin' goods to Gordon and hell, Jessup, Fort Mac, even Hancock. Dollie's man Maddox's freed up—no longer guarding the Huns up at Hancock. He's offered a hand when he can," Tom reasoned, leveling a glare on Wheeler. "People need the farms. They need us to figure out how to keep 'em fed."

He made sure to take in every man at the table before adding, "Nobody's won no war on an empty stomach."

Ruth felt the words falling around her. She'd heard Dollie's beau, Maddox, was guarding the German prisoners. She wondered who was taking his place now. She imagined the Hun hiding in the woods out by the creek or in the cracks and crevices of the Stone Mountain. She imagined the Yankees harboring them. What if Riley and Earl found a real one while they were out playing their war games? Her thoughts begin to spiral in all directions, and tears bit at the backs of her eyes. What if the draft took her family? What if they got lost in France like Uncle Ephraim? Or one of them came back without his legs?

She closed her eyes tight and decided no one would be leaving. Mother said they would be fine. Mama doesn't lie. Her father and

Tom—even Earl and Riley—kept them safe. At least Earl and Riley were too young to sign up for the war. And Tom loved the earth—he would never leave Daddy.

Wheeler was different. She didn't mind him much. Nor did he mind her. In fact, she wasn't sure if Wheeler ever saw her. He never spoke to her. Wheeler talked about things that made no sense—radios and flying machines. He made it clear to the family that he didn't plan on staying on the farm, and he didn't think they should either. Shake off this red dust 'fore it chokes us, he'd say. Fine. Wheeler could leave the farm and go all the way to France for all she cared.

The conversation died down. Papa Perkins and Papa Jefferson rose to say their goodbyes. Father pushed away from the table and approached her hiding place.

"I believe we've had ourselves an interloper," he said as he ambled closer to her. He scooped her into his arms. She gasped. "Time for bed, little miss. You gotta get up early for chores. And I believe ya got school now, don't ya?"

"Ruth Elizabeth!" Mother gave a disapproving huff at Ruth's presence. Mother had been blocking her out of conversations more lately, and her annoyance at Ruth's snooping was clear. Agitation nipped at Ruth. Snooping had been her only recourse for knowing, and there were plenty of things she felt she ought to be allowed to know.

Ruth burrowed into her father, hiding her face, grateful that he kept moving and rescued her from their mother's ire. She tried not to think of the men being called into the camps or, worse, to France. She felt a gnawing in her belly.

"Are you going away?" she whispered against her father's neck, trying not to cry.

"No, Rue. I am not going away," he promised.

He carried her up the stairs, then dropped her down at her door. He tousled her hair and vanished down the dark hall without a look back.

Clara May's baby breath whispered from her crib. Bessie, nestled in her bed against the far wall, snored softly. Ruth leaned over and put her small hand on Clara's back. The peacefulness of her baby sister melded into her. She drew the nourishment deep into her chest, matching the pace of her sister's breathing. She let the thought of war—of a deserted, lifeless farm—seep out of her. She filled the vacant places with the syrupy sweetness of her mother's cobbler and Clara May's soft cotton gown.

Ezekiel 7:15
KJV

The sword is without, and the pestilence and the famine within: he that is in the field shall die with the sword; and he that is in the city, famine and pestilence shall devour him.

Chapter 8

"More cases a'the influenza been reported up at Camp Gordon. It's at Hancock too. Fifty thousand dead, they say. Dayum virus been takin' more folks out than that war. They're askin' the women to make masks to send over to the camps. There's a collectin' box set up at the depot."

Ruth startled as her father tossed the DeKalb paper onto the Talking Table. She and Ruby were tucked around a basket of freshly picked green beans and having a contest to see who could snap the most. Clara May played with the tin coffee cups at their feet beneath the table. Earl, their father's perpetual shadow, slid into the chairs next to his sisters.

Snapping beans was one of Ruth's favorite kitchen chores. Pop off the stem end, and a snap to the middle revealed a small circle of damp dark inside. Sometimes, if you snapped right through the pea, the snap end appeared to be the most uninterested green eye gazing at you. God is watching you, Ruth could hear Brother

Johnson declare. Even through the beans.

Ruth took such an interest in the slender vegetable that her new teacher, Miss Beauchamp, put her in charge of the bean row in the school garden. Ruth had started school a few weeks prior, and her mornings had taken on a new kind of excitement. She left Ruby and Clara May and walked to the two-room schoolhouse with Lola and Bessie. Riley and Earl darted and ran along with them, weaving in and out of the woods and fields that lined the dirt path.

Lola and Bessie didn't talk to her much. They mostly leaned in and laughed with each other. But sometimes they asked her about Miss Beauchamp and told her they were very jealous. Miss Beauchamp was the early grades teacher and was one of Dollie's old classmates. Their own teacher, Miss Alden, was a mean old spinster who'd been the first teacher the school hired—back in 1880 when it was still called the Little Red School.

Mother regarded the newspaper that had been tossed on the table; the pine rolling pin she was using to roll out pie crusts slowed but didn't stop. "Have they now? Well, I'm sure we can make time for stitching in between the double harvest and our hand shortage."

She wasn't one to complain, but her voice sounded strained. She had Eugene fastened to her in a sling, and he reached up and tugged at her mouth as she talked.

"Ida." Father's low, lazy drawl drew out her name like a stretch of warm taffy. "Jus' give the girls some scraps and let 'em make what they can. We been reapin' a right nice return with all the produce goin' out to the camps. Cotton's shot through the roof. We're tuckin' more away this last year than we have in a long time. Hard times, darlin', but profitable times too. Even got ourselves a factory-made motor car, and Tom's done turned that old farm truck into a rollin' market."

The tight lines of her face softened under his gentle chastising.

A strand of silvery amber hair came loose from her old-fashioned knot and grazed her cheek. She tucked it behind her ear and cocked her head.

"Well, with the wedding and all, there's plenty a'scrap. Be nice for Ruthie and Ruby to have a part too, I guess. You want to join in the cause, right girls? Keep our boys healthy so they can finish off those nasty Huns—bring your cousin and your uncles back home?"

She motioned to them with her dimpled chin. "Finish on up with them snap beans and go on and collect the eggs. Then you girls gather the sewing scraps. They'll be a few bits a'white silk in there, I reckon. Maybe we can send those direct to the Red Cross ladies."

He patted her on the hip.

"That's my Ida-girl. Now what about the county fair tomorrow? There's some talk a'cancelin'? Few folks we know won't be goin' over. Worried as winter squirrels 'bout this sickness goin' round."

He eyed her pies hungrily. "Maybe we should be stayin' round here. Keep these here pies for ourselves."

"I don't know about that," she scoffed, cocking her eyebrows at him. "Some folks get themselves wound up over nothing. Bundle a'nerves some a'these city women. Softer than the spring lambs. . . Fair's all outside. County closing orders have only been for indoor events. Not to mention, we been holding services outside the last couple a'Sundays anyways. Fair cain't be much different. I have the exhibit jars ready. Finishing up these pies now."

She emphasized the word pies especially for him. He leaned over her shoulder.

"Seems right to me. If we can gather in the name a'Jesus, we can gather in the name of a good blackberry pie."

She feigned horror at his irreverence and chucked him away with her hip. Ruth and Ruby giggled.

"Dollie and Bea are out helping Charlotte Mobley with the Red Cross exhibit. Bessie's up at school working on the floats, and Riley's out with Sister Johnson's boy trying to sell a few more war stamps. And . . . " She paused to take a breath. "Our new boy is gonna be in the beautiful baby contest too."

She gave Eugene a little pat. Earl sniggered and slipped closer to his sisters, taking up his share of the snapping.

Father grumbled, pulling off his hat and mopping the grime from his forehead.

"Baby contest?"

He leaned in for a peek at his fifth son, furrowing his brow like he was looking at an unexpected squash in the watermelon patch. Mother followed his gaze. She lived for town gatherings and showing off her children. She wasn't going to let worry over a little sickness ruin her day at the much anticipated DeKalb County Fair.

The county fair was a day of friendly (and not so friendly) rivalries: skills contests between the district schools and a flaunting of the town's matrons and belles. Farmers puffed their chests out over eight-hundred-pound hogs and high-producing dairy cows. Canning skills and rifling skills were equally prized, and the woman with the best pie? She was the envy of all.

"Well, yes. Ms. Sams is heading up a showing a'the most beautiful babies. The winner—which will be my Eugene—takes home a big blue ribbon."

Ruth and Ruby exchanged eye rolls. Their father chucked them lightly under the chin.

"Too bad there's no beauty contest for little farm girls. These two'd bring home the prize. Ruthie, you singin' with your class?"

He winked at them both, accepting a glass of sweet tea and pulling up a chair. He reached into the bowl and joined the bean snapping. Riley's habitual war howl floated in from outside. He'd returned from the schoolhouse with Quillan Johnson by his side. Earl tripped over himself to meet them in the yard.

"Yes, sir." Ruth nodded. "We're gonna be up on the school float. Bessie says it's all covered in red, white, and blue stars. She made sure we had our flag and the regulation flag. We're singin' 'Over There.' Caroline's grampy's gonna play the bugle for us." She hummed the happy march for him. He swayed to her pleasant melody.

"Is he now? Well, that should be rather fine. He was the best a'the Old Buglers. You'll be hard to beat—I do hear Doraville schools' got a ringer of a tenor, though." He shifted toward her as a thought caught up to him. "Tell me—how's it feelin', havin' those indoor toilets at school too? Much easier I'd reckon, bit more like home?"

"Yes sir, it is. But Earl and Riley keep tellin' everybody they gonna be sucked down in the ground. It ain't very funny cause some a'em believe 'em, and now they won't use the toilet at school. Lucy wet herself yesterday cause she was too scared to use 'em."

"Riley can be a troublemaker—he's fond of a good riddlin'. You tell Lucy that your brother's a'teasin'. Not a body has been sucked in the ground by these toilets." He paused. "That I know of."

He wagged his eyebrows at her and laughed at the idea of her schoolmate being sucked into the new toilets, his weathered face creasing merrily. Ruth felt a pleasing rush that she'd humored him—making his mustache twitch.

"It's not funny . . . ," Mother corrected her. Ruth looked at her mother confused. "Ain't is not a word, Ruthie. I don't want you sounding like the white trash."

Mother had gone to a special finishing school when she was a girl and learned all the finest manners, which Father mostly tried to mind but also mostly ended up stumbling over. Despite his own farm-grown education and general dismissal of Mother's strict adherence to manners, he valued schooling and made a point of supporting the aggressive push within their community for high-quality schools in DeKalb County. When the county announced there would be a ninth and tenth grade added in the fall, he hadn't hesitated to insist that his children would be attending the new high school.

A tapping resounded from the screen door, followed by the snap of it opening and closing.

"Ida, dear! Ida! Yoo-hoo!" Sister Johnson's melodic soprano floated into the house. Sister Johnson waltzed into the kitchen holding a basket full of treats in either hand, singing, "We have sweeties for sweeties."

Sister Johnson, having brought the boys home from their soliciting, was delivering treats for the schoolchildren to Mother, who would be in charge of doling them out at the fair.

"Oh, aren't you a doll! These are the prettiest bags! Such a talent you have, Berta."

Sister Johnson gave a little curtsy at the compliment and laid her fingertips to her heart in modesty. She turned her attention to the Talking Table.

"Afternoon, Bill," she acknowledged. "Ruby. Ruthie."

She cocked her head and inspected Ruth before turning back to mother.

"Goodness, Ida, that girl a'yours has some pretty red hair. Sweet little voice too. I heard her singing in church last Sundie. Not quite the soprano like my Melody, but she holds a fine tune. A fine tune."

Sister Johnson sang the last of her words, and Ruth blushed. It was hard not to shrink under the bright glare of Sister Johnson's attention.

"Girl's barely six years old, Berta. Give her a year or two, she might be outsingin' your Melody," Ruth's father teased, elbowing Ruth with a wink and a smile. Ruth felt her face flame, and she bowed her head intently over her bean snapping. Father was riling Sister Johnson at her expense, and she knew it.

Mother mercifully jumped in with talk of fair planning. Ruth leaned against her father in relief. He snapped a few more beans with them, then stood up and pushed his hat back on his head.

"Awlright, well . . . Tom and I gonna bring the hog round so the boys can give 'im a good scrub. He's a fine one this year—though Graham's been braggin' bout hizsen—I told Carl Wallace I'd have the stock over first thing. Ruthie and Ruby, we need you to pick the two prettiest hens to show off."

"We picked 'em," Ruth replied with assurance. "Max is the meanest ol' rooster. Peckin' away at all the pretty biddies til they bleed. Me and Mama pulled two out to the barn already to keep 'em nice enough for the fair. We been takin' care a'em there."

Father nodded in approval. Ruth saw her mother give her father a discreet wink and scowled. Ruth wasn't old enough or strong enough to manage the hen run on her own, but she pretended she could. Right down to bossing Ruby and Clara May around, as if they were her own crew of farmhands. Needing her mother's help pricked at her pride.

"The boys racin'?" Her father shifted the subject.

"They are." Mother laughed, "Riley's right excited about it too. He and Quillan are both determined to whip the Clarkston school in the sack races. Earl's pairing up with Quillan's little brother. They're outside practicing."

She slid her perfectly crisscrossed pies into the hot oven and untied her apron. She took out two teacups and gestured toward the Talking Table. She and Sister Johnson would be settling in for an afternoon of gossip.

Ruth peered out the window where Quillan, Riley, and Earl were hopping around in grain sacks. Riley, being older, was a solid foot taller than Earl. Their three-legged sack was a bit whoop-sided, so Quillan, who was closer to Riley's height and age, made a better pairing.

Sister Johnson slid into a seat at the Talking Table. Ruth and Ruby, anxious to escape, finished snapping the beans and filled a handful of canning jars with the bright legumes. Mother added hot pepper slices, peppercorns, and several sprigs of dill before pouring boiling seasoned vinegar over them. Scrambling under the table and over the threshold, the girls bounded toward the door.

"Don't forget you are collecting scrap. We'll go on ahead and make a few masks tonight, girls," Mother called after them as she sealed the jars. "We'll use 'em at the fair just to be mindful. There's extra ribbon in the ribbon box for the ties."

The henhouse, with its tiny roosting porch and sprawling fenced-in space, was filled with colorful, daft birds. Mother collected them— she bought two new hens every month at the Atlanta market so that there'd always be hens laying and always be ones ready for eating. Sometimes she'd indulge herself and pick ones because she liked the look of them. The pen was bursting with birds—autumn-feath-ered in reds and golds, speckled ones, Leghorns with bright red waddles. Some had smooth, tight feathers, while others were fluffy and soft.

They had one rooster—Maxwell—who made Ruth feel sorry for the hens. Maxwell would leave the hens bald with scabby places on their thin chicken skin from his pecking. That was why she had to separate the show hens early. When she complained to Mother that Maxwell was hurting the hens, Mother chucked her under the chin. "It's the way of things. Not a thing to be sorrowful about."

Ruth plopped Clara May down in the dirt while Ruby strewed the feed.

A sway of feathers and an expanse of iridescent flesh caught Ruth's attention. The peacock's head, crowned as it was with delicate spikes of black and white, cocked aside and took her in. Its plumage shook and spread like a harlot's halo. The morning light danced in and out of the weightless strands of blue-green feathers. Its many evil eyes winked haughtily.

Leaning eye to eye with the arrogant creature, Ruth cocked her own head in mimicry. She shook her hips, pretending she too had feathers. "Good mornin' to you, Francis," she whispered. The bird looked away.

"Now, Francis," she continued. "Let's not be unfriendly-like. Come here and eat."

She spread feed along the ground. Francis glanced back at her through one eye. Feathers rustling.

"We're goin' to the fair, Francis. And there's to be a parade. You'd make a right fine strut in that parade too. But I can tell you, you don't wanna come. Somebody'd snatch you for sure what with those feathers you wear. Come now . . ." She ran her fingers through the feed. The peahen chittered up next to her mate. Francis folded his tail feathers, paying no attention to his docile brown counterpart.

Ruby came bounding toward them. All but sliding into the dirt by Ruth's feet. Francis screeched, raised his feathers, and glared. Ruby's chubby hands were filled with warm eggs. She laughed and screeched back at the indignant peacock. Having kept the eggs coddled safely, she let them roll from her hands into the waiting basket. Ruth scowled at Ruby's precociousness and clucked an apology to Francis.

"Beau-tee. Beau-tee. Such a cu-tie. Sell your feathers for some boo-ty." Francis blinked before strutting away, his feathers swaying.

Ruth and Ruby finished filling the egg basket while Clara May gnawed on a stick. Ruth swatted at her chubby fingers. "No, Clara May!" She put her hands on her hips as she'd seen the mothers do. Ruby, momentarily contrite and seeking recompense from both Ruth and Francis, gingerly picked up the egg basket and took Clara May by the hand. The three headed back inside to deposit the eggs.

The kitchen had filled with a covey of women's hands, moving and flapping and fluttering from one surface to another. As Ruth navigated the basket of warm eggs to the counter, she felt like the branch they lighted on, patting her head or handing her a baby or passing a biscuit. And Ruth, inert and still. Aware of their fluttering but unable to join in.

Her sisters had the table spread with sweet bread loaves, canned jams, wrapped butters, and baskets of garden goods. Mother was sitting at the table with her house ledger writing out the items that would be taken to the fair and how much each one might bring them.

"There was thirteen eggs, Mama," she said dutifully. Her mother nodded and wrote the number into the ledger.

"There were thirteen eggs, Ruthie, were," she mumbled in distraction. "It is your choice of words that will separate you from the trash."

Ruth pulled herself taller and nudged her shoulders into her sisters' circle. "There's a bunch a'yella flowers out in the back field if you want 'em, Dollie. Maybe I could pick you some for the weddin'?" Dollie paused, giving her a dismissive motherly smile. Bessie took it upon herself to answer for her.

"That's sure sweet Rue, but those are wiltin' weeds. We're planning to use the asters and the dahlias . . . and a'course Francis's feathers. You are collecting them, aren't you, hmm?"

Bessie looked to her sisters for their approval before closing the circle, leaving Ruth with a prim view of their backs. Ruth thought that Bessie was a much better sister when no one else was around.

She waited outside the circle, thinking about how she might get their attention. Lola Bell looked down at her and tugged lovingly on one of the coils of her hair. Lola bounced down to her heels so they were looking eye to eye and leaned in, whispering, "I'd love some a'those yella flowers for my hair."

Ruth nodded. Lola Bell shooed her away and turned back to the circle.

Ruth and Ruby, with Clara May toddling and stumbling to keep up, passed on through the kitchen like three little dust motes blown about by the September breeze. Before they settled into mask making, they had sticks to gather for the kindling pile and then pulling and tying up spring onions, checking the squashes and late tomatoes in the kitchen garden.

That evening, when preparations for the fair were complete and supper was cleared, the circle opened for Ruth, and even Bessie scooted over and made room for her. With a basket of scrap for mask making in hand, Ruth settled onto the floor near the sewing machine by Dollie's feet. Ruby curled up next to her and laid her head in her lap.

They were all, save Ruth, who was charged with stitching masks, focused on dress making. Maddox had asked Father for Dollie's hand in marriage, and when he gave his permission, Dollie and Maddox decided to marry as soon as the war was over. Every evening since the proposal, Dollie insisted that they all gather in the Great Room to plan and prepare for the wedding. She started their circle time in prayer. Her prayer was the same every time. She wanted God to put an end to the war.

The six girls sat around the fire, humming hymns along with Homer Rodeheaver on the Victrola. Dollie at the Singer—her posture debutante perfect—sewing together the dress panels for her wedding dress. Lola pinned patterns for the bridesmaids' dresses. Bea tatted the lace, pieces of which Bessie stitched with surgical precision to the kerchiefs. Ruth, with Ruby drifting to sleep in her lap, sat crisscross on the floor with needle, thread, and scraps and made masks for Camp Gordon and for their day at the county fair.

Ephesians 6:6-8
KJV

Servants, be obedient to them that are your masters according to the flesh, with fear and trembling, in singleness of your heart, as unto Christ; Not with eyeservice, as men pleasers; but as the servants of Christ, doing the will of God from the heart.

With good will doing service, as to the Lord, and not to men: Knowing that whatsoever good thing any man doeth, the same shall he receive of the Lord, whether he be bond or free.

Chapter 9

The first morning of October debuted bright and clear and warmer than usual. The morning papers were laid out with breakfast, and both the *Atlanta Constitution* and the *Dekalb New Era* boasted of key Allied victories. Buried within the pages was dire news of the Spanish flu raging across the Southeast. But it was Fair Day in Dekalb County, and pestilence was inconsequential to Fair Day.

As soon as breakfast was over, the girls scurried to their room to don their best day dresses and chattered about who they might encounter at the fair. Lola was planning to meet cousin Elmer near the Red Cross exhibit. He was home from France, and she was giddy at the thought of seeing him.

Uncle Lovett had delivered the September edition of *Ladies' Home Journal*, and it lay open on the bed to an article entitled, "The New Way with Hair." Ruth and Ruby had already cut the *Betty Bonnet* paper dolls from it, and Mother had clipped the recipes that intrigued her. Bessie nipped it in the evenings and lost herself in the short stories. Sometimes she tore them out and kept them. *Ladies' Home Journal* stirred more devotion than their family Bible.

"I cain't wait to hear all about France," Lola said, dabbing a touch of Bourjois behind her ear. She paused with a bit of a pout as she settled the wide-brimmed, feathered hat on her head. Her hair was twisted into a loose beribboned chignon at the nape of her neck. Lola studied the hair fashions in the magazine every month and had a talent for recreating them.

"Maybe he was lured in by them French girls. Oh Lord! Maybe he brought one home with him! I hear every single one is beautiful." She spun on her tailbone to face Dollie. "Do you know the French girls are cuttin' their hair off?! Oh, if only! It must be so much cooler!"

Dollie indulged her. "Now, Lola Bell. Elmer has eyes only for you. Besides, if he had brought some French Jezebel home, we would all know it by now."

She put one hand on Lola's shoulder and, with the other, patted her sister's dark chignon.

"Our hair is our glory, Lola. Why would you wanna go and scalp yourself? You know what the Lord says: You'll know a harlot by her painted face and her shaven head. From what I hear tell, most a'those French girls are harlots."

Ruth watched in awe from her seat on the bed, her stockinged feet tucked under her white wool dress. Clara May nestled in her skirts, teething on a well-worn wooden ring their father had whittled for one of the first babies. Dollie's voice had an elegance to it that made Ruth think of the blossoms blowing in spring. She was careful with her speech, never wanting to sound like the poor whites or, even worse, the negroes.

"What's a harlot?" Ruth piped in.

Dollie glanced at her. "Never you mind, Ruthie."

She turned back to Lola and leaned her face close, her siren voice a lullaby to Lola's insecurities. "Elmer is home, Lo. And maybe he won't be going back to France. Maddox says the war is all but won. We can all get back to our everyday living. Maddox and I are getting married . . . you and Elmer will too."

"Do you think he'll ask me to marry him?"

"Do I think? I know it's so, Lola. So do you, silly thing. Our families have been talking about it for months."

Lola's dress was cut in the newest fashion—loose through her torso and falling to her midcalves. She, Dollie, and Bea had pooled their money to buy the drop-waisted pattern and bolts of colorful silk earlier in the summer. To their mother's horror, Lola had foregone traditional corsetry this season and was wearing only a brassiere under her loose dresses. Dollie and Bea opted for the fashionable but conservative longline corset, but even Ruth could see their vexation when they considered the freedom of Lola's wilder undergarments.

Ruth thought her sisters looked like the ladies from their magazines in their colorful dresses—Lola's in purple and Dollie's in green. Bea had made hers in peacock blue. The influx of bright color into women's fashion was the one area of French influence that Dollie chose not to denigrate. The three would trade their dresses back and forth to expand their fashion choices. Dollie's hat, a brand-new New York fashion she'd purchased from Miss Dorothy's shop, held one of Francis's glowing tail feathers, a complement to her green version of the drop-waisted dress.

Lola smiled and relinquished the one small mirror to Dollie. She settled herself around Ruth and set to nestling blue and red crepe paper flowers in among Ruth's curls. She and all the Shurlington women wore a blue star carefully pinned to her collar in honor of all who were in service.

Bessie strode into the room. She too was dressed for the school float—not quite as fashionable as Dollie and Lola, as she wore a pale-blue hand-me-down dress cinched in at the waist. Her hair was done up with red, white, and blue ribbons. Her dress had a white dropped overlay she'd designed herself to disguise the out-of-fashion waistline. She had pinned several blue stars to the bodice. She was in eighth grade. She, like Lola, would be going on to high school. Unlike Lola, she couldn't wait to continue her schooling.

"Mama says she needs everybody downstairs hippity-hop. The truck's in need a'loadin'."

The girls indulged one last preening before bustling down the stairs and out into the kitchen. They blushed when their father let out a whistle.

"I'm a lucky man with such lovely ladies to escort. You girls ready to go?"

He had on his Sunday hat and his good shirt. He'd trimmed his mustache and scoured his hands. Riley arrived in his wake and picked up a stray crate of canned vegetables. He stood tall, imitating his father, though not quite as spit-shined.

"I'll help you, Mama," he said, shifting the crate to his hip and offering to help with her handbag. Bessie scoffed. Mother, cinched tight into her corset and wearing a pale-blue silk dress with pearl buttons, thanked him and let him take her bag. Riley, the prankster, was no less a charmer.

Their caravan of motorcars chugged along the Stone Mountain car line, trailing the incoming commuter train. It was a gay sight—hats with feathers and flowers, ribbons flying from the girls piled in the touring car. Tom honked the car horns, and Earl and Riley whooped from the truck windows. It was a rare day when the whole family dressed and left behind the running of the farm for something other than Sunday service.

Ruth and Ruby sat up on their knees, wind whipping at their clothes, and waved vigorously at the excited faces pressed against the train windows—city folk making their way to the suburban outlands. The raucous melodies of the Stone Mountain Orchestra beckoned them all to the village center. When the truck hit a pothole, they bounced precariously high. Tom's voice floated from the cab: "Sit yourself down before you fall out!"

Ruth tucked her knees close, her arm wrapped securely around Ruby's shoulders, as the burdened truck made its way into the village center. She could hear her father and Tom talking about Richard Sams and his new irrigation system. Richard Sams had come home from Georgia Tech and was coming up with all kinds of ways to make the crops grow strong and hearty.

In town, their caravan slowed to a crawl, deftly navigating the melee of cars, horses, wagons, and trolley lines. The county fairgrounds were at the far end of town, and the festivities of the day spilled from one end to another—taking up the whole village in an obligatory wave of communal celebration.

Familiar faces mingled with visitors at every corner. A quick finger to the brow or a tip of the hat offered a polite hail to neighbors, be they friend or foe. An occasional knowing eye roll passed between the hamlet inhabitants at the site of the overdressed city dwellers. Whispering gossip and bursts of good-natured laughter accompanied the dance of preening girls and straight-backed boys. The DeKalb County Fair was a don't-miss shindig in full swing.

Tom brought the truck to a stop by the line of farmer's goods on Main Street. The wheels hadn't stopped rolling before he jumped out and offered to carry goods to the Women's Exhibit. Bea took the opportunity to load his hands with pies and, with a quick pat to his shoulder, shooed him on. Bessie giggled and nudged

Ruth.

"He's not really trying to help, Mama. He's goin' to meet up with that Carrie Carter. Guess there's no time for piggybacks, hmm? Seems to me you might have to transport yourself like a lady today."

Ruth scowled as she watched the receding backs of the mothers. Tom followed them, balancing pies and sidestepping Ruby and Clara May, who yapped around his feet.

Tom was courting Carrie Carter and had all but vanished from everything but his farm duties. Carrie was kindhearted with remnants of a deep, pulling coastal drawl that made her hard to understand. She reminded Ruth of a spring fawn. There was no reason to dislike Carrie, but Ruth didn't care for the idea that Tom preferred the Carter house to their own.

The Carters, a family long allied with the McGurdys, had migrated from Savannah a century ago and had broken first ground in the county, claiming expansive tracts of dairy land that sat adjacent to the main car line and the Shurlington land. It had become Tom's habit to finish work, scrub up, and head down the road to spend his evenings with Carrie. It was assumed the two families would be happy with a union among their offspring. Ruth only knew that Carrie's presence had come to mean Tom's absence.

Ruth sighed and turned to the truck to help with the hens. Poultry tending was a woman's domain, and Ruth had taken a special interest in picking the show hens for Fair Day. Today, she'd chosen the gentle, brooding Cochin and the elegant Houdan.

"Looks like you lost your shadows to Mama's pies," Riley quipped, lifting his chin toward the receding bodies of Ruby and Clara May. He handed his sister the hen pens before jumping down off the truck bed. Ruth had to admit she was rarely without her little sisters. Her hands, usually held tight by one sister or the other, felt empty.

She lifted the hen pen to her face so she was eye to eye with the golden-eyed Cochin hen inside. She crossed her eyes, and the hen flitted her velvet head. She'd make a good showing with her mottled, puffed-up feathers. She was plump with large wings that broke out into a confetti of orange, yellow, black, and red feathers, ending in smooth, creamy tips. Her spray of shiny tail feathers matched her black head. The Cochin paired well with the Houdan, who wore her short black-and-white feathers like fine evening wear. Her aristocratic black beehive head feathers framed her pale pink face and beak. Her black eyes peered out, bored and unruffled by the swinging pen. Ruth collected the shiny feathers from both and added them to the peacock fronds she sold at their farm table.

Lola peered over their shoulder at the Houdan.

"Little full a'herself if you ask me. Might do to pluck some of them dancin' feathers for a new hat." Lola took the pen from Ruth and lifted it to eye level. "We best get you on over to the exhibition 'fore I decide to do just that."

Ruth started to protest, but Lola had already stepped away. Conveniently, she and Bessie volunteered to take the hen pens to the Exhibition barn and then chaperone Riley and Earl over to the Camp Gordon tent.

Ruth arranged the crates of garden goods on the open truck bed. She filled a Mason jar with Francis's bright feathers and a small basket with the less showy but still elegant offerings from the Cochin and Houdan. She set up a bushel basket full of the first of the pecans and one for the last of the peaches and figs. She attached the small handwritten price signs that Mother had given her to each of the crates.

Her father tied the money apron around her waist. The apron

had been fashioned from scrap fabrics for market use. It had three pockets—one for coins, one for paper bills, and one for the little notebook ledger that Mother required them to keep. Each pocket had a flap that could be secured by a button.

"You are gonna be my sales girl today?" Her father sucked a small match flame into the bowl of his pipe and leaned against the truck. A spasm of coughing overtook him. Ruth waited for him to recover. "You been practicin' your numbers?"

"Yes, sir."

"Let's have a go, then. I want . . . a bag a'pecans, a bundle a'spring onions, one a'em—mmm—make that two a'em delicious pies and six peacock feathers. One for each a'my girls. How much will that be?"

Ruth bit her lip and lifted her eyes to the heavens as she counted the items one by one in her head. A red curl came loose from her bow and bounced on her forehead. "It'll be . . . two dollars and a nickel, please, sir."

"Ah, yes! You are a clever one, Miss Ruthie. Just like your mama's clever. Now you tell me what should we do with the two dollars and a nickel we earned ourselves, hmm?"

"Well, sir, first we pay our tithin' to God, then we put aside half of what's left for a rainy day, then we take the rest to care for the fam'ly." She beamed at her father.

"And what about candies? Is there a penny for candies?"

"Sometimes there is, sir. If we work hard enough."

He winked at her. "You'll make a fine woman someday. Keep listenin' to your mama and keep your eyes on your sister, Dollie."

He took in a puff of his pipe and added, "Maybe don't pay so much attention to Lola Bell, hmm?"

Richard Sams—the county's best hope for reviving the farms—materialized by the side of the truck. His appearance demanded attention, and Ruth knew she'd lost her father's. Everyone was anxious to hear about Mr. Sams new irrigation methods. The two farmers moved to the front of the truck and left Ruth to care for the customers as they began to show for market time.

Ruth was passing off the last of the butter and eggs to one of the McGurdy clan when Bessie and Lola came chattering up. Flushed, Lola bounced over to the truck bed and swept Ruth off her feet, landing her squarely on her hip and tweaking her nose. She jangled the pouch around Ruth's waist and raised her eyebrows in approval.

Lola. Lola with her green sparkling eyes had the spray of yellow flowers Ruth had given her tucked in the waves of her hair. Ruth wanted to be like her no matter what their father said. Lola was happy and bright, and not a thing seemed to fracture her joy. Worry over the war or the farm didn't taint her days. She loved the wild clacking of the streetcars and the train. Her marshmallow mouth tugged in a persistent smile, and her apple-pink cheeks were flush even in her calmest hour. Lola loved hats and ribbons and bright-colored dresses. She drank in every word of *Ladies' Home Journal*, and she reveled in spring and fall all the same. Lately, all she talked of was learning to drive and living in Atlanta.

"Come on, little sister! Mama's been a'lookin' for you. Let's get you to the float!"

Lola tugged loose the money pouch from Ruth and tucked it into the truck. She carried her across Main Street and onto the far sidewalk before plopping her back to earth. As soon as Ruth's feet hit the ground, Bessie tucked in tight to Lola's side, and the two sisters resumed their giggling, leaving Ruth to scamp behind them, weaving in and out of skirts and legs.

Ruth took in the bustle as they made their way up Main Street. A city woman in a sun-yellow dress was kneeling down giving a sip of Coca-Cola to her son, smiling and ruffling his blond hair. A tight circle of roughened men in overalls and squat hats, munching at their pipes, leaned into a lively conversation by Smith's Pharmacy. A tall man in a smart hat and pressed shirt lifted a chubby, peach-skinned babe onto his shoulder. Two little girls with bright-blue bows and bright-blue eyes sat knock-kneed on the curb, their fingers tangled in a spool of string. Smiling faces. Laughing faces. Furrowed faces. White faces. All white faces until her eyes moved all the way to the far end of Main Street, where the darkies had their own special place.

Ruth peeked down at the crowd of coloreds. The coloreds all lived on the opposite side of the village, in a place called Sherman-town. Shermantown had its own grocery and a few other shops, but they didn't have their own parade. The colored folks were laughing among their families, sipping colas while they waited for the parade. Little girls in faded dresses jumped Double Dutch with long stretches of old clothesline rope, chanting rhymes that rolled in percussive waves in Ruth's direction. Instinctually, she wanted to join them. She knew the chant from her own school games. But she wasn't allowed on the negro side of town.

She turned her face back to her side of Main Street. Happy eyes glinted in masked and unmasked faces as hope surged. American victory after American victory assured them that the current war would be coming to an end soon. It was hard not to feel light on a day such as this—the sun bright, soldiers both old and new were crisp and clean, the Confederate battle flag flying in tandem with the regulation Stars and Stripes from the hands of children and billowing behind parade floats.

Ruth found her school float in the staging area just as Riley and his friends tumbled in beside them. The four district school floats were to open the parade festivities with each school performing in front of the judges' stands at the head of the parade route. Ruth and her brothers loaded up on the Stone Mountain School float, ready to wave and sing their anthem.

Ruth sat snug beside her cousin Elly and took in her sunny face. Elly raised her eyebrows high at her. Later in the day, Elly would be representing the first grade class in the spelling contest. She had a flopping blue silk ribbon in her blond hair. She leaned her elbows into Ruth's lap and moaned over her too-big shoes. "Shoes're stupid," she said. The two made a pretty picture all dressed in whites and blues.

A huge crimson feather bounced in the straw hat of their teacher, Miss Beauchamp. She had a particularly large blue star pinned to her white high-collared blouse. Her beau was at the heart of the French battles. The upper-grade teacher—Miss Alden—was grumpy and old and left Fair Day in the hands of the sunnier Miss Beauchamp.

The float jolted as their horse was nudged forward. Miss Beauchamp, as part of her history teaching of the Revolutionary War, taught them all to wave at the crowds like the queen of England. Riley and Quillan were class leaders in war stamp sales and, as such, took their places of honor on either corner of the float, grinning and waving the war stamp books.

Painted tins were tied to the back of their float and bounced against the stone street. The girls all hoisted small flags—one federal regulation and one Confederate. Half the boys sat along the edge of the float, wielding pop guns. The oldest boys stood high in the center of the float with toy drums for tapping. Their float came to a stop in the middle of town, in front of the singing judges. They all straightened up and readied themselves. The old Confederate soldier dressed in his uniform grays, the grandfather of her classmate, bellowed the first notes of their song on his tarnished bugle.

Ruth caught sight of her mother clucking with her many aunts. The women waved happily at their brood. They were brightly dressed and wore feathers in their hats. Ruth thought of her hens penned up and on display over at the poultry exhibit. The old soldier finished the bugle introduction, and they all began to sing . . .

Over there, over there,
Send the word, send the word over there,
That the Yanks are coming, the Yanks are coming,
The drums rum-tumming everywhere.

The boys in the center of the float pounded on their drums in random syncopation. The boys along the edges popped their pop guns to add to the percussive chaos. The girls folded their hands together in mock prayer, flags tucked tightly together.

So prepare, say a prayer,
Send the word, send the word to beware,
We'll be over, we're coming over,
And we won't come back till it's over, over there.
Johnnie get your gun, get your gun, get your gun,
Johnnie show the Hun, you're a son-of-a-gun,
Hoist the flag and let her fly,
Like true heroes do or die.
Pack your little kit, show your grit, do your bit,
Soldiers to the ranks from the towns and the tanks.
Make your mother proud of you,
And to liberty be true.

Applause rang out, and Ruth scanned the crowd, catching sight of Tom. His head was bent into a small circle made by Carrie Carter, Lola Bell, Elmer Vaughn, Maddox Grant, and Dollie. Laughter erupted from their coterie, and they headed away from the bandstand. Carrie had her arm looped through Lola and Dollie's. Ruth watched her sisters flank the pretty Carrie Carter and disappear into the crowds. A dark twist of envy tugged at the corners of her mouth.

"Oh, my Ruthie, don't be sad. We're sure to win," Elly comforted her, misreading her frown.

The float jolted again as it moved to the side to make room for the Clarkston school. One of the ladies from the UDC was standing up and talking about the Liberty bonds. She smiled a toothy, lipstick-smudged smile. She held up a festive box and reminded the crowd to fill a Christmas box for the soldiers. Ruth pushed aside a wave of smug pride. She and her sisters had already made and delivered a dozen Christmas boxes for the soldiers.

They disembarked from the float. She and Elly joined hands and tucked themselves on the curb to watch the rest of the parade, settling down just in time to see the mayor's float. The mayor soared on a horse-drawn wagon all done in red, white, and blue buntings. Two tawny mares paraded in a crisp trot. The prettiest collection of girls in the prettiest patriotic dresses waved from the wagon bed. Their wide-brimmed hats brushed against each other.

Behind the mayor came a high-stepping troop from Camp Gordon. Their guns leaned casually on their shoulders. Behind them came three shiny new cars, honking and sputtering—headlights flashing off and on. Their drivers were dressed in their Sunday best with flag rosettes pinned to their lapels.

Ruth looked about the crowd, her nose twitching at the scent of BBQ and horse manure. Tiny flags were waving, and children were running between the legs of the grown folks. The tall white hats of the Klan came strutting behind the string of shiny autos. They were led by a man on horseback—a fine chestnut mare with a shiny black mane. The horseman's robes bore three black stripes along the sleeves and three along the hem. Two Klansmen flanked him on foot, one carrying the regulation Stars and Stripes and the other lifting the Confederate battle flag. Behind them came two members bearing a banner that read America First. Mud-caked farmer's boots and fine leather city shoes thudded heel to toe, in near perfect formation, against the cobbled street.

The white-robed klavern, its members distinguished only by the shoes they wore, were the same ones that circled the bonfires every Sunday night atop Stone Mountain. There was a red circle patch with a white X stitched in its center sewn on the left breast of each robe. Inside the white X there was a small red flame. At the peak of their hats, a tiny red tassel bounced with each step.

On the heels of the Klansmen came a caravan of Confederate veterans—set fore and aft by a decorated car full of the United Daughters of the Confederacy. The old soldiers were singing Dixie and chatting back and forth with each other. Ruth waved wildly at Papa Jefferson and Papa Perkins. The war-worn Confederate gray uniforms, cragged faces, and drooping caps were a strange contrast to the smart khaki regimentals worn by the Camp Gordon boys.

Mathis's cow Rosebud brought up the rear. Her coat gleamed soft white with patches of black. Her neck was wound with wildflowers. She was followed by a bright-blue wagon with a big sign that read Bring the Family to Mathis Dairy. Mathis's was the biggest dairy farm in a county full of dairy farms, and they, like Richard Sams and his irrigation system, led the state in improving the Southern dairy industry. Mathis's parade wagon marked the rear of the parade, and Ruth and Elly joined the town's children as they filled the street behind the dairy wagon and made their way toward the town center.

The parade of automobiles and soldiers and agricultural icons culminated at the Courthouse steps for the flag presentation. A sea of bodies clad in uniforms of Confederate gray, Allied khaki, and Klansmen white stood in stark relief to the red, white, and blue buntings that framed the presentation stage. They were all very proud when the Atlanta mayor handed over the new regulation Stars and Stripes flag—honking and clanging and back patting congratulations on their efforts to win this war.

Happily worn out, Ruth followed her family back to the farm truck, where they packed the few remaining goods in the truck bed. The money pouch was tucked and ready for Mother to reconcile. The day had been fruitful with all the butter, eggs, and breads gone.

Ruth watched with curiosity as Mother took Father by the arm and pulled him aside. Her face was dark, and her eyes were teary. Ruth slipped along the side of the truck, listening to her mother's whispers.

"It was that flu that took her," Mother was saying. "She came down sick, and within days, she was gone."

"Lord. McGurdy's wife? That is a loss, ain't it," Father said, shaking his head. He put his arms around Ruth's mother and gave her a squeeze. "You be mindful, Ida. All that time you and the girls spend over at the camps? It's spreadin' like wildfire."

Ruth slid through the shadows and climbed into the corner of the truck bed. She perched her chin on the edge and thought of Mrs. McGurdy and the pearl brooch she wore. She thought of the sweet muffins she made. Ruth felt sad for Mr. McGurdy. He'd be lonely without his son and his wife. She gazed at the twinkling box of the Big Dipper and wondered if Mrs. McGurdy was in Heaven dancing with Uncle Henry. The wind felt cool against her cheeks, and the crepe paper flowers in her hair came loose, floating into the darkness behind her.

By the following Monday, the threat of the Huns diminished,

overshadowed by a greater menace. Deaths from the Spanish flu were reported at alarming rates, and not just within the confines of the military camps. Thousands were sick in Atlanta and the surrounding communities. The schools closed down, and public gathering was discouraged. Bessie was charged with teaching them their lessons. Ruth found this to be an unfortunate turn of events, given that Miss Beauchamp was such a nice teacher, and Bessie was a much bossier one.

Ruth 1:16
KJV

*And Ruth said, Intreat me not to leave thee, or to
return from following after thee: for whither thou
goest, I will go; and where thou lodgest,
I will lodge: thy people shall be my people,
and thy God my God:*

Chapter 10

At the very beginning of November, the front page of the *Atlanta Constitution* blazed "President Ends All Draft Calls." Ruth ran straight to her father and jumped into his arms. He laughed and gave her the tightest hug in return. A few days later, on November 11, 1918, Allied victory was declared, and the whole town of Stone Mountain gathered atop the mountain peak. The bonfire pyre was lit in celebration—it had been built higher than ever, and it blazed at a towering height, tickling the underbelly of the night sky. The celebration was so loud, Ruth felt it in her muscles and her stomach and in the rapid pumping of the blood through her veins. Jubilation frolicked and spilled into every unmasked conversation. Horns honked and sparks flew and laughter rang out. At the peak of it all, Sister Johnson rose, her hands high in the air, and led them all in singing "America."

The fabric of fear that the Huns had tightened over their lives loosened, thread by thread, in the days that followed. The buoyancy of hope that came with the end of the war lifted them just above the weight of worry over the flu epidemic. After the jubilation night on the mountaintop, they returned, relieved and renewed, to cloistered homes, separated from neighbors, anxious over every cough.

Ruth's mother decided it was the ideal time to pour their energy into Dollie's wedding. Her union with Maddox was a new beginning, a momentous celebration for them all. A date was set. Since Dollie had already prepared all the wedding details while she waited for the war to end, it was determined they would be married two weeks after Armistice Day—on Thanksgiving Day.

The sentiment of being married on a day of gratitude suited Dollie, and despite the concerns over the flu epidemic, she would not hear of delaying the wedding. She wanted the whole family to celebrate together. She thought it reasonable to believe they would be protected by prayer and good behavior, so the women gathered around the fireplace in deep discussion about the possibility of holding the gathering outside.

"Outside would be a fine choice, and I think the back garden'd be lovely for a wedding. The dahlias'll be blooming. Might be a tad chilly, but we'll light the fires. Set up the food tables in the barn? It'll make the most perfect Thanksgiving," encouraged Bea, as she plucked the pins needed to set the hem on Dollie's dress.

Dollie stood in the center of the room while Bea pinned a few more nips and tucks. The dress was the color of magnolias with pale-green trimmings. The body of the dress was ruched along the sides, and the waist fell all the way to her hips. A sea-green sash cascaded from her right hip. The bottom of the dress had two layers. The top layer was of creamy silk, and the inner layer was the same sea green as the sash. The effect was a full double skirt that swung gaily about her stockinged calves.

"There'll be no worries about folks getting sick if we're all outside. Plus we can make some extra masks from the scrap." Bea looked about the room for Ruth, winking once she lay eyes on her.

"Ruthie has gotten right handy at mask making. Why, she's even been adding some fine stitching to the edges. Learned some new patterns from Miss Beauchamp? Here, gather on up the green silk . . . maybe some a'the lace pieces? We can make up a basketful to put on the porch for anyone who'd like one."

Ruth gathered the squares of sea-green scrap that had fallen around her sister's feet. Discarded ribbons of creamy silk inspired her. She took a tiny square of green and folded it into a pistil. Then she tucked the cream scrap ribbon into small folds around the pistil until it resembled a delicate blossom. She secured it with a quick stitch and decided the tiny flower would make a sweet finishing touch on the masks.

"Oh, that's divine, Rue." Dollie beamed down at her. "You do have a natural touch, don't you?"

The women tutted on—weighing their concerns about the influenza with their desire to celebrate the occasion with family. Ruth made a dozen ribbon blossoms and sorted the scraps into usable mask-sized pieces—listening, wondering what flowers would be blooming. After much conversation, it was decided that the wedding would be held outside in the garden. Anyone coming in from Atlanta would be encouraged to don one of the homemade masks. They'd light bonfires and lay out quilts for extra warmth.

All their family would be invited, and everyone would come too. Dollie's wedding and the end of the war had them all giddy with the need to gather, tempered only by their one missing soldier. Uncle Ephraim's name was whispered in reverence, the women touching their hearts anytime it was uttered. There was still no word of his whereabouts.

Ruth tried not to think of Uncle Ephraim. Thinking of him

made her upset. Instead she thought of the bonnie blond Elly, whom she saw practically every day, and of Lizzie, who still lived in Atlanta. Why, she wondered, as she sometimes did, had her mother given her the same name as two other babies? Why couldn't she have her own name? No one else in the family was named Dollie or Bea or Lola. Or even Ruby or Clara. She snuck a sideways look at Mother chattering with her sisters, ignoring her, leaving her in the corner with the scrap.

Her sisters had their very own names. She, Ruth Elizabeth, had to share her name with two girls who were both smarter and prettier than she. She sat back and glared at the pile of perfect green mask squares and cream-colored blossoms she'd crafted from the rubbish of her sister's dresses.

She picked up the kindling basket—she wanted to fill her lungs with quieter air—and headed out to the woodpile. The faint peeking of the stars slowed her steps. The moon hung woozy in the purple sky. God was up there, watching her, chastising her for her mean thoughts. She found it funny to think of the sky as the floor of Heaven, and she so small beneath the feet of God. She apologized to the sky, to the soles of His divine feet, for thinking badly of her mother.

At the woodpile, a fair distance from the main house, she sat, listening to the pigs rutting and the baying from the barn. The cicadas had long gone quiet. She heard murmuring, and realized Elmer's car was tucked into the space by the barn. He'd stopped by earlier to take Lola out for a drive in his new runabout. Father had given him a short leash, warning him to keep the drive short and safe. Ruth could see them in the shadows of the car.

They were sitting in the backseat. Elmer had Lola perched on his lap. Her skirts were splayed out around them. They were both making soft noises. Ruth watched with curiosity before it occurred to her they were rutting like any other farm animal. She was pretty sure that no one knew Elmer had brought Lola back yet and even more sure she wasn't supposed to be watching them rut. She should run straight to Mother—but Lola. She kept secrets for Lola. She picked up the empty kindling basket and slipped away, leaving them to the falling night.

When the roar of the runabout rang down the drive, Mother clucked at Lola's tardiness. Ruth's four eldest brothers tumbled out to inspect Elmer's new car. The men had a habit of circling about each new toy that landed on their doorstep. Lola slid into the Great Room and took her place in the mending circle.

"Sorry, Mama," she said, speaking to the needle she'd picked up to thread. The voices of the men carried from outside, their words indistinguishable. Father's lilting baritone mixed with Elmer's younger, brassier tones.

"We got to countin' the stars and . . . lost track a'time."

Ruth eyed her. She didn't look any different than when she'd left the house. Jezebel. Lola's needle pierced the corpulent cream silk of the bride's apron with which she'd been charged. A smile played at the dimple in her cheek. Ruth smiled, unnoticed, in response.

Madness reigned the morning of Dollie's wedding. A stack of blankets had been set out for anyone who might need extra layers. Several brush piles for bonfires stood ready for warming the wedding guests.

The main barn had been swept and long tables made from cinder blocks and wood planking were set up inside. The oldest quilts, stacked nearby, were to be used as table coverings. There were sea-green strips of silk hanging from the trees, the cool breeze catching them and twirling them about. Mama Ann and Aunt Norah filled dozens of aqua-blue mason jars with wicks and candle wax and hung them from their wire carrying baskets in the trees for lighting later in the evening. Lola and Bessie decorated the garden bower with late-autumn wildflowers, Francis's feathers, and evergreens.

Aunt Alice made a special cake for the wedding—a light, buttery-yellow masterpiece made with the last of her Swan's Down flour. Swan's Down made a special wartime blend that used both rice and wheat flour. It made the lightest cakes, and everyone agreed it was better than the original one.

Swan's Down was an easy-to-find staple, but sugar still ran scarce. The stark white icing of the double-tiered confection had been the source of many tense kitchen conversations. Several families had contributed their share to sweeten Dollie's wedding cake. Mama Ann passed on a small bag of costume pearls to decorate the edges—she said she'd seen it in *Good Housekeeping* magazine. The center of the cake bloomed with colorful Johnny-jump-up blossoms that had been collected from the fields.

The main cake was flanked by two smaller cakes. Lemon sponge cake for the ladies and an icebox fruitcake for the groomsmen. It was tradition that the two smaller cakes be made by someone who loved the bride and groom. When the wedding ended, a slice would be sent home with each guest to bring love and prosperity to their families. Bea made the sponge cake, and Maddox's mother brought the groom's cake. The rest of the table waited for casseroles and family favorites to be delivered by guests as they arrived.

A new Edison electric Hotpoint percolator had been purchased just for the gathering. The women fawned over how generous, how up-and-coming Bill Shurlington had been in his purchase, who, as a result, strutted about much like Francis the Peacock while pots and pots of steaming coffee were consumed by his spoiled guests.

Riley led a regime of Confederate cousins to war against Earl's diabolic Huns. Their theater of battle raged from the creek bed to the meat house and back again. Wheeler and Tom took Maddox down by the creek for a celebratory nip from Papa Jefferson's still before the wedding day festivities. Wheeler had been sulking for months; he'd enlisted but never made it past training at Camp Gordon. The war was over before he'd taken a step outside Atlanta.

Elly, having arrived with Aunt Alice, and Lizzie with Cousin Frank, joined Ruth in making crepe paper flowers for the tables and tree hangings. Mother had mandated that they stay inside to keep from spoiling their party dresses.

"Ruthie! Ruthie, come here . . ." Lola's voice floated in from the kitchen door. Ruth skipped out to the porch, hoping Lola wanted assistance with the bower. She much preferred to be outside. But Lola was standing by the porch rail, holding out a bouquet.

"Take these into Dollie, won't you?" Lola handed her the bouquet of purple asters and emerald fern fronds. "They're for her crown, so be careful."

Ruth brought the flowers up to her parents' room—which had been turned into a makeshift dressing room. Dollie was sitting on the bed pulling on her stockings while Mother and Bea fussed with her veil and flower crown. Mother's day suit had a high-collared lace blouse peeking from a mildly worn green velvet jacket. Her silvery-strawberry hair was swept low at her neck, waiting for her hat. Bea was dressed like Lola and Bessie in a low-waisted, long-sleeved sheath crafted from green gabardine. Their hair had been set back and intertwined with slim green ribbons and strings of tiny pearls. A removable raccoon fur collar, a recent French trend Lola had insisted upon, had been added for extra warmth. The brown-gray fur came to a perfect point at the center of their chests.

Mother took the ferns and asters, absently straightening the collar of Ruth's white Lolita dress. Ruth and her little sisters had matching dresses that had been ordered from Atlanta. Store-bought dresses were a rare treat. Ruth suspected they had been ordered as compensation for not being bridesmaids.

Dollie looked beautiful, standing in her corset. Thin garter straps secured her stockings. Bea dropped the creamy dress over her head, careful not to disturb her hair. The watery silk fell around Dollie's slim figure. The double skirts sang as she moved. The green accents created an illusion of watery shadows.

Mother tucked a raccoon stole around Dollie's shoulders before draping a filmy veil over her head, securing it with the crown they had made from wisteria vines. She tucked the purple asters and fern into the crown. Bea added a few more of Francis's feathers to the cascading bouquet of colorful dahlias, fern fronds, and asters that waited on the chest of drawers. Pride swelled in Ruth at the generous number of peacock feathers shimmering in iridescent amethyst and emerald. She'd collected them for months.

Mother leaned in with whispered words for Dollie that Ruth tried to hear, but even the few she caught made little sense. There was a warning of Dollie's responsibilities and duty to take care of Maddox. Mother's voice held the anxious edge of caution she used when the smaller children came close to the fires.

Mother and Dollie were wrapped inside their own glowing bubble. Mama Ann and Aunt Norah and Aunt Alice—all the eldest matriarchs of their own families—were the moons orbiting their planets. Sunlight streamed through the waffled glass window like angel smiles washing over them. Ruth wanted to be inside the sun circle with them. She glanced down at the childish flounces of her knee-length dress and thick stockings. Someday, she thought, Mother would whisper secrets to her, and she'd be in the sun circle too.

"You girls ready?" Ruth grinned up at the unexpected appearance of her father. "The family's gather'd. Cousin Davis has that Bible open, and he's chewin' on a soul-savin' sermon if we don't get a bride out soon."

"Did you put the Victrola out?" Mother asked.

"Yes, ma'yam. Record's sittin' on the pin and ready to play. I put Riley in charge a'droppin' the arm."

He caught sight of Ruth. "Run on and let your cousin know we're a'comin'. Tell your brother to start that record."

Ruth roused from her reverie and took off to the garden. Family, masked and unmasked, lined the porch railing. Through the open barn doors, she could make out her aunts fussing over the tables now covered in food, and through the kitchen window she saw the elders observing from the warmth of the Talking Table.

The back garden was filled with family—some sitting in mismatched chairs while others leaned against the old chestnut trees. Papa Jefferson, Papa Perkins, and a few other patriarchs held sentinel in their Confederate grays. Maddox stood by the bower, looking very fine in his khaki uniform.

Ruth ran to the wooden table set up to hold the Victrola and nudged her way through the crowd of younger children. It was clear that Riley considered his post pivotal to the success of the wedding. He started the music just as Dollie and their parents came around the house. They were beautiful, Ruth thought—Mother in her wide-brimmed hat, and Father puffed up in his best Sunday suit.

Dollie walked between them as they headed up an aisle loosely defined by motley groupings of the two families. From the Victrola, Homer Rodeheaver's disembodied voice sang out the strains of "Where He Leads I'll Follow."

> *Sweet are the promises, kind is the word.*
> *Dearer far than any message man ever heard.*
> *Pure was the mind of Christ, sinless I see.*
> *He the great example and pattern for me.*
> *Where he leads I'll follow, follow all the way . . .*

The sounds of children laughing in the distance, accompanied by the honeyed bayings of the barn added to the strangely divine air. The gaze of the crowd was captured by Dollie—except Lola, whose bright eyes strayed to Elmer. Carrie stood under one of the great pecan trees next to Tom. Her face was shining and dreamy as she watched Dollie walk toward Maddox. Mama Ann had found Papa Perkins and hooked her arm into the crook of his elbow. Her head rested on his shoulder.

Where he leads I'll follow, follow all the way . . .

The singer repeated the strain. His deep voice blended with the sounds of the farm. Ruth thought how very pleasant. To follow. The needle skipped, and the singer spun into an unending repetition. Follow all the way, follow all the way, follow all the way . . .

Hand in hand and surrounded by friends and family, Dollie Lee Shurlington exchanged promises with Maddox Feldon Grant. Cousin Davis gave a special prayer for all those suffering from the virus, and he blanketed their family gathering with protection from the illness. He prayed in gratitude for the Allied victory and for the boys still finding their way home and for the farmers trying to pull every last crop from every corner of their lands. He prayed for Dollie and Maddox—for the children they would make and the life they would live. He prayed in thanksgiving for Maddox's studies at the new agricultural school. He prayed for all of them. He blessed the new couple and declared it was time to give their thanks for all that God had given the family and to celebrate this Thanksgiving union.

As soon as Cousin Davis was done with his praying, Ruth saw her brothers head down to the creek. All afternoon, the men went back and forth—even her father, who mostly swore off booze when the Prohibition laws were passed.

Banjos and fiddles appeared, playing hymns from church and old Dixie songs. Appetites were sated. The whole of the day was accompanied by laughing and shouting and running about and the occasional apology to Cousin Davis for their heathen indulgences. Cousin Davis responded with a tilt of his hat and the raising of his own shine-doctored glass of sweet iced tea.

As the evening set in, the younger men, free of the shadow of the draft, got rowdy, spilling past the Shurlington property lines and making their way into town. The yawning stone fireplace in the Great Room warmed the women and small children. Tipsy and graveled with homespun drink and smoke, the older men settled outside around the bonfire burning from the massive old stump pulled from a far field earlier in the month. They stared, mesmerized by the flames licking at the tangled roots of the ancient tree.

The sun set in a blaze just as the Model T laden with young men returned, honking down the long driveway. The men tumbled out and between fits of laughter; they talked about the joke they'd played on the old Prohibition man that had come to Stone Mountain to write about the benefits of it being a bone-dry town. There had been a succession of news articles about the successes of state Prohibition laws in an effort to establish the new amendment.

Tom recounted how he and Wheeler hauled Riley between them, pretending he was too inebriated to walk. When they'd come up on the Prohibition man, they'd all spun into a pile with Riley on top, yelling how he was going to murder them dead if they didn't give him his liquor. The old pharmacist, who'd just decided to join in on the joke, came out yelling he'd been poisoned by the tiger liquor. To finish the prank, Tom ran up to the Probi man with a bottle in his hand and asked if the Probi man had any liquor to spare since it was a mile back to the still. The Probi man was so shocked he called for a car right away and left town. At the retelling of the story, porch sitters and fire watchers alike broke into roars of laughter. Especially when it was added that Miss Dorothy had popped out of her millinery to see what the fuss was about and nearly fainted at the spectacle.

Drunk on victory and good fortune, Ruth's parents agreed the whole of the day was a success. Ruth said her goodbyes to Lizzie and Elly. She kissed each of their cheeks as she had seen her mother do with Aunt Norah and Aunt Alice and promised them both she'd write letters every week.

Inside, she gathered her little sisters and sat them down for nightly prayers.

"He sees you," Ruth warned her sisters. "Everything you do and all the way to your heart. He knows if you felt the sin a'pride today. Our Doll-baby is one of His angels, and that's why God made her to be a beautiful bride. We have to pray every single night and beg forgiveness for all our sinnin'. Then maybe God will bless us to be brides someday too."

She took her sisters' hands and began to pray for their sins and hers. When she was done, she helped them change into their night-clothes. She brushed out their hair and sang soft hymns to them as she tucked them into their beds. She lay down beside Ruby and closed her eyes.

The trees came in her dreams. Yards and yards of silk fell from their branches, and towering columns of sunbeams pushed through. She reached for the light, but it burned her skin. The silk billowed and the wind rose. The creamy sheets whipped and twisted until they were popping in the wind. The sound was so loud and cracking that Ruth covered her ears. Then the sound took shape, sinuous wisps of silver smoke. Sparks flew with every pop until it became a metallic downpour. She sank to her knees, covering her ears and shrinking against the silver rain.

December 1918

It was early when the knock came. Earlier than knocks usually came. Ruth heard her father make his way to the door and held her breath. Then there came a whoop. She listened harder.

"We were awful worried 'bout you, Ephraim. Awful worried." There was a pause. "Good to have you home, brother . . . you look good. Skinny as a whittled-down rail post . . . but good."

Ruth smiled into the dark, barely resisting the urge to jump out of bed and run down the hall. Uncle Ephraim wasn't lost. She said a prayer of thanksgiving.

"Good to be home, Bill," she heard Uncle Ephraim say. "Good to be home. I was sorry to hear about Uncle Henry. Hard one. Hard one. Man was a saint."

An appropriate moment of silence ensued before Uncle Ephraim shifted to happier news. "I hear y'all have a new son-in-law and a fancy new coffee brewer in this house. Think Ida could make us some coffee? Thought if I dropped in early enough, we'd share a cup. I hear some wild talk a'you doin' some motor farmin'?"

"We'll see. Tom's gotta real fire lit under him 'bout makin' changes. Maddox—that's Dollie's new husband—well, that one's plannin' on bein' a preacher, but he's been studyin' at the new ag school too. Got some good learnin' on him. So we gonna head down to Macon for a big showin' a'these tractors."

"Tractors?"

Their voices faded. Uncle Ephraim was home. Ruth burrowed deeper into her covers. Everything would be okay. The war was over. Her brothers were home. And now her father's were too.

Hebrews 4:13
KJV

No creature is hidden from his sight,
but all are naked and exposed to the eyes of Him
to whom we must give account.

Chapter 11

Spring came, and worries over the flu died down. Ruth was relieved, as she found masks very unsettling. She didn't like to see only half a person's face, not to mention she hated how hard it was to breathe when Mother made her wear a mask to church.

As soon as March rolled in, Saturday mornings were dedicated to the farmer's markets in Atlanta. Ruth knew—she'd been told many times—they were luckier than other farmers. Her father had been given their farmland free and clear just a few years back, as had all her uncles. Their connections with the Atlanta relatives made it easy for them to find a market for their goods.

After the market, the families gathered for Saturday dinners at one of the Atlanta family homes. The farm families brought baskets of goods to share, and the city families filled them in on the latest innovations. Gossip from both sides of the car line flowed freely. The newest electric contraptions, from irons to toasters, girded the lively conversation. The city wives lucky enough to have gone to one of the department store demonstrations shared their thoughts in detail, either recommending or advising against each household investment. One by one the younger women bobbed their hair, in response to which there was an equal balance of tsk-ing and aw-ing from the bevy.

The men talked about the full restoration of the railroad—stronger than before the States War—and the impact of new farm machines like the motor tractor. Ruth's father puffed out his chest when he announced his new tractor was due to be delivered any day. The younger men, who attended the new agricultural schools, shared ideas on economic sustainability, pasteurization, and field rotation. The old farmers weighed in—trying to listen to their sons while clinging to what they had always known.

The women slid in the *Good Housekeeping* "Experiment Station" monthly remarks on pasteurization and food safety, rousing the men to agitation. The magazine, targeted to women's work, had a Tested and Approved List that was somehow gaining traction in agricultural policy. Women meddling in men's work, they grumbled.

Ruth loved the Saturdays when they gathered on Logan Street at Cousin Frank's house, for this was where the pretty Ruth Elizabeth lived—the one with the fancy shoes and the store-bought dolls. Cousin Frank had become more and more of a presence in their lives. When Riley turned twelve, Cousin Frank agreed to let him spend the summer in Atlanta and apprentice at one of the job sites.

Cousin Frank and his wife Lucy welcomed a new baby girl named Pearl, and with Pearl's birth, Cousin Frank made it official. The family would relocate to Stone Mountain. Ruth and Lizzie were elated when he shared the news.

While the adults swapped news, Elly, Ruth, and Lizzie found a spot in the garden to play with Lizzie's real Dollie Dimple doll, which Ruth thought to be much better than her own paper doll version. Lizzie had a small trunk of store-bought clothes for the doll and a bed that her father had crafted from an old chair.

Eventually, they grew bored in the garden. They snuck unnoticed into Lizzie's mother's closet and wrapped themselves in her furs. Pulling silk stockings and fine slips from her cedar drawers, slipping their feet into Lucy's patent pumps, they giggled and waltzed and planned their future together. Feeling brazen, they crept into the garage, dolled up as they were, and sat in the fancy new car. They were ladies about the town.

It was after spring had turned to summer that something like misery came, but also something like happiness. Ruth sat on her mother's bed, knees pulled into her chin, debating which prevailed—more misery than happiness? Or perhaps more happiness than misery?

Lola was crying, her crumpled face red and blotchy. She twisted a kerchief in her hands and listened as Mother paced the floor and talked about shame and ruin and sin. Father had threatened to send her away all together and stormed out hours ago.

Dollie, her belly swollen with her first baby, sat next to Lola with her arm around her shoulders. Lola declared her love for Elmer and swore she was going to marry him. Tears dripped from her chin. Ruth yearned to touch her—to hug her—anything to soothe her sister. Lola was miserable and broken. Ruth wanted to beg forgiveness for keeping the secret—for not helping—for letting her sister be ruined. Instead, she sat silent, as she had the night by the barn, drowning in Lola's pain.

The growling of male voices rumbled from the floor below. Their father and Maddox had Elmer cornered. Ruth had never heard her father sound so angry. The only reason she even knew Elmer had been brought into the house was because she kept hearing him say, "Yessir"—over and over. Ruth shrank into the corner and watched the world spool into heaps of unchecked words.

The door to Lola's room swung open, and their father stepped inside. Ruth and her sisters shrank and averted their eyes at his fury. He stared hard at Lola before turning away and speaking only to their mother.

"Maddox is a'gatherin' his thoughts. Elmer's mama and daddy are on their way over," he said, a calm settling on him. He needed to send Lola away but had found a way not to banish her completely. "Have her clean up and put on her nice dress, at least."

Lola heard his decision in those words, and she threw her arms around him. She begged for his forgiveness and blanketed him with gratitude all at once. He took her by the arms and held her at a distance, his fingers biting into her flesh.

"You're gonna marry Elmer this afternoon, Lola Bell. His sister is makin' a place for you both. You'll be helpin' her with her house. Pack your things. Maddox'll deliver your vows. Your mama'll make a nice supper. Then you'll be leavin'."

"Yes, sir, yes, sir." Her head bobbled as if the muscles of her neck had gone slack.

He didn't smile at her or hug her. He released her with a small shove. His face was blank and hard. Lola Bell was a stranger to him. *You're a disappointment, Lola. You've shamed our family.* Ruth didn't recognize her father this way—anger, confusion, and hurt bubbling to his surface, and him not knowing which to embrace.

"Let's get you cleaned up," Mother said, shaking herself and dropping off the pallor of humiliation as one might a summer cloak. "You are gonna be married! Ruthie, grab Ruby and go find some flowers in the gardens. Doll-baby, I'm gonna leave you to help her freshen up—Bea and I'll go prepare a nice meal. I believe we got a fine butt roast still in the meat house? Should have time to put a cake in the oven too?"

That night in the family garden beneath a bare bower, Maddox Grant, who'd taken on a job as small parish pastor, officiated the wedding of Lola Bell and her cousin, Elmer Vaughn. Lola wore her bridesmaid's dress from Dollie's wedding—stifling for a July evening in Georgia, but the prettiest thing she owned. She carried a bouquet of yellow roses Ruth had picked for her. She'd done her best to remove the thorns, but the smallest ones—the prickliest ones—snagged at Lola's lace gloves. It was a hot, somber ceremony followed by a quiet supper that was marked by a sense of relief.

No one could say Lola wasn't happy. She was expecting a baby and had Elmer by her side. She was to go live in Atlanta, just as she wanted. Albeit as a house hand to her sister-in-law.

Elmer had a smile on his face the whole evening, despite the looks he got from his new in-laws. An undertone of peaceful resignation settled on the group. It had long been assumed that Lola and Elmer would marry. It was different than they all had planned. The families hoped to stave off ugly gossip by blessing the marriage a good seven months before the baby arrived.

By the end of the meal, the family was chuckling over the couple's new adventures in Atlanta. Bea and Bessie were both going on about visiting—with Bessie making a list of all the practical reasons why it was good for the family to have two daughters settled in marriage. Elmer reassured them all about his position with the Atlanta Streetcar Company and was sputtering on about having no need to worry over Lola's well-being.

Ruth watched as the men ambled out to the porch; the wafting of spirits assured her it was indeed a special occasion. She leaned against the inside of the door and listened as the last of the tension drained from their voices. She soaked in the musk of their smoldering pipes and the slow drawl of their sporadic conversation.

Lola found her by the door. "Stealin' secrets are we, Rue?" she said with a smile. Ruth lifted her worried green eyes to Lola's. Her sister smiled, the dimples in her cheeks deepening. Her hat sat cocked toward her face with a large plume bouncing out the back. She knelt and held Ruth's hands in hers.

"It'll be just fine, little sister. You can come visit me in the city. We'll have a grand time. I plan to get a real job soon as I can."

Lola took Ruth's hand and opened it. She dropped a sparkling pin into her palm.

"You keep this now. When you miss me, pin it to your dress and know I'm thinkin' of you."

Ruth nodded. She couldn't speak because she didn't want to cry. Lola wrapped her finger into one of Ruth's auburn curls and gave it a gentle tug.

"Come now and say goodbye to me."

There were hugs and tears as the couple drove away in Elmer's runabout to start their new life. The baby growing in Lola's belly would be coming in the early days of winter. Ruth watched until the very last cloud of red dust faded. She held the pin tightly in her hand and waited for something to happen. If she waited long enough, Lola might come driving back, laughing at her own joke. The needlepoint dug into her skin, and a trickle of blood dripped onto the porch railing. The roar of the runabout faded, leaving only the sound of the farm. The same sounds she heard every night. Unchanging. Unyielding. Unaware of her presence.

I Corinthians 4:11-13
KJV

*Even unto this present hour we both hunger,
and thirst, and are naked, and are buffeted,
and have no certain dwelling place.*

*And labour, working with our own hands: being
reviled, we bless; being persecuted, we suffer it:
Being defamed, we entreat: we are made as
the filth of the world, and are the offscouring
of all things unto this day.*

Chapter 12

Between the rising heat and Lola's departure, the summer languished into a plodding dollop of days. Rumors stirred among the neighbors and the church folk but, with no visual confirmation of their suspicions, quickly died away.

Soggy heat seeped under Ruth's clothes and dampened her thoughts. The calefaction of the barns melded with the sultry scent of magnolia and wisteria. Every window in the house was thrown open and chores were done before the temperatures rose. Constant fights erupted about who slept on the porch and who was to meet the iceman and help with loading ice into the icebox. Summer slithered and writhed into every crack, crook, and crevice of human and building alike. A single fan whirred nonstop in the kitchen to deter the unbearable sweltering. Wet scraps of cotton were tied to the front cage and whipped in the artificial breeze. The fan with its wet tentacles did not, in fact, offer any relief—but the stirring of the air made one feel as if at least something was willing to move.

Barefoot and clay-streaked, Ruth and her youngest siblings spent the afternoons down by the creek catching crawdads and tadpoles. They waded through bubbling waters no cooler than the summer air. They swatted at gnats and no-see-ums and rubbed themselves with mud and bee balm to stave off the onslaught of mosquitos. They squatted, knees folded near to their ears, to examine every sparkle beneath the crystalline water, lest it be gold.

On lucky days, they'd find an arrowhead, abandoned and forgotten by the Creek warriors that had lived on their land less than a century ago. Papa Jefferson's daddy had obtained a large parcel when the Creeks left for Oklahoma. Ruth pictured a tall, bright-red man shaking hands with her great-grandfather—handing him the deed to their farmland with a majestic nod of his feathered head. She wondered if there were any of the warriors still living in their woods and shivered at the thought. They were madmen, murderers like the Yanks, savages like the darkies.

She lay on the banks of the creek staring up through the great trees, fingering the pin Lola had given her. She'd worn it every day since Lola left. Mosquitos zinged in and out of earshot—a tinny, piercing pinging that reminded her of the kitchen fan. She watched the sunlight bounce from one leaf to the other. She squinted her eyes and imagined the beams of fractured light were windows opening in Heaven.

Sometimes Riley would lay next to her and talk about how he planned to move off the farm. He wanted to go to Atlanta and become a businessman like Cousin Frank. He'd say, *maybe Cousin Frank will let me stay on if I do good as his apprentice?*

Ruth couldn't wrap her mind around it—even though Lola had been in Atlanta for weeks, and Wheeler talked nonstop about it. If she were really, truly honest about it, Riley and Cousin Frank had a similar way about them. Both brash and confident and wily.

It was one of those wilted days of late August when Mother sent them out to collect blackberries. Riley was warning them all about the snakes in the bushes when a faint wailing came slicing through the thick afternoon. Riley shushed them all.

Gunshots rang out as the wailing grew closer. Ruby buried herself in Ruth's skirt. Ruth pulled Ruby close to her. Billows of dust swirled in the distance, and light burst with each gunshot.

"It's sirens," Riley hissed. "Sirens up on the car line. Police got 'em a runner! Com'mon."

They ran out through the waffling mirage of cornfields toward the house, bursting into the kitchen. Riley and Earl tumbled together, telling their mother what they'd heard. They made up all kinds of reasons why the police cars were wailing so close to their home.

Mother sat them down at the Talking Table and handed them a bucket of snap beans. She believed hands must always be busy. Then she leaned in and asked them for every detail. Once they'd finished their tale, she sat back.

"Awlright, boys, awlright . . . I'm sure your daddy'll hear all about it and can tell us later. Did you bring plenty a'berries?"

Ruth handed her the tin buckets she'd grabbed, half filled with fat blackberries. Mother eyed them in disappointment.

"Tomorrow, I expect these buckets to be full. Little excitement is no excuse for a job poorly done." Mother liked to make up her own proverbs to go with the ones God wrote down.

The next morning, Father did hear all about it when he went into town. Another bank had been robbed. This time down in Duluth by an armed gang. They'd attempted to escape into Atlanta by way of the Stone Mountain car line—disappearing and hiding the money somewhere among the farms. Police were all over Stone Mountain searching for the villains.

Dollie was very upset by the whole thing and wailed that these murdering thieves could be anywhere.

"It's all those military camps," she wailed. "Foreigners been coming in and out because of that war. Brought people up from God knows where. These robbers could be hiding in our barn!"

She was getting so upset that Mother had her go lay down. The baby was due soon, and it didn't serve her well to be spun up.

By the next morning, folks were saying the robbers hid their loot with an accomplice on one of the colored farms. The gang had stolen thirteen hundred dollars and locked up the clerk in the safe. They roared out of Atlanta and through Stone Mountain in stolen cars, shooting at the police. Two of them had been caught out on Indian Island overnight, but police thought at least one was hiding in the farmlands.

Riley, golden brown and bare chested, lay next to Ruth by the creek. He thumbed an arrowhead round and round between his fingers. "I bet we could find that money," he mused. "We could sneak back over to Ezra's and look for it. I bet you a penny they hid it in that ol' barn . . . or maybe down the well. If I was gonna be hidin' somethin', I'd drop it down the well."

Ruth eyed her brother like he'd lost his mind. "You're coo-coo, Riley. We're not goin' over there. You heard what Daddy said— we're not allowed. What makes you think it's at ol' Ezra's place anyways?"

She turned to him, propping herself up on her elbow, slapping a mosquito dead on her arm as she did. It left a bloody streak at its demise.

"Well, if I was tryin' to hide somethin', I'd find me a place far from the car line, one that had lots a'hidin' places and was hard to get to. Ezra's place'd be perfect—you know that ol' darkie don't talk to nobody. He's one a'em ol' Virginia tobacco slaves." Riley paused, thinking, chewing on a wispy green weed.

"What's that got to do with anything? Jus' cause he's from Virginny don't mean he's hidin' things. 'Sides. He was down helpin' daddy with the horses when those robbers came through."

"I'm tellin' you, Ruthie. He's hidin' somethin', sure as shootin'. Maybe he's the accomplice. You scared to go?" Riley cooed, knowing she'd have to prove otherwise.

Ruth bristled. She considered herself very brave. She knew Riley was baiting her. She looked back up at the clouds dragging themselves across the sky. She wondered about that money too.

"What'd you do with it if you found it?" she asked. "Your half, I mean. 'Cause I'd get half too."

"You wouldn't get half. I'm the one who knows where it's hid . . . you'd get maybe . . . a'ten dollar assistance fee."

"Assistance fee?" She mulled it over. Ten dollars was more than she could fathom. It'd buy new hats for all her sisters and a fancy hen for her Mother. "Awl'right fine. What'd you do with the rest?"

"That's easy—buy me a house in A'lanah." He paused with the faintest whiff of guilt. "Maybe buy Daddy another a'em motor tractors they been talkin' 'bout. Somethin' to take my place. . . you in?"

She gave a huffing grin.

He took her smile as agreement. "Earl! Ruby! Com'mon . . . we're goin' over to Ezra's place."

Earl looked up from his crawdadding. "Why would we go over to that old darkie's place? You know we ain't 'posed to."

Riley winked at Ruth. "We're goin' treasure huntin'."

No one knew how old Ezra Harrison was for certain. What was known was that he'd been a field hand and breeding slave in Virginia. It was said he came into Georgia as a company laborer with his master's troop during the Sherman invasion. When the war ended, he decided not to return to Virginia. There was talk he had a wife who was sold into Georgia the year the war broke out. Some say he stayed hoping to find her. No one ever said anything about his children. It wasn't a topic for polite conversation. Since he was a breeding buck, he had no idea how many or where his children were.

Ezra was one of two sharecroppers on the back fields of Papa Jefferson's land. He kept a milk cow, a plow horse, and a chicken pen to care for himself and planted soybeans for livestock feed. He did odd jobs around the farm when their father needed him. During harvest time, Papa Jefferson summoned him to the larger fields to make up for any difference between his rent fees and his soybean profit, which was nearly every season.

The four of them made their way to Papa Jefferson's back fields, crossing over Stone Mountain Creek and climbing upward over outcroppings of granite boulders. Riley instructed them on what to do once they arrived. They would crawl on their bellies to the barn like he'd seen in the war films at the Rialto. That way Ezra wouldn't see them.

On the edge of the woods, they dropped down and started belly crawling toward the old barn. Once inside, they split up, digging beneath the hay and scaling up in the haylofts. Except for a feral old tabby, the barn was empty.

"Must be somewhere else," Riley declared. "Maybe the cellar?"

"We're not goin' down in the cellar, Riley," Ruth said, once again toe to toe with her reckless brother.

"Now why's you chil'ren be wantin' to go in my cellar?"

Ezra leaned against the barn door. His grizzled white hair was cropped close to his scalp, and a corn pipe lazily clung to the side of his mouth. His hands were tucked into the pockets of his overalls, and on one side of his face, there was a long scar that ran from his temple down to the edge of his jaw. On the other was a pale circle of puffed skin with the letter H inside. The mark of his owners.

Riley jumped up, and the other three stood behind him for protection. Ezra towered over them. Ezra was said to have Indian blood too. Warrior blood. Riley stammered before pulling himself tall and blurting out. "W-We know you helped them robbers, boy. You let 'em hide that bank money here."

Ezra stared, caught by surprise, then bellowed out a rich laugh. "You thinks they's money hidden up 'n heyah? You thinks . . . I'd up'n burry a load a'money? If I had me that kinda money, I wouldn't be workin' fer yer pappy, now would I?"

Riley looked confused. Ruth noticed the tremor in his clenched fists. The old man cut his eyes at Riley—menace and amusement flitting across his face. He was twice Riley's size with none of Riley's power.

Riley pushed his chest out and, in what Ruth saw as sheer force of will, met Ezra's eyes. In that tiny space when their two pairs of eyes first connected, there was hesitation. There was a child and a man meeting on a late-summer afternoon. There was a game at hand—an adventure—and nothing more. The moment passed as quick as an intake of air. Ezra gave a slight bow and looked away. Riley's chest puffed out a bit more at his superiority.

"You been listenin' to town talk way more'n's good fer ya, Mistah Riley. They ain't no money—hidden or in plain sight. I ain't seen no gangstas comin' down through heyah. Now you'n yer brother'n sisters head on back home afore I have to send fer ya daddy. I know Mistah Shurlington don' want you chil'ren 'round this place."

He used his chin to indicate the dilapidated barn.

Ruth took Ruby's hand and led her past the burly man and out of the barn. Riley and Earl followed slowly, keeping their chins high and eyes on Ezra. Ezra tipped the edge of his hat in deference to the children.

Ruth looked back as Ezra closed up the barn. He was shaking his head. He looked over at Ruth, and they stared at each other. His eyes glinted. Ruth hoped he might find his wife, even after all this time. A man like that needed a wife, she thought. She watched him for a minute more. She got the impression that Ezra didn't think their treasure hunting was as funny as he let on.

By the time they clamored to the porch, they could make out Maddox pacing the boards. He called to them before they made it to the kitchen door.

"You children com'mon out and help with the garden. Your sister's bout to have that baby. You don't need to be underfoot."

They weeded the entire kitchen garden and swept the barn before Mother came out on the porch and handed Maddox a small bundle. Ruth ran up and peeked into the blankets.

"A little girl," Maddox said to her, leaning down to give her a better look. "We're gonna call her Christine Leona. You wanna hold her?" Ruth nodded and sat down in the rocker. Maddox placed the bundle in her arms, and she looked into the little face.

"Makes you an aunt, Rue," he said and tousled her hair. Ruth beamed at the baby. Christine was a tiny creature with the tiniest hands. Ruth slipped her finger into the powerful grip of Christine's clenched fist. "Where y'all been, anyway? Your mama's been lookin' for you."

"In the back field up at Ol' Ezra's."

As soon as she said it, she bit her tongue. They weren't allowed in the back fields. To be there without permission was a punishable offence. So far Ruth had avoided her father's switch—though the boys caught it all the time. She ventured a look at Maddox, hoping he hadn't heard her, but it was clear that he had.

Dusk gathered, and Ruth held out hope that Maddox hadn't shared their transgression. But when their father's voice rang out—looking for them—Riley gave her a knowing scowl.

"Snitch," he whispered under his breath as they dragged their feet to the woodshed where their father waited.

He stood at the door with a long, thin willow branch grasped loose in his hand. There was no twinkle in his eye or amusement playing at his lips. He caught sight of Ruby hiding behind Ruth's legs.

"Ruby, you go on back inside."

Ruby scrambled across the yard. Ruth turned to follow her. They were one and the same in her mind.

"Ruth. You stay. You are well old enough to know better." Ruth returned to Riley's side, staring at her feet.

"Foolishness is bound in the heart of a child; but the rod of correction shall drive it far from him," Father began. "The word of Gawd for the people of Gawd."

"Thanks be to God," they mumbled in reply.

"'Twas a foolish thing you three did today. Never you mind the trouble you might could a'found back up in there—mountain cats roamin' as they are. Ezra has no need for trespassers in his barn. He was most worried 'bout Ruth and Ruby runnin' wild in the woods. He'd seen two cats prowlin' that mornin'. Never you mind there's an armed fugitive roamin' 'bout."

Their father's displeasure with Riley and Earl was clear. Ruth looked up at him. Maddox hadn't said anything. Ezra had told him. Why would her father be talking to Old Ezra?

"It is my duty as your father to remind you a'your path. Your path is the one I lay for you, as Gawd has assigned me to be your protector. You are not to be in the woods by the back fields or trespassin' on Ezra's place. You are not to be foragin' 'round in his barn."

"Yes, sir," they mumbled in unison.

"Riley. You first." Riley stepped into the woodshed. He was familiar with the routine. Ruth heard the switch whip against his bare legs ten times. Riley didn't make a sound. He walked from the woodshed, refastened his britches, and gave her a dark stare. His eyes shimmered, but no tears fell.

"Earl." Their father waited. Earl started to cry as he crossed the threshold. He yelped at the first lash, and by the tenth he was begging forgiveness and swearing he'd never disobey a rule again. Earl ran, snotty and defeated, toward the house.

"Ruth." Ruth stepped into the dark woodshed. "Lift up your dress."

She started to cry as she lifted her dress. She knew to pull down her bloomers too. The switch was to bite at bare skin. "I'm sorry, Daddy . . . I am . . . we were lookin' for . . ."

"Ruth Elizabeth. I have no interest in your reasonin'. You knew better, and you did it anyway. Were you unclear regardin' the rules?"

"No, sir." She bit at her lip. Her face was wet with snot and shame.

"Your choice was more dire than Riley or Earl's. You took Ruby by the hand and led her astray. You led her into treacherous places. Did you not?"

"Yes, sir. I swear I'm so sorry, Daddy."

"I know that you are. But this is my duty as your father. To deliver your punishment. Turn 'round." She turned, hiking her dress round her waist, and started to pull down her bloomers.

"Leave 'em . . . this is your first switchin'. There's no need to make it your worst."

His voice sounded pained. She left the bloomers in place and put her hands on the woodpile, leaning forward. The first lash stung, but the fabric of her bloomers caught the willow and lessened the blow. He delivered all ten—as he did with the boys—but she was certain he had been merciful. When he'd finished, he knelt down and pulled her into his arms.

"Ruth Elizabeth. It is because I love you that I punish you. You understand that?"

It was a hard thing to understand, and she wasn't entirely sure she believed him. Being whipped with a willow didn't seem like a very loving thing to do. If she took a willow to Ruby, she'd be in a mess of trouble. She considered saying as much to her father. He was bending down in front of her, studying her with his wise eyes, with no trace of displeasure in his expression. The switching had drained him of it. She thought it best to say she did understand, even though she really didn't.

"Yes, sir."

"Now go on. Don't give me any reason to bring you back up in this woodshed."

A fortnight passed. All the Shurlington women save Clara May joined the Mount Zion Baptist Church choir for a singing contest. Singings and Homecomings were a favorite part of Ruth's summer—on par with the county fair in their social importance. She believed her singing voice to be of above-average quality. At least once a year, sometimes twice, Baptist congregations throughout the county gathered together to decide whose choir reigned supreme.

Sister Johnson and her eldest daughter, Melody, were both ringers of first sopranos. Dollie joined them in this vocal stratosphere while Bea, as was natural, supported the two with a silvery second soprano line. Mother and Bessie warmed the bottom tones with their humming alto. Father, on occasion, added his deep voice to the bass section, and Riley and Quillan created a swoon with their pure choirboy tenor. Ruth and Ruby stood in the front and added their voices wherever they fell. Sister Johnson took near-sinful pride in the Mount Zion Baptist Church Choir's mastery of six-part harmony.

The churchyard was packed with families from all over the county. At least six different congregations had gathered to worship together. Long tables were set up under the trees and laden with casseroles and biscuits and pies. Brother Johnson, flanked by his wife and his ten children, opened the afternoon with a rousing prayer of thanksgiving. Then the church doors were thrown open, and folks took turns taking the stage and sharing their testimonies and their songs. The six competing choirs presented one song each at the half hour mark until all had shared. The pastors of the respective congregations made up the panel of judges, and the final verdict would be handed down at the close of their gathering.

The whole family attended the Singing—all twelve of the Shurlington children plus two more by marriage. Heaping plates of food passed among them, and a smug critique veiled as simple observation—perhaps even helpfulness—on the saltiness of one casserole versus the blandness of another weaved through the afternoon. Blankets were strewn about for sitting, and parishioners wandered in and out of the church at will—listening to the singing for a bit, then returning to the food tables—then heading back inside.

Eyes beseeched the heavens when an elderly soprano warbled her yearly rendition of "The Old Rugged Cross." When Riley, Quillan, and two of their friends joined in four-part harmony to deliver their own take on Fanny Crosby's "Blessed Assurance," there was standing room only inside the sanctuary. Ruth was among them. When they finished, she clapped as loud as she could and so long that her hands hurt.

Other than the obvious favorites, Ruth was never sure if people were lured inside by the shade or by the singing. She suspected it was mostly the former.

"Somebody 'round here really likes cel'ry. They's cel'ry in the potato salad. Cel'ry in the eggs. Cel'ry in the chicken cass'a'role. Likes they cel'ry, bless they heart." The elder's voice faded, and she crinkled her nose as she took another bite of celery-laden potato salad.

Recipes were shared with eagerness among the women who all brought extra recipe cards tucked into their pockets just for the occasion. The occasional matriarch jealously guarded her secret ingredient—swearing she'd only share her complete recipe with the angels themselves. Random "Hallelujahs" and "Amens" punctuated the afternoon. Parishioners closed their eyes and nodded along to the faint harmonious singing wafting from the church. If a singer stumbled or hit a sour note, a thick round of "Bless 'em, Jesus" would excuse the error.

When Sister Johnson gave Quillan a stack of extra fans to pass out to the ladies, Ruth volunteered to help. She liked looking at the pictures of Jesus and his disciples on the fans. She liked being a helper. And she liked the quirky, confident nature of Pastor Johnson's angel son. Sister Johnson had a way of correcting him and praising him all in the same breath, and Ruth could only figure it was because his mother loved singing. Quillan had the kind of singing voice that reminded Ruth of a clear summer afternoon by the Stone Mountain creek.

Quillan was ten years old. Three years her senior, his birthday fell right between Riley and Earl. There was always a yo-yo in his pocket and a sideways grin on his face. In Sunday school, he led them in opening prayer and could quote the Bible verse every time from memory. But what Ruth found most curious was that when he was with Riley, Riley got in less trouble.

They spent the next hour passing out fans to the lounging expanse of Baptist believers and clearing away their trash. Quillan brought her a plate of chicken and biscuits, and they sat beneath the pine tree, seeing who could remember the most Bible verses.

Quillan tried to teach her how to yo-yo, which only frustrated her. He told her most girls weren't able to master the mechanics of it, and she found the thought ridiculous. She insisted on trying over and again until she was able to make the wooden cylinder slide up and down the string at least twice. Having accomplished the impossible, she crossed her arms and gave him a look of triumph. He patted her on the head in congratulations and said clearly she was different than most girls. By the time Riley and Earl showed up to drag him away, Ruth felt certain she'd made friends in her own right with the boy whose hair shone like gold in the sun.

As the afternoon waned to evening, Brother Johnson's booming voice quieted the crowd to announce the winner of the choir sing-off. The Mount Zion Church choir, having delivered a rousing rendition of "Nothing but the Blood of Jesus," was awarded the prize of the day. Sister Johnson coddled up next to the ladies and assured them it was the crystalline voices of her children Quillan and Melody—supported by the beautiful harmonies of the Shurlington women, of course—that had taken the day.

Ruth, who had too often heard Sister Johnson exalt her children's talent, strolled away from the food tables toward the old cemetery, where she saw Lola curled close to Elmer under one of the great trees. From a distance they appeared to be a young couple resting beneath the towering pines. But Ruth knew different. Lola had come home from Atlanta last night crying. She'd wept at her mother's feet in the Great Room and told her she'd started bleeding.

Mother said nothing. She stroked Lola's hair and let her weep.

"A life conceived in sin is destined to destruction," Father remarked. "It is the price you pay, Lola Bell."

Mother let the words seep into the room before adding, "You and Elmer gonna come out to church tomorrow. Sing with me and your sisters. Spend some time in prayer. You and Elmer together get down on your knees. God gathered that baby on to Heaven for a reason. We do not question the will of our Lord. There'll be more babies, Lola Bell. There's always more babies. Go on to bed—you're set up on the porch."

The baby Lola had married Elmer over was gone, and she had been forbidden from seeking solace from her church community. As far as they knew, her marriage to Elmer was an honest one. With the loss of the babe, the family breathed a sigh of relief—a scandal avoided.

So Lola organized casseroles on the long tables and made small-talk with their neighbors and sang in the choir. She listened to the elder advice and accepted well-wishings on her new marriage. Now, finally, she sat in the shadow of the squat brick church, under the umbrella of the soaring pines. Granite headstones surrounded her, most marked with their family name. She hadn't looked any different the night she'd sinned with Elmer. But she looked different now. Her sadness dulled the light within her. She closed her eyes and leaned into the crook of Elmer's arm—he with his legs stretched before him and his head resting against the knotted tree—both letting the waning sun warm their tired faces.

Bibb County, Georgia—1919

Crawford hesitated on her front porch. She worked endless days in the secretarial pool—but today hadn't gone well. She'd been laid off and sent home early. Her body, abused and worn, begged her to rest, but she knew that would depend on Leonidas's mood. He'd been laid off from the ironworks company weeks before. His small errors in interpreting the blueprints had added up to his firing. Most of his days started with job hunting and ended with him drinking away his worries with his brother.

Recently he had been talking about selling insurance. He said it was a sure way of making good money. He told her it would require traveling all over the state, and she'd have to be without him sometimes. She responded with the appropriate grief but assured him that the money would be worth the temporary separation.

She stepped into the dim entryway and felt the strangeness in the air. She paused. Helen? She heard Leonidas's voice and Helen whimpering. She struggled to connect. Helen spent the days with her grandmother. She wasn't meant to be picked up for a few hours still.

Fear pricked at her. A knifepoint at her throat. She felt it as sure as if it were really there.

She followed the sounds of her daughter's whimpering. Her feet carrying her faster with each step. She came upon them in her little girl's bedroom. He was sitting in the rocker. His three-year-old daughter perched on his lap, facing away from him. Her tiny, half-clothed body rocking in rhythm with him. Blood. Tears.

Crawford broke in half. She screamed. She rocketed to her daughter and pulled her away with one arm. With the other, she swung at him. She made contact with his jaw. Stunning him.

She ran.

Proverbs 30:30
KJV

Favour is deceitful and beauty is vain: but a woman
that feareth the Lord, she shall be praised.

Chapter 13

The Spanish flu, which the winter before had crippled them into isolation, was promised to be milder and more manageable. Schools and public places remained open as the weather changed, but officials suggested mask-wearing as a precaution. Mother made them wear their masks anytime they left the farm, which they quickly discarded once they were out of her sight.

Morning walks to school with her siblings lifted Ruth, wrapping her safely in their childish world. They talked of the treasure that had yet to be found and what they would do with the spoils should they be lucky enough to discover it. Warm breezes brushed at their faces. Wispy puffs of cottonwood seed danced with celluloid-winged insects over dewy grasses. Squinting her eyes at the watchful trees, Ruth made out gnarly arms and legs and tangled heads. The ancient trunks bowed around them, showering them with red-gold leaves. Fresh-turned earth and the pungency of living and dying things perfumed the air.

Miss Beauchamp was sadder than the last time the children had seen her. Her beau had never returned from the war, and both her parents had been taken by the flu. It was clear she was destined for spinsterhood. She used to laugh more and play games with them outside, but she'd tucked that part of herself somewhere else. Now she rang the bell for them to go outside and to come in—but she didn't join them.

They learned their lessons about how their county was born from a land treaty with the Creek warriors and how, in return, the Creeks were given miles of land under the Oklahoma sun, where they were safe and protected. They learned about the Lost Cause and fine heroes like Robert E. Lee, whose image was to be carved into the face of their great stone mountain.

Miss Beauchamp explained how the white planters had cared for their slaves—how unique and bonded the relationship had been. But now that that relationship had been torn asunder, it was important, for the sake of the common good, to keep the races separate. She explained this was why there were places for the whites only and places for the coloreds.

On Mondays, Miss Beauchamp read the front page of the Sunday *Atlanta Constitution*. She called it "current events." She read about the funds drive for the Confederate reunion and about the small fights still happening overseas. She reminded everyone that it takes a while for peace to settle in among warring people.

On Fridays, Miss Beauchamp ended lessons with a talk on staying clean, washing their hands, and taking care of themselves. Ruth listened carefully to those parts. Once her teacher even collected samples of their poo to send to the doctor in Atlanta, just to make sure they didn't have the worms. Riley and Earl both had them, and they had to take a special medicine. Miss Beauchamp said the new indoor toilets at the school were going to help keep the worms from getting into the children. She gave a serious look at Riley when she said this, her expression telling him to stop scaring the little ones over the toilets.

Ruth spent most of her day hand in hand with Elly. Elly was the clever and outspoken Ruth Elizabeth, while Ruth was the quiet Ruth Elizabeth. The one no one ever looked to find. Sometimes the teacher would forget to use their nicknames, and she'd call out "Ruth." But Miss Beauchamp always meant to be calling on Elly. Ruth wanted to be the one everyone was calling for when she heard her name. "Vanity is a wicked thing," her mother's disembodied voice chastised her.

During recess, Ruth, Elly, and her other cousins played outside under the pine trees. They made plans for Lizzie's return to Stone Mountain and laughed about how poor Miss Beauchamp would have three Ruth Elizabeths in her classroom. They practiced braiding and skipping rope. They chanted poems and fell laughing into flouncing piles of soft cotton skirts.

> *There was a little girl, and she had a little bird,*
> *And she called it by the pretty name of Enza;*
> *But one day it flew away, but it didn't go to stay,*
> *For when she raised the window, in-flu-Enza.*

Ruth felt the seasons change by the number of leaves that fell around her on her morning walks. By the time the leaves had stopped falling and the trees were bare, the sky sunk in on them. The rains came, swelling the creeks and flooding the roads, turning them into sloppy swaths of red mud.

One rainy December afternoon, she was fairly pleased to see no one had driven out to pick them up from school. The roads were often impassable this time of year. She loved being left to walk home, for it meant rain drinking and puddle splashing and, despite the midwinter chill, a detour to the fattening creek. She and Riley and Earl and Ruby careened in and out of the creeks and mudholes that marked their way to the farm.

They rounded the fence to home, soaked and shivering, to discover the yard full of cars. Family was gathered on the porch to avoid the rain. Their faces were somber. Some were crying.

Ruth slipped into the crowded kitchen. Her father was at the Talking Table with his head in his hands and his face grim. Her uncles and brothers were angry, shouting about the railroads. Mother was shushing them, telling them to go on outside if they needed to rail. Ruth looked from one face to the other, finally landing on Dollie, who was rocking Christine in her arms. Maddox stood behind her, his hands kneading at her shoulders.

"What's happened?"

Dollie looked down at her, vacant. She glanced up at Maddox, and he nodded.

"I guess there's no way a'you not knowin'," she finally said. "Frank and Lucy were in an accident. The train. They . . . They never saw it comin'. Baby Pearl n'little Frank . . . they're gone too."

Ruth tried to process what Dollie was saying. She heard the clacking of the train storming through her head. Its black engine plowing over the rails, chugging black smoke. Giant crow wings carrying the winter creature over their fields. Dollie reached out a free arm and offered to comfort her. Ruth leaned into her big sister and laid a hand on Christine's tiny chest. Her shivers grew more violent.

"Lizzie?" she whispered.

"Lizzie's okay . . . and Mary and Margie. They'd just been dropped to school with John. Their Grannie Spivey picked them up and took them home with her."

Ruth buried her head in the baby's belly and breathed in the sweet milk smell. Sadness overcame her, and a lump grew in her throat. This was worse than when Uncle Henry went to be with the Lord. She tightened her eyes against the image of the big black train running over her cousin's car, of the babies inside. She saw the babies. She saw the train breaking them in pieces. She squeezed her eyes tighter until all she could see were small blue spots.

Pictures of Cousin Frank's laughing face and Aunt Lucy's fur-trimmed coats and the pretty, round face of little baby Pearl flipped through her mind. Lizzie is okay, she said to herself over and again. Lizzie wasn't in the car. Pretty, pretty Ruth Elizabeth. A strange regret flicked through her mind, like a fat beetle clicking through a dark corner. Lizzie was still the pretty one. If she'd been in the car . . . ? Ruth shook her head with a violence that startled baby Christine into a wail. She ran from the room and fell to her knees by her bed, clasping her hands and begging God to forgive her for her evil mind.

Matthew 26:39
KJV

O my Father, if it be possible, let this cup pass from me: nevertheless not as I will, but as thou wilt.

Chapter 14

March 1920

"Some darkie got themselves killed by the train yesterday. Carryin' wood and crossin' the tracks, they say. It's a shame. Them darkies can be lazy. Prob'ly thought the train'd stop for her."

It was early, before the sunrise. Wheeler, Maddox, and Tom were sitting at the Talking Table drinking coffee and reading through the morning paper. There wasn't a pause at the thought that Cousin Frank was neither lazy nor stupid enough to think a train could stop on a dime. And yet. He'd gotten himself, his wife, and two of his children killed.

"Looks like the whole dayum country's been takin' by the Drys. That new amendment's got folks dancin' to the Devil's fiddle and they don't even know it." Wheeler scoffed at the article he was reading. "That moonshine river won't stop flowin'. All they did is chase it underground and make the Probis even more of a bother."

"Pish-posh, Wheeler. Probis aren't anything for us to worry on. Our people been side-steppin' them since a'fore Ruthie here was even born. Did you know you were born into a fam'ly a'criminals, baby?" Lola winked at Ruth.

Lola and Elmer had been fighting since she lost the baby, and she'd come home for a while, refusing to speak to him. She too sat with the boys, smoking one cigarette after another and stubbing the butts out into her coffee saucer. Riley held out a fan of poker cards in her direction, and she drew one. He'd moved from sleight of hand tricks to card tricks.

"Ace a'spades," he said with confidence. Lola tossed the two of diamonds on the table.

"Go fish," she said. Riley's face clouded over. He snatched the cards back into a pile and took to shuffling.

"We are not criminals, Lola Bell," Tom chastised. "We simply choose to celebrate—on occasion commiserate—in a fashion true to our forebears. The gov'ment has no place in how we go 'bout our private lives . . . on our private land . . . in our most private ways."

A warming fire raged in the Great Room. A fine haze clung to the ceiling. The constant percussion of their father's cough came from his bedroom—drifting into the kitchen. Mother scowled at her children and refilled her sons' coffee cups. Her brow furrowed as she listened more to her husband than the banter around the Talking Table. Lola lifted her cup for a refill. Mother grimaced and refilled her coffee with some reluctance.

"How's Daddy?" she asked. The question they had all begun to ask. He had battled the flu last month—as had half the family. But it had clung to him; his lungs had never fully recovered from the village fire two years prior. Pneumonia threatened to consume him.

"Doctor's back there," Mother said, her own voice husky from the cough she'd had all month.

There was only one doctor available to the Stone Mountain community. Streetcar strikes and rising flu cases had overwhelmed him. Traveling from the city into the outer communities had all but ceased, thanks to the warring transportation providers. Hospitals were flooded. Medical staff was exhausted. The women of rural Dekalb County were expected—as they embraced with pride—to take care of their own. By February, the doctor came only to the direst of patients. By March, even those approaching Heaven's gates had to wait.

"He's havin' a real hard time breathin'. Don't seem like he's gettin' any better. Been in the bed these last three days. Says he's achin' too bad to move."

"He'll be awlright though, won't he, Mama?" Ruth asked.

"A'course Ruthie, he'll be hoeing corn rows come spring like he always does . . . your daddy's a strong man. It's a touch a'the flu bug still got him down. Few more days rest'll do him right."

Wheeler looked over at the two other men. Their expressions were dark.

"Speakin' of." Mother eyed both Riley and Earl. "You two go on. Hogs need some attention, and with your daddy still down, you're gonna need to mend up the south fence before we have cattle loose."

Riley tucked his cards in his pocket. He and Earl grabbed their coats and headed out without complaining. Everybody had been shifting chores with the winter sickness falling on one or the other of them.

"Bea and Dollie are coming out a'it. They're near right-side up," Bessie added, taking her role as Mother's surrogate helper seriously and changing the subject from their father. She, Ruth, and the babies were the only ones that had escaped the flu this winter. Bessie and Ruth kept the three smallest members, including baby Christine, occupied and away from the sick rooms.

When Mother was recovered enough, she and Bessie got on well as a makeshift medical team. Mother read all the back issues of *Ladies' Home Journal,* scouring them for every thought on how to keep the germs from spreading. Bessie, with her natural penchant for plant medicine and under the guidance of Mama Ann and Aunt Norah, had turned to making homemade tonics and chest ointments to soothe the patients. The women collected every new piece of information that came from the health departments that had opened in Atlanta. They sanitized and washed hands and kept the sick separated.

"I believe they're stirring this morning," Bessie continued with authority. She'd also redistributed the chores based on who was well enough to help. "Dollie said she'd be getting to mending today."

Mother nodded with confidence in Ruth's direction. "Well, see, that's some good news. Everybody's on the mend. Your daddy will be coming out the other side soon too." She glanced at the men, who refused to meet her eyes. "It's a muddy one, boys. Y'all be sure to come through the wash room when y'all come back in."

It was a rainy Wednesday one month after Ruth's eighth birthday. In school, Ruth went through her lessons as best she could. She sat at the front of the room near Ruby. She tried to ignore Earl's voice coming from the back. She could hear him picking a fight with the Hollingsworth boy. Earl was mad that he'd been sent to school and was taking it out on the other boys. Riley had been allowed to stay home, and he thought he should be at home helping too.

The fire crackled in the wood stove, and Miss Beauchamp was tutoring Ruth's group on numbers. Ruth's thoughts drifted to her father. She'd peeked in before leaving for school, hoping to see him sitting up and drinking his coffee. But he was asleep. His breath was short and wheezy. His face was ghostly. She didn't want to be away from home today, so she'd carried the little wooden bunny he'd made her in her pocket. Every time she felt worry, she slipped her hand in her pocket and felt for the smooth wood of the bunny.

When school let out, she ran all the way home and up the long driveway that led to the farmhouse. She slowed as she saw Uncle Ephraim standing on the porch. He was talking to Uncle Lovett, Mother's brother, who never came round unless something bad happened.

She veered to the hen run. Inside, she locked the gate behind her and looked for Francis. The grand bird was loitering in the corner away from the other hens. She went over and sat in the mud next to him. She took out the wooden bunny and cradled it in her hands—running her thumbs up and down its carved flank. She lifted her face and let the drizzle blind her. Francis cocked his head at her.

"Beau-ty, Beau-ty . . . such a cutie . . . ," she whispered to him. Daddy was dead. She knew it. She saw her days without him. She felt the pain of his absence. She cried tears that disappeared into the rain. When she had emptied herself of all the grief, she stood up and headed to the porch.

"You might want to go in and see your Daddy, Rue," Uncle Ephraim said as she approached. Ruth looked at him, confused. He wasn't dead? She walked past her uncles and up the stairs to her parents' bedroom. From the doorway, she watched her father struggling to breathe. His eyes opened, fluttering and lost, before recognition settled back on him. He gestured for her. All the tears she thought she'd finished welled up behind her eyes.

"Ruthie," he whispered, then coughed. "You be good to your

mama now. Don't cause her no trouble."

"Daddy?"

He squeezed her hand. His chest rattled, and he started coughing again. Bright-red splatters of blood were on his kerchief. The room had a rancid smell. "There's nothin' for any a'us to cry 'bout. Nothin' that Gawd hasn't already intended," he said and closed his eyes.

"I'll pray for you, Daddy. I'll pray, and God will make you better."

She knelt by her father's bedside. His hand rested on her head. "Dear God, Look down on my daddy . . . on William Shurlington. He's very sick and he cain't breathe. Whatever you have to do to make him better, then fix him, God. I know you can fix him."

In all her eight years, she'd not prayed so hard. She finished her prayer and sat with her eyes closed and her hands folded. She felt his hand go lifeless on her head as he drifted into a restless sleep. God would fix this. God would save her Daddy and make everything better. All you had to do was ask God. That's what Brother Johnson said every Sunday. That's what Cousin Davis said every time he preached too. Uncle Henry used to say it. Uncle Henry made her memorize the Bible verse: Whosoever shall say unto the mountain, Be removed and cast into the sea; and shall not doubt in his heart, but believes the things which he saith shall come to pass; he shall have whatsoever he saith.

Ruth slipped from beneath his hand and went to her afternoon chores. She was glad she remembered to pray and wasn't sure why she hadn't thought of it sooner. All she had to do was believe and remove all doubt from her heart. The Bible said so.

After supper, she tucked her sisters into bed and curled up next to Ruby. She murmured assurances to her little sisters. She prayed until sleep stole her words.

The dream came that night. The trees with their twisting roots towered over her, and the light all around her was blue. She reached out to touch the bark of the great tree. It bent beneath her fingers, the massive trunk rounding itself over her. All the trees began to bend and shape themselves into a ball—holding her in their center. The blue light deepened, and the twisting roots writhed and tangled until she was cocooned inside their womb. The blue light grew darker and darker until it turned to blackness. She knew there was nothing outside of the root ball. She nested herself into the bottom and surrendered to her cage.

Ruth woke the next morning before dawn, as was her custom. An eerie silence permeated the house, and there was a bite to the air. The fires hadn't been started. Rain echoed against the tin roof. A whimpering came from the Great Room, and she followed the sound.

Mother sat in her father's rocking chair. One arm was wrapped about her waist and the other covered her mouth. Her shoulders shook, and a soft mewing came from her. Her eyes were closed tight, and she rocked rhythmically. Her generous hips snuck out like soft pillows from beneath the curving arm rests.

"Mama?" She looked up slowly, her hand still covering her mouth. Her eyes were colorless against the red-rimmed puffiness surrounding them. She opened her arms, and Ruth ran to her, frightened by her Mother's tears. She wrapped herself around Ruth the way she'd done when Eugene was a babe, and her tears came stronger. She stroked Ruth's unruly red curls. "Your Daddy's gone to be with the Lord, Ruthie."

That couldn't be right. God hadn't heard her? Had she not banished all her doubt? God hadn't listened at all. She buried her face into her mother's breasts and fought the tears. She was stupid for believing God would listen to her. To her! Maybe she should have prayed harder and louder and longer. Maybe if she believed more or didn't get distracted in church, God would have listened to her. Maybe he was punishing her for her evil thoughts about Lizzie. Or for keeping Lola's secrets.

"Ruthie?" Mother pulled her away to look at her face. "Ruthie, baby. Daddy was very sick, and the sickness was stronger than he was. But he's not sick anymore. He can breathe easy. He's up there in Heaven dancin' with your Uncle Henry and Frank and Lucy. He's checking in on sweet baby Pearl. He's looking down on you, watching you."

Her father wasn't dancing. He was sad. From his place in Heaven, he could see how weak her prayers were. That she was a doubter. He could see her horrible thoughts about Lizzie. He could see she had hid Lola's secret, and that she was the reason Lola had been ruined. He could see her jealousy and her vanity. He wasn't dancing. Her father could see everything now, and he was ashamed of her.

"I need to call in the doctor, Ruthie, and wake your brothers and sisters. Can you start up the fires?"

Ruth tried to breathe, but her lungs wouldn't move. The only thing to do was to be better than she'd been. She headed to the kitchen to set the cooking fire. For the second time in as many months, grief came alive in the house. By dinner, the house was once again full of food and cousins and aunts and uncles.

Ruth kept her head down. She made sure there was butter and jam on the table and that her father's coffeepot stayed hot. She cleaned up after anybody that left a mess. She arranged the casseroles on the table and kept the plates washed. No one seemed to notice her at all. They talked around her. Weeping, grotesque faces with bleary eyes and dripping noses loomed about the tables, talking, talking, talking. She wanted to shout. Shout in somebody's face that she wanted her Daddy back. She wanted someone to tell the Lord that she still needed her Daddy.

The scream grew so loud inside her head she thought she might explode, so she swallowed it whole. The screaming went into her belly, but her head felt clearer, and her eyes were dry. Placidness enveloped her, and she cleared the empty dishes away from the grieving grown-ups.

"Ruth?" A hushed voice broke through her stupor. She was standing in the kitchen, holding onto the counter. "Ruth?" She turned to meet the sad eyes of Quillan Johnson.

"I-I wanted to say to you it was your Daddy that taught me how to tie a proper fishin' line. H-he happened on me at the creek one day, and I guess I'd never got it quite right—that funny knot on the hook? He sat with me a long while til I could do it easy."

Quillan looked down at the rim of his hat held tight in his hands. His bottom lip quivered. "I . . . well, I know you're gonna miss your daddy. We all will. I'm real sorry."

Quillan gave her a nod and turned and walked away. His shoulders slumped and his hand-me-down shoes, a size too big for his feet, gave a faint clop against the wood floors. She let out a breath.

"He taught me how to tie a fishing line too," she whispered.

When the house eventually quieted, Ruth, Earl, Ruby, Clara May, and Eugene curled up together like a kitten litter by the fire. All the feelings inside her stormed. She swallowed them into her belly, and the screaming that waited there ate them. She would be a good girl. She would take care of her brothers and her sisters. She would make sure that when she prayed God would be willing to listen to her.

Bibb County, Georgia—1920

Leonidas maintained his innocence of assault. He claimed disgust at

Crawford's allegations and campaigned against her, telling his sisters and his mother and anyone who would listen that Crawford wanted to take Helen away from him. He claimed Crawford was a bitter woman who wanted to hurt him with her lies. The courts agreed that there was no evidence of assault. The council of his fraternal order circled around him, protecting him and handling the rumor of his transgressions amongst themselves. After two weeks in jail, he was released with no official charges filed.

Crawford persisted in claims of child assault and filed for divorce on the basis of cruelty. She called a newspaper reporter and detailed his abuses. Leonidas, infuriated by her betrayal, refused to show up for the hearings, prolonging his control over her.

Crawford's family encouraged her to move on, and so she dropped the assault charges in an effort to focus on the divorce. She moved herself and her daughter into her mother's home and began to piece her life back together, refusing to let Leonidas anywhere near Helen. He stalked her when she went out and feigned innocence when he was confronted by the police. Despite the advice of her family, she refused to be intimidated by him, locked in her home by fear. She went to church. She shopped. She applied for a new job. She told anyone who would listen what Leonidas Brantley had done to her daughter.

It was inevitable that he would catch up to her.

"Isn't that Lee?" Crawford turned to where her friend was pointing. They were shopping in downtown, and Lee was strolling toward them, deliberate in his movements and too close to avoid. He caught her by the arm before she could get away, flicking his knife open and holding it to her side. Crawford's friend slipped quickly into a nearby shop.

"You nasty little cunt," he hissed. "What have you done to our family? What have done with my Helen? Tellin' her your lies?"

"Lee?" Crawford whispered. She caught sight of her friend urgently talking to the shopkeeper. "Agree to the divorce. Let us go."

He leaned in close to her ear and pressed the knife tip into her side, breaking through fabric and skin. "You belong with me. My wife. Ain't no piece a'paper changin' that."

"It might be best if you let that little girl go."

A man's voice rang from behind Leonidas, and as quick as he'd opened the knife, he folded it closed. His face softened, and he turned to face the officer. Blood bloomed bright on Crawford's dress, and she buckled into the arms of her friend.

Crawford filed assault charges for the second time and as a result was granted the divorce on the grounds of marital cruelty. Upon his release from jail, Crawford's father and her brothers paid Leonidas a visit that left him with a few broken ribs and the clarity that he was no longer a welcome face around town.

Given the scandal and the threat of bodily harm, Leonidas decided to lean into his insurance sales. He packed his bags and headed up the Dixie Highway toward DeKalb County. He had an uncle living there and had done some fieldwork off and on in the outlying farmlands. All the building and changing meant people were ripe with insurance needs, not to mention Atlanta and the outlying Stone Mountain was making waves as the center of automobile ingenuity. He had a knack for engines and figured if the insurance sales went sour, he could find a machine shop. Worse case, he'd return to the fields for a harvest or two until he sorted out his situation.

Crawford shielded herself and Helen deep within her family circles. She fell in love and married again. She legally changed her daughter's name, erasing Leonidas from her life and from her daughter's.

Judges 6:37
KJV

Behold, I will put a fleece of wool in the floor; and if the dew be on the fleece only, and it be dry upon all the earth beside, then shall I know that thou wilt save Israel by mine hand, as thou hast said.

Chapter 15

Silence descended on the farmhouse. Ruth felt it to the very center of her being. The morning papers reported dozens of tornadoes swirling through the state of Georgia, stopping just south of their little town. The worst of them hit LaGrange, and all kinds of people died. Ruth heard her father's voice: Nothing happens without God intending it to.

God must have sent the tornados to take away those people, just as he sent the pestilence to take away her father.

Every day there's pain, that's just part of living.

When she thought of it that way, she felt less sad for their families. She felt less of everything. God decided. She followed. She ran her thumb over the little wooden bunny that had found a permanent home in her pocket.

The house and everyone in it felt empty. Even when Dollie told them all she was going to be having a new baby, they hardly stirred. Mother made a big show of moving out of the big downstairs bedroom she shared with their father and upstairs to one of the smaller rooms. She said Dollie and Maddox needed it more since it was big enough for the two of them, their baby Christine, and the new baby. Her moving upstairs felt like she was working her way closer to Heaven.

Ruth had never noticed the worn corners of their furniture or the frayed edges of the quilts. She'd not seen the graying paint peeling from the side of the house or the bowed steps leading onto their porch or how dirty Francis's feathers got from being trailed across the henyard. But after her father took his last breath, the signs of dying swirled around her, pulling at her arms and her fingers and her eyes until she was certain she could feel the very weight of her father's ghost piggybacking on her shoulders.

Lola's separation from Elmer became permanent. She stared out the window and smoked most days.

"You thinkin' about Daddy?" Ruth asked. Lola shook herself at the sound of Ruth's voice and stubbed out her cigarette.

"I am not. I'm thinkin' about this candy factory I know of. They're hirin' candy girls, and I'm thinkin' about askin' for a job."

"You gonna move back with Elmer?"

"Well, that's the dingus, little sister. I'm not feelin' all too fond of Elmer."

"You're really not goin' back to him?"

"I am not."

Lola told Elmer to stay away, but he came knocking on their door all summer long under the guise of offering comfort to Lola over losing their father. True to her word, she refused to see him, and he went mad with grief over it. He showed up more often, calling for her and demanding she return home. Ruth felt sorry for him. It was clear he was taking the beating for all of Lola's sadness.

"Tell 'im I'm unwell," Lola hissed at Ruth whenever he came

around and locked herself in her room.

Ruth gave Elmer all kinds of reasons why Lola wasn't around. To Ruth's relief, sometimes he'd catch Lola outside so she had to talk to him and Ruth didn't have to lie for her. On those days, Elmer and Lola would go for long walks or take off in Elmer's runabout.

Mother chastised her regularly for refusing to go home with him and said she was shirking her duties as a wife. Ruth figured that Lola must have done her wifely duties because by the end of summer and with much less enthusiasm than the first time, Lola announced she'd be moving back to Atlanta with Elmer. She was going to have another baby. Ruth dug out Lola's pin that she had hidden when Lola returned the previous summer and pinned it to her day dress.

While Lola and Elmer were fighting each other, Carrie Carter wrapped her pretty arms around Tom in love and comfort. On a Sunday afternoon in September, Tom knelt in front of Carrie and asked her to marry him. The Carters planned a wedding bigger than Dollie's, and Ruth figured everybody from one side of Stone Mountain to the other side of Atlanta showed up. As a wedding gift, Mother gave them a parcel of land, and the Carters gave them a chunk of money. With the help of Wheeler, Riley, and Earl, Tom built a whitewashed two-bedroom house for his new wife. Within months, the couple announced they were expecting a baby too. Ruth had never known Tom to be happier. His own man on his own land.

Maddox, a man of great integrity but of little means, had moved into their house after he married Dollie. Maddox was kind to her and looked at her with sad eyes. Ruth could tell he wanted to find his place in their house, but he wasn't like Tom or Wheeler, and he certainly wasn't like her father. He tried, though, sitting down with Wheeler and Mother every Sunday evening to go over what the farm demanded of them. Papa Jefferson started joining them too. Wheeler made a habit of announcing the current land prices at every gathering. Papa Jefferson and Maddox thanked him for his diligence and went on to discussing the distribution of the week's work.

Ruth turned nine years old ten months and eight days after her father died—though no one noticed. There was no special cake or cousins over. When Mother reminded her to stack the kindling, rather than relieving her of her chores, she understood that without her father, there were no birthdays. That made sense to her, and so she thought nothing more of it.

In the spring of 1921, Mother and Aunt Norah helped bring Lola's baby into the world. Ruth had to stay home and tend to the younger children while the two women nursed Lola in her Atlanta home. Lola named the baby Marshall, and within six weeks of his birth she took a job at the candy factory, leaving Marshall to be tended by her sister-in-law. It wasn't long before she and Elmer split again. Only this time, Elmer left and went all the way to California without a word. Ruth didn't mind that at all because Elmer made her sister sad.

After Elmer left, Lola boarded with an older couple in Atlanta so that she could keep her job at the Sophie Mae Candy Shop. She brought Marshall back to live at the farm in Stone Mountain, and during the week, Ruth tended him. Lola came back to the farm on the weekends but didn't pay him much mind. When she came home, she preferred to catch up on the gossip at the Talking Table and leave most of the child-tending to the other women in the house. Dollie's second baby arrived by summer, and Lola figured that Marshall could pile in with Dollie's children without too much trouble.

Ruth devoted herself to sainthood. Memories of her unheard prayers crept in her mind, and if she wasn't careful she'd sink beneath the knowledge that she had failed God. In failing God, she failed her father. She read her Bible in the mornings and said her prayers at night. She memorized a new scripture from Proverbs every week and helped Bea teach Sunday school to the little children.

During the week, she studied the fine art of domestic science, as everyone was calling it. Lola said that made perfect sense because women were having to learn all kinds of new technology and that running a household required as much skill as any job. It was a science. "Just read the papers," she said. Ruth knew Lola had gone to suffrage meetings in Atlanta. Out of habit, she kept Lola's secrets. Nevermind there didn't seem to be anybody to tell.

Ruth laid out dress patterns for her older sisters and hemmed the hand-me-downs for the younger ones. She stayed close to her mother in the kitchen and honed her canning and preservation skills. She sat with Mother to balance the monthly expenses and learned all kinds of small ways to make a penny last, a skill that was becoming more essential by the week.

In the months after Father's funeral, there'd been a steady stream of family dropping by with food and kind words. The stream had dried to a trickle until only Aunt Norah continued to make a habit of coming by for coffee in the late mornings. "Just checking on you, baby," she'd say to Mother. Ruth made sure there was coffee in her father's coffeepot for Aunt Norah's visits. She didn't bother to tend the coffee for Papa Jefferson, whose visits came more and more often, reviewing the books and ordering the boys to this task or another.

When Wheeler married a girl named Bonnie and announced he'd found a house and a job in Atlanta, Ruth might not have noticed his absence, except for how obviously relieved Maddox seemed to be.

"Mama has Tom and Papa a shout away, and Maddox has the work here in hand," he said without meeting anyone's eyes. "I'm gonna make manager at the machine shop in no time. Plenty a'money to be made. Bonnie's set up in a house that's got one a'em washin' machines! You hear about those, Mama?"

"Ruthie here's my washing machine, and she does a fine job," Mother replied and winked at Ruth. Ruth wanted to ask more about this washing machine. Wheeler might be half crazy about most things, but a washing machine sounded like a fine idea.

Wheeler and Bonnie drove back the first Sunday of every month to attend church at Mount Zion Baptist and have dinner with the family. Most of the family, all except Mother, could see those Sundays were a self-inflicted penance. A few months after Wheeler married, Bea married a soldier by the name of Martin. They too moved to Atlanta, a few doors down from Wheeler and Bonnie.

Ruth had the strangest feeling that she could hear the world whirring around her. Everything was changing. Tom, Wheeler, Bea, and Lola had all left the farmhouse. Her father had been replaced by Maddox and Papa Jefferson. People were vanishing from her days, and yet she was standing still.

Riley—who'd planned an apprenticeship in Atlanta that died with Cousin Frank—took the weight of Wheeler and Tom's absence. Riley, who'd yet to show signs of hair on his chin, made every effort to step into his father's shoes. Ruth saw him stretch his back as straight and tall as he could, doting on Mother and doubling his work on the land. He no longer joined them by the creek and paid little attention to his sisters. "I got no time for lazin', Ruthie." Riley sat at the Talking Table, alongside Papa Jefferson and Maddox and, on occasion, Tom. Ruth thought he looked skinny and lost when she saw him there, tin coffee cup gripped tight, clinging to the banter of his kin.

When Marshall was a year old and on a high-heat summer day, Mama Ann died of heart troubles. Papa Perkins held her hand as she took in her last breath. Mama Ann was the second wife Papa Perkins buried. Mother cried for a long time when Mama Ann died. Maybe longer than when Father died. She said that Ann Perkins was the most godly woman she had ever known. One that had loved her like her own.

Before Mama Ann had grown cold in her grave, Uncle Lovett, who'd been living with Aunt Norah, moved to Augusta with his long-time friend Ivan. They opened a cigar shop together—Ivan managed the store while Uncle Lovett handled the books. Uncle Lovett had always walked in the shadows of their lives, leaving books and magazines for them to read and whispering to his nieces to be brave and bold—they could learn from the characters in the stories. Ruth only knew he was gone when the new *Ladies' Home Journal* didn't show up, and she overheard Aunt Norah and Mother's conspiratorial whispering at the Talking Table. The two sisters had a lot to say about their brother and his friend Ivan—neither approved.

On a hot August morning that same summer—Lola and Bessie started singing Hallelujahs over their morning coffee. "Praise Jesus!" Lola, giddy with tears, took Ruth's hands and swung her around in happy circles and then rained kisses on her face. Lola sank to her knees and took Ruth by the shoulders.

"We been given a voice, Ruth Elizabeth. We can go out and vote like any man!" she sang. Mother, who was hunched over the sink peeling potatoes, gave an uninterested grunt. Her shoulders had slumped the day Mama Ann died and stayed that way.

"Leave Ruthie to her chores," Mother grumbled. "Don't be filling her head with your nonsense, Lola Bell."

Lola was turned inside out because women had begrudgingly been given the right to vote in Georgia. For the last two years, Lola had mourned the prehistoric nature of the state of Georgia, which, along with Alabama, voted against ratification of the nineteenth amendment and took every opportunity to stall the inevitable tide of female voices within the halls of government. The state and Papa Jefferson considered it yet another interference by the Yankees in their business. But they could no longer find their way around the law (save another war), and the polls opened to Georgia's women.

Once the vote was established, women started popping up more and more in places other than the society pages. Old Ms. Felton of Lithonia ended up on the front page of the *Atlanta Constitution* the week before Thanksgiving. She became the first woman senator. For exactly one day. Lola and Bessie were on a high for weeks. Lola continued to sneak away to the suffrage meetings (even though Mother refused to let her talk about it), dragging Bessie with her whenever Bessie came to Atlanta to visit. Lola, a newly minted divorcee at the ripe old age of nineteen, was also a suffragette—in secret.

Ruth didn't much see what the fuss was about. Old Ms. Felton only had a job for the day, and what interest did any of them have in voting? Ms. Felton didn't even get paid. She asked her mother about it, who snapped, "It is not what God intended, Ruthie. Women are not to be messin' in men's work. It's the Devil got things stirred up. Now hand me over them canning jars."

Lola, who'd been seething on the outskirts of their conversation, got flaming mad.

"Good heavens, Mama, cain't you see! You are oppressed. Livin' your whole life in this kitchen. Cowtailin' to Papa Jefferson and his kind. We are oppressed. We have as much right as any man to have our own money and our own opinions. Votin' is the first step."

Mother, more unkempt as the days went on, gave Lola a tired look.

"Lola," her once melodic voice had grown bored and flat, "you got a baby to take care of and dishes to do. Your man run off and left you with nothing to speak of. You living off my table and barely clinging to a dime. You the one's oppressed, Lola. It's not voting that's gonna help you. Finding that baby a new daddy's what'll help you."

When word came that Uncle Lovett had gone under with the flu and then died of the pneumonia—the same way that Father had gone—Mother became obsessed with cleanliness. She turned her mind to endless housework. She scrubbed floors and windows until her hands were raw. Ruth sometimes heard her rustling in the kitchen in the middle of the night. If any of them so much as coughed, they had to go right to bed with a smelly compress on their chest. Mother collected a medicine cabinet full of salves, pills, and tonics—all touting their powers of immunity.

Ruth said her prayers faithfully. Deep down she wondered if God could hear her yet. Sometimes she would test it. She'd ask God for something—like rain or a dozen of Francis's feathers or for Mother to make extra biscuits. Sometimes it seemed that God heard her. When He didn't, she knew she had to work harder.

Ruth took to working so hard with Mother and the new babies that she decided she had no need for going on to the new high school as Riley and her older sisters had. She could read and write and was good with her numbers. Those extra years hadn't done Lola any good—and she had no use for what Bessie had to say. Neither Mother nor Papa Jefferson saw any reason for it either.

They saw no reason for Ruby to continue either, when it would be easier to have both girls helping at home. When Ruby protested, Ruth told her it wasn't her place to decide. There were more things to worry about than schooling. So Ruth and Ruby said goodbye to Miss Beauchamp on the last day of their seventh and eighth grade years with no plans to return.

Dekalb County, Georgia—1922

The insurance salesman smiled at her from the porch, sunlight glinting off the red stone of the ring he wore. On his right hand, not his left, Annie noted. She blushed under his blue-eyed stare and looked down to study the slats of the porch. It wasn't often men looked at her with such interest. At twenty-five, she'd resigned herself to fate. She was destined to be a spinster caring for her aging parents.

"Yer daddy home, miss? I got some real important things to be sharin' with 'im."

Leonidas paused for effect and leaned in close enough that Annie could feel his warmth. "It's right clear t'me that he's got some real valuable possessions that need protectin' in this house."

The man's soothing drawl snaked under her chin, and Annie glanced up, confused.

"By valuable, I mean you, a'course, ma'yam. Beautiful little gurl like yer'self? I know yer daddy wants t'be sure yer proper cared for."

Annie felt the corners of her mouth stretch near to her ears.

"I cain't speak for my daddy none, sir. He should be home right soon, though."

Leonidas stepped a bit closer and lounged against the door frame.

"I don' mean to impose on ya, ma'yam, but it's been one mighty long hot mornin'. Any chance I might could take a sit on yer porch step for a spell? Maybe trouble ya for a glass a'water?"

Annie hesitated. He was a fine-looking man with a cerulean gaze that was impossible to break. His clothes were worn but clean and pressed. He wore a brown suit and a white shirt. A gold tie bar glinted from either side of his brown-and-blue-striped tie. His shoes were spit-shined, and a sharp crease had been ironed into his slacks. He'd taken off his hat and seemed to have important things to say. She nodded toward the step and told him she'd be back momentarily with a glass of water.

Leonidas sat on the front step, considering how many more doors he might be willing to knock on before he gave up selling insurance. The screen door cracked behind him, and Annie sat down next to him on the step.

"Maybe a lemonade'd suit you better than water? My name's Annie by the way. You don't really have to call me ma'yam."

He took a long sip.

"You make this yer'self, Annie?"

She nodded.

"'Bout the finest lemonade I've ever had the pleasure a'sippin' on."

Annie blushed and looked at the toes of her shoes.

"Why don' you tell me the story behind that mountain over there. Am I seein' buildin'?" Leonidas squinted at the rising granite mound that dominated the horizon. He was certain he saw the makings of scaffolding along its smooth surface.

"Don't you read the papers?" Annie chuckled, oblivious to the cloud that passed over his eyes at the question. "That is bound to be the world's largest sculpture. Greatest monument to the greatest cause there ever was. They're planning to carve General Robert E. Lee riding on his horse up there. Him and a coupla other generals.

You ain't heard of it?"

Annie seemed astounded that anyone breathing was unaware of the Stone Mountain memorial project.

"Naw. Naw . . . cain't say I have."

PART TWO

The Lost Cause

(1924–1931)

By 1924—long before the Stock Market Crash of 1929—more than half of Georgia households fell below the poverty line due to the escalating agricultural crisis. Sharecropping, established as a survival mechanism post-Civil War, was a way of life. Unprecedented drought conditions left both people and crops parched. Rural migration overburdened urban resources and created a labor crisis on the farms. Rumblings of arrogant government interference and a conspiracy to oppress Southern people undergirded porch conversations as belts grew tighter and tensions higher.

Lawlessness throughout the state of Georgia was being referred to as "domestic terrorism" by major news outlets. Cotton gins were being burned in a rogue effort to push up cotton prices. Lynchings and floggings were a regular part of the daily news, and accusing eyes began to turn toward the resurrected Knights of the Ku Klux Klan. The Klan, a white supremacist organization whose membership included respected business-men and community leaders throughout the state, publicly denied any role in these acts of terrorism.

Calcium arsenate, a highly toxic form of arsenic, was regularly applied to dwindling cotton crops in a futile attempt to combat the boll weevil. Unbeknownst to farmers at the time, the pesticide was seeping into streams and soils, leaving a lasting toxic legacy. In addition to damaging the neurological system, arsenic is now recognized as a carcinogen. But in 1924, Southern farm families unknowingly ingested trace amounts daily through their skin and the air—a poison that would impact their hearts, bodies, and minds for generations.

In the aftermath of the first world war, the United Daughters of the Confederacy, in union with the Venable Family, reinvigorated their campaign to turn Stone Mountain into a Confederate war memorial. The Yankee Borglum was fired, and this time they hired a sculptor by the name of Henry Augustus Lukeman. Blasting for the relief sculpture began with the sculpting of the head of General Robert E. Lee in 1926. Schoolchildren were used to collect funds not for aid in the poverty epidemic but to commemorate the Lost Cause.

In October of 1929, when the whole American economy collapsed, the Southern states had yet to recover from the economic ruin of the Civil War and were free-falling in a downward spiral caused by the agricultural crisis. Georgia, the land of cotton crop in crisis, spent the 1920s enduring the boll weevil plague, and from 1924 to 1927, the worst drought in the state's history destroyed thousands of acres of cash crop. With the onset of the Great Depression, more than 80 percent of Georgia residents fell below the poverty line. Banks collapsed, factories and businesses shut down, and declining cotton prices plummeted to six cents per pound, devastating farm-dependent families. Worse yet, overworked and undernourished land eroded, forming deep canyons in the fields.

Work on the Confederate memorial was halted for a second time as funds ran dry and schoolchildren were pulled out of class to become wage earners. DeKalb and Fulton Counties became the epicenter of a desperate rural migration, and county resources were overwhelmed by the mass population increase. The streets became sewers. Fields became homesteads. Clean water became scarce. The divisive vitriol of the Klan reached the peak of a meteoric rise to social power.

I John 3:15
KJV

*Whosoever hateth his brother is a murderer:
and ye know that no murderer hath
eternal life abiding in him.*

Chapter 16

When the Night Riders began burning down the cotton gins, dragging both colored and white people from their houses and flogging the negroes, a constant fear settled over Ruth's mind. All kinds of people were becoming victims of the attacks—lawyers, preachers, business owners, women. A couple of Tennessee lawyers were murdered over defending the need for a fishing license. Another man's wife was murdered because he spoke out against moonshining. Signs were posted on all the cotton gins, threatening anybody who tried to turn them on and gin their crop.

Now that Ruth was home with her mother all day, having not returned to school, she found herself eavesdropping more and more on the grown-up conversations around her, picking up words and turning over their meaning. The animated discussions of the men in her family revolved around whether or not the Night Riders were doing what was right or what was wrong. Outsiders were threatening their way of life, the inflow of rural migrants was causing all kinds of problems, and shutting down the gins in order to drive the price of cotton back up made reasonable sense. The everyday farmer held little sway in the chaos of change that swirled around them—the Night Riders were sending a message to the powers that be.

"What does rural mean?" Ruth whispered to Bessie one evening.

Bessie answered with impatience. "Oh, it's a fancy word for the country folk and the pinelanders."

"Aren't we country folk?"

Bessie set down her embroidery wheel with exaggerated patience. "We're a different kind a'country folk, Ruthie. We aren't backward. We are . . . agrarians. And we are Atlantans." She hesitated and added for more clarity. "Nearly Atlantans. We've gotten to be more urban. Urban means city dwellers. We have electric lights and indoor facilities."

"They don't have electricity?"

Ruth thought of all the things in their house that were powered by the electric lines that hung along the car line. She tried to remember their house before the electric lines and indoor toilets. The faint memory of lanterns and midnight walks to the privy tickled at her thoughts.

"The pinelanders?" Bessie continued without answering Ruth. "They're coming here with nothing more than a bag and their shoes. Sometimes they don't even bother with the shoes. And that's only the ones a'substance. They're doing business in the ditches. Sleeping in the fields and creating eyesores with their camps. Leaving their own people 'cause they heard there's money to be made here. Then there's the low-country negroes and the Gullahs. They don't belong here, Ruthie."

The Night Riders were making it clear who belonged and who

didn't. Any insinuation that the Klan and the assaulting Night Riders were one in the same angered Ruth's brothers. They contended that the Klan was the one organization that was doing right by the Southern states, and even as they insisted it was a few bad seeds that wore the Klan regalia who carried out the violence of the night raids, they mumbled in agreement that at least someone was doing something to address the migration problem.

Every morning Papa Jefferson made his way across the field from his own small house to the front steps of Ruth's. Maddox strode out onto the porch at the same time, and the two started the day with a survey of the family's expansive property. There was tension between them that extended past the land troubles. Papa Jefferson was invigorated by the aggressive tactics of the Night Riders while Maddox argued it would only lead to more violence and more trouble.

"Burnin' those gins makes cotton scarce. Pushes the price back up." Papa Jefferson lifted his chin toward the cotton fields under their care.

"Sure it will, Jeff," Maddox drawled. "But destroyin' a man's property? Beatin' a man for disagreein' with your way a'thinkin'? It ain't Christian. It ain't right."

"Vengeance is mine, saith our Lord," Papa Jefferson grunted.

"Burnin'? Killin'? Hangin'? That ain't what it means, Jeff," Maddox said as he walked away toward the barns. Maddox would speak his mind to Papa Jefferson, but only so much.

The women were warned not to be out alone or in the village after dark. They were warned to stay away from the growing tide of negroes and displaced sharecroppers trudging in looking for any hope of a foothold. Negro men and dirty sharecroppers were dangerous, even more so now that they were hungry.

The Klan and the strangers and the nightly attacks became familiar. The questions that nudged at Ruth waned under the weight of her fear. Avoidance was the only recourse for handling the poor and the violent, and so they averted their eyes from the growing shanties and encampments that sprung up along the car line. Acceptance was the only path to peace with Papa Jefferson, so they made no effort to defy him. Silence about the gin burnings and the attacks on those who spoke out against them was the only way to keep the Night Riders from their family, and so they remained silent. Mother took to reading the society pages to them in the evenings and skipping over the newspaper articles that detailed the injustices being visited upon their neighbors.

"Looky here," she said one night. "Wheeler's Bonnie is in the paper! Isn't this grand?"

She cleared her throat and read to them aloud. "The Brookhaven Garden Club will hold a flower display on Wednesday, September 2. The exhibit is free, and there will be a musical program arranged by Mrs. Wheeler Shurlington."

She closed the paper, neatly folding over the blazing front-page headline: "Minister Attacked by Night Riders. Sermons Directed against Crime."

"Bonnie has the nicest singing voice. I'm sure she'll do a fine job," she said and picked up her Bible, turning to the Psalms for their reading.

Ruth sometimes thought of Old Ezra and wondered if the Night Riders had visited him. The idea of Old Ezra as dangerous had long melted away. Ezra had quietly shown up day after day when Father died, helping in the fields, driving Mother into town, and offering his presence wherever it might be needed. He'd behaved as much like family as anyone else in her life. He wasn't the same as her brothers; she knew that. She understood where the colored folks belonged in the hierarchy of their lives, but she thought it absurd to be afraid of him.

Ezra sidestepped Papa Jefferson the best he could, but Papa Jefferson had a hold over Ezra, a stranglehold Ruth couldn't quite work out. Ezra bent low, hat in hand, when Papa Jefferson spoke to him, and avoided meeting his eyes. Papa Jefferson spoke more kindly to his horse than he did to Ezra—and yet he called on Ezra daily to some task that needed handling. If she were braver, she might say something to Papa Jefferson. She might tell him that her father was never mean to Old Ezra and that her father trusted him. But she wasn't brave. At least not brave enough to endure her grandfather's wrath.

Papa Jefferson's morning routine grew past his conversation with Maddox about the fields. Every few days, he asked to review the house ledger and proffered his insight. "To keep abreast of things," he told Mother, who, as quick as she was with farm business, understood she needed Papa Jefferson's protection from the land developers and Night Riders.

He stayed around their house all day, mostly holding court from the rocker, and took all three of his daily meals with them.

"Riley! Earl!" he'd yell when something had him riled, pulling out his belt. Mother would hear him and stroll onto the porch.

"I sent 'em into town, Jeff. They'll be back after a bit," she deflected. Or she might say, "Tom's got 'em helpin' in the fields."

Papa Jefferson found small ways to corner the girls. He ran a rough hand along their bottoms or insisted on one of them sitting in his lap while he rocked on the porch. If refused, he'd laugh and grab hold of an arm or a waist and pull them in anyway. Anytime he did, Mother had a way of knowing.

"Jeff? Jeff? You seen the girls?" she'd call from some place close by. "I need 'em in the kitchen. Send 'em on in, won't you?"

After supper, he'd stretch and say his goodnights before ambling back across the field to his own little house. Mother tolerated his rantings about migrants and government and the insults of modernization. She gave him leeway in making field decisions and let him deal with the land developers when they came sniffing. In time, Mother and Dollie and Bessie grew immune to his bluster, filling his pipes and ignoring his moonshine.

Lola, however, made it her weekend habit to rile him about both negroes and women. She fought with him, and Ruth worried for her. It was one such evening that Lola said she didn't see any difference between a black man and a white man. She didn't think it was right the way the negroes were being treated. Papa Jefferson, well into his cups, lifted himself over her like a barn shadow rising at the sunfall. Lola ignored the menace in his voice.

"What'd you say, girl?"

"I said I don't see how the color of a man's skin can tell you a thing about what he's worth," she repeated with her chin in the air and her eyes unblinking. Papa Jefferson used the weight of his body to back her against the porch railing. She paled.

"Ain't none a mine gonna be a niggah lovah," he panted. "You a niggah lovah, Lola?"

"I didn't say I was, Papa. I said I jus don't see the diff'rence from one man to another."

She struggled to keep her voice steady. Ruth watched her hold her ground and wondered if her sister had gone soft in the head.

Lola didn't see it coming. Papa Jefferson grabbed her by the hair and shoved her down the porch steps. She lost her footing and landed with a thud. He followed and kicked her in the stomach. Maddox and the other men who had gathered on the porch rocked silently. No man interfered in the discipline of another man's family. His agreement with the matter was irrelevant. Ruth felt sick.

"Let me ask you again, Lola. You a niggah lovah?"

Ruth held her breath and silently begged Lola to just agree with Papa. Mother rushed to the porch at the commotion but stopped short when she saw Papa looming over Lola. Much like the rest of their lives, Papa had taken over doling out discipline.

Tears streamed down Lola's face, but her eyes snapped as they met Ruth's. They were full of anger—and surrender. She shook her head, mumbling a denial.

"Go on, girl. Get back in the house." He shoved her with the toe of his mud-caked boot. She rose with care and dusted off her dress.

"Yes, sir." She walked gingerly back up the stairs, avoiding her mother, and retreated through the screen door.

Papa Jefferson returned to his rocker and sucked a flame into the bowl of his pipe. The conversation among the men resumed as if Lola hadn't been there at all. A resignation settled over Ruth. For the first time, she understood how firm her father had stood between Papa Jefferson and their family. She saw it clearly. It was her father that had kept Papa Jefferson at an acceptable distance. Without him, Papa Jefferson's vitriol was a torrent that raged unchecked into their lives and their minds. They were powerless. Quietly, she slipped back into the house to find Lola.

Lola was at the Talking Table smoking a cigarette, her hand shaking as she sucked the smoke deep into her lungs. Mother set a cup of coffee in front of her.

"Lola, baby. You cain't go riling your Papa. He's not gonna suffer none of your nonsense 'bout them black folks. Or women neither. Hush with this, now, Lola Bell. Hush with it." There was a pleading in Mother's words.

Lola stubbed out her half-finished cigarette in the coffee saucer, and without looking up, she nodded. Ruth slid into a chair across from her.

"You awlright, Lola?"

Lola stared at Ruth for an eternity. Her cat-like eyes shimmered and brewed.

"Ruthie," she stated, clipping at her words with an unfamiliar harshness. "You make sure you mind Papa. Keep yourself quiet, and do as you're told. If he asks you a question, you be sure to ask him right back what your answer oughta be. Well. That is until you find yourself a husband. Then you'll need to do as he says. Think as he says. Eat, sleep and rut as he says. You'll spread your legs when he says and let him plant one baby after another in your belly. 'Cause little sister, we are not worth much more than that."

"Lola Bell!" Mother gasped and took hold of a counter for balance. Ruth thought her mother might actually faint at Lola's words. Lola stared at her snuffed-out cigarette.

"What, Mama? She's old enough to hear it, isn't she? To know her place. Isn't that it? We gotta know our place or take a boot to the belly?" Lola laughed an ugly laugh and patted her stomach. "That's what this is for, isn't it? Mama? Babies and boots?"

She stood up and leaned in close to Ruth. "I'm just fine, Ruthie. I just gotta learn to be quiet. Right, Mama?"

Mother turned to the sink.

"Right?! Mama?!"

Ruth watched as her mother's body stilled and turned slowly to Lola. Ruth felt their silent words in the air, penetrating every surface of the kitchen. She could hear them pinging off one surface to another with no sense of what was being said in the silence. When Mother finally spoke to her wildest daughter, it was without apology.

"Yes, Lola Bell. You gotta learn to be quiet."

DeKalb County, Georgia—1924

"I'm gonna need you to shut yer mouth, Annie," Leonidas growled. Annie's voice was grating on him, clawing at the insides of his head and making him want to choke her into silence. She was sitting on the front porch of her parents' home. He knew better than to touch her, so instead he paced in front of her. Annie chewed at her nails, tears running down her face.

"You sure it's mine?"

Annie's eyes grew wide at the insult.

"A'course it is, Lee! How could you ask me that?"

"It wasn't hard to get up yer skirt, Annie. I don' reckon I'm the first that's been there."

Leonidas hadn't planned on marrying again after Crawford. Her betrayal had left him bitter, and he'd vowed not to commit himself to the institution a second time. But he wasn't certain how to avoid it. DeKalb had grown on him—the future was happening here. He'd sent word to his parents and his sisters, telling them they could build a life here, a better one. They'd believed him, sold off some land and emptied their savings, boarded the train and moved themselves into a quiet little neighborhood in Atlanta. Three small bungalows all on the same street.

He'd left off insurance selling and taken to doing odd jobs. Working on buildings. Working on cars. A bit of fieldwork here and there. The constant shifting suited him. If he didn't marry Annie, he'd have to explain things to his family. He might have to leave town, and he wasn't done with Atlanta.

"I suppose you expect me to marry ya?"

Annie crumbled, standing up and heading toward her front door.

"Fine, Annie. I'll marry ya! Let's get married!" He felt the words leave his mouth and watched Annie turn back to him, shyly at first. He considered that trying to have a family again might not be all that bad.

"You do love me?" she asked.

"A'course I love ya, Annie." It was an easy thing for him to say. She didn't care whether or not he meant it. She just needed him to say it.

Leviticus 15:19-20
KJV

And if a woman have an issue, and her issue in her flesh be blood, she shall be put apart seven days: and whosoever toucheth her shall be unclean until the even.

And every thing that she lieth upon in her separation shall be unclean: every thing also that she sitteth upon shall be unclean.

Chapter 17

July 1925

De boll weevil say to de farmer: "You better leave me alone;
I done eat all yo' cotton, now I'm goin' to start on yo' corn,
I'll have a home, I'll have a home."

De merchant got half de cotton, De boll weevil got de res'.
Didn't leave de farmer's wife but one old cotton dress,
An' it's full of holes, it's full of holes.

Ruth hummed as she plucked a small-snouted creature from the burgeoning cotton boll and dropped it in her bag. She found an infected square and snapped it off the young plant. The square was full of weevil eggs and if left alone would burst open with hungry babies. The old Kroger grain sack, secured by a makeshift shoulder strap, hung loosely about her body. She could feel the tickle of the bugs wriggling against the woven fabric. Sweat ran rivulets through the red dust that clung to the back of her neck. She glanced a few rows over. Squinting, she could make out Ruby and Clara May through the humid edges of the small cotton field.

Georgia had slipped into a drought state, and all the farms were feeling the strain. Wells all across the county were drying up. Self-imposed water restrictions were being encouraged. The fields rippled with malnourished cotton plants under the unrelenting sun. Ruth and her sisters and the thirsty plants were but a small layer of earth beneath the expansive Southern sky.

Stories of red-and-purple canyons forming in the fields ran from one town to another. Some said the canyons came because the ground had grown tired of the cotton fields. Some said it was God's vengeance for the many sins of the people. God was angry with them all for the arrogance of invention and for the crumbling of their morality. They were all among the Sodomites. So He'd sent the drought and the canyons and the plague of boll weevils.

All manner of insects flitted and slithered about. But it was the weevil that was destroying the cotton crops. While nothing could be done to pull water from the cloudless sky, plucking weevils earned Ruth and her sisters a dollar a week in June and July. For the last few summers, they had pinched the bugs for the cotton farmers. The farmers paid one penny for each bug collected and destroyed.

Ruth scratched at her arms. The thin white dust the farmers used on the cotton bolls killed most of the weevils. It was the stragglers they were picking off. The farmers' dust reminded her of the talc Mother used on the babies' bottoms. Only this one made her skin itch and her chest heavy.

Ruth called out to her sisters. Ruby and Clara May came running with their weevil bags, and the girls combined their haul into one for the farmer to count. They'd take home close to fifty cents. The farmer thanked them with a well-worn coin and a few slices of cold watermelon from his patch before sending them back down the dusty terra cotta road to their own farm. Their skin tanned to a deep golden brown from their days in the sun—though this did little to hide the mottled red rashes that appeared along their arms.

By the time the cotton harvest began, the girls had made a handful of dollars collecting weevils from the cotton bolls—money they put in their mother's hands, to Ruth's relief. She wasn't sure she could take her mother's humiliation at not being trusted with even the smallest of their everyday income.

Papa Jefferson shifted from taking a look at the house ledger to managing it. He settled into his seat at the head of the family, overseeing the property of his dead son along with his own. He stopped speaking to Mother about the major decisions, relegating her to refilling coffee and sweeping away crumbs while he sat with Tom and Riley and Maddox at the Talking Table. He took control of the money generated through the farm markets and stock breeding, doling out enough to support their family's immediate needs. He allowed Mother to manage the meager income the children brought in for household items.

More farms all across the state went under as summer waned, and the rain refused to come. More desperate farmers poured into the Atlanta area from the south counties, hoping for a job or an adventure or a better life. As far as Ruth could tell, they weren't finding any of it. Farmland was being turned not by the plow but by the giant excavators run by the building companies. When the real estate men came to chat with Papa Jefferson, Ruth knew—or did she pretend?—they were Yankees. Yankees had come to take away their home. Even Papa Jefferson wouldn't allow that.

Maddox spent hours planning the crop rotation, and at least

once a week, Tom came over to walk the fields and offer counsel. At times, Richard Sams joined them to discuss irrigation strategies. All three men were leaders in the DeKalb Agricultural Association and took part in searching for long-term solutions to the land decline.

Despite these efforts, the Shurlington farm, once neatly maintained and producing a healthy profit, devolved into a hand-to-mouth family homestead, their land dwindling to pay bills. The fences bowed, the buildings sagged, and the fields produced less than they ever had. By root harvest time and without regular rainfall, the earth hardened and red dust covered every open surface—and some that weren't—in a thin crimson film. When the canyons began to form on their own land, a hushed pall fell over the Talking Table.

It was a hot day at the end of August when Papa Jefferson sat with a slender man Ruth vaguely recognized, smoking on the porch. Maddox and Riley were sipping sweet tea and rocking in the shadows. All four were furrowed in farm talk. Ruth found it odd that her grandfather outlived his son and now held court with the family men. Papa Jefferson wasn't like her Daddy. Though she knew it was an evil thought, she wished God had taken him instead.

Papa Jefferson was heavy-handed when he was drunk—which was often. He pulled out his belt at the slightest offense, using the buckle end to drive home his aggravation. He didn't bother with the ritual of the woodshed switchings. He roared at Mother more as the farm produced less and money became tighter.

"Why, Ruthie," he said as she walked up the porch stairs, "are those little teets I see growin'? Come on over here and let your papa see you."

Ruth obeyed. Her eyes scanned the splinters in the sagging

wooden porch boards. Her face flamed. Papa Jefferson reached up and gave her small breasts a squeeze. "Why, I think they are. You're growing into a right pretty mare." The other men glanced away.

"What do ya think a'our Ruth, Charlie. Little plain. Not quite as pretty as our Lola Bell but still good stock, hmm? Birthin' hips this one." He swatted her on the bottom. The young man nodded noncommittally in her direction. She recognized him now as the oldest of the Hollingsworth children.

"Yes, sir, she is, Jeff. You do have yourself some pretty girls here." He tipped his hat in her direction. "I'm Charlie. I believe I've seen you in services with your sisters."

Mother came to the screen door. She noted Ruth's flaming cheeks. "Never you mind, Ruthie. He's nothing more than an old man eyein' young teets. He don't mean ya no harm." She turned to Papa. "And maybe save those hands for the dairy cows, Jeff. She don't need milkin'."

Lola came splashing onto the porch, her three-year-old son Marshall perched on her hip. Mud-streaked, the toddler was naked except for a stained nappy pinned loose about his hips.

"Why, hello there," she said, flashing a smile in Charlie's direction. Lola's flirtatiousness had lost its spontaneity. Ruth recognized the undertone of intent. It was the same calculation she conveyed when teaching her younger sisters how to turn their eyes just so when speaking to a boy. "Papa said you were comin' over today to take a look-see at the horses?"

Charlie gave Lola a slight bow of acknowledgment. Papa Jefferson suggested Lola take Charlie out to the barns to see the newest mare. Lola shifted Marshall off her hip and passed the lanky boy to Ruth.

Mother opened the door, tweaked Marshall's ruddy cheeks, and shooed Ruth and the other children into the house.

"There's biscuits and butter on the table for y'all," she sang after them.

Papa Jefferson had recently informed Mother that he and Maddox had agreed on a price for a significant tract of their best land. He and Maddox weren't seeing eye to eye on most things, and Maddox had appealed to the mercenary in Papa Jefferson, offering a generous monthly payment in exchange for autonomy. Mother argued that it would only be harder to further divide the land and the chores. There was no extra money for hired hands, and she needed all the boys for the spring planting.

Ruth wondered if Mother argued over it not because she worried over the division of the land—she'd been fine with Tom taking a share—but because she suspected that Papa Jefferson was sending away the last of his equals. Without Maddox in the house, there would be only Riley, Earl, and the women and children. At seventeen and fifteen, Riley and Earl, though men in their own minds, were mere boys to Papa. Riley had attempted to step in after their father's death and had the bruises to show for it.

Ruth was torn between anger for her Mother's humiliation and excitement for the departure of the Maddox family. There were seven siblings living in the old farmhouse, plus Maddox and Dollie had three babies now, with another to arrive any day. If Dollie had her own house, that'd be five—soon to be six—less people taking up space.

"I'm goin' down to Tom's, Mama," Ruth called. Tom's wife Carrie had a new baby boy who was six weeks along, and Ruth visited twice a week to offer a hand with chores.

"Take Marshall and Eugene with you. I don't need 'em underfoot."

Ruth hoisted Marshall onto her shoulders and whistled Eugene to follow. Marshall knit his tiny, grimy fingers together beneath her chin. She grabbed the basket of clean nappies she'd laundered for Carrie and headed out through the dead cornfield that separated their farms. The field was unkempt, and though the meager harvest of stunted corn had been taken in, the stalks were yet to be mulched down. Sunbeams kissed at the few remaining silks, and even in this late season, ethereal tufts of cottonwood seed floated on the air. Ruth walked with an exaggerated bounce as Marshall giggled and grabbed at the cornstalks. Seven-year-old Eugene, having not yet hit his growth spurt, jumped up and down by her side, trying to capture Marshall's bouncing fists in his own.

She envied Carrie and Dollie and Lola with their beautiful babies. Even Bonnie, Wheeler's wife, was due for a baby when winter came. Pink cheeks and bright eyes made her smile. She loved the way they fit in the crook of your arm, as if that was the very purpose of bending it. She could soothe their tears and tickle their tummies. They needed her—and so she needed them.

A tugging in the bottom of her belly slowed her step. The tugging had become familiar in the last few weeks. It made her feel like folding over or stretching long. She was never sure which one would help. Ruth hoisted Marshall from her shoulders and set him to the ground just as they broke through the edge of the cornfield. Eugene grabbed his cousin's hand, and they stumble-ran toward Tom's house. The small bungalow gleamed in the sun—the wood still strong and square and freshly painted. The tin roof was silvery blue, not yet reddened and rusted with age.

Carrie's kitchen garden was a large plot at the back of the house, encircled by a woven-willow fence. Despite the bone-dry days, it teemed with cucumbers and tomatoes, squash and okra, pole beans and watermelon. Along the outer perimeter, a root garden flourished with onions, potatoes, and beets. A second, smaller fenced area marked her medicine garden, heady with kitchen herbs.

There were whispers that Carrie came out at night and watered her garden—even though the creeks were dried up and the wells were dangerously low.

Her stomach knotted harder—pulling at her. She felt warm wetness on her underpants and thought she'd peed herself. Then she remembered. Lola had told her all about Eve's curse and the blood that came. It was God's way, she knew. She bent over, her arms wrapped around her stomach, unsure of what to do. She needed the ladies' basket filled with the homemade monthlies, but that was on the other side of the cornfield.

Carrie came out on her porch, wiping her hands against her apron. "Ruthie," she drawled, "where you been, girl? I gotta feed Harold, and dinner needs doin'."

Carrie's Georgia drawl was thicker than most. "What are you standing around like a dodo for?"

Ruth felt the blood seeping through her underpants. A small river of red ran down inside her leg.

"I . . . I . . ." She set down the basket full of Harold's fresh nappies. "I forgot. Mama wanted me to bring over . . . um . . . the summer jams. I—I gotta go back."

She turned and ran back to the cornfield before Carrie could say anything, leaving Marshall and Eugene picking up stones at the edge of Carrie's porch. Carrie's high-nasal drawl soaked into the hot air as Ruth ran through the corn.

She stopped, her breath ragged. She felt the bitter tang of shame. She would have to walk by Papa Jefferson to get into the house. Lola had once told her that corn husks could be used in a pinch for her bleeding time. She pulled an errant ear of corn from the stalks and collected the silks into a soft, cushioned pillow. She sandwiched the corn-silk pillow between two pieces of soft husk and slid the makeshift pad into her underpants. She used another corn husk to wipe the trickles of blood from her thighs. Gnats swarmed about her face and stuck to the sweat on her neck. She scratched at her irritated arms.

Using her thighs to hold the pad in place, she walked out of the cornfield toward her own porch. Lola was sliding her eyes at Charlie by the barn. Papa was snoring, mouth open, on the porch rocker. She was a shadow moving through the creaky screen door.

"Ruth!" Mother said sharply. "Why am I seeing you here? Carrie's in need a'you. Where's the boys?"

Ruth tried to make her mother see what had happened without using any words, but her Mother's patience was short. "Come out with it, girl."

Ruth mumbled.

"I . . . I need the ladies' basket, Mama."

Understanding spread across her mother's face. "I see. Well, you go on ahead and wash up. You know where the basket and the pins are."

She walked over to Ruth and smoothed her hair out of her eyes. She gave her forehead a quick kiss. "I'll send Ruby over after the boys. You stay on out a'the kitchen. I'm churning up the butter and don't want it not to set on account a'your bleeding."

Ruth went to the washroom, washed her legs and hands, and discarded the wet corn silks. She pulled the ladies' basket from the cabinet. It was full of oblong cloth bags stuffed with cotton sewing scraps. Mother made the bags using the darkest fabric so they wouldn't show stains. She took one of the pads and placed it on the crotch of her panties. Taking two safety pins that were kept in a Mason jar with the pads, she pinned either end in place.

She went to the room she shared with her sisters. She lay on the bed and rolled into a tight ball, holding her thighs tight against each other to keep the pad safely against her crotch. She felt ugly and sinful and dirty.

Ruth's nightgown, underpants, and sheets were bright with blood. With haste she rose, stripping the soiled clothes, and washed as best she could. She nudged at Ruby—still deep in her dreams—and pulled the bedding from beneath her. She took the bloodied laundry along with the soiled pads from the previous day out to the wash-basin. Beneath the last of the night's stars, she scrubbed the blood from her things and hung them crisp and clean to dry on the line.

Since it was her bleeding time, she settled herself into the Great Room to take care of the mending. Later in the morning she'd be in charge of the wash and the sweeping. She wasn't allowed to do any kitchen chores or go near the smokehouse. She had volunteered to help out with the Mount Zion Vacation Bible School, but due to her bleeding time, she'd have to stay home until it had passed.

Dollie ambled into the Great Room with her youngest on her hip and settled into the rocker opposite her. Dollie's belly was round and hard with the final months of her fourth pregnancy. She was more tired and puffy than she'd been with her other babies and had to sit more often.

"You cain't be in here, Dollie. I've got my bleedin' time, and it's not good for the baby."

Among all the other things Ruth had been told, it was common knowledge that you didn't want a bleeding woman around pregnant animals—and that included people. It hindered the births.

"Yes, I heard you did. I wouldn't worry about that ol' tale. This baby's just fine."

They rocked in rhythm, both finding the motion soothing for their own reasons. Sadness teased the edges of Ruth's thoughts as memories of their Celebration Day drifted into her mind. She missed her sister, who had vanished into the vortex of motherhood.

"The coming of your monthlies means you are a woman, Rue," Dollie assured her. "Soon enough you'll be getting married and having babies of your own. Your bleeding is a blessing."

"I don't expect I'd have to be married for a baby," Ruth reflected. "Lola and Elmer weren't married when Lola came to expectin'."

Dollie scowled. "How did that turn out for Lola Bell, hmm? That baby withered up in her womb as payment for her sin. God has shown us the way through his holy scriptures, Ruth Elizabeth. We are given to our husbands. Then we are blessed with their children. Lola Bell went against the ways of God, and He took that baby from her. She wasn't worthy a'mothering yet. It's a'right blessing God saw fit to let her keep Marshall."

Dollie stroked the cheek of her littlest, who lay dozing on her belly. Dollie looked like the pictures Ruth had seen of the Virgin Mary holding the baby Jesus.

The two returned to their silent rocking. Finally Dollie stood and nestled the sleeping toddler into the wooden crib kept in the Great Room for all the babies. She was headed to the kitchen for her morning work. She turned with a last thought.

"You are a godly woman, Ruth. Don't go making something out of Lola Bell's doin's. She plays with the ways of Jezebel. Too often, it is the Devil himself who has her ear."

Ruth bowed her head back over the mending, listening to the peaceful breathing of her nephew. She felt the stirrings of her blood between her legs, soaking into the rags. She would be a godly woman. The Lord would bless her.

By Saturday, Ruth's bleeding waned. Mother told her she'd be able to help with the vacation bible school at Mount Zion Baptist in the coming week. Ruth was glad of it as she enjoyed spending time with Brother Johnson's family.

Her friendship with Quillan had anchored her through her father's death. He'd told her stories of her father's kindnesses and sat quietly next to her when she started to cry. Not once did he suggest she stop crying.

She considered herself a master yo-yoer under his tutelage, and his wit and curiosity made him a handy adventuring partner when she wanted to explore in the woods or along the creeks. No one worried after her if she said she'd be with him. She often had to compete with Riley for his attention but not when it came to church things. Riley made every excuse to avoid helping at church, while Quillan was the first to volunteer. Partly for this reason, assisting with vacation bible school was one of her favorite things to do.

Mother and Dollie were busy putting away summer vegetables, and, now allowed back in the kitchen, Ruth sat with Ruby snapping beans at the table. Dollie had been agitated all morning, complaining again of a headache and short-tempered with everyone around her. She was pale, and her face was clammy. Dark circles shadowed her eyes. She stretched, putting her hands on her lower back and wriggling a bit. Dollie's ankles were so swollen the bones had vanished.

"This baby, Mama," she groaned. "This one's giving me a fuss."

"Mmm," Mother purred. "They do, Doll-baby. You need to sit?"

Dollie shook her head and returned to the stove. She doubled over with a suddenness that sent a ladle clattering to the floor. Her hands clutched at the bottom curve of her stomach.

Mother, more spry than she'd been in months, came to Dollie's side. "Doll-baby?" she cooed. "Dollie . . . ?"

Dollie let out a pained yelp. It was weeks before Dollie's baby was due.

"Oh heavens, Mama," Dollie cried. Bloody, mucousy waters

flowed down her legs.

"Ruth! Get Maddox and tell him we need the doctor. The baby's coming." Mother shooed her with urgency as she guided Dollie to the sleeping pallet in the Great Room.

Ruth ran to the barn to warn Maddox, returning just as quick to her mother's side. Mother barked instructions at her. The baby was coming. To Ruth's relief, Bessie appeared and took over her duties. Mother and Bessie fell into the rhythm of delivery.

Foreboding descended over Ruth. Dollie had sat with her in the Great Room when her bleeding time had started. She shouldn't have done that. Ruth knew Dollie shouldn't have done that. The baby was coming early because of her.

Dollie labored for less than an hour. The doctor arrived just as the baby slid from Dollie's body. Ruth gasped and covered her mouth for fear she might cry out. A white creamy layer covered the bruised baby. His eyes were sealed closed, and his tiny mouth was parted by the ghost breath. He was so small that he fit like a fallen bird in Mother's hands. He made no sound.

"Mama?" Dollie pleaded. "Mama?"

The whole room was motionless, staring at the still baby. Mother opened and closed her mouth, before lifting heavy eyes to Dollie. Ruth watched with dread, clutching at her treacherous belly, as the tiny creature was laid to rest in Dollie's arms.

"I'm sorry, Dollie . . . he's an angel baby."

Dollie's face, worn from the onslaught of labor, melted into misery. She laid her hand atop the baby's head, tears flowing. Dollie's keening filled the Great Room and seeped out the windows until even the trees fell still in mourning. Bessie bowed her head, murmuring in prayer. Ruth couldn't take her eyes off her sister. She was sure she was going to be sick. The doctor looked at Mother, and she reached with trembling hands for the infant. "Doll-baby, you got a little more work to do."

Mother left the room with the dead baby as Dollie delivered the afterbirth. Ruth backed in horror into the far corner of the room, away from Bessie and her fervent incantations, and watched Dollie vanish into herself.

Dollie and Maddox and their three children bore witness as the tiny casket was lowered into the grave. The baby was buried in the family cemetery next to their father. The tiny stone marker said Baby Grant. Brother Johnson, with his wife by his side, said a few quiet words of prayer. He gave a gentle pat to Maddox's shoulder and whispered words of condolence to Dollie before he and Sister Johnson slipped away.

The family remained in silence around the small rectangular grave. It was an empty moment when all things lost their color. Grief possessed them, nestled into their corners. Ruth stared at the box holding her ill-formed nephew. This was different from Uncle Henry, who had come to the natural end of his journey. It was different from Cousin Frank and her father because the train and the sickness gave Ruth a reason for their loss. There was no reason for the loss of Baby Grant. No explanation. He wasn't even a person. He was a promise unfulfilled. A happiness she was meant to feel but never would.

Time spun out. School started and leaves changed. It seemed that winter descended all at once. Thanksgiving, Christmas, and on its heels the New Year came under a pall of penance. The stories of the baby Jesus rooted Dollie in an unyielding state of melancholy. God had taken her baby. She beseeched the Lord daily to be forgiven of her unknown sin—flogging herself with her failures morning and night. Ruth avoided her sister—avoided asking if she was to blame for the baby's death and, in so doing, accepted that she was.

It was her sin, not Dollie's, that had taken the baby.

DeKalb County, Georgia—1925

Leonidas kicked Annie hard in the belly. She reflexively coiled around the growing baby. Praying—begging—that God spare the child as he raged on. The baby was seven months along, and Annie, in her weary state, had done something wrong. What was it she did wrong? Why was he kicking her?

Leonidas panted, exerted from doling out the beating.

"Git up," he said. His voice as calm as if he'd just come in from work. She didn't stir. He nudged her with the toe of his boot.

"I said git up."

He lounged back into a kitchen chair and took out his cigarettes. He snapped the match head between his thumbnail and his forefinger, and it sprung to life. He watched his wife inch herself into a ball before rising with care to her feet. He watched her cradle her heavy belly and felt a tremor of remorse. She shouldn't have agitated him, he thought. Shouldn't have made his day even harder. She shouldn't have forced him to marry her in the first place.

One foot in front of the other—her limbs heavy and rubbery— Annie moved to the stove to start dinner. Was this it? She hadn't started dinner? Fog settled on her. She couldn't remember.

A wash of water, and blood broke between her legs, and she cried out.

"Lee? The baby."

Leonidas looked at the floor. "Gawd-dayum it, Annie."

At the hospital, the doctor told her that her baby boy had died. He never met her eyes. Or those of Leonidas.

Leonidas helped her to the car and drove her to her parents' home. He stood, hat in hand, and explained to her mother that she had fallen down the front steps. The baby came too soon, and the doctor couldn't save him. He had no interest in staying with her at her parents' home while she recovered, so he left her there and promised to come back.

Two weeks later, he returned. Her father answered the door and made it clear that Leonidas was no longer welcome in Annie's life. He made a handful of threats, and Leonidas, unwilling to fight the old man and having learned the futility of fighting a father over his daughter, gave his assurances that he would honor Annie's wishes.

He whistled as he made his way back down the walk away from Annie's house. He'd done right by her. He'd married her so she wouldn't be ruined. Now that there was no baby, which it probably wasn't his baby anyway, there was no need for him to remain obligated. The marriage to Annie had left him with a nagging, though.

He was thirty-one years old. He'd had two wives and two children. One child stolen from him and the other born dead. His oldest brother had married but died within a year of the marriage, leaving no children to carry on the family name. His youngest brother, his partner in many a crime, had fallen in love, married a girl, and taken to insurance selling in Detroit. Leonidas considered that it might be time to settle down. A real kind of settling down—not the way Annie had tricked him. Not with a woman like Crawford, who thought herself better than him. It might be time to start looking for the kind of woman with whom he could build a real family.

I Corinthians 9:22
KJV

I am made all things to all men,
that I might by all means save some.

Chapter 18

September 1926

A siren wailed in the distance. Ruth startled. Her heart beat into her throat. The feed she'd been spreading for the hens slid unnoticed from her hands. The sun had just broken the horizon, and even that great orb held a breath—waiting. An eerie silence followed the siren. She searched her mind—tornado? War? Perhaps she'd imagined it. She turned back to the hens.

A booming vibrated through the earth beneath her feet—as if a thousand trains had rushed down a thousand rails. The trains must have all broken loose from their tracks. Panic rushed through her, and tears sprung to her eyes. She wailed, dropping her basket and running to the house.

She came face-to-face with her family, shaken and running toward the cellar for shelter, panicked, eyes wide. Riley—his hands waving—was trying to head them off. He reached the cellar first and slammed the doors shut, standing atop it like a preacher ready to deliver his sermon.

"Hush, now, y'all! Hush!" Riley raised his hands in the air and patted his palms over them as if he could tamp down their dread. He chuckled at the hysterical women clucking about him. Earl, taking his brother's lead and edging himself to the side of the cellar doors, laughed nervously.

"Don't y'all remember? They're startin' the blastin' for the monument today." Riley, who had taken a part-time job as a grocery clerk in town, had told them about the impending blasting, but they had forgotten—and were perhaps naive of its meaning.

The siren wailed in the distance again. Their alarm reignited.

"That siren is lettin' ever'body know that some a'the mountain is about to come down. Wait . . . wait . . . listen careful," he said. Within moments, a thundering rippled under their feet. Their chatter resumed—relieved, nervous—and what had been passing news a few days ago was now the only thing they wanted to discuss.

"They're up there blastin' off the granite to make a flat surface. Called planin'," Riley explained. With his town connections, he was their informant in much the same way father had been. "Makin' it ready for the sculptor to come. There's drillers loosening it up. Then the siren tells ever'body to move away so they can let loose the rocks. The rocks hit the ground, makin' ever'thing get all shaky. There's a line a'trucks waitin' to take it to the train cars. Builders'll buy it up as quick as we can get it to 'em."

The drilling and dropping that began that morning continued throughout the day—a siren, a silence, and then a crash. It continued through the next day and the next. Within a week, they'd stopped flinching at the siren, and the rumbling blended itself into the sounds of the perpetual train. By the end of the month, forty-four thousand tons of granite had been removed, and the stone canvas upon which the great Confederate monument was to be carved began to reveal itself.

Six days a week, a rhythm set in—siren—silence—crash. It began at dawn and continued to dusk. The United Daughters of the Confederacy commissioned a composer to write an anthem to the dream of the memorial. They started a magazine praising the efforts of the men who worked on the mountain and encouraged all good citizens to become part of the great history of the Confederacy by purchasing a Stone Mountain half-dollar. Ms. Plane even took a trolley out to Stone Mountain to gather with all the Stone Mountain ladies—including Mama and Aunt Alice and Aunt Norah. Dollie and Bea joined them too—but Lola refused. She had no use for Ms. Plane's kind of campaigning.

Ruth sat in the family pew at Mount Zion Baptist Church, picking at her nails. Mother elbowed her to stop. Lola and Charlie stood side by side at the altar. Lola, her wild, wavy hair recently bobbed, stood in an olive-green travel suit, holding a bouquet of daisies and chrysanthemums. Jezebel, Ruth thought with an indulgent smile. Charlie, dressed in his Sunday best, smiled down at her as he slid the simple gold band on her finger. Little Marshall toddled about their feet, and the family was content to leave him be. Cousin Davis pronounced the two wed, and those gathered gave a smattering of applause.

Siren—silence—crash.

The family trickled into the crisp October afternoon and gathered in the covered picnic area just behind the square brick church. A large platter of fried chicken stood sentinel at one end of the table, and a white cake decorated with pink flowers guarded the other. In between, countless casseroles, biscuits stuffed with salted ham and pimento cheese, fried okra, corn cobs and bacon-soaked butter beans, Karo pies, and three different kinds of banana pudding formed an aromatic landscape. The women migrated into service, and the men took up court along the benches and scattered chairs.

Mother, Aunt Alice, and Aunt Norah dished up plates for the wedding guests. Ruby and Clara May led a game of hide-and-seek with the younger children. Ruth's older sisters fussed about the men and children, feeding them and clearing their rubble.

Riley, a man of eighteen, sat elbow to elbow at the picnic table with his brothers, no longer a part of the pack he'd formed with his sisters. His awkwardness and the prankish nature that had marked his boyhood had evolved into an insistent, if still humorous, doggishness.

"Here it comes," Ruth whispered over Riley's shoulder as Wheeler shoveled the last of his dinner in his face. Wheeler needed fuel for his unending campaign to sell. "Ready your troops."

"Aww . . . this is no war, Rue. It's nothin' more than treasure huntin'. Hardest part is tryin' to figure out who has the map." He winked at her as Wheeler wiped his greasy face and leaned forward. She laughed over her shoulder and dodged out of earshot.

She smiled weakly at Elly, who was holding court with a group of cousins. She and Elly had grown apart when Ruth left school— an unsalvageable truth now that Elly was excelling in the new high school, and her family was saving to send her to the Agnes Scott College in Atlanta. Neither had seen Lizzie since Cousin Frank had passed. The Spivey family, who blamed Cousin Frank and by proxy the whole Shurlington family for the accident, had swallowed her.

Elly gave her a passing nod as the interminable argument about the travails of the farm and the godlessness of the city and what was best for the family began. The argument had become as constant as the train, and not a new thought had been introduced since Wheeler took up his stance in the city and Tom had planted his shovel in the field. Riley and Wheeler sat on one side of the table—Tom, Maddox, and Earl eyed them from the opposite. Charlie and Martin, those brothers that had come late by marriage, remained on the outskirts of the discussion. Both were men of commerce making their way in Atlanta.

Siren—silence—crash.

Ruth leaned up against one of the tall pines, observing her family and averting her eyes from Elly and her coterie. She was four months shy of fifteen and artless. She tugged self-consciously at her knee-length yellow-flowered dress that had come secondhand from Bessie. Thanks to hand-me-downs and the girls' skill at tailoring, they had yet to resort to the flour-sack fabrics that many families had begun to convert into clothing. Ruth rubbed her back against the gristly pine bark, scratching at the endless agitation caused by the white talc on the cotton plants. Her skin had lost its smoothness. Ruddy, agitated patches mottled her arms. It was a condition her older sisters did not suffer.

"Hi-ya." Overall-clad and grinning, Quillan swooped from the other side of the pine. Ruth jumped. He chuckled, gripping a piece of sugarcane between his back teeth.

"Quillan! You scared me!"

Over the summer, Quillan had grown a solid two inches and was all legs and arms and sharp angles. He looked down at her with wide-set brown eyes and a lazy smile. His hair was straight as corn silk and sun-kissed into a kaleidoscope of amber and golden strands. Quillan and his friendship with Ruth were common topics among her mother and her sisters.

"Didn't mean to," he said, leaning against the tree next to her. He pulled a short stick of sugarcane from his pocket and offered it to her. His father had brought back several plants from a visit to the Georgia islands and nurtured a small field of it behind their house. Despite the drought, the cane field had produced a healthy crop for the preacher, which everyone attributed to his close relationship with God. Ruth took the cane stick and bit into the blunt end, sucking at the sweet juices. She loved chewing on sugarcane.

Quillan nodded toward Lola. "Your sister's done gone and cut all her hair off. Hope it ain't catchin'."

Ruth took the cane from her mouth and glanced up at him under her lashes, reaching for a thick curl that hung over her shoulder. She was tall for a girl, but Quillan was still taller. Being around him made her feel petite and feminine.

"No-wa. Why would I go and do such a thing, hmm? Lola's a little coo-coo is'all." She leaned in with a whisper. "Charlie's her second husband, ya know. Her first one ran off to California."

He nodded at her, satisfied that she was in agreement. "Want me to dip you up a plate?"

Her fingers fiddled with the frayed Peter Pan collar of the dress. She bounced her hips against the tree and wondered why her tongue felt thick and slow in her mouth. Her body was confusing her. It was Quillan—just another of the boys with whom she'd grown up playing with in the creeks. Never mind that the creek beds had been all but dried up since last summer.

"I can get it. I need to be helpin' Mama anyways," she replied, pushing herself off the tree and starting toward the pavilion. She stuck the sugarcane back in her mouth, chewing at the sinewy fibers. She was aware of the way her legs were working, her arms swinging, her feet hitting heel to toe on the dirt path. She straightened her back and tried to walk naturally, which, she feared, only made it worse.

"I'll come with ya." Quillan loped beside her.

Siren—silence—crash.

Quillan's unexpected attention caused her stomach to roll in queasy waves. Their mothers watched them from the pavilion.

"Well . . . I should be helpin' Mama," she said again, aware that she was repeating herself. Heat flooded her cheeks, and she dashed off. When did Quillan Johnson start making her feel weird? She'd been fishing with him last week, and it hadn't been weird at all. They'd laughed about how they both tied knots the same way. The way her father had taught them both to do.

Ruth, unsettled by her feelings, avoided Quillan by helping serve throughout the afternoon. She busied herself combining casserole dishes, clearing plates, and keeping track of the toddlers.

"Quillan's a nice boy," Mother ventured. "Gets along well with your brothers. Kept Riley out a'trouble more than once. Hard worker too. Did you know he's planning to be a preacher like his daddy?"

"I did, Mama. You mentioned it three times last Sunday," Ruth groaned. She caught him staring at her from across the churchyard, where he had joined up with Earl and the other boys to throw horseshoes.

Quillan had a kind, easygoing nature that made everyone around him feel at ease. She decided if Earl and Riley were merged into one person, he'd be a lot like Quillan Johnson. It wasn't hard to picture him standing before a crowd delivering a Sunday sermon with charm and conviction. Like Maddox, she thought to herself.

Dollie, though more subdued, had physically recovered from losing Baby Grant and was once again expecting. Her best Sunday dress was clean and pressed, despite the last few hours outdoors. Her long hair was wound into old-fashioned coils at the nape of her neck and pinned with a silver comb. Her skin had a faint glow from the summer, and freckles dotted her cheeks. She and Bea had their heads together, sharing secrets. Ruth imagined Dollie giving Bea advice about making babies. Bea and Martin wanted a baby, but after four years of marriage, they had not been blessed.

Her eyes wandered to Lola, uninhibited and bold, her head thrown back in laughter—her bobbed hair bouncing, her rouged cheeks flushed. She seemed free of concern—even for her own tugging child that stumbled at her feet.

"Ruthie," Mother said, breaking through her thoughts, "I need you to round up the little ones. It's 'bout time to pack up."

Ruth nodded and began herding the youngest of their kin into a loose formation. Ruby refused to fall in line and instead walked side by side with Ruth. Ever since the two had left school, Ruby ignored her or questioned her. At family gatherings such as these, she stared with envy at their cousin Elly and often threw barbed, accusatory words in Ruth's direction. Ruth felt the early draft of their divide. Ruby hadn't wanted to leave school. It was clear she blamed Ruth for this loss.

The smaller children held hands in a marching chain, and Ruth took them winding back toward the front of the church, detouring through the cemetery for an extra bit of fun. She recited each name on the gravestone and told them one thing she knew about the person who'd been laid to rest. She paused longer at her father's stone. She realized she'd been without him for near as long as she'd been with him. She said his name. "William Shurlington. Everybody called him Bill. He told the very best stories." Ruby turned and walked away. Clara May and Eugene blinked blankly at the mention of their father's name. They had no memory of him. Ruth stared at Ruby's receding back. She wanted to grab all three of them and scream in their faces. How could they have forgotten him?

The train roared past. The new laws required the engineer to blow the whistle in three short bursts to warn anyone who might be on the track crossings. Even with the whistle warning people of the danger, train accidents persisted. The little ones squealed and covered their ears at the high-pitched triplet and watched in fascination as the metal beast powered down the tracks. Ruth led them to the church steps, warning them to stay still until the adults were ready.

The train. The blasting. The cacophony of voices overlapped in a dissonant harmony. Unless you were listening real close, you could hardly make out one from the other.

Small groups of family ambled up the hill, carrying a dish or a basket to be returned home. Earl and Riley shoved at each other in a good-natured game. Eugene escaped to join them—wanting their attention. Ruth looked for Quillan. She saw him wrestling with his brothers, making their way toward the parsonage. Clara May followed her eyes and began chanting.

"Ruthie and Quillan sittin' in a tree. K-I-S-S-I-N-G . . ." Ruby smirked. Ruth gave them a playful shove.

"Hush it, you two!"

Clara May stood on her tiptoes, amber waves of tangled hair swirling about her round face, pursed her beautiful, rosy mouth, and gave Ruth a quick peck to the cheek. Clara's skin, like Ruth's and Ruby's, had taken on the same itchy ruddiness. Clara giggled and plopped back down, snuggling closer to Ruby. Ruby wrapped her arm around Clara May's shoulders, taking possession of her and resting her chin atop her head.

The winter Sundays of 1926 became the highlight of Ruth's days. On one hand, it was the only day that the Stone Mountain memorial builders rested. On the other, it was the day she saw Quillan. Which was more pleasing to her, she couldn't say. On Sundays, she mimicked Dollie—taking extra care with her hair and her dress. Bessie reformulated her burn salve with hog grease and bee balm for her younger sisters to calm the incessant itchiness—and thus the redness—of their skin.

Ruth listened for the lucent tenor of Quillan's voice to guide her alto crooning. There'd been a time when he'd struggled. His voice had cracked and warbled, but in the last year, his tone had settled into a silkiness, richer and clearer than it had ever been.

For Ruth, all other voices faded when he sang. She harmonized strong and clear on every hymn, imagining herself in a private duet with him. She demonstrated her piety with enthusiasm. She listened with close attention to Brother Johnson's sermons right up until he made some interesting point that she could mention to Quillan. She often missed whatever part of the sermon that came after that. She repeated in her head the idea she snagged over and over so that she wouldn't forget. She had to, as sometimes her brain felt full of fog.

After service, her mother and Sister Johnson had a habit of putting their heads together and sending encouraging smiles to their two children. While Ruth gathered her things, Quillan loitered on the church porch waiting for her. He smiled when she emerged and tapped his fingers to the brim of his hat. Ruth's habit was to visit the family graves nestled under the pine copse, and it became Quillan's to join her.

Her father's grave was the first to be tended. Quillan plopped beside her, sitting cross-legged and chewing on his sugarcane. Ruth focused on the bits of weeds as she found; she couldn't so much as peek at him without blushing. She directed her sparse responses at the gravestone, pretending he wasn't sitting within arm's length of her. After her father's grave, she moved to Baby Grant's stone. Quillan followed and rattled on about the streetcars and the trains and the giant carving of Robert E. Lee and his fellow heroes being blasted into the face of the stone mountain.

"Can you believe they're actually doin' it? After all that talk?" He waffled between admiration for the general and wonderings about whether or not God would consider it a graven image.

"I mean, it is a graven image, right? But I don't think it counts as a sin if you don't go bowin' down to it? And ya cain't have no plans for callin' people to go bowin' down to it."

"I don't plan to go bowin' down at the mountain," she remarked.

"Yeah. Me neither," he reflected. "So I'm thinkin' that means it's an honorin', not a'worshippin', ya know. Like we're doin' what God would want us to do. Honorin' the gen'ral, I mean."

"I think there might be some that worship that ol' general. Like Papa. I think he goes way past honorin'. You know those half-dollars they been sellin' to raise money for the carvin'? He's collected a dozen of 'em. It's a Memorial to the Valor of the Southern Soldier—says so right on the coin."

"That makes things right complicated with your ol' pappy, then. He's a'worshippin' coin and country."

Quillan grinned at his own alliteration. Ruth watched him make a mental note of the phrase for later use. He sometimes practiced mini sermons with her and took great pride in his developing oratory skills.

"He does keep a tight fist on 'em—even when Mama says we need money for things 'bout the house."

"Well, then . . . I s'pose that goes and makes it a sin. A dishon-

or. But that's your pappy's dark road, not ours. We ain't seein' that memorial for a'worshippin'. We're seein' it for a'honorin'."

Ruth considered correcting his grammar as Mother corrected hers—but the way he talked appealed to her. He was schooled but not overly so. Laughter underscored the mixed drawl of his thoughts. His faith formed from a combining of family tradition and a good knowledge of the scriptures one needed to affirm those traditions. He'd make a fine preacher.

He sat back, reassured that his whole town was not committing a sin by erecting a ninety-foot image of the great General Lee and his trusty horse Traveller. Whatever sin was being committed, it was not one of the whole.

When he was near, she had to remind herself to breathe. She felt coarse and stupid and had trouble tying her thoughts together. She'd spend the week planning her conversation and practicing looking up from beneath her thin lashes. If only she were as calm as Dollie or had Lola's flirtatious nature. She envied them. Lola—who moved liked the cane fields under the breeze—was stunning and unassuming. Dollie's polished perfection made Ruth feel oafish in comparison. Bea, saintly and sweet. Bessie, clever and confident. They all wore their femaleness like a robe and crown.

Kneeling before the graves of her forebears, listening to Quillan dream of Atlanta, Ruth pieced together a mélange of womanhood. Fragments of her mother and her sisters came to rest in her. Mother and Dollie and Bea and Lola and Bessie melded into a Frankenstein image that suffocated the tentative blooming of her own. She—Ruth—couldn't catch her breath beneath their weight. Looming above them all was the woman of Proverbs. The woman a boy like Quillan would want to marry.

I Timothy 12:2
KJV

*I suffer not a woman to usurp authority
over a man but to remain in silence.*

Chapter 19

On the iridescent predawn hours, Ruth stepped out onto the porch of the farmhouse and took her first deep breath of the day. Just as she had as a child. No matter the season, that first intake of air felt clean in her lungs. She inhaled the soft awakenings of the land, believing that there was a balm in that sovereign morning sigh. Her father whispered to her—his whittling, his soft chuckle, the ringing of his hammer—permeated those sacred minutes. She glanced up to the pinking sky and wondered. Could he see her?

She smiled to herself. Four months after the blasting on the mountain had begun, it stopped—the face of General Lee stared down at them, watching their comings and goings. Quillan was conflicted by the sacred nature of the whole project and refused to look at it. He was concerned the whole thing might be idol worshipping and wasn't willing to take any chances of sinning. Even accidentally. Ruth found his piety endearing, and when he was near, she too refused to acknowledge the carving.

They were distracted from the great monument when the papers reported that the daring wing walker Charlie Lindbergh had flown the single-engine *Spirit of St. Louis* across the Atlantic. She, like most Georgians, took a personal interest in the captains' antics. After all, he'd purchased his first plane and taken his first solo flight from Souther Field down in Americus. Without that old Jenny plane and some barnstorming lessons from one of their own, Lucky Lindy might never have gotten off the ground. Or at least that was how any Georgian worth their salt told it.

Quillan dismissed Lindy, suspicious of his character. Whenever she talked about the wing walker, Quillan shifted the subject and reminded her of the Bible story about the tower of Babel. It is the arrogance of the sinful man, Quillan noted, that leads him to seek self-glory and believe himself equal to God. Pride will lead to destruction. The people of Babel were scattered when they assumed themselves capable of building a tower that could reach the heavens, Quillan warned.

Despite Quillan's admonishments, Ruth wondered about men like Lindy who weren't afraid to play among the clouds. Men who dared touch the face of God. Were they closer to Heaven? Men of such adventure—of such ambition—didn't exist in her world. The men she knew were of the earth, not of the sky.

At fifteen, Ruth moved between three households. She was the first to rise—starting the fires and feeding their small herd of animals. She'd been relieved of supervising Eugene and Clara May. Ruby, self-appointed guardian of Clara May's education, had shoved herself into this role. After her chores, no longer needed by her own younger siblings, Ruth walked to the Grant house to help Dollie, who had given birth to her fourth living child, get the smaller children off to school. Dollie had named the little boy Henry Eugene, Henry to honor their ancestors and Eugene in hopes for their future.

By the late morning, she was in Carrie's garden, tending the kitchen vegetables and playing with little Harold, while Carrie focused on her new baby, Betty Sarah.

A few days a week, she walked into town to earn extra coin; a bundle of Francis's feathers for the milliner and a stop in at the. McGurdy's three-gable house to do up the laundry and mending could bring in two or three dollars a week. At all hours, she was surrounded by some collection of her nieces and nephews. She'd take them into the henhouse with her or set them to the churn. She schooled her firstborn niece, Christine, on stitching and did her best to keep Marshall corralled. In the evenings, she read to them or taught them to make paper chains.

Despite her will to remain present with Papa Jefferson, Mother grew quiet. Fully ensconced as their patriarch, Papa Jefferson handled all of the dwindling farm assets, including its women and the accounting books, with an aggressive hand. Ruth had come to suspect that Papa Jefferson insisted on wifely duties from her mother—though she had no proof of such.

Her mother's only rebellion was the coffee tin of money she ferreted away when she was able to do neighborly favors. Only Ruth knew they weren't of the kind sort. She worked as a maid here and there for that precious clink of independence. "People don't need to be knowin' about our business," she said to Ruth. "And by people, I mean your papa."

Father had been with the Lord for seven years. Mother had been in partnership with him—running a business and standing by his side. Under Papa Jefferson, she grew meek one concession at a time and had long stopped offering her opinions for fear of retribution. Age had made Papa Jefferson menacing, and he released a low drone of homegrown violence that undergirded their lives.

He contended that it was the Yanks and negroes who were to blame for the way the city was spilling into their fields. It was the Yanks and the negroes that caused the work shortages and the food shortages. The federal government, with their progressive agriculture policy, was driving cotton prices down and plotting to ruin the South.

Ruth rarely saw Tom or Maddox. Both spent late hours hashing out the ultimate fate of their own farms. Their growing families had made them both determined to protect their simple rural lives. Even as their world dipped deeper into poverty. Even as it was becoming more obvious that Atlanta was bound to swallow Stone Mountain. Neither had the resources of time or finance to check in with the family farm as they once did. Neither was willing to usurp Papa Jefferson.

Bessie, having finished high school and in full mastery of her own brilliant mind, side-stepped Papa by taking an office job at the Stone Mountain quarry. Her skill and finesse with organization and accounting—not to mention the balms and salves she set up for sale to the quarry miners—made her an immediate asset. Demand for quality granite throughout the county kept the quarry in endless orders—some for businesses and some for private building. The paper had recently valued the high-quality granite in their mountain at five billion dollars. Ruth read it over and again—five billion dollars. She tried to comprehend the number before finally deciding it was a made-up thing.

Each evening, Bessie came home from the bustling quarry as smartly dressed as a farm girl could manage with stories about all the county families. She referred to herself as a businesswoman and had a particular interest in the newly arrived Vining family. The Vinings had migrated from way down in Tift County, and their son James had taken on odd jobs for the local builders, putting him in the quarry office on a regular basis. *For hand salve*, she added to anyone who might question his perpetual presence.

Riley and Earl toiled long hours to maintain the family farm. When their youngest brother, Eugene, insisted he should be allowed to quit school to help, Riley refused to allow it.

"Daddy would never have considered it," he insisted.

It was one of the few times Riley stood up to Papa Jefferson, who considered Riley's argument that migrant labor was cheap and plentiful, and there was no need to cheat Eugene of his schooling. Papa Jefferson acquiesced when Riley added that Eugene could leave school once he finished eighth grade.

Like Tom and Maddox, Earl worked hard from the time he woke until his head touched the pillow at night. The farm invigorated him. He was happiest covered top to bottom in red Georgia earth. It was Earl who sat with Mother at the Talking Table, assuring her the farm could survive. She doted on him the way she once did with their father. When Earl sat eating her cobbler and talking about the farm, she was herself again.

Riley, much like many of the young Stone Mountain boys, grew restless and talked nonstop of joining Wheeler in Atlanta. After a full day on the farm, he'd head to town by four in the afternoon for his job as a grocery clerk. He'd taken the job to support the family finances, but, Ruth knew, it took the edge off the farming, for which he could no longer disguise his distaste. He was courting Sarah Elliott—their union inevitable. His ambition was to find a job in finance in Atlanta and buy a big three-gabled house like the McGurdys.

"Treasure huntin', Riley?" Ruth would say some nights when he trudged up the porch steps. He'd smile and nod. It was their code for—remember?

The erosion of their life was audible in the constant building springing up around them. Papa Jefferson continued selling off the far parcels to keep them afloat until Ruth could see the edges of their land from the front porch step. The land was receding against the tide of change. Migrant farmhands were begging for odd jobs, and squatter camps were common in the outskirts of DeKalb County. The smell of manure mingled with a more acrid, human smell on warm nights.

During the spring harvest season, the men who were familiar to them—the laborers from years past—were scarce. They'd moved on to different lives. Papa resorted to hiring a half dozen of the migrants. Strangers had never worked their land before. These sullen men from the pinelands frightened Ruth.

Papa Jefferson let the white migrant workers sleep in the barn. Late at night, Ruth heard them rustle about and could hardly discern them from the livestock. One evening, she set out across the yard to retrieve a side of ham from the meat house. As she headed back toward the house, she noticed one of the workers leaning against the barn door, watching her. His dark hair was matted with sweat, and his face was streaked in dirt. His clothes were worn thin. In the fading light, his eyes reflected the bruised setting of the sun. He took a long drag on his cigarette—the orange tip glowing. He stared at her.

"Wanna smoke?" he drawled.

She shook her head but didn't move. Something about him stunned her to stillness—a lightning strike that rooted her into the ground.

"That's a mighty purty dress yer a'wearin. Yer like a firefly flittin' about here in the dark."

Ruth looked down at her faded yellow hand-me-down she'd worn to Lola's second wedding, smoothing it with her free hand. Papa had warned them not to speak to the migrants.

He ambled toward her in feline strides. He took out a fresh cigarette and a match. He flicked the match head between his thumbnail and forefinger, and it burst to life. The flame of the match glinted against the gold ring he wore. It had the same signet she'd seen on her father's things.

"Magic," he said, winking at her. He offered her the cigarette. Again, she shook her head. Her green eyes met his blue ones. He looked to be near Wheeler's age, and the mischievous light behind his eyes reminded her of her father.

"Aww . . . come on. Makes a man lonely t'smoke alone."

He gestured the cigarette toward her mouth. It was a good-natured dare from a dark stranger capable of a little magic. She rose to the occasion. She took the cigarette and sucked the smoke into her lungs as she'd seen Lola do. It burned, and she coughed. Her naivete reflected back at her through the amusement in his eyes. She stepped back and averted her gaze from his. She felt childish and indecisive on where to look. He was lean and sinewy like the mountain lions that sometimes lurked at the edges of the cattle fields.

The man tilted his head and chuckled. "There's not a'cause to be bashful. I ain't gonna hurt ya. Just enjoyin' a'bite a conversation with a purty gurl. What more could a man ask for, huh?"

She smiled in spite of herself. The purr of his deep Georgia drawl lingered. He wasn't from DeKalb. That particular warm hypnotic timbre came from much further south.

"I gotta get back to the house." She shifted the ham against her hip. Her skin had begun to feel the chill of it through the thin cotton dress.

"Well, I'd sure like to know yer name a'fore ya go disappearin' on me. Firefly." He sat back on his heels, one hand in his pocket. The other fiddled with his cigarette.

"Ruth," she said.

"Well, Ruth. It is right fine to meet the lady a'the farm. Name's Leonidas Brantley."

"Nice to meet you, Mr. Brantley." He was indeed quite a bit older than she.

"Aw, now, you make me feel like an ol' man. You can call me Lee." He paused for effect. "Ruth."

Ruth left Leonidas standing in the dark and made her way back to the house. The feral stench of moonshine stumbled down the porch steps with Papa Jefferson. She stepped into the shadows so he wouldn't see her. She noticed Leonidas too watched as Papa Jefferson turned and headed toward his own house.

Inside, Mother was sitting in her rocker by the fire, their family bible opened on her lap. The mournful record from Dollie's wedding played on the Victrola, popping and scratching against the low bass of the Sunday hymn. Where you lead me, I will follow . . .

Mother was staring into the fire. Her day dress had faded, the original pattern of playful ivy barely visible. Ruth came and sat beside her. Fresh bruising was beginning to appear along Mother's upper arm.

"Mama?" The scene was becoming familiar. Her mother sitting by the fire, worn, sometimes bruised, sometimes not. Ruth wondered what had angered Papa Jefferson tonight. She didn't ask, as her mother always had an excuse for him—for his anger and aggression. He hadn't been right since the war, she'd say, or losing his son had been a shock, or it was hard on him, being responsible for a house full of women and children.

Mother turned her head and mustered a faint smile. She'd lost most of her teeth, and her once-full lips had receded into a thin line. Her skin was dry and cracked, and an unnatural tinge of blue brushed her edges.

"A woman has to know her place, Ruthie. Says so right here in

His word. You see?" She gestured toward the Bible in her lap. "Not something we can go forgetting."

"Mama . . . ?"

"Did I hear you talking out there? Who were you talking to, hmm?"

Mother was having no more discussion of the state of herself. Ruth, accustomed to the intricate weavings of alluded conversation, shifted with her.

"Was one a'the hands. He was outside smokin'."

"You be careful about that, Ruthie. I don't wanna see you out there talking to the low-country folk. Those pinelanders don't have so much as a wooden nickel to lose. And I know the one you were talking to—a snake charmer, that one."

"How do you know?" Ruth felt a stirring of defiance at her mother's admonishment. Her mother sat straighter and leaned forward, agitated at Ruth's back talking.

"I know him 'cause your daddy hired him and his brothers some years back for a harvest. Them Brantley boys been passing in and outta here for years. Good hands. But rough living. That one strode on in here a few weeks ago. Without his brothers this time. Smiling and sweet talking. Something off about him. That sweet talk's too sweet if you ask me. You steer clear, hmm? Now go on to bed. And don't let me catch you smoking. Makes a woman ugly. Makes her smell ugly too," she added, her words catching Ruth before she left the room.

"Yes, ma'yam." Ruth knew better than to question her mother any further. Mother might bow to Papa Jefferson, but she suffered no back talk from her children.

Songs of Solomon 2:3
KJV

As the apple tree among the trees of the wood,
so is my beloved among the sons. I sat down
under his shadow with great delight, and
his fruit was sweet to my taste.

Chapter 20

The terrible drought that plagued them for the last three years, a trial more devastating than even the boll weevil, broke. Rains filled the wells and gave a deep watering to the land. Creek beds and rivers flooded as the rains came faster than the parched earth could take in. But with rain came hope.

June brought a warm, nourishing sun, and the fields vibrated with life. Clara May and Ruby drew a tight circle around themselves. Papa Jefferson had declared Clara May would not be returning to school in the fall. She, like Ruby, would finish her education with the seventh grade. The two girls, in some unspoken way, treated Ruth as if she were to blame for their exit from formal education. Their older sisters, after all, had gone onto the high school. Bessie and Lola had jobs and were sophisticated and connected. But when Ruth left school, Mother thought it natural that both Ruby and Clara May would follow.

Ruby, in her search for knowledge, convinced Clara to sign up for the vacation reading program at the brand new Decatur library down at the Decatur Bank & Trust. It was their first real library. Before the Decatur library opened, their neighbor, Miss Lula would let children borrow books from her library room. The two were nose-deep in the Oz series and were up to Book 5, *The Patchwork Girl of Oz.*

Ruth, devoted to putting her hands to good use wherever needed, was nudged outside their circle. Ruby and Clara had secrets they no longer shared. They were carefree, lighthearted girls that seemed to be troubled for nothing. They made friends with ease and had a constant urge for adventure. Ruth felt slighted that her little sisters were moving past her—away from her.

Tom and Maddox latched onto the news that the demand for Georgia peaches was on the rise. They entertained the idea of adding a peach orchard and planting peanuts, perhaps expanding the soybean fields when soybeans began to be seen as a source of human consumption—not just livestock feed. Ruth wondered if Old Ezra's patch of soybean might be worth enough to cover his expenses now.

"Not a need for all this fancy testin' you're doin', Tom," Papa Jefferson ranted one afternoon. "Your tubes and your charts? How much that gonna cost us, huh? All these fields need is some rest and some sun. Soakin' in the rains. There'll be back to bounty by next spring."

Tom pinched the bridge of his nose in frustration. Papa Jefferson was convinced the government was lying about the depletion of land nutrients—insisting their need for research was a fabrication meant to keep Georgia farmers poor and under their thumb. He refused to invest in revitalizing the farmlands. Instead, he sold off the fallowed fields to the builders one lot at a time.

"Papa. All the sun a'summer's not gonna change them canyons.

The farm is dyin'. The soil is useless. It's a fool's way to keep plan-tin' the same and expect things to get any better."

"You call me a fool, boy," Papa Jefferson drew his sagging, knobby frame to its full height, towering over his grandson. Tom took a step back and deferred.

"No, sir. No, sir. I am not. I'm offerin' the courtesy a'informin'. Me and Maddox been workin' to figure out what'll grow best with what we got. Thought you might want us to do the same here. We're considerin' peaches . . . peanuts . . . expandin' the soybeans."

"Tom's always had a knack for it, Jeff," Mother interjected. She'd been listening in on the conversation. "Maybe consider what he has to say?"

"I don't recall askin' for your thoughts, Ida. I do recall askin' for a fresh cup a'coffee." Mother opened and then closed her mouth, exiting the conversation as quickly as she had entered it.

On the first Sunday in June of 1927, Wheeler showed up at the farm bearing a brand-new radio.

"All the people in the city have one," he said, bustling about the kitchen and clearing a spot for the large wooden box.

Ruth wondered about Wheeler's gifts. He brought her new things anytime Papa Jefferson sold a part of the property. All Ruth's brothers received compensation from the land sales—though Tom mourned every loss. He reinvested the money into his own farm. Wheeler bought gadgets. Wheeler told Mother he wanted her to have the radio in time to hear of Lindbergh's return from Paris, and he made her promise to have everyone over on the Tuesday that Captain Lindbergh flew into New York.

He set the radio up by the Talking Table. It was an Atwater Kent Model E with an elegant mahogany speaker that everyone could hear at once. The compact receiver had the new one-dial feature, and Wheeler set about tuning it to Roxy and his gang on WSB.

"This here is happenin' in New York, Mama!" Wheeler's face was bright with excitement. "There's music and stories. Or you can tune it to Reverend Baldwin and The Happy Bible Hour."

Mother walked around the rectangular wooden box, inspecting it, and looked dumbfounded at Wheeler. She peered into the round speaker bowl. She mumbled that it was the Devil's work, and Ruth muffled a laugh with her hand. Her mother thought the Devil was working in everything from movie films to the new electric refrigerators. Wheeler's face fell.

"I'm tryin' to help you, Mama, you know? Bring somethin' good into this old place."

"Bringing my grandbabies 'round for supper every now and again is good enough for me, Wheeler," she said. She glanced back at the radio, then slid her eyes back to him. "You say there's a Happy Bible Hour?"

Wheeler came back alive from her pummeling. "There is, Mama, . . . and Ruth." He turned to her. Hearing her name come from his lips startled her. A foreign sound. "Ruth, go on and grab the paper so Mama can see all she can listen in on."

Ruth, who loved listening to the radio anytime she visited Lola or Bea, ran for the Sunday paper to look up the radio shows. She sat with Mother and read out all the radio shows one by one. Long after Wheeler had slipped back into his fancy car and driven the half-hour back to Atlanta, they sat awestruck, as James Melton's tenor vibrato serenaded them with Mendelssohn's "On the Wings of Song."

The summer remained mercifully mild and rainy. Temperatures climbed to a mere ninety degrees by July Fourth. Their small town was engulfed by daily visitors lounging near Stone Mountain or out for a drive on the car line.

"Got my car up to fifty miles an hour," Riley boasted. He'd purchased a secondhand roadster from one of their cousins. "They say they're only gettin' faster. Eighty. Ninety miles an hour before you know it."

Ruth rolled her eyes at him. "That's nonsense, Riley. People's sayin' everybody'll be flyin' like Lindy too. That'll never happen."

"Oh, it'll be happenin', Ruthie. You wait and see."

Charlie and Lola convinced the family to come into the city to Lakewood Park for the July Fourth fireworks show. Lakewood was a hub of high-octane entertainment. Aside from the traditional fair games and fun rides, it was home to the Greyhound roller coaster and the Atlanta Speedway.

It was an oddity for their mother to make the trip into the city for the Independence Day festivities, especially on a weekday. But this year was special. There was going to be a fifty-foot replica of the new Stone Mountain memorial all done up in fireworks.

The Shurlingtons, like most of the Stone Mountain people, were proud of their famous rock, and it seemed cause enough to give the day to celebration. A good number of their neighbors, including Brother Johnson and his family, would be joining them at the fairgrounds, which, for Ruth, meant an afternoon with Quillan.

Mother and Bessie spent the day before packing a day's worth of food. Ruth smiled to herself as she heard Bessie bossing their mother about the kitchen. Bessie was well-organized and a natural leader, and though Mother bit right back, her bite had lost its sting.

Ruth was in charge of pulling out the oldest quilts to take along for the picnic. She added wooden-handled fans and wide-brimmed hats to the supplies that were piling by the door. The following morning, after a hearty breakfast, they all caught the Stone Mountain trolley to Lakewood Park. It would be a long trip, but Mother preferred the trolley to the car on holidays. She found the congestion of the city endurable only on foot.

Aboard the trolley, Ruth watched her simple village morph into an urban landscape. The quick swish of paper fans enlivened the broiling interior—colorful images of Jesus flashed back and forth like a swarm of cardboard moths caught by a wing. As they neared Lakewood, she could just make out Joyland, the negro amusement park. An involuntary shudder passed through her shoulders. Joyland was a desolate place marked by dilapidated buildings and overfilled trash cans.

At the Lakewood Park entrance, the trolley emptied its belly of rural outliers. Ruth's pale-green dress, one of the old bridesmaids' dresses from Dollie's wedding that Ruth had altered for sunnier weather, wilted in the sultry afternoon air. Her curly hair sprang free of her bun in a frenzy. She glanced around their motley crew of women and children. Earl folded their mother's hand into the crook of his elbow to help her navigate the sudden surge of humanity. Dollie, as usual, appeared unmussed by the heat and chaos. She gathered the smaller children in a line, linking their hands, and led them forward like a garden snake winding through weeds.

The plan was to meet Charlie and Lola outside the Lakewood gates at noon. Lakewood had been built on fifteen acres of the old Creek Indian land parcel and existed in a perpetual cloud of red dust and auto fumes. Most Atlantans were consumed by Flivver Fever, gawking over every new car that came down the line. Their obsession with the latest automobile advances made them immune to the respiratory discomfort of the speedway.

Young boys hawked newspapers, novelty toys, and handheld fireworks on the corners. Tom bought a couple of cracker cannons, several strings of firecrackers, and a handful of spit devils and tucked them away for later.

Mother clucked. "I don't like them things, Tom. They are dangerous! Wasn't a few months ago that all them children died in Cartersville 'cause of those things. One stray cigarette and they turned the mercantile into a fireball a'fore you could sing 'Dixie.' Poor babies burned past any recognition."

She raised her eyebrows at him, shaking her finger at the collection of fireworks in his hand. "Never mind that if you get yourself shot with one of them, you could get the lockjaw. Those little ones? They are poisonous."

Tom laughed. "Well, Mama, I reckon they are if ya go puttin' 'em in your mouth—which I don't plan on doin'. Nor do I plan on shootin' anybody with 'em. At least not today. How 'bout you, Ruthie? Plannin' on eatin' any fireworks with your chicken and collards?"

Ruth, overwhelmed by the crowd and following close behind Tom and Carrie, shook her head. Her stomach roiled. A carousel of conversation and color spun around her. She had never been to Lakewood Park. She couldn't tell if the jittering of her insides was from fear or excitement.

Mother scoffed and gave Tom a warning look. Ahead, Lola was leaning against the sagging wood of the park fence; a cigarette dangled between her fingers. A Whites Only sign was tacked next to her. Charlie stood at her side, rocking on his heels and chatting with Riley, who'd driven their car up the night before. When Lola spied them, she squealed and came running—showering them with hugs and kisses.

"Oh! It's wonderful y'all are here, Mama! Clara May, you get prettier and prettier ever' day!" She leaned in to give Ruth a kiss to her cheek. "And you? Why you're quite nearly a woman. I hear tell there's a certain preacher's son who's gone sweet on you."

Ruth turned crimson and looked away. She was rescued from further comment by Tom, who swept Lola into a bear hug, then delivered her to his wife. Carrie and Lola linked arms and hurried ahead to catch up on Stone Mountain gossip.

In the designated picnic areas, Maddox claimed an empty table beneath one of the massive oaks. Dollie spread out their blankets, and the women began to lay out dinner for the smaller children. A few of the men passed around a flat brown bottle of whiskey, some declining, before heading to the livestock exhibition. It was an hour before the motor revue event opened on the one-mile dirt track that wrapped around the lake. They planned to place a few friendly bets on the upcoming races. The "Flying Norwegian," Sig Haugdahl, and his Duesenberg 8 was favored for the big win. But the men were sentimental and backed their hometown boy, JD Andrews, aptly known as the "Atlanta Daredevil."

Barber's Band blared a quick-tempo foxtrot in full brass from the center pavilion. Ruth felt the booming of the bass drum vibrating against her chest and she wondered if her heart might pick up its rhythm. Firecrackers bounced and cackled in all directions. On occasion, an errant spark met flesh, invoking a cry of pain. The whooshing of the Greyhound roller coaster came at regular intervals—clackety-clack—high above their heads, flying along a complex tower of wooden scaffolding.

From a few tables over, Sister Johnson hailed Mother. Her own offspring had their heads bowed into their dinner. She swooped up a small platter of corn cakes and headed toward them. Behind her, Quillan gave Ruth a sheepish smile over a piece of crispy fried chicken. Sister Johnson tugged at him, and he hopped off the table to follow his mother.

Sister Johnson offered the corn cakes to Mother, who in turn brought out a jar of blackberry jam. Mother and Sister Johnson had been friends as far back as Ruth could remember. She found it curious that Sister Johnson had remained soft and pink and powdery while her own mother had taken on the same gray tinge of their crumbling farmhouse.

Sister Johnson gave Quillan a gentle nudge in Ruth's direction. He made a show of removing his hat and bowing to Ruth with one of his mother's corn cakes perched on his fingertips.

"For you," he said. "Mama's are the best in the county."

His nails were chewed to the quick and rimmed with a permanent line of dirt. His mouth had the faint gleam of chicken grease. His chestnut eyes glinted at her under dark lashes. He wore his overalls loose over his bare chest. His hand-me-down leather boots lacked laces. His poreless skin was bronzed by endless days in the Southern sun.

"I was wonderin' if you might be willin' to join me for a walk to the mirror house?"

Ruth glanced over at their mothers, noticing the gleam had returned to her mother's eyes in the company of her friend. The two women were watching them with approval and waved them on, adding that they'd be expected back at the oak before dark.

Colorful pennant flags snapped in single file along the roofline of the mirror house. Quillan paid the attendant two nickels—one for each of them. He took her hand and led her through the red-and-green-checkerboard entrance. The stifling interior hall was dark, and the cacophony of revelry faded to a din. Quillan led her around the corner into a room full of waffling mirrors.

She was startled by her own image. At home, there was one small mirror, which was mostly dominated by Lola, and so Ruth had rarely observed her own outward appearance. She saw herself through the reflection of her inner thoughts, through the passing comments of others. Here, surrounded by external mirrors, she took in the full length of herself, distorted and multiplied. In one direction her legs were short and her torso bulbous, and in others, she appeared to be three feet tall. In another, her face was pulled like a tug of taffy. In all of them, she could see the blotchiness of her skin, the plainness of her features, the wild frizziness of her hair, the square shape of her body. The ugliness horrified her.

Quillan, unaware of her distress, made faces and danced about, laughing at the morphing images of himself. He raised his arms and flexed to see if his muscles would appear bigger. He was silly and animated.

The room was a box, and at the same time the succession of mirrors gave the appearance of endless tunnels. She reached her hands forward only to be met by the hard surface of a mirror and a grotesque, misshapen version of her face. She took a deep breath, fighting the rising panic. Another mirror. Another wall. Another dead end. She started spinning, frantic to find the exit, her hands in front of her, seeking escape and finding only glass.

"Hey, hey, hey," Quillan said against her ear. He wrapped his arms around her from behind and soothed her as if she were a wild beast. He caught her hands in his and laced their fingers.

His body was hot against her.

"Breathe, now."

She closed her eyes and took in a breath. The tang of red clay and tanned skin tickled her nose. She opened her eyes. Her gaze met his in the contorted mirror. They two intertwined into a crea-ture with four arms and four legs but one head with four wide eyes, and the strangeness of it was beautiful to her. This she preferred over the singular horror of her own image standing alone. She breathed in a ragged breath. He brushed his lashes against her ear, and she giggled at the shiver.

"See? You're safe. Safe here with me, and we are havin' a good time."

Embarrassed by her panic but desperate to escape the onslaught of her reflection, she turned toward him, playfully swatting at his chest. He took her hands and led her around one of the mirrors, back into the darkened hall. He continued to hold her hand as he walked her back into the sun. Outside, he pulled two pieces of sugarcane from his pocket and handed her one.

"Makes ever'thing better," he assured her and nudged her with his shoulder. She looked at him and he at her.

"You awlright now?" Concern painted his voice.

She nodded. She bit into the hard sinewy stalk and groaned in pleasure at the syrupy juices her teeth had released. She shivered away her panic and shifted her focus back to the world outside of herself.

A crowd was gathering near the pavilion. Their heads were lifted to the sky in unison. An announcer was calling for everyone to watch over the lake for a stunt plane—due any minute. Grady Dunn would be making his second attempt to parachute right into the center of the racetrack. Red dust from the first of the car races filled the air. Ruth's eyes stung as she squinted up at the sun.

Men who play among the clouds, she thought.

The plane came in low, and the crowd erupted in cheers. Its wings wobbled back and forth. Grady stood on the wing, visible from the jumping platform. With the wink of a sunbeam, he was plummeting toward the speedway. His parachute opened in a great white whip, and with a jerk, he vanished into the thicket of trees.

The crowd let out a disappointed sigh. The announcer stuttered to life.

"That's awlright, folks. I'm sure he's just taking a detour through the pines! We'll have to wait yet another day to see if Grady will ever hit that bullseye."

The band struck up a lively March, and the crowd dispersed. The Greyhound coaster made another whoosh as it dipped sixty-six feet in the air. Ruth furrowed her brow at the racing roller coaster.

"Scared to ride?" Quillan teased.

"There isn't much to be scared of," Ruth sidestepped. She headed toward the entrance to the roller coaster, and Quillan bounded after her in admiration.

The roller coaster clacked overhead, drowning out all other sound. They boarded the coaster side by side. Quillan vibrated with excitement while she sat holding tight to the safety bar. As they left the coaster house, he leaned over.

"Gonna put your hands in the air when we go down the hill?"

She shook her head vigorously.

"Scared?" he challenged again.

At the top of the climb, she took a deep breath. The clacking of the wheels slowed, and the entire world teetered on the edge of two wooden tracks. The coaster was so high she could see all of Atlanta. She flung her hands in the air just as the coaster started its descent.

For an instant, she was beyond sound.

Weightless. Free. Flying. Playing among the clouds.

Then she screamed—loud and long—as the reins of sound caught up with her. The coaster reached the bottom of the first drop with a jerk, and she slammed her hands back to the safety bar. She closed her eyes. The feeling of freedom was gone. She was being jerked from one side to another—slamming between Quillan and the hard wooden side panel of the coaster car. Her neck hurt, and she dug her feet into the floor in an effort to keep her body from flinging about. Her ears started to ring just as the coaster shuddered to a halt. Quillan let out a whoop. She'd made it. She trembled and started to laugh.

"Wanna go again?"

He looked at her expectant, his eyes bright and eager. He saw her falter, and his face softened.

"Aww . . . I'm teasin' ya. It's 'bout time we got back. Mama'll be mad as a nest a'hornets if I bring you back late."

She might have loved him at that moment. The moment he saw her hesitation and released her from his grasp. She would've gone a thousand times more if he'd insisted. She would've endured the whipping and cracking and pounding of her head if he had asked. He knew she would, but he didn't ask.

They made their way back to the oak. The Stone Mountain people melded together, gossiping and laughing. Maddox, Cousin Davis, and Brother Johnson were debating the many meanings of the book of Revelations. Tom, Wheeler, Earl, and Riley were at temporary peace—tossing horseshoes and laughing with the other men. A pack of small bodies, led by Clara May and Eugene, ran about playing tag and lighting off firecrackers behind unsuspecting adults. The sing-song voices of the women wafted between them all, knitting their community together in a home-spun tapestry of summer sonance.

Ruth and Quillan climbed high into the big oak tree. The Battle of Fort McHenry was reenacted in booming splendor, Captain Lindbergh's flight to Paris was memorialized in incandescent luminosity, and a recreation of the newly unveiled Stone Mountain rendering of Robert E. Lee and his trusted steed Traveller burst into spinning phosphorescence.

"Honorin'," Quillan whispered to her with a grin. It was the most beautiful thing Ruth had ever seen.

To end the display, one hundred rockets flew from the center of the speedway—all at once—bursting in air. The sky was alive and immensely bigger than she'd ever conceived.

"You're cryin'," Quillan remarked.

"How could you not?"

She pulled her eyes away from the sky and met his. He leaned in and brushed his lips against hers. His lips were sweet, glazed in sun and sugarcane. They both pulled away, shy and uncertain. She could swear his beautiful bronzed face took on a reddish hue.

Sometime approaching midnight, they all piled into the back of the old Ford truck that Riley had driven into town. Ruth didn't even register the constant bumping and swaying on the ride back to the farm. She might as well have ridden a cloud home. She didn't even mind her younger sisters teasing her. Dollie and Bessie leaned against the back of the truck with the smaller children tucked into the spaces between them.

Dollie leaned her head against Bessie's and gazed in amusement at Ruth.

"Who knows? We might be hearin' weddin' bells before long," Dollie drawled with a tired smile.

Ruth sighed deep in herself and pulled her knees beneath her chin. In the moonlight, she could see the red dust from the track clinging to the tiny hairs on her arms. She was sixteen. The connection she felt with Quillan was comfortable and peaceful—like laying by the creek bed with her brothers—only Quillan gave her that flip in her stomach.

It was love. Wasn't it? Mother and Sister Johnson thought so. Her sisters thought so.

The old Ford came to stop in front of their sagging porch. Ruby and Clara May carried the sleeping children to the pallets set up on the sleeping porch. It was late enough that the women had decided to nestle everyone in together for the night.

Ruth dawdled in the empty truck bed, lost in her thoughts and staring up at the stars—wondering what God thought of fireworks. The starlight was steady and constant—unlike the blaze of sparks that she had watched tonight. Quillan, she decided, was starlight. Heaven-meant. The sounds of her family receded into the house, replaced by the shrill ring of the tree frogs and crickets. An owl hooted somewhere near.

Climbing down from the truck bed, she was so caught up in her revelry that she jumped when a noise came from the barn. She peered into the dark and saw the glow of a cigarette, a waterfall of dying embers flicked from the tip. Her breath caught when she realized the glow was moving toward her. Leonidas half emerged from the shadows.

"Evenin' there, Firefly." The burr of his voice blended into the night sounds. She thought she heard the low growl of a wild dog. "Yer lookin' . . . dusty. Git in a fight?"

He came out of the shadows and walked up so close she could taste the rich whiskey on his breath.

What was he celebrating? she wondered.

She stuttered. "No-wa, I haven't been in no fight. We all went up to the Lakewood track today for the fireworks."

He nodded in understanding and took a long draw of his cigarette. He blew the smoke away from her, out of one corner of his mouth. His eyes took in the plump rosiness of her cheeks and the carelessness of her loose red curls.

"Beautiful night, ain't it?" He paused and took another drag from his cigarette. He swept his arm wide toward the sky. "The heavens declare the glory of Gawd and the firmament shows . . . his handiwork."

He didn't take his eyes off her as he drawled out the snippet of Psalms. He studied her face before dropping his eyes to her chest.

She crossed her arms over her breasts and tried to pretend she didn't notice. He clucked. "They ain't that interestin', Firefly."

Her cheeks burned. This man who was both hard and soft, who knew about the land and quoted the Bible, frightened her and enlivened her curiosity all at once. She wondered about the places he'd been—where he'd come from and where he was going. She was drawn to the way his words felt like windows and suspected that if she could keep him talking she'd discover secrets to places and ideas that everyone else kept hidden from her. She had the suspicion that all she had to do was ask the right question, and he'd give her the answer. Tell her things. What things? She couldn't say, and that was the lure of him. His gaze left her and drifted skyward.

"I've always wondered what it looks like from up there. Tried to fly once. Back durin' the war. But had me a wife, so . . . " He trailed off.

"You're married?" she blurted without thinking. The corner of his mouth tilted upward. His eyes remained skyward.

"Coupla times. Both gone on t'be with our Maker."

He huffed out smoke rings, redirecting his attention from the sky to her face, smiling at her. "Gotta girl not much younger than you, I'd reckon."

"You have a child?" He didn't seem like a man who would have children.

"I do. Don' see her much. She's a'livin' with her grandparents since her mama passed on. She's over at Battle Hill—consumption." He picked a few tobacco leaves off the tip of his tongue. "Had a boy once too. Dead now."

"Oh," Ruth lamented. An urge to comfort him stirred in her. "I'm sorry."

The pull of him unnerved her. The mellow glow of Quillan's lips against hers faded in this strange man's presence. Standing beside him, she felt the breeze tickling the tiny gossamer hairs on her arms, and she lifted her face into its touch. Without looking at him, she was aware of the muscles in his arms and calluses on his hands.

Something wild roused in her. A memory of Lola and Elmer by the barn. She shivered at the intrusion of the recollection, clearing her throat and rubbing her arms in an effort to sidestep the unfamiliar craving.

His eyes rested on her, taking in all of her. He tilted his head and let her feel the reflection of his unchecked admiration. Sparks of silence bounced off the fields. He took another drag of his cigarette before dropping it to the ground and crushing it with his boot tip.

"My gurl? Helen's her name. Well, I hope she turns out as purty as you, Ruth. She's not quite a woman yet. Not like you."

Ruth considered the man and envisioned him as a father. He was old enough—that was clear. She thought of her own father and how she had failed him. She heard his laughter in the corners of her mind, and she felt the sting of his absence.

"Do you miss her? Your daughter, I mean?"

His thoughts were palpable. His presence filled the space between them.

"I do."

"I should go in," she said. She felt unsettled by him.

She turned toward him to say goodnight and was surprised by how close he stood. She lost her balance and fell against him. He was stronger than she imagined and radiated dark earth and rotting moss. She felt the scratch of his beard against her cheek. He ran his hand along the slope of her hip, pulling her tight against his own. The yearning that only moments before whispered in her now bloomed in her belly. He made a sound like a cornered wolf before shoving her hips away from him.

"Goodnight, little Firefly." He receded back into the shadows.

The heavy sound of his boots blended into the night chorus.

With all the children laid out on the sleeping porch, Ruth had the rare luxury of a bed to herself. She lay on her back—staring up at the rough-hewn ceiling. She put her fingers against her lips and thought of Quillan—his eyelashes brushing her skin, the sweetness of his scent. He moved and he laughed—all the time—reminding her of Riley before the tensions of the farm seized him. His skin was impossibly bronzed, and she blushed when she thought of tracing the clear, firm muscle in his arms. I got you, his ghost whispered.

She closed her eyes to pray. She prayed for Quillan and his family and for her brothers and sisters and all her nieces and nephews. She hesitated at the thought of Leonidas bunking on the scratchy hay of their barn. It was Christian-like to include him in her prayers. She prayed for him. And for his daughter. She asked God to comfort him and walk with him so that he wasn't so alone. She prayed for forgiveness for the yearning she felt. She was most shamed that the yearning was not for Quillan.

She fell into the dream from somewhere high above. She thought it must be the roller coaster, but there was nothing beneath her. She floated, weightless through a swirling mass of translucent leaves. The leaves shifted in color from pearlescent to golden-honey to ivy-green—pulsing and changing and dancing in a cloud of sunbeams. Waves of laughter intertwined with the swirling leaves. She hit the ground with a jolt. The roots beneath her arched up and around, encasing her in a viny seat of branches. The roots beneath her feet continued to writhe until one pulled loose. The smooth grain surface shimmered until it became silver scales and a snake's head formed at its tip. The snake slithered about her, winding around her arms and her legs. She knew she should be afraid. And yet, the snake's skin was warm. He wound his way to her neck and hissed, nearly inaudible in her ear. She leaned closer. She closed her eyes. The hissing grew louder until it was all she could hear.

The rains, becoming more menace than blessing, intensified by August, and the sky swole over the granite mountain. Flooding started in the south along the Chattahoochee River—Clark and Stone Mountain Creek broke their banks and made the local roads impassable. The promise of a late-summer harvest drowned in the unending torrent. Fields flooded and bridges were washed away. Drought gave way to deluge.

Without a full harvest, Papa Jefferson dismissed the temporary farmhands and relied on the family to bring in the fall crop. Ruth leaned against the porch railing and watched Leonidas leave the barn. He slowed as he came near the house. Mud clung to his boots. His overalls hung shapeless about his shrinking frame. He smiled his crooked smile. Wrinkles brought on by time and sun framed his blue eyes. Rain dripped from the brim of his old hat.

"Maybe you'll be wantin' a bite for the road?"

The sadness at his departure was unexplainable. He struck her as a lone man against the whole world. She felt an overwhelming desire to soothe him. She ran inside and wrapped a corn muffin and a small side of ham in a cloth. He was on the porch when she returned.

"I'll be missin' you, Firefly. You've made these days fair bearable." He took the wrapped bundle from her hands, lingering on her fingers. "I think you might be the purtiest sister on this farm."

She found it impossible to look away from him. He tipped his fingers against his hat and disappeared through the endless summer rain.

Lola was screeching through the telephone about Captain Lindbergh's visit to Atlanta. Ruth held the receiver a bit away from her ear.

"Do what?" Ruth was struggling to make sense of her sister's babbling over the noise of the house. Babies were howling despite Clara May's attempts to calm them. Mother, elbow deep chopping up the apple harvest and putting away the autumn greens, hollered from the kitchen.

"I said! Lucky Lindy will be in A'lanah next week, and we just gotta have the fam'ly in to see him. They're gonna be puttin' up grandstands and everything, and Wheeler? Well, he has connections—God bless him. We're gonna have a spot right on Peachtree. You'll convince Mama, won't you Rue?"

"I'll tell her, Lo. It couldn't be a worse time, though. Papa had to let the hands go, and we been gettin' everything in and put away ourselves. Sides, you know Papa, he's not gonna go nowhere."

In fact, both Papa and Mother were having nothing to do with air travel or any celebration of its kind. Last week, leaden clouds had hovered over the stone mountain until the sky and the mountain looked one and the same. One of the new airmail planes crashed into it. Both pilots died in a fiery explosion. Mother said this was God's way of saying people ought to stay on the ground.

"Pish-posh, Ruthie. Papa's an old goat—mind you, you need to keep clear a'him." She paused. "Either way, you come. Maybe you can come out all next week. I been needin' some help with my baby too. Ruby and Clara May are plenty help for Dollie and Carrie. You can bring us up some a'the okry and Mama's spiced apples."

Ruth agreed to ask about spending time with Lola and Charlie. She wasn't near as excited about Captain Lindbergh's visit as she was about time with Lola—not to mention Marshall, her favorite nephew, and her brand-new niece, Eva.

Ruth tried not to notice her mother's relief when she told her of Lola's request. Mother had four daughters to feed and care for in the deteriorating house. Earl was the only hand left on their land. Eugene, who wasn't yet ten, was being kept home from school to help Earl despite Riley's objections. The tension between Riley and the other men had escalated, and Riley had taken a small room in the village. He and Sarah were to marry once the winter passed.

Ruth packed a small personal bag, intending to stay for a week. Bessie gave her a collection of salves and tonics to share with Lola and Bea, and her mother packed a crate of okra, dilly beans, tomatoes, and spiced apples. Ruth snuggled the little ones and assured them she'd be back soon.

When she arrived, Lola bounced with excitement and led her to her own room. It was a small room with a twin bed, neatly made with a quilt Ruth didn't recognize. She scoffed at the idea that Lola might have made it herself. There was a small closet and a vanity table with two drawers set to the left and right side. There was a delicate wire chair tucked under the center of the table. On top of the vanity was a tall mirror and a vanity tray. On the tray there was a silver hairbrush and bottle of Bourjois Lily of the Valley.

"Thought you might like a little something special. To celebrate your move to A'lanah," Lola cooed from the doorway.

"I'm not movin' to A'lanah, Lola Bell," Ruth laughed. "I'm here to help out for a few days."

Lola winked at her. "Sure thing, little sister."

Ruth had never had her own room. She relished the privacy of it and spent the next hour filling the two vanity drawers with her things before sitting in front of the mirror and brushing her hair, smiling at her reflection. She peered about the room as if someone might be watching before picking up the perfume bottle and dabbing a touch at the back of each of her ears. The tiniest flicker of missing Ruby and Clara May danced through her thoughts, which she easily pushed aside—given their recent habit of circling themselves together, leaving her out of their world.

Ruth settled in with ease. Lola's house was quieter and newer. Charlie worked all day, and when he came home in the evenings, Lola made him a meal and listened to his unwindings with her chin perched in her hand, waiting for him to finish so she could get on with her evening. After supper, he ambled into their family room to read his paper and smoke his pipe. He was content in his life with Lola and Marshall and Eva, with no desire to lord over them or rant about injustices, and it showed in the way he relaxed into his chair and left them to their own conversations.

Marshall and Eva were happy children. Ruth bundled them in their coats and took them for morning walks. She entertained them through midday while Lola busied herself with being a wife and upstanding member of the community. She brushed aside the tickle of sadness she felt when Ruby and Clara May crossed her mind. They no longer had a need for her. Marshall and Eva did. She did the grocery shopping at the big grocery store and tried to look like she fit in, fighting back her urge to gawk at the bustle of cars and people. Charlie wanted to treat them one evening and took them all to the Rialto to see Margarita Fischer in Uncle Tom's Cabin.

"Maybe you want to stay on?" Lola ventured as the week came to an end and they sat gossiping on the porch swing—mostly about their brothers' wives. "Marshall and Eva adore you. And so do I. And Charlie's not the beast that Papa Jefferson is, now is he?"

Ruth looped her arm through her sister's and laid her head on her shoulder. It had been the loveliest week she could remember. She told Lola she'd be happy to stay on and help with Marshall and Eva. Lola called Mother and informed her that she was in desperate need of Ruth's assistance. Mother made no objection, and so Ruth settled into her room at Lola's in Atlanta.

Songs of Solomon 5:16
KJV

His mouth is most sweet: yea, he is altogether
lovely. This is my beloved, and this is my friend,
O daughters of Jerusalem.

Chapter 21

Quillan was waiting for her at the trolley station with his hat in his hands. After a full six weeks in the city with Lola and Charlie, she was returning home for Christmas. She adjusted the chocolate velvet beret she'd thrifted and patted self-consciously at her hair. Lola insisted that if she refused to bob her hair, the least she could do was put it into a fashionable twist.

She stepped off the trolley, and he reached to take her bag. The stillness of the Stone Mountain trolley station stunned her. She'd become accustomed to the frenetic energy of the Atlanta streets, the honking horns and babbling of overlapping conversation. The clinking of china teacups at the garden club and the colorful spray of hats and dresses. It was colder too—as if the body heat of two hundred thousand tightly packed Atlantans kept the city warmer than the outlying suburbs. Her village street that only weeks before filled her with expectation and intrigue now stretched before her—docile and provincial. She watched a stray farmer in dusty overalls amble into the pharmacy. A plump mother in a pale-blue dress hefted a crying child onto her hip.

Quillan took her hand and suggested they walk for a bit before he drove her home. Ruth's eyes began to adjust to the softer sights of her village, and she felt herself relax into the gentle bustle of her hometown. The festive decor of the main street winked at them as they strolled. Shiny glass balls caught the afternoon sun, and streams of velvet ribbon danced in the breeze. The ladies of Stone Mountain had purchased several strings of new electric lights for the town beautification. Ruth cooed with surprise at the glittery gleamings that were just becoming visible in the spruce trees lining the outside of the trolley station.

"It's as if they've captured the stars inside the trees," she said, leaning into Quillan. They walked past the woman in the blue dress, and Ruth smiled at her. The child was suckling a lollipop and content in his mother's arms.

"You smell nice," he said, leaning down to take in the scent. "Are you wearing perfume?"

Ruth blushed and nodded. She'd dabbed on a touch of the perfume Lola had given her.

"Pretty new hat. Sweet smellin'. You're like a different girl, Ruth Elizabeth."

Ruth's face fell, and she reached self-consciously for the hat. "You don't like it?"

"No, no, no . . . I like it," he assured her, then glanced away and added, "Different's all."

They sat on a bench. Ruth tilted her head in curiosity at the new red light installed atop Stone Mountain. It seemed more part of the decorations on this clear December afternoon—rather than a consequence of the recent tragedy, a warning light to future pilots.

"I been thinkin'," Quillan started. "Maybe you don't go back after Christmas. I mean, I know your sister needs your help and all, but . . . well . . . maybe it's not a good thing. You galavantin' about A'lanah. I was thinkin' maybe we could . . . maybe we get married and . . ."

Ruth's eyes flew wide. Again, she reached her hand to her hair in an attempt to calm her reaction. Beneath her excitement, something else stirred, a stubborn feeling made of reluctance and selfishness.

"Married?" she gasped, averting her eyes, unsettled by her own response.

Both she and Quillan had long been aware that their families encouraged—were even hopeful for—their union. But Ruth still found herself caught off guard. Quillan Johnson, handsome soon-to-be minister, thought well enough of her to ask her to be his wife.

The Shurlington family had a history of producing fine Baptist ministers, Uncle Henry and Cousin Davis among them. Maddox, Dollie's husband, had taken on a full-time parish, and the idea that Ruth would bring yet another minister into their fold assured their place in Heaven. As for the Johnsons, the Shurlingtons' urban connections were helping them all weather the rapid changes in their county. They weren't wealthy, but they had enough squirreled away to keep them in house and home. Marrying a preacher would make her sisters proud.

"Well, yeah. I mean." Quillan leaned back so he could look directly in her eyes. "I spoke to your papa and your brother Tom too. They both said it was a fine idea. If you'll have me. I was thinkin' I needed to find us a place and . . . times is hard right now. I know. But Daddy said I might could go on ahead and start my Bible studies. Maybe take on at a church down in Americus . . . or Perry. I mean, what do ya reckon? Wanna get married?"

He stumbled to the end of his proposal with a grin, warming

Ruth's heart.

"I'd love to marry you," she whispered. "I mean . . . soon enough I would."

Ruth shifted uncomfortably, balancing her answer with care. She didn't want to let Quillan think he wasn't the most important thing to her. An image of her neat room at Lola's teased her. She'd been free to do as she pleased for the last six weeks—with Marshall and Eva in tow. Her mornings had lingered in Lola's sunny kitchen, and her afternoons had strolled through parks, and her evenings were spent laughing with Lola's friends. There'd been the parade for Lucky Lindy and the sky full of colorful confetti. Even Wheeler had grown on her. Bonnie, who'd given birth to a plump little girl named Gertrude, whom Ruth immediately nicknamed Gertie, had a house that was practically space-age with all the gadgets he bought for her.

"Lola is in need a'me for a time. And I haven't had a second to say, but Bea found me a position at that new mattress company? I can help Mama . . ."

Her words tumbled, and she grabbed for any thought that wasn't the truth. She didn't want to return home to the farm. Not yet. She wanted more time.

She looked past Quillan and caught sight of the woman in the blue dress. The child was crying again. The man in the overalls came out of the pharmacy and joined them, lifting the child over his head and planting him firmly on his shoulders. The child laughed and snuggled around his father's neck. They were a comfortable little family.

"You were able to find work?" He interrupted her words and her thoughts, scrambling forward as he sensed her hesitation. He touched her chin with his fingers and brought her attention back to him. "That's real good, Ruthie. I mean, not that I'll have you workin' when we're married, but there's a time for savin', right? We don't have to get married right away. It is my intention to make you my wife. I wanna know if you're willin'. To have me. In due time."

She laced her fingers with his and assured him that she couldn't think of anything that would make her happier. For the next hour they talked of the future. She assured him she knew her Mama's secret banana pudding recipe. Quillan thought it a grand idea to keep a pen for peacocks and a garden dedicated to flowers. Ruth vowed to learn from Bessie how to make salves and tonics from the medicine garden they'd undoubtedly plant. Quillan talked of finding lodgings and a situation in one of the southern churches.

They decided they would each set aside a small amount from their respective work to start their savings. They'd spend the week apart but meet every Sunday at the Mount Zion Baptist Church. It'd be a year—maybe two—and they could start a life of their own.

Happiness wrapped around Ruth's thoughts. She'd have a year—maybe two—on her own terms. Then she'd settled into the perfect marriage just as Dollie had. She'd love Quillan the way her mother had loved her father. She'd have a dozen babies and a peacock.

By the time they ran out of words, the new Christmas lights twinkled in the dusk. The cold settled into their bones. They jogged their way back to the car to get their blood warm. Quillan took his time returning Ruth to her front porch, lingering on every step as he walked her to her front door. He leaned down to brush his sugarcane lips against hers, as he had done in the oak tree that summer.

"You are gonna make a good wife, Ruth Elizabeth Shurlington."

Her eyes shone, but she said nothing. She turned and left him standing on the porch wanting more of her. Just as Lola Bell had taught her to do.

It was raining on the first day of 1928. The New Year had come with the promise of more babies to feed and tend but little else. Papa Jefferson shuffled across the field from his little house and sat at the Talking Table gulping his coffee and reading the morning paper. Mother brought him his breakfast, and when he finished, he made his way to the rocker on the porch.

Ruth felt her body tighten as she listened to him bully Earl and Eugene. By midafternoon, the slur in his voice told her he was under the shine. She whispered to herself, "One more day."

She folded most of her things into her small bag. She took a moment to admire the garment she laid out on her bed. Mother had gifted her with three yards of pretty green cotton material for Christmas, and she was feeling proud of the new dress she'd made. It was a simple day dress, but her stitching was fine, and she felt savvy when she added the two deep pockets to the front. She planned to wear the dress tomorrow when she returned to her little room at Lola's.

When evening came, she called Papa Jefferson for supper. He didn't respond, and she blew out a huff of air in exasperation. He was sleeping or drunk or both. She tried not to think of him around her mother every day and ignored the guilt she felt over her freedom in Atlanta. She stepped out on the porch to wake him. The rocker was still, and he was slumped to one side, slack-jawed. He was pale, and his lips had a blue tinge. His eyes stared glassy and unseeing out into the fields.

"Mama," Ruth croaked, and then louder, "Mama!"

Mother stepped onto the porch. She regarded his lifeless body with indifference. The moment was silent, laced with dirt and ash. The pungent odor of his bowels releasing perfumed the air.

I Peter 4:12-13
KJV

*Beloved, think it not strange concerning the fiery
trial which is to try you, as though some strange
thing happened unto you: But rejoice, inasmuch
as ye are partakers of Christ's sufferings;
that, when his glory shall be revealed,
ye may be glad also with exceeding joy.*

Chapter 22

January 1929

"I cain't believe how grown you are, Ruth Elizabeth," Bessie admired. "I mean, I swear it seems like yesterday you were picking your bloomers out a'your butt crack."

Ruth turned herself this way and that, admiring her store-bought brown silk dress. She was to be a bridesmaid in Bessie's wedding. Bessie had taken the trolley into the city to spend the day wedding planning with her sisters. She'd stopped first at Lola's to have Ruth try on the dress she was to wear. Ruth was so pleased to be included that she nudged away the nagging thought that Bessie had asked her only because Dollie was pregnant again and couldn't be in the wedding. James Vining had proposed, and unlike their other siblings, Bessie had convinced him to stay close to Mother by settling into Scottsdale, one of the many chic communities rising on the outskirts of Atlanta. Since half their family had moved to Atlanta, Bessie's decision to stay close to Mother was a relief to them all.

"Thanks . . . ?" Ruth pulled her hair into a twist at her neck, poofing it forward so it appeared bobbed. "Mama says you're gonna be keepin' your job up at the quarry too. James say you could?"

"He did. He's very progressive, my James. Seems like everybody's looking for work these days, and James thought it might be reckless to let go a'my income too soon. We're saving it. Plus Wheeler says it's helpful to have ears at the quarry. Not a one a'those boys thinks twice about what they say when I'm around, so I get intel."

"You mean like a spy? Wheeler has you workin' as a spy now?"

"Not Wheeler . . . not really, anyway. Ever since he started that construction company, he's been working one angle after another. He likes knowing what jobs are coming through. He and Tom have been going gangbusters. I suppose a little inside information can only help us all, hmm?"

"I cannot believe Tom threw in with Wheeler. Of all our brothers, I was certain Tom would figure it out. Keep the garden alive? I guess between the pestilence, the drought, the government—and Wheeler's high-flyin' ideas—he toppled."

Lola sailed into the room, joining the conversation as if she'd been there the whole time. Bessie scooted over so Lola could join her on the bed and weigh in on Ruth's dress fitting. Lola winked at them, teasing, "Weak kneed, our Tom."

"That and Carrie's no farmer's wife," Bessie scoffed at Lola's analysis. "At least not a poor farmer's wife. I think once Riley took off to A'lanah, and Earl jumped on board with Wheeler? . . . Tom's tired. Needs new inspiration. He's handy with a hammer anyhows. Did a fine job on his and Carrie's house."

"Why did Earl give in to Wheeler?" Ruth asked.

"Lucille." Lola laughed. "He's been smitten by the love bug. A fancy love bug who told him she'd never marry a farmer. I swear these brothers a'ours have a habit a'chasin' expensive skirts."

"Speakin' a'skirts. I was over at Riley's this week." Ruth slipped off the bridesmaid's dress and back into her day dress. She gave her sisters a sideways glance. "Sarah has . . . taken to motherhood slow. She lets that new baby cry all the time. When she picks him up? She holds him like he's a rotten cantaloupe about to break open. She even crinkles her nose at the smell."

"Mmm . . . Bea told me," Lola affirmed. "Says she's practically motherin' that baby. Sarah cain't bring herself to so much as brush her own hair. Bea don't mind much. Poor thing's been seein' the doctor."

Bessie leaned in and whispered. "She might be barren. I'm thinking Baby Elliott's making the whole thing less devastating. But poor Riley. Married himself a potato."

"Maybe," Ruth acknowledged. "What about you, hmm? You gonna keep spyin' for Wheeler once you have a baby?"

"Oh my heavens, no! Even now I have to admit it is a struggle at the quarry office. The way they left the mountain with just the giant head of General Lee floating? Folks come in and ask why we only blasted a head into the mountain? Where's his body? Where's his horse? They ask me. It's embarrassing. Having to explain to strangers the bankruptcy."

"It's not like it's your bankruptcy." Ruth gave her sister an amused look.

"Isn't it, though? Aren't we all goin' bankrupt?" Lola quipped.

"All but Maddox and Dollie," Bessie noted. They all nodded in agreement.

Maddox and Dollie, with soon-to-be-five children in tow, dug their boots into the nutrient-depleted Georgia earth and were making a go of their farming business. Dollie, like all of them, had been well-schooled on how to turn a profit in every part of the farming life. The two pivoted into consumer demands, investing in hogs and planting the fields with more secure cash crops. Maddox the farmer kept his thumb on the pulse of agricultural innovation. Maddox the minister received a small stipend from his parish. Combined with Dollie's odd jobs, the Grant family was self-sufficient.

Fussing came from the children's room. Eva had woken from her nap. Lola gave Ruth a pleading look. "Would you mind, Rue? She quiets so easy in your care. Me and Bessie need to finish up a few more things here before we head over to Rich's."

"A'course, Lola. I got her."

"And maybe get her dressed too? Pull out her buggy?" Lola added. Ruth nodded and slipped out of the room to care for Lola's little girl. Eva was growing into a sweet toddler—she'd turned one in December—and Ruth adored dressing her to go out. They were all going to Rich's Department Store to pick up a few things from Bessie's wedding list.

After the initial good tidings brought by her unofficial engagement to Quillan, Ruth's siblings reimmersed themselves in the perpetual motion of their lives. Weddings and babies and businesses kept them focused on their own households. Ruth garnered attention only when she intersected with those households—if she was needed to tend a child or cook a meal or deliver a package or stand up at an altar to celebrate another. Their need for her created a redundancy to her days—habit propelled her between her sister's homes in Stone Mountain and East Atlanta.

On Mondays, she took the trolley from Stone Mountain straight to Woodbine Avenue to bring her siblings goods from the Stone Mountain farm. She helped with the children or ran errands for her brother's wives before starting the afternoon shift at the mattress company. On the other weekday mornings, she helped Lola get Marshall off to school. In the evenings, she tended Lola's baby Eva while Lola made supper or entertained friends. The time in between was spent stitching mattress covers until her fingers bled so she could pad her savings for a life with Quillan.

On Saturday mornings, she packed a small bag with penny candies for the farm children and weekend necessities. She took the trolley back to Stone Mountain to spend the day with Mother and give Dollie and Bessie a reprieve. Mother would be waiting for her on the porch with a strong cup of coffee, laced with sugar and milk, and they rocked and sipped as Ruth filled her in on Bea and Lola and her brothers.

Sundays she got up early and dressed her best. She visited her father's grave with fresh flowers before service. Quillan was always there waiting for her. Their Sunday meetings were the only time they were able to spend together.

They talked about children. Ruth wanted to have as many babies as God would give her. Quillan praised her for her godliness. He talked about where they'd live once they married and about spreading God's word. He had this idea that he could give services in the squatter camps. They laughed about General Lee's head and decided it was neither honoring nor worshipping but, like most human endeavors, a failed attempt to harness the divine.

She told Quillan all about Lola's midtown apartment and the people she met in the building. She described the neat square cottages with the small square lawns on Woodbine, where Wheeler, Riley, and Bea lived. She told him about the small porches that looked out onto the street and how there was always someone walking by.

On Sunday evenings, he said goodnight to her on her porch

with the same light kiss and same sweet tip to his hat. Quillan saw everything as savable and fixable. He believed the world could be rid of war and anger if people loved hard enough. He loved pie and iced tea and refused to take a smoke. So Ruth never told him she'd taken up smoking or that the warm smell of whiskey reminded her of celebrations with her father. Quillan told her all his dreams. She listened and nodded and tried to reply with words of which she hoped he'd approve. When he asked her of her dreams, she replied that his dreams were hers.

Monday mornings, she started the cycle over. She drifted in and out of sleep as the streetcar clanged and jerked and clattered back to the other half of her family. She was becoming vaguely aware that when she left Quillan she felt very little—and that when she returned to the city, she felt very little. The days blended in a toxic fog of red dust and auto fumes. She wondered if this was the dust that she'd return to—she wondered if anyone would even notice.

It was a Friday afternoon as she and Bea were clocking out that she heard a familiar voice.

"I was a'wonderin' when I'd run into you, Firefly."

Electricity shot through her as she replaced her punch card and turned to meet the blue eyes of Leonidas Brantley. He was thinner than when she'd last seen him, and the lines of his face had deepened. He held a cigarette between his teeth, and his hat sat sideways over his black hair. He reminded her of Valentino.

"Hey there, Bea." He tipped his hat in her sister's direction. Bea gave him a hard look.

"Aww, what'sa matter, Bea? Didn't Martin tell ya I'd come back to town? I'm doin' some repair work here for a coupla weeks. Better than starvin', yeah?"

Bea gave him a tight smile. "No, Martin didn't say a thing 'bout you being back in town." Bea added an odd emphasis to the words *back in town.* "And I don't think it's a good idea for you to be talking to Ruth. She's got no use for you."

Bea gave Ruth a tug, and they started the walk back home. She glanced back to see Leonidas watching them, one hand in his pocket and the other tapping out his cigarette.

"What was that about?" she asked Bea.

Bea pursed her lips. "That one's not our kind, Ruthie. I don't know how you know him, but I mean it when I say he's no good."

"Papa hired him on a few years back for a harvest. That's how I came to know him. How do you know him?"

"Martin's come across both the Brantley boys. They did some auto repairs for his daddy just after the war ended. Leonidas and his kid brother Hoyt sold him some insurance on the car too. Turns out the insurance company went bankrupt not long after. Those brothers swore they knew nothing of it, but Martin's daddy lost a fair penny. Hoyt ran off to Michigan the very next month. Took a girl with him too. Fair ruined her. She came back a year later divorced and with a baby on her hip."

"Divorced?" Ruth was enthralled by the story.

"Extreme cruelty was what she told the courts. That brother's still in Michigan. One likes to think he's too ashamed of himself to cross back over the Georgia state line. Probably not why though. There's probably a warrant out for him, and he's avoiding retribution by staying in Michigan."

They walked along in silence. Bea, contemplating.

"Honey, the thing is—there's more you don't know about men like Leonidas Brantley than you do know. Men like that'll ruin a girl just by getting close to her. Is that what you want? That one's run through a couple of wives. Both dead now, and truth is no one seems to be familiar with the finer points of how either one of them passed on. And that brother of his? He'll be burning, I'm sure, for the things he's done. Let me ask you: where's Leonidas Brantley been the last two years? Hmm? I'll tell you. He's been in prison, that's where. Martin says he killed a man."

Ruth expressed the appropriate sense of horror at the things Bea had said and assured her sister she'd walk the other way if Leonidas tried to speak to her again. She shivered at the thought of him and the vague memory of his touch.

The first time he waited for her against the brick wall of the sewing company was on a Monday—the day she went in for the afternoon shift without Bea. She pretended not to see him. When he spoke to her, she nodded curtly and went straight inside.

The third time he came, he brought her wild violets. The freshly dug roots were tucked into an old tin can. He stepped into her path and extended the delicate plant as an offering. She took the tin can with hesitation.

"It's kind of you, Lee," she murmured, fighting between her promise to walk away and the manners her mother had ingrained in her.

"They're my daughter's favorite," he said, shifting shyly from one foot to the other. He looked down at his hands and, with distraction, twisted the ring on his finger. "You remind me a'her. Figured if I cain't give 'em to her, maybe you might like 'em. I didn't mean to bother you none."

He gave her a slight bow, shoved his hands in his pockets, and bid her a pleasant day. He whistled as he walked away,

The fifth time, he brought wild blackberries he'd found out in the woods.

"You like blackberries?" he asked.

"I do. Mama used to have me and Ruby and Riley collect 'em

for her cobblers. Daddy loved her blackberry cobblers." Ruth let the memory of her father fall between them.

"Must a been hard," he consoled. "Losin' yer daddy like you did. You wanna tell me 'bout him? I'm gonna bet he was a fine man."

The words spilled from her. She ate blackberries and laughed over the stories her father used to tell. Her sharing spilled past her father and she told him a little about her sisters and brothers. She didn't think to ask him much—he was so good at listening to her. She stopped seeing his worn, dirty clothes, and the stench of his unwashed body added to her recollection. He smelled like her brothers after a long day of work. She saw only his smile and his sky-blue eyes and the tender purple violets and the plump ripeness of late-summer blackberries.

"Ain't a thing wrong with havin' a friend, is there?" he said to her finally. "Sounds to me like you could use one. Cain't say I have too many myself."

He held out his hand to her, a gesture of his friendship.

"I'm engaged, you know," she answered with some hesitation. His laughter at her answer was good-natured. He dropped his hand.

"I got no designs on ya, Firefly. Old man like me? Naw." He nudged her shoulder and looked at her sideways, his eyes crinkling with his grin. "Just bein' yer friend seems blessin' enough."

Ruth narrowed her eyes at him. but couldn't stop the amusement from shining through on her face.

"Awlright, then. Got myself a new friend. What a day this is."

He winked at her and walked away.

It became his habit to show up at the mattress company once a week. When he offered her a smoke on one of those afternoons, she took it, and she let him light it for her. She leaned against the brick wall with him and let him ask her things. No one else asked her things. They told her things.

He commented on how hard it must be for her to go back and forth between her family every weekend, pulled from one world into the other. He asked about Quillan and said he sounded like a fine boy. She thought it odd when he admitted he could neither read nor write. When she offered to help him, he waved her away. He told her letters never had made sense to him, and given that he worked better with his hands than his mind, he'd given up trying to decipher them long ago.

Sometimes she'd ask why he kept coming around. "You remind me of my daughter," he might say. He said she made him feel happy and lighter about the world. He only came on Mondays. He insisted that if Bea knew he was coming round, she wouldn't understand. Bea had the wrong idea about things. He softened his words by saying that he understood why Bea would want to protect her. She, Ruth, was a special girl. He, too, wanted to protect her.

"Bea says you've spent time in jail," she ventured.

"Sent me away on a passel a'lies. People needin' someone to blame." He bit at the end of his cigarette. "There was an accident and somebody died. A real good friend a'mine, name a'Hodges, mind you. Me and Hodges? We were tight. I ain't the kinda man that'd go and kill a friend. But then he died, and somebody had to be blamed for it. Guess I was that somebody."

His face grew dark. He stepped away from her, pacing up and down the dirt-bare strip butted against the brick wall. He gave his cigarette a hard flick to the ground.

"'Course you're not that kinda man . . ." She reached to reassure him, but he brushed her away. He pounded his cigarette pack against the heel of his hand, freeing a fresh light. He stuck it between his lips without lighting it.

"What am I supposed to say when you ask me these sorta things? Bea ain't gonna tell you the truth 'bout me, Ruth. She's gonna keep passin' on the lie that I was to blame for that accident that killed Hodges."

He paused, considering his words.

"Y'sisters wanna keep you under their thumb—takin' care a their houses and their children. Don' serve 'em well to have you makin' friends outside a'their control, does it? I am yer friend, ain't I? How you think it makes me feel havin' you—you—question me 'bout things that I cain't do a gawd-dayumed thing about, huh? For long, yer gonna believe these terrible lies yer sisters tell 'bout me. Tell me we cain't be friends no more."

The cigarette bounced as he spoke. Sullenness oozed off his shoulders. He lit the cigarette, ignoring the imploring look in her eyes. He tossed the match and started walking away.

"No, Lee, I know who you are. They don't. Maybe come round and meet 'em?" She spoke to his receding back. "Where you goin'?"

"I ain't got no room for this kind a'condemnation, Ruth. You done got me thinkin' about ol' Hodges. Got my brain all stuck back there. You made it hard for me . . . too hard for me to talk."

He strode away without looking back at her. She wanted to call after him and undo the dark mood that had descended over him.

In the days that followed, she replayed the conversation over and again in her mind, picking through his words. His anger made little sense to her, so she chose to see it as sadness and hurt. He was hurt that she had questioned his character. Why wouldn't he be? She would feel the same.

By the end of the week, she wondered if she'd see him again. She went back to Stone Mountain for the weekend, distracted by her thoughts. She was angry for thinking of him at all, and she tried to push him aside, focusing instead on the bevy of nieces and nephews who clamored for her attention.

"Penny for your thoughts," Quillan nudged when she failed to respond to his conversation.

"No thoughts," she dismissed, "Feeling a bit poorly is'all."

She feigned a cough.

"Lord I hope it ain't the flu." He furrowed his brow and laid a hand on her back, inspecting her as if he might see the germs crawling on her.

Later when he leaned in for his Sunday night kiss, she turned her head away, clearing her throat. She didn't want to risk passing on her germs.

When Monday came, Leonidas was waiting by the brick wall. He told her he had been so upset thinking about his dead friend that he needed to be alone. She could understand that, couldn't she? He said she was the one person he could be himself around. She leaned in and met his eyes.

"I don't mind a bad mood none, Lee." She smiled, confused by her relief that he had returned. "I feel plenty sad when I get to rememberin' my daddy or Cousin Frank. Sounds like you miss your friend. I'm sorry if I made it worse on you."

"I forgive ya, Firefly. You were bein' curious. Don' blame ya for wonderin' why an old man like me'd been locked up."

"You're not an old man, Lee."

"I am, though. Next to a purty girl like you? You could be my daughter. Cain't reckon ya see more than a broken-down poor sap moonin' over a girl who's out a'my reach."

Ruth tried to understand his words. She felt the need to reassure him.

"I think you are plenty handsome, Leonidas Brantley. Like Valentino if he were a farmer. Any girl'd be lucky to have your attention. I like when you come by here.”

She felt awkward. Aware of herself. Her words danced around a shadow of a thought she couldn't quite grasp. When he waited for her, she felt less invisible. She'd come to rely on his presence and on their conversations. She'd tuck away thoughts throughout the week that she knew she could share with him. Thoughts she knew he'd listen to and mull over and offer his perspective on.

It was one of those Monday conversations when he asked her if Quillan had ever kissed her. She blushed and told him she didn't see how that was any of his business. He flicked his cigarette and leaned toward her, closer to her than was his habit. His eyes danced with amusement.

"Well, I'm just wonderin' if this little church boy has any idea how to kiss a girl a'tall."

His eyes dropped to her mouth. Her heart pounded against her throat. It was the first time his tone suggested he didn't think much of Quillan.

"I-I mean, he does," she stuttered. "I-I like his kisses fine, and I think you're bein' very rude, Leonidas Brantley."

"How ya gonna be certain 'less ya been kissed by someone other than this Quillan Johnson?" He stepped closer to her, letting his hand rest on her hip.

She didn't answer and instead looked down at her feet, her mind on Quillan's gentle brush against her lips and tilt of his hat. Every Sunday night, the same.

"How 'bout we test it out? Ya think? I'll give ya a little kiss, and you can decide if yer church boy's kissin' yer right. Little kiss ain't gonna matter, is it?"

Her eyes met his, and she said neither yes or no, but she didn't look away. This was a game—a dare. She nearly heard Riley whispering, "You ain't scared, are ya?"

He put his hand to her face and rubbed her jawline with the pad of his calloused thumb. He teased her. Leaning in just enough that she could taste the earthiness of his breath. She felt captured. Spellbound by something she couldn't name. The corner of his mouth lifted in a faint smile, and the wolfish rumble of his voice sent a chill down her spine.

His lips were warm and soft, a strange contrast to the cool scruff of his beard scratching against her face. His grip on her neck tightened. He teased at her lips with his tongue, smiling against her mouth. Before she could protest, his tongue forced her mouth wider, and he shed the cloak of gentleness. His kiss became bestial, as if he'd been released cold and starving from a chain. The hand that had rested on her hip pulled her against him.

He released her mouth; she shivered at the sound of his breath against her ear. He clutched her hair and inhaled.

Free. Flying. Playing among the clouds. Her hands lifted to his face. Then fear swept through her. She was being slammed between shame and desire. She pushed away—freeing herself. She held her hand against his chest, keeping him at an arm's length. He made no effort to bring her back to him.

"Is that how yer church boy kisses you?"

There was no more playfulness in his voice. The contours of his brow—the setting of his mouth—hardened. He took a step back. Disoriented, she turned without a word and left him standing there—relaxed and rapacious against the brick wall.

I Corinthians 7:9
KJV

But if they cannot contain, let them marry:
for it is better to marry than to burn.

Chapter 23

Quillan waited at her father's headstone. August sun glinted off his corn silk hair. His amber eyes lit up when he caught sight of her, and regret coursed through her. Quillan—so pure and bright. She—a Jezebel. A Jezebel like Lola. She told herself she hadn't let Leonidas kiss her at all. He'd done it without waiting for her answer. It had been a dare. A joke. She had stopped him, and she had walked away. She refused to acknowledge the ache in her belly or the way she trembled when he let her go.

She loved Quillan. She wanted to marry Quillan. Her family was proud of her—happy. Leonidas was a scoundrel, a goblin from the mountain, a temptation of Satan. The yearnings he stirred in her were evil and sinful and wrong. Wrong. She—she—was evil and sinful and wrong. The dream snake hissed through her thoughts.

That night when Quillan leaned in to kiss her goodbye, she wound her arms around his neck and tried to deepen the kiss. She needed him to make her feel what Leonidas had made her feel. He pulled away, eyeing her with a hard look. He ran a hand nervously through his hair and took a firm step back from her.

"What's the matter with you, Ruthie?" He glanced around him as if he'd misplaced something before kissing her hurriedly on the forehead.

This time, it was he who walked away, leaving her humiliated and betrayed by her own longings.

Leonidas didn't show up at the mattress company on Monday. Ruth convinced herself she was relieved. Leonidas was older than Wheeler. He compromised her promise to Quillan and stirred in her the lusts of the flesh. Lusts that Brother Johnson called evil and Quillan found disdainful.

Leonidas wasn't her kind—as Bea had said. She forced her thoughts on Quillan. Recollection of his disappointment and of his obvious discomfort made her cringe. She felt stupid. Of course, he wouldn't kiss her as Leonidas had. Leonidas was a temptation, and temptations were of the Devil. Quillan was a man of God.

Her sisters were married to men of faith—ambitious men of means. Her picture book thoughts flipped through images of them in their kitchens with their cherub babies—images of them in pressed day dresses kneeling before their husbands, removing their shoes and filling their pipes. She tried to put herself in those pictures. Instead, she saw Leonidas shaking his head at her willingness to be used by them. Leonidas saw her as a woman with ideas and not as a girl with two hands to spare.

She was awkward, not as pretty as they. Lola was gregarious, while Ruth struggled to speak up. Dollie was unflappable. Ruth was uncertain. Bea was kind, but Ruth battled her mean thoughts. Bessie was smart enough to finish high school, and Ruth had chosen to quit. Shame flared at thoughts of Ruby and Clara May—both surpassing her, discarding her, having no more use for her. She ticked off all the ways she couldn't be like her sisters. Unless she married Quillan. Marrying Quillan would make them all proud—by marrying Quillan she would belong inside their circle.

The week crawled by. Guilt crept across her skin. Leonidas was a friend. She touched her lips and winced at the memory of Quillan's rejection. Dear Jesus, Forgive me. I will never let it happen again, she promised to the unseen.

When she saw Quillan again, she begged his forgiveness for the way she'd kissed him, just as she had begged the Lord's forgiveness. He told her if he were a better man he'd not need to marry. He'd be like the apostle Paul and live only for the work of the Lord. He chastised her for her lustful behavior. He took her hands in his, and they prayed together.

Quillan asked God to forgive her for tempting God's servant and to strengthen their resolve as they kept themselves holy for the sanctuary of marriage. He put his arms around her, offering his own forgiveness to her and, with piety, kissed the top of her head.

Each Monday came and went without any sign of Leonidas. She missed him, as if the color had drained from her days, but she'd been given respite from his consuming presence. Quillan didn't mention the night on the porch again, and they returned to the innocence of their Sunday night routine.

The call from the farm came early on a December morning. Dollie informed Lola that Ruth would not be coming back into town, and instead the family needed to make their way to the farm. Papa Perkins had passed on peacefully in his sleep.

At the funeral, there was an ever-shrinking contingent of the old boys in gray. The Perkins family were a small lot compared to the Shurlington clan. Mother and Aunt Norah, having lost their brother Lovett and stepmother Ann a few years back, stood comforting each other by the grave. The bugler played taps, and the kind old shoemaker was lowered back into the earth.

The family gathered at the farm to mourn and break bread. It was becoming more common that their gatherings were instigated by mourning rather than celebration. Quillan and his father had joined them, offering pastoral comfort. Ruth organized the casseroles and served coffee from her father's rusting coffeepot. A short in the cord had been mended with a wrapping of electrical tape, and kitchen grease had made a permanent home in the joints of the old appliance. No one was willing to replace the coffeepot—not while it still made a pot of coffee, no matter how begrudgingly.

"Mama, it makes no sense for you to stay here anymore." Bessie reached for Mother's hands. Mother, dry-eyed and stoic, scoffed and waved her away. She'd returned to her old self since Papa Jefferson's death. Quillan leaned against the counter listening. He lifted his empty cup in Ruth's direction. Ruth refilled it without thinking. She hesitated, vaguely aware of the automation of her servitude.

"Really, Mama, I've got enough room to house a circus. It's not like I live all the way in the city. I'm just over in Scottsdale. It's nearer the church too," Bessie cajoled as if she were speaking to a small child.

Dollie and Bea chimed in. Lola rocked back and took a drag on her cigarette, watching her mother and sisters beneath tired eyes. Mother wouldn't even consider moving into the city, so Lola and Bea were pretty much off the hook.

"She's gotta fancy new kitchen too, Mama. An icebox. And her toilet room is real nice," purred Dollie. Ruth knew that Dollie felt guilty for not having the room to take their mother in. Lola eyed Dollie with contempt.

"Y'all aren't coming round and helping me. This house is wearing down about as fast as I am." Mother grunted. She reached for a napkin to dab at her nose, unused to idle hands.

Tom strolled over and kissed her head. He kneeled down in front of her and looked up into her eyes. "Mama, Bessie wants to help. We all wanna help. You been takin' care a'ever'body for so long. Me and Wheeler could really use an extra hand with the buildin' business—I was thinkin' Eugene could come on over. Stay with me and Carrie. Bessie's house'll be full a'babies before long, and she'll be needin' your help again."

Tom swallowed as if he were choking on his own tongue before continuing. "We can sell the land here and tuck away some money."

Mother softened at Tom's words. No place in Georgia had higher land values than Dekalb County. Tom glanced over at Ruth and winked. She shook her head at his smooth talking. She leaned against the counter next to Quillan and rested against his shoulder. Despite the reasons, it was satisfying to have the family all together in the old farmhouse.

"What about the girls?" She twisted the napkin in her hands.

Lola leaned in and joined the conversation. "Ruthie is practically livin' with me and Charlie already. Ruby and Clara May's gonna move in over at Bea's. They're excited about it."

"I don't wanna be trouble, Bessie. Gotta earn my keep—you'll likely be needing help once them babies come. You've never been good with the young ones."

Bessie clapped her hands together. "No, no, Mama, I'm terrible with the babies—so you'll be no trouble a'tall."

Dollie looked relieved that Mother would be ensconced at Bessie's. Lola blew a cloud of smoke into the air and gave a half smile. Ruth knew what Lola was thinking. She'd heard her talking to Charlie. Once Mother sold the land, there'd be a nest egg, all right. There'd be a little nest egg for all of them.

Proverbs 14:12
KJV

There is a way which seemeth right unto a man,
but the end thereof are the ways of death.

Chapter 24

It was her eighteenth birthday. In the past three months, the world had plummeted into a death spiral of poverty and want. Ruth didn't grasp how it had happened—though her brothers talked of nothing else. They were calling it the Great Depression—the Slump of 1929. Jobs somehow became more scarce than they already were. Yet more and more people flooded Atlanta, hoping to find work. They didn't find work. Instead, the squatter camps grew, and there were food lines all over the city. The ghettos were rife with the diseases of overcrowding, and the city resources—from water to sanitation—reached their breaking point.

Ruth finished her shift at the mattress factory and stepped out into the cool February air. Leonidas was leaning against the brick as if he hadn't disappeared for six months. She stared at him. She took a cigarette from her purse and put it between her lips. He flicked a match between his fingers, bringing it to life, and held it under the tip of her handroll and then stepped back a respectful distance.

"You done gone married that church boy yet?" He kept his eyes downcast, picking at some invisible irritation on his fingertips.

She blew smoke into the air with what she hoped was Lola-esque nonchalance. She gave a slight shake to her head and kept walking. He caught up to her and matched her gait.

"I brought ya somethin'." He held out a small box tied with twine. It was clear the box was used. It was marked with the Sophie Mae candy logo—the shop that once employed Lola as a candy girl. "It ain't much, but I was thinkin' about it bein' yer birthday n'all."

She slowed—wary of him—and took the old candy box. Not one other person had remembered her birthday. Not even Quillan. She untied the twine and opened the box. It was filled with bright-red hawthorn berries. Nestled within the berries was a tiny carved animal. The familiar gnarled surface of a peach pit had been honed and shined into a warm, gleaming fox. She smiled, removing the tiny fox from the box. She blushed at her own fascination—popping one of the wild treats in her mouth to give herself an excuse for the silence.

"Those are right perfect haws, Leonidas Brantley. Where'd you find 'em?"

"Outskirts o' town. Bunch of bushes there." He removed his hat and placed it on his heart. "Listen, I was thinkin' maybe we could spend some time together. Maybe you don' take the trolley tonight. I bought me a truck. Lemme give you a ride home, huh? Save you the nickel."

"Lee. I really do appreciate you rememberin' my birthday. That's awful sweet, but I am engaged. It's best you don't show up here no more."

Her words lacked the undergirding of conviction as she ran her fingers over the tiny lines that defined the fox's face—the grooves of his curved tail carved in delicate detail. She'd only ever seen whittling this fine from her own daddy's hand. Leonidas, hearing her hesitation, stepped toward her and laid a tentative hand on her arm.

"Listen, Ruth. I didn't mean nothin' by disappearin'. I had some things that needed doin'. You kept sayin' how you was gonna marry that church boy. I didn't wanna hear it no more. I figure you'd a'married him by now. Yer belly roundin' out with a young'un. But I saw ol' Martin, and I admit, I asked after ya. He said you were still workin' here and well . . . , I-I wanted to see ya. We been friends for a while , and I cain't see no harm in catchin' up."

She felt the breath moving in and out of her lungs. The little fox peered up at her, cool and sweet in her fingers. The heat of his hand on her arm seeped into her blood.

"We're friends?"

"If that's what you want. Hard bein' friends with a woman as purty as you, but . . ." He stepped closer and seemed to make a decision. "I take that back. It might be an impossibility to only be yer friend. I missed you, Firefly. I ain't never felt like this. Not with anybody. Feels like you were chasin' me in my dreams."

"Lee, I . . ." The wrong words came out then. Words she hadn't meant to say. "I missed you too."

He was kissing her again. Hungrier than before. She tasted the tart sweetness of hawthorn and didn't resist when he pulled her closer. He was full of heat. She felt it radiating from him, and he kissed her as if she was the only thing that would ever satisfy him.

He pulled away, and she laid her hands against his chest to steady herself. She had missed him. She hunched her shoulders into his arms. He was strong, and she felt it.

"I wanna take you for a drive," he whispered and led her to an old Ford truck parked on the roadside. He opened the door and held out his hand to help her in.

The truck lunged out onto the road. She wouldn't be forgiven for stepping out on Quillan. She stole a look at Leonidas and his profile etched against the purple sky. Maybe she didn't want Quillan at all. She wasn't like Dollie, and a man such as Quillan needed a woman like Dollie. Leonidas made the hairs on her arms stand up. He made her feel smart and beautiful.

The lights of Atlanta began to recede. The stars woke in the night sky. Leonidas turned down an old farm road, and in the distance, Ruth could make out the sloping lines of the old out-buildings crumbling back to the earth. Leonidas came to a stop at a pull-off tucked into an overgrown and abandoned sugarcane field. Ruth took in the endless stretch of land and field around them. They were in a dead space—all the inhabitants of the farm had vanished, and the city lights had yet to consume it. Nothing moved or lived here save the yellowed and severed remnants of the sugarcane. She shifted uncomfortably on the bench seat, shoving aside Bea's warnings with a shiver.

"You cold?"

He handed her a flask. She took a long draught the way she'd seen Lola do. The homemade liquid burned as it went down. It was sharper than the stuff her brothers made. He turned to her and took the nape of her hair in his hand, exposing the winter white of her neck.

"It's okay. I ain't gonna hurt ya," he purred against her skin. "Relax."

He leaned in and bit at her throat. She shivered.

He freed her hair and caught her mouth with his. His kiss was insistent. She tried to push him back, but his arms were steel girders wrapped around her.

He hummed in her ear, "Yer awlright, darlin'. Little kissin's all. I haven't been able to think a'nothin' but you. I think I love ya. I want ya to feel good. You want me to feel good too, don' ya?"

His hand slid beneath her dress. In one swift movement he had pushed her panties aside and shoved his fingers inside of her. She cried out. Confused by the rush of desire and dread. His eyes glazed into a dark, stormy blue, and he nipped at her flesh as if she were his last meal.

He pushed her backward on the truck seat. She heard the heavy buckle of his belt clank.

"No, Lee . . . I . . ."

He pressed his hand against her throat and wedged himself between her legs. He was inside her with one hard thrust. She gasped in pain as her head hit the window crank on the passenger door.

His voice slithered against her ear. "Oh Gawd, Ruth. I knew you was mine. You ain't never done this."

His own revelation gave him no pause, and he thrust harder. She could feel him inside of her, the rush of liquid as she bled. He let his weight lay on her, pushing her thigh against the hard dashboard. He anchored himself with his hands atop her head, protecting her from the window crank. She felt this as a kindness—a consideration of her comfort. He pulled her downward as he thrust up, grunting against her shoulder until he curled into her. He pounded her with one last stroke as his need was satisfied. Then he lay limp on her chest. His weight made it hard for her to breathe. They were wet with sweat and sex and blood.

It was over. Before she could think about it. Before she could say whether or not she wanted him. It had happened. All she'd been told—everything that led up to this loss of her purity—remained unmoved. Nothing changed. Nothing grand or dangerous or shattering happened. The train whistled in the distance. A man lay catching his breath on her sweaty body.

It seemed forever before he came back to life. Ruth felt the awkwardness of her limbs splayed against the dashboard and the door and the steering wheel. He sat up, pulling her with him.

"Thank you," he said.

Should she say you're welcome? She adjusted her dress, grateful for its whimsical cherry pattern. Her mind was empty—not a single thought stirred. She'd had the same feeling the morning her father died. Suspended between what was before and what was to come. She had no idea who she was.

He grabbed her by the neck again and kissed her deeply before starting the truck.

"I should be gittin' you back. That sister a'yers is wound about as tight as them mattress coils."

He looked over at her. She was leaning away from him, staring out the window at the passing trees. He reached over and pulled her close, tucking her into the crook of his shoulder.

"It's best you don' say nothin to yer sister, Ruth. This is private stuff between a man and his woman. You don' want nobody know-in' what we done, do ya? Don' want nobody thinkin' yer a whore. I don' think ya are, but yer sister? She will. They all will. Think yer a whore."

Ruth nodded and tried to relax against him. He felt foreign and familiar at the same time. He was a memory she had yet to make. Her sister's voices spitting out "Jezebel" echoed in her mind. He was right. She was a whore. Not a whore—a harlot was what Dollie would say. But she didn't care. She couldn't care. She leaned into the way he needed her. The way he cried out against her pulled at a dark, vacant place inside of her. The heat and energy in him excited her more than she'd ever been in her life. Maybe this was love. And if it was, then what was it she felt when she was with Quillan?

She ventured her hand to the hard plane of his stomach and craned her neck to look up at him. He smiled at her. There was a foreboding in her chest, and despite his proximity, she felt alone.

What have I done?

Thoughts tumbled over one another. She had given herself to him. Jezebel. He had marked her—branded her—as his own. Temptress. Whore. Harlot. Her head ached, and there was an unpleasant stickiness between her thighs. She curled tighter into him. The closer she was to him, the further she could be from herself.

He stopped the truck by the mattress factory. He leaned away, separating himself from her.

"I think it's best if I let ya off here, Firefly. I don' wanna git ya in trouble droppin' you at yer sister's."

He slipped a nickel into her palm for the trolley.

"I had a real good time tonight." He inhaled the scent on his fingers. "I'll be thinkin' 'bout ya later."

She was confused, the nickel warm in her palm. Then it dawned on her that his hands must smell of their intimacy. Waves of shame engulfed her. This had happened. But it hadn't. She couldn't think of it. She slid out of the truck and started toward the trolley stop. She lifted her eyes to the sky, to the heavens, to the God who was disgusted by her.

Ruth pretended to be sick the following Sunday and excused herself from church—from seeing Quillan. She looked different. She smelled different. She was sure he would notice the minute he saw her. She didn't have the courage to face what she knew he'd see. She pretended to be asleep when he came by to check on her. She was staying at Bessie's, and Bessie eyed her with suspicion. An eternity passed before Monday morning came and she could take the trolley back to Lola's.

Leonidas stood by the brick wall. Eyeing her. He was smartly dressed in slacks and a loose button-up shirt. He must have come into some money. He'd most certainly come by a shower and a shave somewhere. He was a handsome man. A different kind of handsome than Quillan—dark and brooding. She joined him, leaning against the wall, close to him.

"You doin' awlright," he said, caution edging his voice.

She nodded.

"You ain't goin' back to that church boy, Ruth."

He emphasized her name, every word a declaration.

She took in a long drag of her cigarette—avoiding his eyes. She felt it. The unraveling of her future with Quillan. She let her thoughts drift to the way he danced in the mirror house, laughing and morphing from one image to another but always himself. And she, so afraid of her own reflection, so incapable of understanding the way the mirrors distorted her.

"Breathe now," he'd said. "You're safe here with me."

When did his Sunday kiss become another chore? When did she begin to long for something more than the safety of his arms? How it happened, she couldn't say. To stay with him—to choose Quillan—meant looking in the waffling mirror every morning and seeing a whore. A liar. A cheat. The weight of it suffocated her. Everywhere she turned within her own mind she saw no other image. Jezebel.

Her only redemption was to believe that Leonidas had been her fate all along. She had given herself to him. It was scripture. The word of God. Once she had lain with a man, she belonged to him. Remaining his alone.

"No," she finally said. "No. I am not."

He stubbed out his own cigarette with the toe of his heavy boot. He pushed himself off the wall and walked away.

Leonidas made a habit of picking her up in his flatbed truck after her Monday shift. He'd pull the truck discreetly off an old road and have her before dropping her back at Lola's. He told her they couldn't spend too much time together. They didn't want Lola to get suspicious. Sometimes, if they'd been quick, he'd take her hand and help her down from the truck. He waltzed her about to the rhythm of the night sounds.

Monday was the day she flew well under the radar of her family. Monday could be given over to her temporary secret. It was temporary. The lie she told Lola and Bea about the addition of an hour to her shift time was a necessary one—a lie meant to protect them from worry. In God's eyes, she was married—and there was no sin, not if she committed herself to Leonidas. In her prayer time, she took to reading the first book of Corinthians over and again—affirming her belief. When the time was right, she'd set things right with her family. She and Leonidas would officially marry in the back garden, as all her sisters had.

Leonidas consumed her. He ran his hands over every part of her body, commenting on the silk of her more intimate places or squeezing at her thighs. He mourned the rough patches on her arms left by the cotton talc. He kissed her and told her he'd protect her. He'd never ask her to do anything that harmed her. Under his eyes—under his hands—she was alive in a way she had never conceived she could be. Not Mother nor Dollie nor Bea had spoken of men like this. This, she thought, was flying.

She made up any excuse to avoid Stone Mountain. She didn't have the courage to face Quillan—to tell him she couldn't marry him. Outside of Leonidas's cocoon, ugly thoughts chased her and made her turn away from herself in humiliation. As long as she stayed with Leonidas, she could justify her sinfulness. Her lust for his attention—which he lavished with generosity—overpowered her conscience. Away from him, in the shadow of the Stone Mountain, the disappointment of her family crashed in on her with an unbearable weight. She couldn't face the devastation of their disappointment in her.

The tenderness of spring broke into summer when Bea confronted her.

"I saw you," she spat. "I saw you with that man, Ruthie."

Ruth walked silently beside her sister. Her thoughts racing. Deny it? Admit it?

"Ruthie!" Bea stopped short. "I said I saw you with him. I saw you kissing him. This is why you been coming up with one excuse after another for not going home to help with Mama? You been avoiding Quillan Johnson, haven't you? You went and got yourself tangled up with that Lee Brantley."

"Lee's a good man, Bea. Different than Quillan, but not in the ways you think. He's kind and sweet. He's been all over, and we talk about everything. You should see his whittlin' work. Finer than Daddy's. He needs me, Bea. I'm all he has."

Ruth couldn't meet her sister's eyes. Bea let out a whoosh of frustrated air.

"What's Mama gonna say, hmm? Me and Lola are supposed to be looking after you, and you done tangled yourself up with some . . . some pinelander? Ruthie, that boy lives over in the camps. Were you aware a'that?"

Ruth tried not to react to this news. They'd only ever talked about the places he'd been. She'd assumed he lived somewhere in Atlanta.

"You are not allowed to see him anymore, Ruthie. God have mercy on us all if he's ruined you." Bea choked on a sob. "And don't think Lola and Bessie and I haven't talked about it. You and

I will be having all the same shifts from here on out. You'll not be leaving Lola's unless she knows where you are going. I swear, Ruth Elizabeth. You are going back to Bessie's and you are gonna set a wedding date with Quillan."

Ruth knew better than to argue with Bea. Bea's decisions—as one of the mothers—were final. Bea spoke to their supervisor and had Ruth taken off the Monday shift. All their shifts were together.

Lola didn't say much to her—how could she, given her own history?—but she kept a close eye on Ruth's comings and goings. Bessie called to tell her that in two weeks Brother Johnson and his family had been invited to Sunday dinner. Ruth would be there. She would apologize for being distracted by all the activities in Atlanta. Bessie too said nothing about Leonidas. Instead she prattled on about a new dress pattern she wanted Ruth to try. She had the fabric all picked out and ready for her.

Bea was true to her word. Her sisters created a gentle wall of activity around her. She wasn't alone at work or on her way home. Bea passed her to Lola in the evenings with the vigilance of a mother hen who senses the fox. Lola did her part by needing more help than ever with Marshall and Eva. She declared that each one needed a new quilt for the upcoming winter. This couldn't be done without Ruth's assistance. She wanted a center panel embroidered with the children's names.

At times, Ruth would wake up to find a small wooden animal carved from a peach pit sitting on her windowsill. A hen. A bear. A cat. She knew Leonidas left them there as a message. She knew she should tell Lola and Charlie. Or at least toss them out. But she couldn't bring herself to do it. She collected them in a small box she kept hidden in the vanity drawer. Telling herself it would be wrong to discard something so pretty.

Bessie and Dollie met her at the trolley station every time she came into Stone Mountain. Chaperoned by her sisters and their husbands, she went on walks with Quillan and had picnics at Arabia Mountain. Quillan, having been told by Bessie that Ruth was not feeling like herself, did his best to ferret out her unhappiness. He asked about her job. He asked her about Marshall and Eva. He asked if anything was bothering her about Charlie or Wheeler or Martin. Ruth looked him in the eyes, reassured him that she was content, and promised him she'd try not to be so distracted. She meant it too. She wanted to live within the circle of her sisters. She wanted to do what was right for her family. Quillan was where she belonged.

She said her prayers faithfully, though it felt like her words fell back to her without any notice from the heavens. She lifted her chin on Sunday nights for Quillan's warm, soft lips and hated herself for the lie. She split in two. Her days played out as they should—each the same, each devoted to her family.

Her sisters played their roles and continued to pass her the babes and congratulate her on bringing another man of God into their fold. They extolled the godliness and purity of her relationship with Quillan at every opportunity and shushed Ruth anytime she attempted to talk about Leonidas. They were banishing him the way women do. They were pretending he never existed at all.

The feminine blockade whirled around her with not a word of judgment or acknowledgment about her indiscretion with Leonidas. If anything, her sisters reiterated her virginal purity—often saying that God washes away every sin and makes a person new like a babe. Leonidas was an unspoken sin, and surely she had prayed for God's forgiveness. Prayer erased sin. Prayer erased Leonidas.

Arthur Grant, Maddox's brother, shot himself in September. He'd come home from the war a different man. Dollie had often whispered that he still felt the pain of his leg, even though it'd been amputated. She'd say he had nightmares that woke the whole family. Maddox, distraught, struggled to find a way to believe his brother had crossed through the pearly gates. It seemed to Ruth that that was the hardest part for Maddox—accepting that his brother was burning in Hell.

For Dollie, Maddox's need for her love in the aftermath of his brother's suicide outweighed Ruth's need for supervision. Dollie turned her attention to her own family and left Bessie to chaperone Ruth when she was in Stone Mountain. Bessie, occupied with tending their mother, sent word to Ruth that she was to wait for Riley to finish his shift at the grocery, and he would give her a ride from the village to Bessie's for the weekend. When Ruth arrived in the village, the air was cool, and she decided to wander down to meet Riley rather than waiting for him.

She ambled into the grocery store where Riley stood sentinel behind the cash register. She waved at him, a stranger since he'd married Sarah and Elliott had come along. She meandered around the large square vegetable island located in the middle of the store. The fall crops from the local farms spilled from the crates—okra and squash, green beans and late-summer corn.

"You're early, Ruthie. Wasn't expectin' you for another hour," Riley called. He watched her tap a melon squash and listen to the hollow sound. "Those melons came from Dollie and Maddox's place."

Ruth nodded, making her way to the counter. She turned and hoisted herself up to sit on its edge. "Thought I'd come in and say hi to a stranger. Maybe see if he wants to skip out early and go treasure huntin'." She smiled at him. He chucked her hip with the tail of his towel.

"Ain't never gonna let me live that one down, are ya? Shame

'bout Ezra. Thought that ol' niggah might live forever."

Riley coughed and banged at his chest a bit. He took a swig of his Coke before offering her a sip.

She shook her head. "How's Elliott? He seems to be with Bea an awful lot—Sarah doin' awlright?"

"Elliot's my little man," Riley chuckled, and a spark of the prankster in him flashed through his eyes. "Sarah? Well, she's havin' a hard time adjustin'. Bea's been real good about helpin' her out."

Ruth pulled a black licorice stick from the candy jar sitting near the register.

"That'll be a penny, ma'yam," Riley warned.

"Mm-hmm." She smiled. "I'll let you cover it. Bea's not the only one that helps out with that wild thing you call a child."

Ruth pushed herself off the counter. She reached her hand up to his cheek and rubbed her fingers against the stubble on his face. It was patchy on the one side where he'd been burned as a child.

"It's not like you to let that beard grow in, Riley. You feelin' good?"

Riley took hold of her hand and pulled it away from his face. He'd always been self-conscious about the scarring left by the village fire.

"Sleep got the better a'me. Had me runnin' late today. What about you? Seems you've been the center of unwanted attention lately? I mean, with the engagement and all. Mama says it's gonna be a spring weddin'?"

Ruth avoided his eyes. The train whistle cut through the air as it pulled in for the afternoon commuters.

"You ever think, Riley, that we're stuck here. That we're never gonna be any different?" She leaned in. "That maybe Wheeler's right? There's more out there than this?"

"I wouldn't let Wheeler hear you say that." Riley chuckled. "I think life is dandy, Rue. No need for upheavals—Lord knows we've had our share. I think Quillan Johnson will do right by you and by the fam'ly. He'll take care a'you, and that'll be all you need. Mama won't worry."

He paused.

"I won't worry neither, girlie. 'Cause I do worry sometimes. The others may not know it, but I do. You got a secret streak a'wild in you. Somebody's gotta look after you. Keep you safe. Daddy always thought well of the Johnson family. Of Quillan."

"Taught him how to tie a fishing line," Ruth mused.

"What?" Riley answered in confusion.

"Nothin' . . . an old memory . . ." Ruth leaned in and kissed her brother on the cheek. She couldn't help but notice the mild clamminess of his skin. "We should go treasure huntin' soon, Riley. I find myself missin' you."

"Me too, darlin'. Me too." He reached behind her ear and pulled out a Stone Mountain half-dollar. He laid it in her hand with a grin. "Still got some magic left in me."

The bell over the door tinkled in warning, and Riley straightened himself to greet the rush of customers that had disembarked from the commuter train.

"I'm gonna walk a bit. I'll wait for you outside. 'Bout an hour, you said?"

Riley nodded. Ruth slipped out the door—a sad sort of contentment settled on her. The train whistle blew again. The soft, rhythmic chugging of the steamer warned of its departure.

Ruth followed Lola and Charlie up the wide steps of the Grant farmhouse. Maddox and Dollie invited everyone to share Christmas dinner at their house. Dollie confessed the dinner was an effort to distract Maddox from Arthur's suicide. Despite her most focused efforts, Maddox struggled in his grief.

The house roared with children running about, and the clatter of the kitchen summoned memories of years past. Lola and Charlie leaned into a corner together—drinking corn whiskey from chipped coffee cups and blowing clouds of smoke into the air. Maddox and Tom had their heads together over the ever-fluctuating demands of the Grant farm—the only profitable one left in the family. Their wives clucked about the kitchen—migrating off and on into the side rooms to admonish children.

Riley and Sarah arrived with candies from the store for all the children. They were a bedraggled pair. Sarah looked as if she'd been crying. Riley was thin and pale. When Ruth asked after him, he brushed her off.

"Don't be lettin' him fool you," Sarah said with agitation. "This man's been sick for weeks. Coughin' all night. Keepin' me and the baby up. I keep tellin' him he might have that parrot flu. But he won't go the doctor. Stubborn as a flat-footed mule. Like your Daddy." Sarah paused, unaware of the silence that seeped into the room.

"You heard a'that? Been killin' people all over the country, and we done had our first case in A'lanah. Dirty niggahs brought it from Africa. Or India. Or one a'them places."

Riley laughed at Sarah. "Sarah, darlin', I haven't been 'round any parrots. It's nothin' more than a little winter gotta hold a'me. Now, pass those candies to my nieces, and if there's any left over, them boys can have one too."

Ruth peered at Riley. "Parrot flu? Like you're some kinda pirate? That wife a'yours little loose in the head?"

"She reads too much, Rue. Maybe I am a pirate—been rowin' up back creek more than usual if you catch my meanin'."

He winked at her. It was no stretch to imagine her brother in his skiff checking on the still in the wee hours of the morning. Ruth cocked her head at him. He'd given himself a clean shave, and Ruth could barely make out the smooth scarring on his jaw. It pulled at the corner of his mouth, as it had done since it happened.

"You still tellin' people there was a Hun soldier in that barn the night a'the village fire?"

He blinked at her, startled at the memory, and just as rapidly broke into his sideways grin.

"There was a Hun soldier in the barn that night, Ruthie. Probably the one that started the fire in the first place. He saw me, runnin' buckets, and he stepped in my path. I could see it. The fire dancin' in his eyes. Him wantin' to get out and me runnin' in. I fought him. Hard. Hand-to-hand combat. When the timbers started fallin', I knew it was him or me. So I gave him one last shove into the fire and turned and ran. Probably saved us all, if you ask me. He mighta made a habit a'startin' up fires. He might a'crept about among us undetected for years."

Ruth gave him a wry look.

"You are lyin', Riley Shurlington."

Riley nudged her with his shoulder.

"Does it matter, Ruthie? It's a good story. And I'm the hero. I kinda like bein' the hero. Maybe you oughta be thankin' me? Mighta been that I saved you too."

"You are coo-coo," Ruth whispered in delight.

"I am."

Deuteronomy 30:19
KJV

*I call Heaven and earth to record this day against
you, that I have set before you life and death,
blessing and cursing: therefore choose life,
that both thou and thy seed may live:*

Chapter 25

Lola crushed her cigarette in her plate as they sipped an after-dinner coffee. Ruby cut herself another slice of the cake she'd baked for Ruth's birthday. She cut a second slice and slid it onto Clara May's plate. The four women had settled around the table after dinner. They were waiting for Bea and Wheeler's wife Bonnie to arrive for a night of bridge and gossip.

"Saw Riley today," Lola said. "Lookin' pekid that one. Didn't even go into work. Which you know Riley. He's not stayin' home with Sarah less he has no choice."

"Parrot flu." Ruth chuckled.

"Pish-posh. I told him it's high time he called in a doctor. Gave him my quinine just in case. He's been out in them creeks so much he might've picked up the malaria."

"He could have parrot flu, Ruth," Ruby noted with authority. "All walks of people come in and out of that store he works at."

"It's not parrot flu, Ruby. Lola might be right—malaria maybe, flu—but either way the quinine'll take care of it. Sarah hasn't called in the doctor?" Bea took more interest in Riley and Sarah than the rest of them. She kept Elliott so often he seemed like her own.

"Sarah cain't see a thing past her own upturned little nose. She cain't take care of her own son—much less her husband. Poor Riley's been makin' dinner for all three of 'em. That girl has no constitution. She's been mopin' ever since the day Elliott was born, passin' all her mothering to Bea here—and to you, Ruthie. Takin' my extra hands."

Lola pointed her cigarette in Ruth's direction. "I just hope Riley has some sense and doesn't make too many babies with that one. Lord knows he wants 'em—but she's not fit for it."

Four days after Ruth's nineteenth birthday, the phone rang in Lola's neatly kept bungalow. Charlie was at work. Lola was out, and the children were sleeping. Ruth, who had been finishing up the breakfast dishes, dried her hands and picked up the receiver.

"Hollingsworth residence," she chimed.

"Ruthie?" her mother's voice rasped from the other end of the line. Ruth heard the ticking of the clock. A warbler sang from the tree in the front yard. She felt the molecules of air that surrounded her grow still. She knew this sound in her mother's voice.

"Mama?"

"Ruthie, baby. I need you to sit down."

Ruth sat in the chair by the phone table.

"You sittin', baby?"

Ruth nodded into the phone. Her mother cleared her throat.

"Our Riley . . ." There was a choking sound. Silence. Then she started again. "Our Riley has gone on to be with the Lord."

"What do you mean he's gone on to be with the Lord? Riley's not with the Lord. He's with Sarah and Elliot. He's with Sarah,

Mama?"

"He's not, baby. He's . . . he's passed." Mother made a sound as if she'd been punched in the stomach, a gasp for air that collided with a groan.

"How, Mama?" The screaming in Ruth's mind began again. As it had when her mother had told her about her father. It came from deep in her belly and trembled out through her muscles and rippled along her skin.

"He stopped breathing, baby. In the middle a'the night. Just couldn't . . . breathe anymore."

The crackling of the open phone line sizzled and popped. Ruth could hear her mother's ragged breathing. Ruth opened and closed her mouth, attempting to find words but feeling only the choking onslaught of disbelief. Finally, Ruth found a voice, though it sounded nothing like her own.

"Lola's . . . umm . . . Lola's . . . somewhere . . . we'll be there soon, Mama."

Sarah told them Riley hadn't made a sound. He just didn't wake up, but that was about all she could say. She'd slipped from hysteria to catatonia and sat by the window staring out into nothingness. Bea took Elliott to her house. It was Bea who explained to Elliott that his father wasn't going to wake up.

The doctor called it intestinal hemorrhaging caused by pneumonia. At his funeral, half of Stone Mountain mourned as Riley was lowered into the grave next to his father, next to Dollie's baby. When the family dragged themselves away from the graveside, Ruth remained. Grateful that the service had come to a merciful end. She couldn't stand the placating that came from men of God like Brother Johnson and Cousin Davis and Maddox. And Quillan. It was God's will. Riley is rejoicing in Heaven. She might scream if she heard it again.

Quillan reached for her. She shook him away—insisted that she be left alone. She didn't care that he grieved as deeply for his friend as she did for her brother. Looking at him made her grief worse. Quillan and Riley were wrapped together in her memories, and when she looked at Quillan there was pain so intense in the very center of her chest that she was certain she too would die from the sadness.

She knelt at the edge of Riley's grave and laid her hand on the warm earth. It wasn't possible. There was so much life in Riley. He nearly burst from his own skin. She wrapped her arms around her belly and rocked as the screaming tried to rise to her surface. But she swallowed the screams, as she had since the day her father died. She pulled the small wooden bunny and Lola's silver pin from her pocket and the Stone Mountain half-dollar Riley had given her. She dug her fingers into the loose earth and buried her treasures in his grave. She curled up on the ground between her father and her brother and laid her cheek over the hidden treasures. "I miss you, treasure hunter," she whispered into the earth.

The blockade broke.

Riley was twenty-three years old when he passed, and the energy of his sisters shifted to fortifying his frail widow and raising his orphaned son. Bea changed her schedule so that she could help Sarah full-time with Elliott. Ruth was left alone with her thoughts and her days, unsupervised.

As if he'd been watching, waiting, she found Leonidas leaning up against the brick wall of the mattress company. He wore a blue coat that matched his eyes and a bright-green collared shirt. She stopped a few feet from him and shook her head at the combination. He spread his arms and turned in a circle for her to admire.

He was impossibly handsome with an expression that said he knew her—every part of her. She was drawn to the idea of being known. Of being seen as he saw her.

"Hey there, Firefly," he purred. There was a magnetic pull to him that she knew would drag her toward him every time. She blushed and glanced away. He was like the stone mountain, she thought. Her mountain.

She walked up to him and let her head drop onto his chest. She started to cry, and he wrapped his arms around her.

"Hush now, Firefly, hush. It's a terrible, terrible pain. I know this. I lost a brother once too."

Ruth stilled. She wiped her tears before looking up at him.

"You did?"

"I did." He put his hands on her face, and an old hurt flared in his eyes. "Not much different than you. He died of tuberculosis when I was nineteen. Near about killed my mama. Homer was his name. He was my big brother too."

"I'm nineteen."

He pulled her close to him, bundling her in his arms as he might a child.

"I know, darlin'. I know. And I wish I could take all this pain away from you. Maybe we feel it together? Maybe if we share it, it won't hurt so bad?"

She let herself lean into him, feeling the mingling of their common grief.

Ruth lay awake in her bed, the window open to let in the cool April air. It had been a little more than a year since that first night with Leonidas and two months since Riley's death. Leonidas had managed to slip back into her life, stealing an evening or an afternoon one week at a time. He'd gotten a message to her that he needed to see her. She was to meet him at the end of Lola's street once the house was asleep.

Part of her wanted so badly to be that Ruth Elizabeth—the one who marries the preacher's son and makes her family proud. If Leonidas would disappear, maybe she could love Quillan again. But Leonidas and her love for him was bigger than all of them.

Maybe he wouldn't be there tonight. Maybe it was all in her imagination. Maybe the entire year was one of her horrible nightmares. Papa Perkins's death. Arthur's suicide. Riley's death. The first night in the truck with Leonidas. Maybe she'd get up in the morning, go home, and stay home. She'd quit the mattress factory and see if she could get a job at the quarry with Bessie.

She lay for a minute more. Her mind drifted back to her old room in the farmhouse. She was part of them—needed by them. You can ignore him, she told herself. You can pretend he isn't waiting. You belong here. She slipped from underneath her covers. Stay here. She swung her legs over the windowsill. She thought of his need for her—the way he clung to her. He needs you.

She hugged the tree line as she walked the block to the end of Woodbine Avenue. He was there. Waiting.

Ruth slid into the seat next to him. She told him all about her conversation with Bea and about Bessie's plans as he drove them into seclusion. She told him what she knew he wanted her to say. She was going to attend church on Sunday with her family and see Quillan. She was going to tell Quillan the engagement was off. She didn't care what Bea said. Her family would have to accept her choice.

He smoldered in the dark. "I'm yer family, Ruth. I'm gonna be yer husband. You understand that, don'you?"

"Yes, Lee, but Mama is callin' all the time askin' why I'm not in church. Lola and Bea and Bessie's planned this dinner. They don't know you, Lee. I gotta give 'em a chance to get over the shock. Then it'll work out. They'll love you same as I do. And well, Quillan . . . It's only right that I speak directly to him. Get everything out in the open."

She blew the smoke of her cigarette into the night air.

"Marry me," he said.

She turned to him.

"I . . . you know I cain't marry you yet. They won't like it. You didn't see how mad Bea was, and Mama's goin' to be hellfire mad. I gotta tell Quillan the truth."

"It ain't about what they want anymore, is it? You can see that, cain't you?" he pleaded. "It's 'bout you and me, and I ain't lettin' nobody come between us, Ruth."

She waved him off and sat thinking about Quillan. He deserved to hear from her. She had to face her mother and Bessie and the rest of them. She owed them all an explanation for her disappearance. She'd tell them about Leonidas. Lola had done it—faced them all when she'd wanted Elmer.

"Listen Lee . . . Quillan—" She never saw him raise his hand. She only felt the jolt of it against her face. The silvery cold metal of the ring he wore on his hand stunned her. She shrank into the corner. His cajoling was usurped by fury.

"Maybe yer still in love with this church boy? You been whorin' with me to bide yer time til he marries you. He ain't gonna marry ya, Ruth. You know how I know that? Huh?"

He grabbed her by both arms and growled, "Because I'll blow his gawd-dayumed church boy head off a'fore that happens."

He shoved her back against the car door.

"I . . . I'm sorry, Lee. I just need to talk to 'em . . . to set this right. I . . . " She touched the warmth of her cheek. He'd never struck her before.

"The right thing for you to do is me, Ruth. I'm the one that loves you. I'm the one that needs you. They got ever'thing, Ruth, ever'thing. All I got is you. All you got is me. I lost myself thinkin' a'losin' you."

He pulled her to him and kissed her hard, then backed away long enough to unbuckle his belt and release himself.

"Show me you love me," he pleaded. His voice was inaudible in its fierceness. Confusion goaded her. "Show me you don' want that church boy."

He wrapped his hand in her hair and pulled her head down to his lap. He pushed himself into her mouth. She gagged, and he tightened his grip on her neck, thrusting upward.

"Show me, Ruth. Show me it's me you want."

He leaned back against the seat and moaned, pumping her against him, thrusting harder every time she gagged. He was taking his time pleasuring himself. She focused on softening her mouth around him. Tears stung at her eyes. She was certain she would vomit. He came against the back of her throat, holding her there until he was finished. She sat up and wiped her mouth. He lit a cigarette, took a drag, and offered it to her. She shook her head.

"Yer my girl." He leaned over and kissed her sore mouth and wiped the tears from her cheek. "Who else gonna kiss this dirty mouth a'yers, huh?"

They sat in the darkness while he finished his cigarette. He flicked the butt out of the open window and cranked the old truck. She heard the buckle of his belt clank as he closed up his pants.

"You make me crazy, Ruth. I been losin' my mind not seein ya. You cain't be actin' like this. I wouldn't hurt ya. But yer pushin' me." He pulled her to him, stroking her cheek with remorse. His voice took on the soothing sound of a parent reassuring a child.

Ruth nodded, swallowing the metallic taste in her mouth. " I'm sorry," she mumbled.

Leonidas reached out and stroked her hair. They had passion between them, he said. He loved her so much it burst in him. He needed to be certain she loved him too. That's why she'd pleased him that way—to prove she loved him.

"I do love you, Lee. I'm doin' my best to sort things out. To do right by everybody. Especially you."

He was calmed by her contrition.

"I understand ya feel like ya gotta do the right thing, Ruth. Yer a good woman like that, and I admire it. I do. Me bein' upset about all this? Losin' my temper?" He took her face in his hands. "I ain't mad at you. I'm mad at them. They're doin' this to us. Me? I'm lookin' out for ya. For us. Makin' sure we don' get sucked back into their lies."

He knit his brows together and looked as if he might cry. As if his next words caused him physical pain.

"You go on into church on Sunday, and you tell the church boy y'ain't never gonna see him again. You be sure he understands. I'll be waitin' for ya outside after service. So you don' have to go to this dinner yer sisters are connivin' over. Ain't no reason for you to be goin' back to your sister's house. They been usin' you. They gonna do ever'thing they can to keep us apart. Why don' they want ya with me, huh? Cause they'd be losin' free help, that's why. You belong with me. Look at me, Ruth."

She turned toward him, and he took her right hand in his.

"I didn't mean for things to go haywire like that. I wanted to see ya tonight to bring ya this."

With his other hand, he reached into his shirt pocket and pulled out a wooden ring. It had the distinct pitted markings of his peach pit whittlings. He slid the ring onto her finger.

"Marry me," he said again.

She crumbled. Quillan was lost to her. Lost to her filthy mouth and her lustful thoughts. Her lies and her secrets. Leonidas loved her. Truly loved her. And she loved him. The wildness in him. The heat and passion. She loved the hum of his voice and the mischief in his eyes. She loved how free he was, and she too wanted to be that free. She ran her finger along the smooth surface of the ring he'd carved for her.

"Yes. I will marry you."

Ruth slipped back through the open window just as the sun rose.

"Hello, little sister."

Ruth's heart jumped into her throat. Lola Bell sat on her bed. Her legs stretched out in front of her. She flipped the page of the *Ladies' Home Journal* that she appeared to be reading.

"Sleep walkin', are we?" Lola glanced up and back down. Ruth thought she'd missed it, but Lola's chin snapped right back up. "Into a tree?"

Ruth gingerly touched the bruising at her temple.

"I tripped."

Lola closed the magazine.

"Little sister, we are not gonna bother with the hemmin' and the hawin'. You and I both are aware you didn't trip. And I'm not gonna ask you to tell me exactly where you've been. Save you the trouble of addin' to your sinnin' with lyin'."

Ruth sank to the end of the bed. Her eyes on her sister.

"Do you love him?" Lola asked.

Ruth nodded.

"And is that shiner his way a'lovin' you?"

Ruth came alive.

"No, Lola, no. This?" She touched her temple again. "He cain't stand what y'all are doin' with Quillan. He wants to marry me, and I want to marry him, and he just got worked up over the whole mess. He didn't even mean for it to happen. He's been leavin' me these pretty little things the whole time. Look. Look at what he's been doin'."

Ruth retrieved the box with the whittlings and showed them to her sister.

Lola nodded. It was clear she knew about the offerings.

"I've seen them. You really think some prowler's gonna go completely unnoticed week after week?"

Ruth closed the box and held it to her heart. She turned her face to the window.

"Are you pregnant?"

"Good heavens, Lola Bell, no!" Ruth delivered her denial with extra indignation. Lola tilted her head in amusement.

"If you were pregnant, would we be clear about who the father is? Not that you are pregnant. And not that you been foolin' around. But if it turned out you were expectin', would you have any troubles sayin' who's to blame?"

Ruth studied her sister, understanding the question and resigning herself to answering.

"I am not pregnant. But if I were, I wouldn't have any trouble knowin' who the father might be."

"That's not surprisin'. It would've shocked my knickers off to hear that sweet Quillan Johnson had ventured outside the sacred boundaries of matrimony. Devilishly beautiful as that boy is, he's got the moral fabric of a saint. Not a sin in him, I imagine."

Lola reached for her and tugged Ruth into her arms. She gave Ruth a firm squeeze and then released her.

"Ruth Elizabeth, you've gotten yourself into a pickle, and I am rather interested in seein' how you get yourself out of it. If I can offer you a word of advice? Make your choice and then move on with it. It's not fair the way you're leadin' Quillan on. And I'm guessin' by the look a'you that keepin' that other one simmerin' is not the wisest thing for you to do either."

Lola laid a hand on her knee and offered, "All of us interferin' cain't have made things any easier for you."

"What would you do?" Ruth asked quietly, lacing her fingers through her sister's. Lola considered the question.

"I'd do the thing that made me feel the most alive, little sister. You know that."

Sunday came. Ruth wasn't surprised to see Quillan waiting by her father's tombstone. She averted her gaze from the edges of her brother's freshly dug grave. Quillan's expression changed from relief to anger to confusion as she walked toward him. She told him she didn't want to marry him. She made up a lie about wanting to be a single girl in the city for a while. She left him sitting there and walked into church to sit with her family.

She sat motionless through the sermon, her head bowed. When Brother Johnson asked them to prepare for the last prayer, she reached into her pocket and slipped the wooden ring onto her finger. She tiptoed out of the church while her family's heads bowed and their eyes closed in prayer.

Leonidas was waiting outside as he promised. The tension and uncertainty of the last hour melted. His wildness. His passion. His love for her and hers for him pushed aside her doubts. She was with him. He understood her. He had promised her a new world if she came with him. Now and forever. He whooped and banged the side of his truck with the flat of his hand.

"Com'mon, girl—let's go."

She took one last look over her shoulder and saw Quillan watching her from the side of the church. She hesitated but only for a moment before jumping into the old Ford. Leonidas grabbed her by the back of the head and kissed her hard, then leaned past her to give Quillan a wave.

Red dust clouds billowed as he revved the truck out onto Memorial Highway and headed north. The clacking of the train raced beside them. She flung her hands in the air just as they came side by side with the heaving black engine. For an instant, she was beyond sound. Weightless. Free. Flying. Playing among the clouds. Then the train whistle blew—loud and long as the reins of sound caught up with her.

Epilogue

Atlanta, Georgia—1932

The heat. The poverty. The smell. The unrest and anger. Automobiles honking and crashing and people protesting. Speakeasies hiding and booming in plain sight, and Probi men threatening on every corner. People growing fat and rich on the clacking railroad. More people—dirty and begging. The train. Whistling and clacking and roaring. Carrying bums and profits. Buildings coming down, and bigger ones going up. Hoover making promises he never kept and driving the farms—driving the whole of Georgia—deeper into change and uncertainty. Ruth could sense the weight on her chest. She began to wonder if the air itself might suffocate her.

In late July, the heat oozed past one hundred degrees. There were bodies lying lifeless in Buttermilk Bottom, and the stench of roasting flesh and fetid sewage had settled in every corner of

Atlanta. Ruth and Dollie sat motionless on the front porch, fanning themselves. Ruth felt sweat pouring down her back, her belly taut and her dress clinging damply to her skin. She watched little knobs rise and fall across her stomach as the baby turned and punched to be released. The pain began midmorning. Dollie called Bessie, who came right to their side.

"It's awlright, Rue. Breathe easy now, baby," Bessie cooed, even as she began brewing her birthing tea. Her presence was calm and brought with it an assuring stillness. "I'm gonna help you bring this baby into the world."

Ruth was delirious with heat and pain. Somewhere along the way she became aware of Lola and her mother. Her mother sat in the corner chair, whispering prayers. Those incantations—her mama swishing through the kitchen and humming hymns. Light fell through the trees, and she was by the creek with Riley and Ruby and Clara May and Earl. Except when she opened her eyes, the light came harsh and hot through the open window, and it was Lola who wet her brow with a cool wet cloth.

When night fell, she was certain she heard the cacophony of men's voices coming from the small lawn, and for a passing second, she heard her father's voice. Men's voices, rough and dark. Her brothers. Her husband. Her nephews. Growling voices that talked over her agony as if her own moaning, aching sounds were irrelevant to their conversation. Bea had taken up her mother's place of prayer in the corner chair, and Dollie was fanning her. Lola brought chunks of ice. She was descending into Hell.

Then the baby ripped her in half. She existed for a breath on the edge of nowhere—time suspended and her very spirit rent. She howled. And there were no voices of men, only the sweet, swishing whispers of her mother and her sisters urging her forward.

Her first child was born on July 26, 1932. She named him after his father, Leonidas Walker Brantley. Someone told him. Someone passed the bundle of baby to him, and she heard his slurred sigh of satisfaction.

"Look a'here," he whispered, breathing his moonshine-laced breath into the baby's face. "Welcome, Leonidas Walker Brantley. Yer my boy, ain't ya. My Sonny boy."

Acknowledgments

As I reflect on the five year journey of researching and writing the books of Ruth, I am overwhelmed with gratitude for those who listened when I needed to talk, encouraged me when I felt stuck, and reminded me why I started. Sugarcane Saint is the first part of this adventure, and your kindness, patience, and unwavering support have played a vital role in bringing this story to life. To Linda and Harry, Suz, Jen, Kat, my music community, and my hockey community—to all those who read drafts, offered feedback, or simply reminded me to take care of myself—thank you.

To Rebekah—who read the same passage more times than any reasonable person should have to and still managed to offer fresh insight every single time. Just when I thought I knew my own characters, you would casually point out something so profound about them that I'd wonder if you knew them better than I. I loved that you got to know them and stood up for them when you felt I hadn't seen them for who they truly were. Yes, you were right. Ida wouldn't have given up easily, and I am grateful that you spoke up for her. I can only hope this book in its finished form offers some reward for your perspective and truly heroic tolerance for repetition.

To Haydee, my publishing partner and dear friend, the person who somehow knew exactly when to push me forward and when to let me sit in the mess of it all. You let me be angry when I needed to be, cry when I had to, and feel every last emotion without ever once telling me to "calm down" (which is precisely why we're still friends). You reminded me that stories aren't just written—they're felt, they're fought for, and they're lived. And on the days when I wanted to throw this book into the abyss, you handed it back to me with a smirk and said, "Not today," along with a helpful, "Maybe tone down the dialect?" I truly could not have done this without you.

A special note of gratitude goes to my editor, Lindsey, who not only understood the complex and layered history of the cultural setting with a depth that leant both support and affirmation to my concerns, but who also possessed an unexpected (and wildly impressive) expertise in poultry tending. Because, as it turns out, shaping a manuscript and managing a flock both require patience, intuition, and a willingness to deal with some unruly characters.

My deepest admiration goes to the incredibly talented MacKenzie, who brought the visual soul of this book to life. Your artistry is a gift. Thank you for working with me through each tweak and adjustment, always willing to make just one more change until it felt right. Your talent is young, but your vision is already strong. I can't wait to see the many things you create in the future.

To my beautiful family—Doug, Clare, Jackson, and Cooper—who loved me through the long hours, the late nights, and the moments when I was physically present but mentally lost somewhere back in time. Thank you for your patience, for understanding when I needed space, and for reminding me when it was time to step away from the screen and just be with you. Your love is the foundation of my world, and I am deeply humbled by the gift of you.

Above all, this book could not have come to life without the courage of my mother. She sees the good in people when no one else can and holds on to love in the face of unimaginable pain. She taught me what it means to face adversity, to speak my truth even when it trembles, and to believe in the power of storytelling. Sharing her memories and allowing herself to be vulnerable in the telling of this story has been an act of extraordinary faith and valor. Her courage is woven into every chapter, every sentence, every word.

Finally, to my cousins and my aunts—I see you, and I will love you always.

her sister Lola and befriends Elmira Keen, a nosy, but well-meaning neighbor who becomes a key ally.

Death mercilessly invades their family—taking one after another into its icy clutches. An ultimatum is given and Ruth, now the mother of four small children, must reckon with the choices she has made. She must decide whether she has the courage to take her children and leave her destructive marriage or succumb to the man who has gained control of every aspect of her life.